Heart's Desire

By T. J. Kline

Rodeo Novels
Rodeo Queen
The Cowboy and the Angel
Learning the Ropes
Runaway Cowboy

A Healing Harts Novel
Heart's Desire

Heart's Desire

T. J. KLINE

Excerpt from *Rebel on the Run* copyright © 2015 by T. J. Kline.

HEART'S DESIRE. Copyright © 2015 by Tina Klinesmith. All rights reserved under International and Pan-American Copyright Conventions. By payment of the required fees, you have been granted the nonexclusive, nontransferable right to access and read the text of this e-book on screen. No part of this text may be reproduced, transmitted, downloaded, decompiled, reverse-engineered, or stored in or introduced into any information storage and retrieval system, in any form or by any means, whether electronic or mechanical, now known or hereinafter invented, without the express written permission of HarperCollins e-books.

First Edition AVON IMPULSE ebook edition JUNE 2015

First Avon Impulse ebook printing: June 2015

ISBN 9780062396532

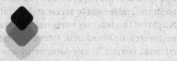

AVONIMPULSE
An Imprint of HarperCollinsPublishers

Excerpt from *Taking Heart* copyright © 2015 by Tina Klinesmith.

EPub Edition APRIL 2015 ISBN: 9780062396518

Print Edition ISBN: 9780062396532

AM 10 9 8 7 6 5 4 3 2 1

For my Little Stink.
The path ahead is rocky and rough but
always trust in your heart.
You know where you belong.
Don't ever give up on your dreams
no matter what anyone says.

Chapter One

"I GOT ANOTHER call from Brendon, Jessie. We can't keep pouring money into Heart Fire without some sort of income. If you won't take in guests right now, you need to think about selling a few of the horses."

Jessie Hart held the phone away from her ear, taking a deep breath and trying to contain herself before she blasted her brother with the anger bubbling like lava in her chest. How many times did she need to explain that she didn't care what their accountant said or how many times he called, the horses weren't ready to be sold yet? She couldn't rush them. These were abused horses, for goodness' sake. Several of them were still recovering, psychologically as well as physically, from the mistreatment they'd faced. She couldn't just sell them to the highest bidder and wash her hands of the situation.

Justin was a veterinarian; he should understand. Why couldn't he see how much this meant to her? She just needed a little more time to figure out how to turn the ranch into a rescue facility; she couldn't give up and go back to running the property as a dude ranch now. Maybe she should just explain what she and their father had been planning, how he'd agreed to let her turn the ranch—at least part of it—into a horse rescue. But Justin had always seen it as another waste of time, a drain on the family finances. In his own words, horses were a money pit unless she was buying and selling quickly.

"I don't tell you how to run your vet clinic, so don't tell me how to run *my* ranch." She clenched her jaw, barely able to stem the flow of angry words before her mouth got her into trouble again.

Justin sighed. She could picture him, rubbing his temples the way he always did when he was growing impatient with her.

"I'm not telling you how to run it, Jess, but we need to figure out something. Right now, my clinic is the only thing keeping *your* ranch in the black. I can't keep delaying buying new equipment in order to fund a place that used to turn a profit."

"I bet you didn't ask Julia to sell any of her dogs," Jessie snapped, instantly regretting her quick temper. It was her worst trait, the one thing her mother had left her that she wished she hadn't. It wasn't fair to drag her sister or her service dogs into this argument.

She didn't need to hear the words come from his mouth to know what he was thinking: Julia wasn't the one driving the family ranch into ruin; Jessie was.

"No, I didn't." Justin's voice softened, the way it did when he was trying to soothe terrified animals in his vet clinic. Jessie was beginning to feel a bit trapped herself. "Maybe it's time to think about taking in guests again. It's been months since Mom and Dad—"

"No!" She couldn't give up her dream, not yet. This plan had been in its first stages when their parents were killed in the car accident. She had to see it through to fruition. She just needed to buy herself a little more time to figure out how to get cash flowing into the ranch again. Maybe she should sit down and talk with Brendon about getting another loan. If nothing else, it would get her brother off her back.

The thought sent shivers of dread up her spine. She couldn't stand the creepy way Brendon watched her every move, as if he owned her. He'd always been overly possessive, but lately he'd been dropping by unannounced and following her around the ranch. He'd never wanted to be around when her parents were alive. She certainly didn't need him stalking her now.

"Then will you please take my advice and talk to Nathan? I'm sure if I call him, he'll help out. He's been all over the news for the last five years, turning huge corporations around. He's a financial genius."

"I don't need help from some—"

Justin sighed. "Yes, we do, Jessie. You could at least talk to him—see what kind of advice he offers."

She'd spent too long trying to forget Nathan Kerrington. She didn't want to think about how it had felt to be in his arms and the longing that had sent her young heart falling hard for a man who didn't belong in her world. She didn't want to think about the last time she'd seen him, climbing into the truck with her brother on their way back to college. Or the way he'd promised to stay in touch, to come back the summer after graduation.

What a stupid, naïve girl she'd been at eighteen. She had never heard from him again after that. Two weeks after returning to college, Nathan had moved out of the apartment he shared with Justin and never spoke to either of them again. According to Justin, the only reason Nathan gave for ending their friendship was that it was for the best.

She refused to ask for Nathan's help. She'd rather punch his rich kid face. Unfortunately, she couldn't tell her brother that. He had no idea what happened between Nathan and her that summer. No one did. She should have known better when he'd asked her to keep their relationship a secret until he talked to Justin about it.

Jessie sighed heavily into the phone. "What does some stuffy CEO know about running a horse ranch?"

"This isn't a regular horse ranch though, is it? It's a *dude* ranch, a resort, Jess. At least, it would be if we had guests."

"Don't start again, Justin. I'm doing the best I can."

"Then let me help. Let Nathan help."

She wasn't sure why she was letting him talk her into this. The last thing she wanted was a stiff Wall Street tycoon wreaking havoc on her ranch, especially one who lied, used people, and then threw them away. She didn't need that kind of help. She couldn't risk Nathan flipping the ranch on its head and leaving her worse off than before.

She wasn't going to allow Nathan to tell her how to run the ranch that she'd been working with her parents for years. She and her two siblings were born and raised on this ranch, cutting their teeth on snaffle bits and western saddles. She knew and loved every inch of the two-thousand-acre spread, even if only a third of it was hers to operate now.

Jessie inhaled deeply, trying to settle the anxiety twisting in her gut. She also couldn't let her siblings down again. Justin and Julia loved the ranch just as much as she did. She might run the daily operations of Heart Fire Ranch while her brother ran the vet clinic and her sister headed Heart Fire Training, but each of them held a one-third partnership in the other businesses. If one was having trouble, they all were. And right now, Jessie was the one on the edge of financial ruin. She was the one single-handedly destroying the legacy their parents had spent their lives creating. She was beginning to believe *that* was her only area of expertise—letting everyone down.

She couldn't let her siblings suffer so she could chase her dream of turning Heart Fire Ranch into a horse rescue and rehabilitation facility. Even if the thought of running Heart Fire as a dude ranch again made her skin crawl. She had only done it because it was what her parents wanted. When she was a teenager, they had needed her help. Justin and Julia had wanted to go to college, but she'd stepped up. Still she had always hated the constant influx of people who saw her way of life as a novelty. She would much rather work with people who understood her love for the animals. Not just city slickers looking for a vacation retreat. Unfortunately, her dreams and sense of pride weren't paying the bills.

"Fine," she finally agreed. "Call him. I'll hear him out, but only because I love you."

"I was hoping you'd say that. He's flying in on Friday. I'll tell Bailey to clean one of the guest cottages this week and pick him up at the airport."

"Wait, what? He can't stay here. You said *talk*, not have him come for a visit."

"He offered, and I'm not about to turn down a chance like that. Besides, he was my best friend."

"Some friend, Justin. You haven't spoken to him since your senior year of college. He bailed on you, remember?"

"And I'm sure he had his reasons for leaving. I have to go. Mrs. James just brought in that damn cat again. I'll come by later."

"No, wait! He can't stay here."

The click of Justin disconnecting the call was confirmation that he had gone ahead and done what he wanted without asking her again. Irritation burned in her chest. Her idiot brother had actually invited Nathan out to her ranch without asking her. Jessie shook her head. Just because she rescued horses didn't mean she wanted a jackass on her ranch.

NATHAN KERRINGTON SCANNED the arrivals hall of the Sacramento International Airport as he waited for his luggage to come around the carousel. Justin had promised to send someone to pick him up, but he had no idea who he should be watching for. He prayed it wouldn't be Jessie. After the way he'd left things with her, he was surprised she'd even agreed to him coming. Not that he could blame her. He owed her an apology, at the very least, but how did you apologize for taking a woman's virginity then abandoning her? Hallmark didn't have a card for that.

He'd done what he had to protect her, but it didn't change the fact that he'd hurt two people he'd cared about. He hoped that saving Jessie's ranch might prove to her he hadn't meant to hurt either of them. Eventually, he was going to have to tell her the truth: how his father had been prepared to use his wealth and influence to destroy her family's business, just to maintain control over his son. But Jessie had never been the forgiving type. Nathan pushed aside the memories of the curvaceous eighteen-year-old girl who'd stolen his heart and searched the terminal for a friendly face.

Nathan half-expected to see a ranch hand waiting for him with some dirty pickup truck belching out smoke and country twang. Justin would do it just to drive him crazy. He couldn't help but grin as he thought about the trouble they'd caused in college. When he'd initially moved into the residence hall and found out his roommate was a hillbilly country boy, Nathan had cringed. Back then, neither would've guessed they had anything in common, let alone that they would become inseparable. At least, until his father realized he could use the friendship to twist Nathan to do his bidding. It wasn't the first time his father had tried to use people Nathan cared about to get his way, but turning his back on Justin and Jess had cost him more than any other.

He reached for his Balenciaga bag, slinging it over his shoulder, and looked around the nearly deserted airport. Arriving at two in the morning wasn't his usual style, but something in Justin's voice told him this matter was urgent, so he caught the first flight out. He rubbed his eyes, feeling the grit behind the lids.

What he wouldn't give for a limo and a nice aged scotch right now. He took a few steps toward the front doors, wondering where his ride was, when he saw the young girl, barely awake in a plastic chair. With her hair pulled back in a ponytail, ripped jeans, and worn T-shirt bearing the name of a band he didn't recognize, she reminded him of a street-smart version of his little sister.

She looked too much like Justin to not assume she was family. She rose when he walked toward her. "Nathan?"

He narrowed his green eyes. "Yes, and you are?"

She thrust out a hand. "I'm Bailey. Justin asked me to come pick you up."

He crossed his arms, wondering if he was really going to let this teenager drive him to the ranch or if he should just call a cab. "How old are you, sixteen?"

She cocked her head to the side and glared at him, planting her fists at her hips. "Almost twenty-two, thank you very much."

Nathan quirked a brow at her tone. The girl had spunk; he'd give her that. Few people dared talk to him the way she did, and he grinned, feeling like Dorothy. This wasn't his Kansas anymore. He was definitely out of his element. "I'm sorry. But don't sweat looking young, kid. You'll love it when you're my age."

She eyed him skeptically. "Because you're so ancient, right?" She headed for the front doors, pulling the keys from her pocket and spinning them around her finger, leaving him no choice but to follow. "And, don't ever call me kid again, if you know what's good for you."

"I remember you." Nathan chuckled at her spirit and hurried after her, his long legs eating up the distance between them quickly. "You were that skinny cheerleader who followed Justin and me around when I stayed at the ranch that summer."

She stopped midstride and spun back toward him. Nathan almost ran into the back of her, catching himself with his hands on her shoulders. At the sudden stop, his bag swung forward and banged against her ribs, knocking her back a step. "Slow down, Wall Street. We're not in a hurry, and we've got a long drive ahead of us." She eyed him, taking in his gray Armani suit. "Justin says you're some kind of genius."

Genius wasn't the term he would use. Leave it to Justin to exaggerate. He was pretty successful at restructuring flailing businesses, and it had become something of a niche for him as a consultant. But he was used to financial renovations, not rebuilding them from nothing. From the sound of things, Jessie needed a small miracle. He wasn't sure about all the details but, according to Justin, after their parents' death six months ago, the dude ranch had sunk into the red.

"Not the way I'd put it."

Bailey laughed. "What kind of genius wears *that* to a dude ranch? I mean I thought I'd seen a lot of people come and go on the ranch but you beat them all."

He arched a brow and, for the hundredth time in the last few hours, regretted caving to Justin's request. He didn't belong out here. A horse ranch didn't fall into his wheelhouse of expertise. The summer he'd spent here, he'd been completely useless until Justin had taught him how to use a hammer and nails to help mend fences. Stacking hay and building corrals didn't take a business degree to figure out, but the Harts had welcomed him anyway. He owed Jessie, and from the worry he'd heard in his friend's voice, there wasn't time to waste.

He followed Bailey across the street to the short-term parking lot. She pressed a button on her key fob, and he heard an alarm chirp in the distance and a truck roar to life. Nathan's brows shot up on his forehead. If the truck had an autostart function, it was fairly new. His cynical nature immediately kicked in as Bailey unlocked the enormous black four-door 4×4. Nathan dropped his bag on the immaculate leather seat in the back before climbing in.

"Nice truck," he said, hoping Bailey might provide him with a little more information. If this was a recent purchase on behalf of the horse ranch, it might be indicative of Jessie's spending habits and explain the trouble she was in. He didn't remember Jessie being a diva, but it had been nearly eight years. People changed. He sure had.

"I wish it was mine." She hopped into the driver's seat and slipped the key into the ignition. "But when Uncle

Colton's truck died on Jessie, my dad made sure his dealership gave her a great deal on this one."

"So, your father owns a car dealership?" She nodded, glancing his way as she maneuvered onto the highway. "Do you work for him? Or Justin?"

She frowned, watching the traffic. "I'm sort of all over the place, wherever my cousins need me. Today, that meant cleaning your cabin at the ranch and picking you up. Most days, I'm at Justin's clinic." Bailey glanced his way and waved a hand dramatically. "I guess you could say I go wherever the wind blows."

The sarcasm in her voice wasn't lost on him, and Nathan let the conversation drop as she turned off the main highway and headed out of town. There was no sense in alienating his best informational resource within the first hour of this trip.

"Do you mind if I turn on the radio?" he asked. AC/DC blared in the cab, and Nathan hid the smile that wanted to creep to his lips. Not exactly what he'd expected from the petite girl in worn cowboy boots, but obviously she was more like Jessie than he first expected and just as full of surprises.

He couldn't help but smile as he thought about the first time he'd seen Jessie giving a group of wannabe cowboys a lesson in manners when they'd dared to catcall her. Like Bailey, she had an indomitable spirit and a smart mouth to match. With her fiery temper and quick laughter, she'd kept him on his toes all summer. When she wasn't teasing him about trying to learn something new like fixing fences and building a lean-to, she was tempting him with her sweet lips and quiet sighs in the darkness. Like a lightning storm, their time together had been electric and exciting but too short-lived.

He'd allowed his father's threats to cloud his judgment and let her slip through his fingers. By the time he'd realized what he'd given up, it was too late.

Nathan sighed. He'd burned his bridge with Jessie a long time ago. He'd been shocked when his secretary told him Justin Hart had called, but even more flabbergasted when he mentioned that Jessie wanted his help. Knowing Justin as well as he had, the fact that Nathan's face had never been beaten meant Jessie hadn't told him about what happened between them.

Maybe she'd never cared about him the way he thought she had; maybe she'd moved on. Maybe she'd never even thought twice about the fact that he'd never called. If she'd held a grudge, she never would have allowed Justin to reach out to him at all. He tried to convince himself this job would be easy. If he could pinpoint the issue quickly, he could be back in New York before the weekend. And maybe this was all wishful thinking.

Chapter Two

JESSIE HEARD THE crunch of tires on the gravel driveway and stepped onto the porch of the enormous log home. Her parents had raised their family here, in the house her father had built just before her brother was born. The scent of pine surrounded her, warming her insides. Even after her brother and sister had built houses of their own on either end of the property, she'd remained here with her parents, helping them operate the dude ranch and training their horses. She inhaled deeply, wishing again that circumstances hadn't been so cruel as to leave her to figure out how to make the transition from dude ranch to horse rescue alone.

Leaning against the porch railing, she sipped her coffee and enjoyed the quiet of the morning. When a teen girl walked toward the barn to feed the horses, she lifted her hand in a wave. The poor girl was spending more time at the ranch than away from it these days, since her mother had violated parole again, but Jessie loved having her here. Aleta's foster mother, June, had been close friends with Jessie's own mother, and she understood the healing power horses had on kids who needed someone, or something, just to listen. Now that Aleta was living with June again, she was spending a lot of time at the ranch.

Jessie looked down the driveway as Bailey drove her truck closer to the house. She could just make out Nathan through the glare on the windshield. The resentment in her belly grew with each ticking second at the sight of him. Clenching her jaw and squaring her shoulders for the battle ahead, Jessie walked down the stairs to meet Justin's former best friend and the man who'd broken her heart.

The truck pulled to a stop in front of her, and Bailey jumped from the driver's seat wearing a shit-eating grin. Jessie narrowed her eyes, knowing exactly what that meant—she was in for a week of hell from this pain-in-the-ass, penny-pinching bean counter.

She didn't understand why he'd insisted on returning to the ranch. If Justin hadn't begged her to give Nathan a chance to help, she would have been perfectly content never to speak to his lying ass again.

She watched him turn his broad shoulders to her as he removed his luggage from the back seat. When he faced her, Jessie was barely able to contain her gasp of surprise. After he left, she'd avoided any mention of Nathan Kerrington like the plague, going as far as changing the channel when his name was mentioned on the news. She'd been praying that the past eight years had been cruel, that he'd gained a potbelly, or that he'd developed a receding hairline. She pictured him turning into a stereotypical computer geek.

This guy was perfection. Well, if she was into muscular men who looked like Hollywood actors and wore suits that cost several thousand dollars. Every strand of his dark brown hair was combed into place, even at six in the morning, after a flight from New York. There wasn't a wrinkle in his stiffly starched shirt.

His green eyes slid over her dirty jeans and T-shirt before climbing back up to focus on her face. Memories of stolen kisses and lingering caresses filled her mind before she could cast them aside. His slow perusal sent heat curling in her belly, spreading through her veins, making her feel uncomfortable. Was he just trying to be an ass? If so, it was working. She felt on edge immediately, but she wasn't about to let him know it. She crossed her arms over her chest and kicked her hip to the side.

"Nathan Kerrington. You've got some brass ones showing up here."

A smile slid over his full lips, as if he'd expected this reaction from her. If she wasn't so irritated by his mere presence, she might have thought it was sexy, but under these circumstances, it only made her palm itch to smack him more than it already did. He probably wasn't lacking when it came to female attention, but he must have forgotten Jessie didn't fawn over him the way most women did. She didn't care how much money he was worth, what family he came from or how attractive he was. As far as she was concerned, he'd shown her his true colors a long time ago. She hadn't stroked his ego before and she wouldn't now.

"Hi, Jessie." She narrowed her eyes as he covered the few steps separating them, holding out his hand. His eyes slid over her again but this time she felt the heat rise to her cheeks as his gaze lingered on her lips. Her body responded to his nearness without her brain's permission, warming instantly as he moved closer. She felt the butterflies in her stomach wake at the thought of taking his hand.

"You look...amazing. It's been a long time."

"Not nearly long enough." Ignoring his outstretched hand, she turned her attention to Bailey. "Can you show him to the cabin? I'm sure he'd like a chance to change and freshen up."

She eyed his suit and wondered at his choice of apparel. He knew as well as anyone how dirty the ranch could get. Unless he was just trying to flaunt how much he'd accomplished since walking out on her. Nathan arched a tapered brow, and she saw annoyance simmering just below the surface, a state she was sure was foreign to him but that she was thrilled to trigger. He took a deep breath and met her gaze with an animosity she hadn't expected.

What did he have to be annoyed about? She was the one being forced to be hospitable. She would have preferred this entire matter be done via e-mail or a conference call. He and Justin were the ones who'd insisted on Nathan coming back to point out her failures in person. As if she didn't already know her many shortcomings. Let him be irritated. She was, too.

"Jess," he began, taking a deep breath. "I'd like to get started right away. I was hoping to remedy your predicament as soon as possible and get back before this weekend."

Jessie glared at him, allowing herself the luxury of a momentary fantasy where she walked down the steps and slapped the arrogant smile from the bastard's face. She hadn't wanted him here in the first place. He was more than welcome to turn around get on the first plane out of Sacramento.

She reined in her whim and mimicked his self-important tone. "*Mr.* Kerrington, please don't feel any obligation to stay at all. In fact, in light of how much work I have to do here on Heart Fire Ranch, I'd suggest you stay with Justin, a hotel in town, or simply to head to where ever it is you plan on going next. I didn't ask for your help with my *predicament*, and I don't want it either."

Jessie glanced at Bailey, who was pinching her lips together in an effort to hide a smile, before looking back at Nathan. His eyes flashed with indignation, but the emotion disappeared just as quickly, as if her tirade was only a minor annoyance. The slick smile and formal speech were back on his lips in the blink of an eye.

"While I appreciate your candor, your brother did invite me, and as a vested party in the success of this ranch, he does have the right to request my intervention."

It rankled her that, from the sound of things, Justin had divulged the details of their parents' will to this man already. She'd specifically told him to wait until they could discuss it together. She didn't understand why

Justin refused to figure this out as a family. Nathan had already proven he couldn't be trusted. Just because Justin forgave Nathan didn't mean she had.

"Then by all means, discuss his vested interest all you want, *with him*. I have work to do and a ranch to run. Bailey can show you the way to your cabin. Lunch is at one sharp. Be there or go hungry."

Jessie spun on her heel and headed for the barn, not giving him a chance to respond. She wasn't about to give this pompous, arrogant city slicker the satisfaction of having the last word. Not this time.

It didn't matter that her body was practically aching to be touched by him again. She had locked her heart away a long time ago, and she wasn't about to let Nathan near it again.

JESSIE HURRIED TO the barn, intent on getting as far away from Nathan as possible. She wasn't sure what to think about the reaction his presence had stirred in her. She hated Nathan. At least, she thought she did. But how could you hate someone who made your insides quiver and your entire body weak with just a look? She looked up as Aleta led one of the older, very pregnant rescue mares into the aisle way and clipped the crossties to both sides of her halter.

"Hey, Jess. What was that all about?" Aleta jerked her chin toward the barn door.

Jessie turned to see Nathan heading toward the biggest of the log cabins on the other side of the barn. Cabins once filled with paying clientele now sat empty, like a miniature ghost town, reminding her of how she was failing her parents. What would her father say if he could see what she had done to his ranch? Jessie glanced toward the hay room, where the supply was dwindling and she had no money to replenish it. The grain and supplements were getting low as well. At least when her parents had been here, they'd been able to run the ranch and bring in the income to support her attempts to rehabilitate the horses. Soon she would have several ready to be sold to new homes, but she just needed a little more time. If Justin had already spoken with Nathan, it was unlikely that she'd get it. They'd probably turn the ranch back into a resort in a week, and that would be the end of her dream.

"New guest? He's a hottie!" Aleta's comment broke through the worries swirling in her head like wasps.

"Just a nuisance." She brushed her hair back over a shoulder. "And he'll be here for only a few days, I hope."

Jessie grabbed a currycomb from the caddy and began to rub down the other side of the mare as they groomed her together. She was trying hard to ignore Aleta's comment about how attractive Nathan was.

She glanced up as he walked past the barn, carrying an expensive leather bag slung over one shoulder as he chatted with Bailey. His green eyes glimmered with humor, and his smile seemed genuine. He was still just as good looking as he'd been at twenty-two, but he was too clean-cut now for her taste. At least, that was the story she vowed to repeat to herself until she believed it.

When Nathan had first stolen her heart at eighteen years old, he'd had a five o'clock shadow coloring his jaw, and his dark good looks had practically melted her in her cowboy boots. When he turned those green eyes on her, she could almost feel the sizzle between them. It had taken every bit of self-control she had not to drag him into one of the empty cabins and find out what she'd been holding out for. She'd flirted with him, trying to get his attention, but he'd ignored her, pushing her away in some misguided sense of loyalty to Justin. At first.

That first kiss from him nearly set her on fire.

She didn't see anything left of the mischievous boy who'd stayed on the ranch to help that summer. In his place was an overconfident, arrogant ass. She hated that she was only fueling his ego by asking for his help.

Still, she thought, he did fill out that expensive suit nicely. And if those broad shoulders and trim waist were any indication of what lay below the material...

"Nuisance, huh?" Aleta's eyes twinkled with merriment.

Jessie tossed the currycomb back into the grooming caddy, embarrassed at being caught fantasizing about the jerk. "Don't you mess with me, young lady, or I won't let you stay here tonight. I'll call June to come pick you up now instead of after breakfast."

Aleta laughed off Jessie's threat. "Sure you will. We both know you're a softie. Besides"—Aleta shrugged a narrow shoulder—"you love me too much to try to get rid of me."

Jessie stuck her tongue out at the teenage girl. Aleta had seen too much of the shady side of life in her short fifteen years, but in spite of her mother's drug use and her own run-ins with the law, she had a sense of humor and a sweet, feisty spirit that she showed when she was at the ranch and working with the horses. It was at Aleta's suggestion that Jessie had begun to invite other troubled teens out to the ranch to help out in exchange for riding lessons.

A smiled tugged at the corners of Jessie's lips. "Well, you don't have to be so cocky about it," she teased. "I'm going to go get lunch ready. We have a couple more horses coming in late tomorrow, so can you get three stalls ready?"

"Sure. Want me to turn Gilly out with the other mares?"

"Yeah." She patted the mare's shoulder. "Put her in the nearest pasture, and we'll bring her back in as soon as I evaluate the others tomorrow. Once I know what sort of temperament I'm dealing with, I'll know how many stalls we'll have left."

"You got it, boss."

Jessie laughed at the girl's enthusiasm. One of the things she loved and envied most about Aleta was her ability to ignore the garbage life had thrown at her and let it fall from her too-thin shoulders. Jessie hoped she could learn the same lesson. Since her parents' accident, life had thrown nothing but refuse her way, and she was having a hard time wading through it. Dealing with Nathan Kerrington was going to be just one more stink pile to get past in order to move forward with her dream.

Chapter Three

NATHAN WASN'T SURE what he'd expected from Jessie's lunch invitation. Maybe pork and beans flung at his head as he walked through the kitchen door? Whatever assumptions he'd made, he hadn't expected to see Jessie rocking out in the kitchen to music pumping through her earphones, as she made enough sandwiches to feed a small army. She cut into another and laid the halves on a tray to her left as she belted out a country song he'd never heard before. Something about a woman going home to load her shotgun. A nervous tremor coursed through his belly. It sounded too much like a personal anthem, and he worried, with their past and her attitude upon his arrival, the song might prove prophetic.

She hadn't noticed him yet, so he leaned against the doorframe, enjoying the show. He didn't remember ever hearing her sing before. She had a great voice, rich and smooth, mellow yet seductive. She twisted her hips, gyrating in time with the song, and he had to admit, what she lacked in height, she made up for in sex appeal. Jessie was a tiny thing, petite but athletically built, with curves that could make a grown man cry. His eyes traveled down her back to her narrow waist and rounded hips. Nathan couldn't help but notice how well her rear filled out the denim of her jeans.

He felt the desire he'd buried years ago reawaken. He pushed himself from the doorway, trying to cast the feeling aside. If her ice-cold welcome was any indication, his chance at wooing Jessie was long gone. He tried to be grateful for her noticeable animosity. If nothing else, it made it easy to remember the only lingering feeling on her part was loathing.

Besides, he tried to console himself, *Jessie Hart isn't your type—at least not anymore.*

His last girlfriend, a sleek, waifish model, was the type of woman he'd grown accustomed to spending his nights with—a woman who could stay on his arm at any function, engaging and beautiful but demanding nothing more than a good time and a few connections to further her career. No emotional risk there.

He couldn't deny that had always been a problem with Jessie. She left him feeling too much. His father had seen it and exploited it, demanding Nathan to help him doctor his campaign finances or else see Jessie's family business ruined. While there was something irresistible about this feisty cowgirl dancing around the kitchen, he couldn't allow himself the freedom to explore it. Nor did she seem to want him to.

"There you are!" Nathan spun in surprise as Justin smacked his shoulder and walked past him to grab one of the sandwiches, tugging the cord to Jessie's headphones. "Hey, Jess. Can't stay too long. Nathan and I have an appointment right after lunch with Brendon Gray."

She pulled the other earpiece out and smiled up at her hulking brother. "Already? Sit and—"

As soon as she saw Nathan standing in the doorway, her eyes changed. The deep blue he'd lost himself in for a whole summer instantly hardened to ice.

"Please, have a seat." Her formal tone left Nathan certain where he stood.

Jessie carried the tray to the table, her eyes sliding over him judgmentally. It wasn't a foreign exchange. In his line of work, people often evaluated his qualifications and likelihood of success by how expensive his suit or the watch encircling his wrist was. But he'd never felt lacking while wearing a Rolex and Armani. Jessie's appraisal made him feel inadequate, as if she pitied him. It irked him that this cowgirl could get a rise from him when millionaires hadn't been able to. Even after changing into a casual outfit of Balmain jeans and a polo shirt that probably cost more than this ranch grossed each month, she still had a way of making him feel like he was lacking. He arched a brow, daring her to comment, and saw her lips pinch together into a thin line.

Jessie looked away from the doorway, ignoring Nathan. "Where's Julia?"

"Waiting for one of her dogs to get picked up by its new handler, a little boy with autism. She told us not to wait to eat because she'd be late." Justin reached for a second sandwich, oblivious to his sister's annoyance with Nathan's presence at the table. "What are you waiting for, Nathan? Dig in."

Nathan reached for one of the sandwiches, wondering again what sort of hell he'd just gotten himself into. He was used to catered meals, expensive wine, and high-rise buildings, not ham sandwiches in the kitchen of a log cabin.

"Want a beer?" Justin asked him, and Jessie eyed him expectantly, ready to pounce regardless of his answer.

"Water is fine."

She stood and reached for a glass from the cabinet, filling it from the faucet. No ice, and she didn't even bother to turn the faucet to cold.

He reached for the glass as she slid it in front of him, and when his hand touched hers, he felt a tingle of electricity. She jerked her hand away from his as if he'd just shocked her, spilling water on the table.

"Sorry," she muttered, narrowing her eyes and watching him warily as she slowly eased back into her seat.

Nathan took a long drink of the lukewarm water, if only to spite her, and used a napkin to wipe up the puddle on the table.

"I'd like a beer!" Bailey strolled in, immediately breaking the tension in the room, smiling from ear to ear as she winked at Nathan.

She plopped down beside him at the table and reached for one of the sandwiches. Her energy was contagious and Nathan bit back a grin. At one time, this was how Jessie had acted around him—vivacious and full of life.

"You're still on the clock at the clinic, and I need you after lunch, so no," Justin scolded.

"Party pooper," she muttered under her breath.

Nathan choked on his water as Bailey chuckled, slapping his back. "Relax, Wall Street. It might not be Voss but it's not that bad. Straight from the well."

Jessie rolled her eyes at Bailey. Irritation seemed to seep from her, directed pointedly at Nathan. "Can we get this over with? I have stalls to get ready."

"For what? Please, tell me you didn't take in more horses," Justin said.

She chewed the bite of sandwich in her mouth slowly and tipped up her chin. "Okay."

"Okay, what?"

"Okay, I won't tell you."

A shadow of a smile played at the corners her lips. Bailey didn't even bother to hide her mirth and laughed loudly. Nathan had seen Justin lose his temper enough in the past to know Jessie was treading on very thin ice. She wasn't just tempting her brother, she was outright poking a bear of a man with a temper to match, and it made him wonder if the years had made her stupid or just incredibly brave.

"Jessie," he growled through clenched teeth. "I thought I told you—"

"And I told *you* to let me handle it." She leaned back in her chair, not looking the slightest bit worried about the impending eruption from Mt. Justin. The air practically sparked with the tension. "I've got this," she assured him.

"You *don't* have this. Unless you're on a mission to put us all in the poor house, there are too many useless mouths to feed and not enough hay to do it."

"I don't recall asking you for money."

"And, yet, I don't recall you turning it down when I offered," Justin countered.

"I know what I'm doing," she insisted.

"Then why am I here?" Three sets of eyes turned toward Nathan.

Nathan was used to moving when his instinct directed him. Usually it meant hanging back and supervising operations, watching for opportunities others might miss, not jumping headfirst in to a hornet's nest of sibling drama. Jessie's blue eyes grew even colder, her sharp glance cutting.

"Good question." She glared back at her brother. "Why is he here? What can he do that we can't manage on our own?"

Nathan wasn't about to sit back and let this slip of a woman insult him. She might have every right to be angry with him for what happened in the past, but his business acumen was above reproach, and he was proud of the success he'd achieved in the past few years.

"Well, for one thing, I can look at your books and see where there might be corners you can cut. My goal is to make sure that you're operating within the optimal tax benefits, legal structure, and primarily, making the best business decisions possible for every dollar spent." Nathan crossed his arms and locked eyes with her. "And I'm damn good at my job."

"Modest much?" Jessie quirked a dark brow, not bothering to hide her distaste.

"Just statin' facts, ma'am," he teased, a smile tugging at the corners of his lips.

This was where he was most comfortable, on the offensive. He didn't want to make her mad, but he needed her to realize how serious her situation was. This wasn't about his past mistakes; this was about her future. However, he had to admit it was a thrill to push Jessie's buttons, making her eyes spark with blue fire. To make those perfect lips round in outrage. What he wouldn't give to kiss her again.

Nathan cleared his throat, forcing himself to concentrate on the reason he was here. "We need to sit down and talk with your accountant to get a clear perspective on your finances. Justin and I are doing that later today, right?" He looked to Justin for confirmation. "And we need to talk about what you're each planning for this ranch."

"I can't put everything here on hold to chat. I barely have time to train the horses after I've finished with barn chores."

"Then maybe you shouldn't be bringing in more," Justin muttered under his breath.

Jessie rose, glaring at him before marching toward the kitchen sink, the island between them. Nathan could see by her defensive stance that she was fighting the desire to escape the conversation altogether.

He saw Jessie pull out her cell phone and frown at the screen. "Crap," she muttered.

"What?" Bailey looked at the phone screen as well. "Go. Justin and I will clean up lunch."

Whatever she saw on her phone must have been important, because Jessie snatched her keys from the hook by the back door and hurried out the front door to her truck. He heard the roar of the diesel engine and the crunch of gravel as the massive tires rolled down the tree-lined driveway.

Nathan raised a hand to his temple, rubbing at the headache beginning to form. "We are never going to get anything accomplished this way."

He had a life to get back to in LA and, if Jessie didn't become more cooperative, this job was going to last forever.

"Don't worry." Justin laughed, pulling out his cell phone. "We'll take a trip into town to meet with Brendon today, get that out of the way. Then we can have a drink and catch up." He cocked his head and frowned. "Loosen up. I don't remember you being such a tight-ass in college. Maybe you need this visit more than you think."

Yeah, the way I need a hole in my head.

JESSIE HATED SITTING outside the principal's office. She hadn't liked it that time she'd been caught cutting class in high school, and she hated it even more now. She shook her head and frowned at the sixteen-year-old boy seated beside her, his long hair draped over his eyes. "What in the world were you thinking, Michael? Vandalizing the locker room?"

"I told you, it's Ice."

"Really? *Ice?*" She sighed. "Because you don't have enough trouble in your life right now without getting involved with that gang again? They're bad news and going nowhere." Jessie glanced through the window where two other students sat, their wrists handcuffed behind their backs. "You're not like them."

He eyed her through his shaggy bangs. "Maybe you don't know me as well as you think you do."

"Quit doing what your brother tells you to and start living the way you want. Do you want to end up in jail like him? You told me you wanted out, remember? I know you don't want to be part of a gang, so why would you even take part in their initiation? You're better than this."

Luckily, the office door opened, ending their conversation. Two deputy sheriffs escorted the other street-tough teens toward patrol cars she'd seen parked in front of the school. Ellie, Jessie's friend and Michael's foster mother, was next, followed by the principal. Ellie looked tired, much older than her twenty-eight years, as she turned her eyes toward the pair.

"Come on, Michael, let's go." Jessie could hear the exhaustion in Ellie's voice as she shook the principal's hand and thanked him for his help with the police.

Michael stared after the other boys before turning back to her. She could read at least a thousand questions in his eyes, but he left them unspoken. "You mean, I'm not—"

"No, you're coming with us. So let's go," Ellie ordered, raising her voice slightly.

Jessie stood, following her exasperated friend to her truck, watching as the police cruiser pulled away from the curb. She still wasn't sure whether Ellie had asked her to come because she simply needed moral support or if there was something else on her mind. She waited, knowing Ellie would make her intentions clear soon enough.

Michael's shoulders slumped forward as he opened the passenger door and tossed his backpack to the floorboard.

"Take your things with you. You're going home with Jessie tonight," Ellie instructed.

"What?"

"What?" Jessie repeated, as confused as the teen.

"I'll be out later, but I think some ranch work might help *Ice* put things into perspective while he's suspended from school. Don't you agree, Jessie?"

Jessie bit her lip as understanding dawned. If Ellie wanted to teach the boy a lesson, she could come up with plenty of chores to accommodate her. "I have fences to be mended, and there are always stalls that need cleaning."

Ellie gave her a grin and a quick wink. "I figured as much." She turned back to Michael. "You head out and get started. I'll be out later, after I get off work."

The boy opened his mouth to protest, but Ellie held up her hand. "Don't say a word! You're lucky you're not in the back of that patrol car with those two boys after the stunt you pulled today. You're getting off easy with just three days suspension. So, show some gratitude."

Jessie could see his jaw clenching. He was at that age where everything set him off. He wanted to fight the system and declare his independence, but he hadn't realized yet how far was too far. Today he'd crossed the line when he'd vandalized the locker room. At least he hadn't pushed as far as his older brother had, landing him in prison for armed robbery.

Ellie had taken Michael in—an impressionable boy who looked up to his troubled older brother—and offered him the world, but she could only do so much as a foster parent. The choices were still his to make, and thanks to his brother's influence, he was making bad ones.

"Come on," Jessie threw her arm around his slim shoulders and gave him a quick squeeze. "We're getting in three new horses tomorrow. You can help me get ready for them." She saw the light return to his eyes. "Besides, Grady's been missing you." At the mention of the old gelding, she saw Michael try to hide a smile.

"Fine," he sighed. He heaved his shoulders dramatically, but Jessie didn't miss the relief in his eyes.

Jessie pulled out her phone to let Justin know they would have two more people tonight for dinner.

How did she manage to go from being alone last night to having a packed house before lunch? Nathan's arrogant grin filled her mind. How was she going to explain having two juvenile delinquents at the ranch when Nathan started asking questions?

Chapter Four

NATHAN SAT AT the kitchen table of the cabin Jessie had relegated to him, staring down at the countless documents her accountant had compiled. Besides an external hard drive filled with account information, more payable than receivable, there were loans, both personal and business, as well as the will from her parents. Since Justin hadn't really talked about his parents' death, Nathan knew he would have to press one of them for details eventually. Reading the will now, he could see none of the Harts fully understood the value and desirability of their property.

With two thousand acres split equally between them, each of the siblings had been given a portion of the property to use for separate business ventures, yet the entirety remained in joint ownership. Wading his way through the legal jargon, grateful for his years in law school, he finally found what made them think they had more than a familial interest in one another's businesses. Each business was run as a separate entity, meaning that Jessie was in full control of the dude ranch portion of the property and could operate it however she chose. But, because of the way their parents had structured it, if one business went under, the others were forced to compensate or help fund it. According to the documents, their father insisted they keep the property whole, or it was to be sold in its entirety. In other words, if one failed, they all failed.

"Colton, what were you thinking?" he muttered to himself. The knock at the front door interrupted his thoughts. "Come in." He looked up in time to see Justin peer around the entrance.

"Aren't you coming for dinner?"

Nathan glanced at his watch and looked out the window to see the sun setting behind the tall pines. He hadn't realized how much time had passed since he'd started looking into their finances. He slid the will into a folder and rose from the small table. "Would you mind if I borrow your truck to head into town and grab a burger?"

Justin laughed. "Afraid of the pip-squeak? When did that happen?"

"I'm not afraid. I'd just rather avoid getting my head served to me on a platter."

"Yeah, sorry about that. She's not happy you're here."

"That's a bit of an understatement."

Nathan moved to the sink, wishing he'd thought to buy groceries when they'd been in town earlier. He grabbed a glass from the cupboard stocked with dishes for guests and filled it with water from the tap.

"Didn't you talk to her before you invited me? Maybe if you would've explained why I was coming…"

"I tried." Justin brushed past him and opened the refrigerator. "I even gave her a list of things to get you. See? But Jess has a temper and thinks this should be a family matter."

Nathan bent down and stared at the fully stocked refrigerator, complete with a six-pack of his favorite beer, sandwich fixings, fresh produce, and dairy. There was enough food to feed him for at least a week. Guilt hovered over Nathan's head like a rain cloud, and he wondered if Justin still would have apologized if he knew what had transpired between Jessie and Nathan. He would have to confess the truth to Justin eventually. But not quite yet.

They'd barely spoken in the last eight years. He wanted to renew their friendship on a good note before he jumped off that ledge. Once he'd helped Jessie, it would be easier to confess the truth to Justin. He reached for two beer bottles, holding one out to Justin, wondering if he really trusted Jessie not to poison him.

"So, she's taking her frustration out on me instead of you?" Nathan had no doubt Jessie's ire had more to do with his silence after leaving and his reappearance now than it did with Justin.

"Trust me," Justin assured him with a laugh. "You're getting the PG version. I've been chewed out several times for even suggesting she call you. Be glad you're staying out here instead of one of the guest rooms in the house."

"Yeah, that makes me want to join you for dinner."

Nathan tipped his head back, enjoying the yeasty brew as it slid down his throat, warming his belly. At least, he wanted to believe it was the beer and not the memory of the last time he'd been alone in the house with Jessie. He hadn't prepared himself for this onslaught of memories. It wasn't like him not to be ready for every possible scenario, but he'd been too busy equipping himself for her hatred to think that feelings of his own might resurface.

Not that he didn't deserve her anger. He'd had eight years to set the record straight and should have done so as soon as he'd worked his way from under his father's thumb, but there was more to her anger than simply a failed summer romance.

"She's overreacting a bit, wouldn't you say? I mean, most people don't enjoy having their finances scrutinized, but wouldn't the possibility of saving this place be enough to make her at least somewhat civil?"

"Jessie's always had a chip on her shoulder about you. I think she had a crush on you that summer and when you never came back…" Justin took a long draw from his beer and shrugged. "But who knows. Ever since our parents were killed in that car accident, she's been working herself to the bone trying to keep this ranch in the black, but she won't admit that she can't do it alone. Everyone sees that except for her." He tipped back the bottle again, finishing off the last swallow. "It's turned into this vicious cycle. She isn't taking reservations, so we're losing money hand over fist trying to afford all these horses no one is coming to ride. We even had to cut our crew loose because we couldn't afford to keep paying them. When I try to talk to her, she shuts me out. We're going horse-poor."

"Horse-poor?"

Justin twisted his lips, pulling his mouth to the side humorlessly. "Yeah, it's what we call it when you have too many horses to feed. They're nothing more than a money pit at this point. Jess is a great trainer, and we could recoup a lot if she would just sell a few, but she refuses and keeps taking in more projects."

"Projects?" He was sure he sounded like an idiot, but as far as he was concerned, Justin might as well be speaking a foreign tongue. "What sort of projects?"

"She's been rescuing a lot of abused horses since our parents died. I don't know if it's her way to cope or what."

"Have you asked her about it?"

Justin shook his head. "Every time I try to talk to her about the horses, she gets defensive. It doesn't really matter why she's taking them in though, we still have more mouths to feed than we can afford. Speaking of which, we have guests for dinner tonight, so let's keep all the money discussions for later, in private, okay?"

"Paying guests?" Nathan had seen enough of Heart Fire's finances to know a few paying guests each month could go a long way to salvaging the ranch. It would be enough to keep it afloat until he could come up with a concrete plan of action for Jessie.

Justin chuckled and gave Nathan a wry look. "I wish. A friend of Jessie's and a couple of foster kids."

Foster kids? Abused horses? Nathan glanced out the window and saw the shadow of a woman stepping onto the back patio, staring toward the barn. He watched Jessie wander down the steps of the patio and make her way toward the pool. Jessie had always had a tender heart for the broken and those in need of rescue. In the weeks he'd spent here, she rescued a litter of kittens, hand-nursed a calf, and saved an orphaned raccoon cub.

He turned away from the dark-haired beauty as she walked through the gate and headed toward the barn. "When was the last time anyone paid to stay here?"

"We had a full house when we found out about Mom and Dad's accident," he said quietly. "We canceled all of our reservations and since the funeral Jess hasn't booked anything. I know she's having a hard time, but she just keeps saying she's not ready. Honestly, I'm not sure she's ever going to be ready, and we can't have anyone stay without a bare-bones crew at least."

Nathan pulled aside one of the curtains to peer out the front window. Jessie had turned her face toward the cabin, as if she was looking directly at him. There was a slight frown marring her forehead, pinching her brows together, and he wondered if his presence had caused it. When she wasn't biting his head off, fuming with anger, she was beautiful. She gathered her hair to one side, tucking stray locks behind her ear and brushing several strands from her eyes as the wind tossed them around her face. Even from this distance, he could see the sadness that haunted her blue eyes. It hadn't been there before.

"You think she's telling the truth?"

"Why wouldn't I? We're not the kind of family that keeps secrets."

Nathan felt his heart lurch. Justin had no idea the secret she'd kept from him. Justin rose and walked behind him. Nathan clenched his hand around the beer bottle, every instinct pressing him to confess the truth to his friend.

Justin followed his gaze and laughed, slapping his shoulder before heading toward the door. "You'd better not fall for my sister, man. She'll chew you up and spit you out." Waves of guilt washed over him again. "And when she got finished with you, I'd have to kick your ass. Besides, I thought you liked your women tall, leggy, and skinny as a stick—or is that just for the tabloids? Now come on. If we're late, Julia is going to have my hide."

"If I didn't know better, I'd think *you're* the one afraid of your sisters." Nathan shot his friend a smirk.

"I'm not stupid." Justin rolled his eyes. "Of course I'm afraid of them. You should be too, for that matter. Between those two and Bailey, I swore off women a long time ago. Females are too hard to please."

Nathan laughed as he followed his friend to the main house. No matter how much time passed or how different their circumstances seemed on the surface, they still got along like college roommates, bonded over their mutual desire to change the world. For Justin that meant healing animals. For Nathan it meant reviving struggling businesses.

At least one of them had remained optimistic about life, because Nathan sure wasn't that same idealistic, pie-eyed kid he'd been when he left Heart Fire Ranch. His father had made sure of that.

JESSIE SET THE rake against the wall and turned off the barn lights. She swiped her arm over her forehead, grimacing when it came away sweaty. Great, now there was probably dirt smeared across her face.

It was hot and muggy, even at this late hour with the moon high in the sky. The weather had her feeling irritable. Or maybe it was the pig-headed chauvinist in the cabin a few feet away. A house full of company didn't help either. She was on edge, and getting out of the house to clean stalls provided her with an excuse to escape the chaos. She wanted to shut her mind down a while, to put life back into its proper perspective.

Normally, she loved having the kids stay and work with the horses, but with every move she made under the green-eyed scrutiny of that suit-wearing number cruncher, everything grated on her nerves tonight. She couldn't help but wonder how Nathan might overanalyze and interpret her every word and deed.

She'd told Michael to live for himself; she needed to take her own advice. Her father knew she wanted to rescue horses, even encouraged her to do it. He told her they would take care of the details when he returned from vacation. Jessie shook her head slightly as she opened the back gate, refusing to allow herself to get lost in the sadness that always followed memories of her parents. The only thing she could focus on right now was doing her best to make sure this ranch started making a profit, so she could afford to continue taking in horses to rehabilitate.

She didn't want to think about her financial woes anymore tonight. She wanted nothing more than to bask in the comfort of her parents' home, *her* home. She stepped into the oasis that made up her backyard. One of the best features of the ranch, it was the one area her parents had splurged on for the pleasure of guests.

The quiet gurgle of the waterfall releasing into the pool mingled with the soothing chirp of the crickets and the low, throaty hum of the bullfrogs. There were no lights on in the house, so only the stars reflected in the dark water. The symphony of the night enveloped Jessie like a down blanket, making her feel warm and secure.

A trickle of sweat slid between her breasts as she slumped into one of the lounge chairs circling the pool. Jessie watched the moon's reflection ripple slightly on the water as a bug landed on the surface. The water called her name, inviting her to take a plunge, to wash away the day's stresses and doubts. She glanced back at the house, wondering if anyone would notice if she just jumped in, fully clothed. She doubted anyone inside would even care but didn't want the dust from her clothes in the newly cleaned pool, and skinny-dipping wasn't an option with so many people around. A few late-night laps were just what she needed to still the hamsters racing on the nonstop treadmill of her worries. Her mind made up, she hurried back to her room and changed into her suit.

She returned to the pool and dropped a towel on the chaise before diving into the water, letting the cool liquid flow over her skin like satin as she moved to the other end, barely making a sound. She somersaulted underwater, pressing off the wall and gliding back as effortlessly as a dolphin; then she heard a splash and felt someone move past her through the water.

Jessie bolted upright and swam away from the intruder, reacting without understanding the fear that tightened in her belly. She pressed her back against the tile of the pool wall. "What the—"

"Sorry. Sorry, I didn't mean to scare you."

She swiped the water from her face, pushing the soaked tendrils of her dark hair from her eyes and saw Nathan's laughing eyes gleaming at her in the moonlight as he held his hands up toward her.

"What in the hell are you doing out here?" She felt the urge to cross her arms over her chest as she swam backward toward the shallow end of the pool until her feet could touch the bottom. How dare he come into her backyard uninvited? To violate her sanctuary?

"I just came out for a swim. It was quiet so I assumed everyone was already in bed."

Nathan's brows drooped as he moved toward her, the water only reaching his lower ribs. She didn't remember him being so tall, or his presence being so imposing. Nathan had always been impressive but now he seemed larger than life. She wasn't sure what it was about this man that set her so on edge. Or how he could make her stomach feel like it had suddenly broken out with a deadly case of butterflies at the same time. She realized she was still retreating and stopped, standing her ground and arching a brow in defiance.

"Well, some of us still had work to finish. I'm so sorry I couldn't take the day off to entertain you." She swam toward the stairs, dismissing him, but felt a hand gently circle her wrist.

The butterflies in her stomach took off, beating against her ribs, making it difficult for her to breath. How could his touch still do this to her? How dare he touch her? Her traitorous body had held onto the memories of Nathan without her permission.

It shouldn't still bother her that he'd never called, but after the last night they'd spent together, she'd thought it meant something to him, that *she'd* meant something. But as it turned out, he'd done her a favor. He'd saved her the embarrassment of telling him she loved him, and he'd made it easy to despise him. It sure made him a convenient target for her ire now.

She shot him a scathing look over her shoulder, then down to his hand still holding her captive.

"Look, I think we've gotten off on the wrong foot, Jess. I'm just here to help you."

"Yeah?" Jessie jerked her arm from his grasp. "I don't remember asking for your help. I don't need your help, and I don't want it."

"Wow, I remembered you being a pistol, Jessie, but it would have been nice if someone warned me that you'd taken bitchiness to a new level."

"Excuse me?" She turned back to him slowly, appalled at his audacity and hoping for his sake she hadn't heard him correctly.

"I just don't understand this whole two-year-old, I'll-do-it-myself thing." He shrugged. "It's obviously not working. I get that you hate me and you're scared but—"

She walked toward him, moving through the water, until she stood toe-to-toe, looking up at him, her eyes barely reaching his shoulder. "I am *not* scared."

Nathan noticed she didn't correct his assumption about him. He let it slide and arched a brow, cocking his head to the side as a grin tugged at the corner of his mouth. "You sure about that?"

"I'm not."

"You're running a dude ranch, *alone* I might add. One that normally takes several people to operate. You've got no clients booked now and none for the future. This place is sinking faster than the Titanic, and you're not scared?" He scoffed, his green eyes looking down on her. "You should be scared because, if you're not, I don't think I'm going to be able to help you."

Jessie took another step toward him and narrowed her eyes. "Did you miss the part where I didn't ask for your—"

"I heard you. You don't want my help," he mimicked. "But, let's face it; I'm your best option right now."

She turned her back on him and climbed out of the pool. "You're my *only* option or you wouldn't be here. I doubt you can help anyway. If I remember right, you were pretty hopeless the last time you were here. You could barely mend a fence. What do you know about running a dude ranch?"

"Apparently, almost as much as you do." She glared at him as she reached for her towel. "Jessie, you might know horses, but I know business. I can save *this* business, but only if you quit fighting me and cooperate." Nathan shook his head and followed her out of the pool. "Look, I get that I hurt you. It was never my intention. But it was a long time ago."

She laughed, but the sound was sad and bitter, even to her own ears. "Don't flatter yourself, Nathan."

He ran his fingers through his hair. Jessie's mouth dried up as her eyes followed the water sliding down the planes of his face, the moonlight making shadows over his jawline. She forced herself not to not follow the path of the water any farther than his broad shoulders. She might tell herself that he wasn't her type anymore, but she was treading into dangerous territory. There was no sense looking for temptation.

Nathan was walking, talking, raw sexual attraction, and she was sure he used it to bend women to his will often. Her body might not know the difference between the past and the present, but Jessie wasn't about to let his sexy smile and hard muscles distract her focus again. She wasn't the same innocent girl who had believed in fairy tales eight years ago. He'd taught her a lesson she wasn't likely to forget.

"I'm sorry. I owe you that. After I left here, things got…complicated. I was wrong not to call."

How long had she wanted to hear those words? She realized she'd been staring at the planes of his chest, highlighted by the moonlight. She flicked her eyes up to meet his, trying to get her brain operating again.

"I'm surprised you never told Justin."

"Of course not! What should I tell him? That his best friend seduced me and then left without another word?"

She moved to stand in front of him and poked a finger against the solid wall of his chest. "Besides, I didn't see the point after you turned your back on him, too. I didn't think he'd be stupid enough to ever trust your lying ass again."

"That wasn't what happened." His voice was husky, seductively mesmerizing as his fingers brushed over the back of her hand.

She could barely make out his face in the near darkness, but she could feel the gentle invitation in his touch. It transported her back in time. To a time when she was young and trusting and naïve. A time when she believed in love that could withstand any trial.

She tried to ignore the grief and the loneliness that washed over her. It made her wish Nathan would make the first move, that he would wrap his arms around her, allow her to bury her face against his chest and seek the comfort she longed for, if only for a moment. The isolation she'd felt for the past few months filled her and tears threatened, burning at the back of her eyes.

Damn it, she couldn't cry in front of this man, or anyone else, just because she felt a little sad. She quickly pulled her hand away from his grasp. She didn't need sympathy. She didn't *want* it, especially from this man. She just wanted him to go away.

She could almost hear her father's voice. *Cowgirl up, Jess.*

As if sensing the change in her demeanor, Nathan laughed quietly. "Don't worry, Jessie, your secret's safe with me. I won't tell anyone you aren't always a hard ass."

Jessie smiled sweetly before lifting her hands and giving him a quick shove backward.

Droplets of water splashed over her feet as he fell into the deep end of the pool. She heard him rise to the surface, sputtering and cursing. She wrapped her towel around her waist.

"I don't know what my brother told you, but neither of you has any idea about what is best for me or this ranch. I have plans, and neither one of you is going to mess them up. Enjoy your swim, Mr. Kerrington."

Once again, she left him behind, heading into the house without giving him to opportunity to have the last word. Exactly the way she wanted it.

Chapter Five

NATHAN RUBBED HIS tired eyes. The sun was just starting to climb over the horizon and peek through the trees, but he'd already been up for several hours. He had just polished off his third cup of coffee when Jessie made her way into the kitchen.

She barely glanced his way as she walked by. "Been up a while?"

He was surprised she said anything, but at least she seemed friendlier this morning. Then again, why wouldn't she be as chipper as hell after shoving him into the pool last night? "Since about four a.m. I was just getting ready to start another pot if you want me to do it."

"I'll get it." She reached for a mug and poured what was left in the pot into her cup before adding cream, sipping it as she started brewing a new pot. "Why are you up so early? I know we get up with the chickens but I thought you city boys liked your sleep. And why are you in my kitchen instead of your cabin?"

He let her veiled insult slide. He didn't even want to attempt to verbally spar with her when he was this tired. It was just easier to be civil. After his dunking last night, he wouldn't put it past her to dump the coffee over his head. "I started there, but I wanted to catch you before you got too busy this morning. Justin stopped by and let me in before he headed to the clinic." He held up a file folder. "I thought maybe we could go over some of these files today. Most importantly, the profit-loss statements for the ranch for the past few years."

She glanced back at him over her shoulder before topping off her coffee with the fresh brew, and her eyes clouded with suspicion. "I don't have time. There are other things that are more urgent today."

"More important than figuring out where your money is going? Why it's disappearing so quickly with nothing to show for it?"

Jessie sighed and turned to glare at him, leaning one hip against the counter. "I have three horses coming in this morning, and I need to evaluate them. If I get finished with them early enough, I'll meet with you, okay?"

Nathan folded his hands over the spreadsheets covering the surface of the kitchen table and met her gaze. He could be just as stubborn as she was. He would figure out a way to reach her, some sort of compromise that would gain her trust again. He was here to help *her*, not Justin or his own reputation, but for some reason, she was still balking at his help.

"I'll tell you what, why don't we talk about these files over dinner? That way you can finish your work." Leaving her with no other excuse for avoiding him.

"Dinner?" Her brows arched high on her forehead in surprise, but she ducked her chin and tried to hide it by sipping her coffee. "I don't think so. You might ply me with a little liquor and convince me to *cuddle* with you again."

It was a low blow. It was supposed to be a reminder of what happened the night before he left, but that wasn't the way he remembered it, not even close. She might have been only eighteen, but the one bottle of beer they'd shared hadn't impaired her judgment. By the time they'd made love that night, she'd been completely sober. Sober enough that when he tried to stay in control, she'd clung to him like a lifeline, her body hot against his, and he couldn't fight any longer.

"It's pretty hard to cuddle with a porcupine," he retorted.

She lowered her mug and pursed her lips, but he didn't wait for her reply.

"Look, Jessie, I promise, this is entirely about the ranch. I'm trying to figure out how to bring Heart Fire back into the black, but I need to find out from you which expenses are nonnegotiable. Like this stable mix—what is it and why does it cost so much?"

She chewed at the inside of her lower lip and took a deep breath, looking suddenly unsure and, for the first time since his arrival, slightly vulnerable. "Fine. But only on one condition."

He crossed his arms over his chest, not wanting to appear too acquiescent. "That depends."

"Before you go making any recommendations, I want you to see the horses coming in today and watch the evaluation. Then we can talk about the future of the ranch."

"Why?"

She took another sip from the mug. "You'll see, but it's the only way I'll agree to do this."

He wasn't about to waste the rare opportunity to gain this stubborn woman's cooperation. It didn't to come easily or often. "Fine, tell me what I need to do."

She twisted her mouth to the side, trying to hide a smirk as her eyes slid over him. "The first thing you need to do is change into something suitable for working outside."

"What's wrong with what I have on?" He looked down at his polo shirt.

Jessie shook her head. "I can't believe those are the clothes you brought. Don't you remember anything?" She finished her coffee and chuckled as she put the cup into the dishwasher. "I'll have Bailey grab you some of Justin's clothes and swing them by your cabin before she heads to the clinic. You'll thank me later."

"Justin's clothes will be too big and you know it. I'll be swimming in them."

Jessie didn't even bother to hide her grin as she raised her hands in mock apology. Nathan stood and leaned over the table, straightening the documents. It was the first bit of humor he'd seen from her, the first genuine smile she'd even directed his way, and he found himself enjoying the glimpse far more than he should.

"I get the feeling you're going to make me regret this." When he looked up, the moment of good-natured teasing had passed. She stopped with her hand on the kitchen door.

"You probably *will* regret it, but it won't be my fault." A frown marred Jessie's brow, and her eyes looked sad again. "I'll meet you at the pasture by the barn in an hour."

NATHAN SHIFTED AGAIN from his position on the porch. How in the world did Justin wear these jeans all day long? They were too big in the waist, so he'd cinched them with a belt, but they were still falling off. He adjusted the weather-beaten baseball cap on his head and sent up a prayer of thanks that no paparazzi had found him here. He'd never live down a picture of him looking like the most uncomfortable redneck alive in an oversized, ratty T-shirt, beat-up cowboy boots, and a camouflage John Deere cap.

He watched Jessie as she stood in the smallest pasture, waiting for the truck and stock trailer creeping down the driveway. She glanced back at him nervously and then leaned over to say something to her brother. Justin was standing beside her wearing the same redneck attire as Nathan, although his hat was on backward. Nathan made his way down the steps to where the pair waited and saw Jessie tense, her shoulders rising and her hands clenching into fists at her side. He wondered how many times he was going to have to apologize before she stopped getting defensive whenever he approached.

"Why don't you stand over there, Nathan?" Justin pointed near the fence. "We don't know how these horses are going to act, and it's better to be safe."

Nathan took a step backward. "What do you mean 'safe'?"

"Be as quiet as possible," Jessie ordered. "Stay out of the way and don't come in here, no matter what happens."

Her instructions weren't putting him any more at ease. With anxiety bunching in his muscles like a current with no release, he watched the pair as the truck pulled up to the pasture and came to a slow, easy stop.

A woman leaned out the window toward Jessie. "You want them in here?"

Jessie took a few steps toward the truck. "Are they okay together?"

The woman nodded and Justin move toward the gate, opening it as the woman backed her aluminum stock trailer inside. The near silence from Jessie and Justin had him curious. He could feel the tension coursing through them, but with nothing to base it on, it seemed odd. He felt out of place, like he was missing some crucial clue, and he gripped the fence hard enough for his knuckles to turn white.

Justin stood by the gate, while the woman parked the truck and moved to the back of the trailer. Unlatching the back door and swinging it wide, she blocked Nathan's view of the animals inside, but he didn't miss the look of horror on Jessie's face. Her eyes immediately widened before welling with tears, as she pinched her lips together, trying not to cry. He recognized pain and anger waging war within her and felt the desire to pull her close, to protect her from the emotions he could see written clearly in her face.

Jessie stepped into the trailer and he heard her murmuring quiet words and nonsense phrases. Slow thumps of what he assumed were hooves came from inside. While he watched in silence from the fence, Jessie led the first animal to Justin for inspection.

What little he was able to see was gut-wrenching.

The animal was nothing but skin stretched tightly over large bones, sunken in unnatural places. Ribs were plainly visible, and he could see each and every bump and ridge of the animal's hip bones. It looked as if the miserable creature was wasting away from disease with open, festering sores dotting the mangy coat, oozing sickeningly. Its hooves were so unkempt they curled up from the ground, and the weak animal could barely lift its head.

Jessie ran a careful hand over the animal's neck, speaking quietly in a soothing tone, almost a purr, and he watched in amazement as the neglected animal buried its head against her chest, seeking comfort.

"Okay, Justin, this girl's going to need your help more than mine."

Nathan heard the hitch in her voice, as if she was choking back tears, and he tried to swallow the lump lodged in his own throat at the sight of the defeated animal. Justin ran his hands over the horse's shoulders, inspecting the festering sores. His friend had always had a soft spot for animals in need. It didn't surprise him that, for all his talk of Jessie making them horse-poor, Justin couldn't turn the abused animals away without helping them, any more than Jessie could.

"She needs to be in a stall, Jess." Justin's voice was thick, as if he was having difficulty speaking as well. "She's going to need antibiotics, and these sores need to be cleaned several times a day, but I think they will heal up, although they might leave some discoloration on her hide. We should give her a dose of wormer and her shot series. I doubt she's had them. Let's get her some food and water first."

A loud, shrill whinny came from inside the trailer where two other horses waited. There was a crash, and Jessie's head snapped back to the trailer.

"Deb," she called to the woman who'd delivered the animals, "why don't you take her into the first stall on the left so we can get these other two out?"

"You might want to be careful of the next one, Jess," the other woman said. "He's pretty attached to the other two, and we had a tough time getting him haltered. I had to tranquilize him and put him between the mares just to get him into the trailer. He's pretty rank."

"Sounds like it's worn off." Jessie gave Deb a wary glance before looking back at Justin, who simply raised a solitary brow at her stubborn determination before shaking his head. "Relax, I'll be fine," she insisted. "Why don't you man the gate and I'll let this one come out on his own? We'll give him some space to explore first."

Nathan watched as Jessie headed to the side of the trailer, out of his line of sight. He quickly shot a glance at

Justin, shocked he'd let his slip of a sister near that metal coffin with what sounded like a crazed animal. He heard several loud *bangs* come from inside. This situation was dangerous, and he felt completely helpless. He wanted to intercede, to grab Jessie, and to yank her back to safety, but he doubted she'd appreciate him butting into her business, especially after her warning. But if this animal was anywhere close to as dangerous as this woman claimed, Jessie was sure to get hurt.

Why the hell was Justin still standing at the gate? Why didn't he go check on her?

"Justin, is that horse dangerous?"

"Of course he is."

"Then go get her. Why are you letting her in there?" His friend's glance instantly silenced him.

The damn fool woman was going to get herself killed. He heard another slam from inside the trailer and saw Jessie pressed up against the side through the slats. If Justin wasn't going to make sure she wasn't being killed, he would. He wasn't about to stand by and watch it happen.

Nathan opened the gate to the corral and stepped inside as a jet black horse bolted from the back of the trailer like a flash of dark lightning. Baring teeth, the animal reared, striking the ground with his front hooves, intent on doing damage to whomever or whatever might be unlucky enough to cross his path. Right now, that was Nathan.

As the horse charged, rough hands yanked him backward by the collar of his shirt. Jessie ran from the side of the trailer in time to see his butt hit the ground with a thud outside the pasture. Justin jerked the gate shut just as the horse's teeth snapped the air where Nathan's head had been moments before. The horse spun back toward Jessie, pawing at the dirt.

Justin glared down at Nathan as he latched the gate. "What the hell are you doing? She said, 'stay out'!"

"What the hell are *you* doing leaving her in there with that insane horse? She's going to get herself hurt." He jumped up and headed for the gate again but Justin grasped his arm.

"She knows what she's doing. The only one who's going to get hurt around here is you."

Nathan watched Jessie calmly stand her ground, even as the animal reared high into the air, kicking out with his front hooves. He looked far healthier than the other two, at least physically, but he was completely out of control. As the horse dropped back onto all fours, Jessie edged away from the trailer and along the side of the fence, across from where the two of them waited. She cocked her head slightly, peering at the horse as the animal snorted loudly, eyes wide. He pawed at the ground again, watching her intently. When she didn't react, the animal took a few steps toward her and paused, ears flicking nervously back and forth.

"You're not so bad, are you?" She was completely focused on the horse, tuning out everything else. "You've just got a lot of spirit."

Nathan's fingers gripped the top rail, using every ounce of self-control he possessed to remain outside the fence when everything in him screamed to rescue her. The horse bounced on his front feet threateningly, but

Jessie remained alert, yet oddly relaxed, turning to face the beast before taking another step toward him.

"Come on, boy. You know better than this. I'm not going to hurt you."

Nathan couldn't hold his tongue any longer. "Jessie, could you get your ass out of there before you give me a heart attack?"

Her eyes darted to him, and the horse snapped his teeth at her, his ears flat against his head. She immediately looked back at the horse, but a slight smile slid to her lips as she reached behind a post and grabbed what appeared to be a long stick with a piece of material tied to the end. "Watch and learn, Wall Street." She took a length of rope from the post.

Nathan cringed as Justin laughed. "Wall Street?"

"Yes, Bailey's been calling me that, and it appears it's sticking."

His eyes never left her as she pointed the end of the stick toward the ground and swung the rope at her side in circles. The horse immediately jumped into motion, taking off in a gallop around the pasture. Jessie moved to the center of the area and let the horse move out. Nathan watched as the animal circled the pasture twice before stopping and turning to face her. She stopped spinning the rope as he quieted.

He didn't look any less dangerous to Nathan, but Jessie saw what she wanted and walked slowly toward the horse. The animal pinned his ears against his head, lunging forward slightly. Calmly, she circled the rope, and he took off at a run, circling the pasture again. When he started to come too close, she would lift the stick straight in front of her, pointing ahead, and the animal immediately moved away from it.

Seeing that she seemed to not only be safe but also in control of the animal, at least for the moment, Nathan relaxed his grip on the railing and turned to Justin. "Isn't she just scaring him more?"

"He's aggressive because he's afraid. She's just making him realize he can't dominate or scare her. He's trying to bluff her, and she's not taking it from him. Watch," he instructed.

After repeating the sequence several times, Nathan saw the horse stop and turn toward Jessie, this time, hanging his head slightly and licking his lips. He took a few steps toward her and stopped. Jessie dropped her hands to her sides, the rope hanging against her leg, but she didn't move toward the horse.

"He's quiet now; why doesn't she just lead him out like Deb did the other one?"

He'd been watching Jessie so intently, he hadn't even noticed Deb's return until she laughed beside him. "She's reading his body language. Dropping her hands like that and softening her body language means he's welcome to approach. But making him move toward her means he trusts her and respects her authority. He's acknowledging her as the leader of his 'herd.' It's almost like she knows exactly what he's thinking. That's what makes her one of the best I've ever seen."

Nathan arched a brow in disbelief. "She's *his* leader? She's five foot nothing and that animal has to weigh over a thousand pounds."

"Yep, and if anyone can gentle that horse, it's Jessie. She'll teach him to lose his fear, but he will respect her."

They watched as the horse approached her warily, his ears continually moving back and forth, as Jessie spoke softly to him. The animal stopped, stretching his neck as far as he could, sniffing at her while still trying to remain too far away for her to touch. Nathan was surprised to see her take a few steps back, away from the horse. He moved toward her again, his head low, but this time she allowed him to sniff her before sliding a rope halter around his neck. When he didn't pull away, she moved it over his nose and tied it on one side.

Nathan stared at Jessie, walking the horse around the pasture as the animal tried to bite her twice. What in the hell was she thinking? That thing was twelve hundred pounds of muscle and temperamental hooves. He was too dangerous ever to be sellable. Even if she could, who would want to ride something that mean? She was obviously great with horses, so why was she wasting time with animals like this when she could be training animals that would make the ranch money?

"Is this what you were talking about?" Nathan asked Justin.

Justin unlatched the gate for Jessie to exit. "Yep. It's a pretty rare gift, but now you can say you've seen a 'horse whisperer' in action."

Jessie walked past them, pretending not to hear the conversation, but Nathan saw a flicker of frustration in her blue eyes.

"Too bad it doesn't make us a dime," Justin muttered.

Chapter Six

WHAT THE HELL was Nathan thinking, coming into the pasture like that?

"A better question might be, what I was thinking," she murmured to the stallion as she led him to the stall.

She should never have suggested Nathan watch. He shouldn't even be on the ranch, let alone near these horses. Resignation settled in her chest, followed closely by a burning resentment that found its target square on Nathan's broad back.

She'd hoped seeing the brutality done to these horses would give him a small understanding of what she was trying to do. That maybe he would help her find a way to keep the ranch afloat while she continued to rescue abused horses for rehabilitation. She'd assumed when Nathan saw how much these horses needed her, how much she could help them, she could explain how she and her father had planned to make the change before the accident and he'd be onboard. His approval would go a long way to convincing Justin.

But after what he'd just seen, she was certain Nathan wasn't going to help. Instead of seeing a scared animal in need, he saw a wild, dangerous beast. He'd questioned her methods and thought her incapable because of her size. She'd specifically told him just to watch and not get involved. When that stallion bolted from the trailer, charging Nathan, her heart dropped to her toes before speeding ahead like a locomotive. He'd nearly gotten himself killed because he couldn't follow her simple instructions—stay quiet and stay out. As soon as she finished with these horses, she was going to rip that pain-in-the-ass accountant a new one.

The stud balked several times on the way to the barn, but when he heard the other horses, he entered the stall eagerly. Still, getting him settled took longer than she expected. Jessie knew she had to be patient with him and take her time if she wanted him to respond with trust instead of fear. By the time she made her way back to the pasture, Deb was leading the third horse from the trailer. The mare looked battle weary, barely bothering to look at her new surroundings, even when the stallion whinnied shrilly from the barn.

Jessie hurried past, ignoring her brother and Nathan as she entered the pasture again, her eyes focused on the mare. "Has she been like this the entire time?"

The mare was in dire need of some good food, but the dulled look in her eyes spoke of an entirely different kind of need. This animal was depressed. Jessie ran a hand over the mare's shoulders and back, feeling her bones protruding.

Neglect had that effect on many horses. As long as this girl didn't show any signs of aggression in the next few days, she would be a great prospect for Michael and Aleta to work with on the ground. The love and attention they could give her would remind the mare that humans were friends instead of enemies and give all three of them direction.

Deb passed Jessie the lead rope, leaning in to her. "Who's the stiff?"

"Just a friend of Justin's who should be gone in a couple days." She ran a hand over the mare's face, and the horse tucked her head against Jessie's side. The gesture of trust wasn't lost on Jessie, and she scratched behind the mare's ears.

"So, the stallion is the only one with behavioral issues?" she asked, changing the subject. She didn't want to talk about Nathan. She'd like to forget his presence altogether and hoped Deb would catch the hint.

"This one has been pretty down, but I think with some attention, she'll come around to be a nice mare. You know that stud colt is going to test you again, right?" Deb said.

"Of course."

Deb jerked her chin toward Nathan who was still watching them intently from the gate, not about to let Jessie get away without telling her more. "I wouldn't turn that one away if he wanted to come by my place." She winked at him, and Nathan quickly looked away, pretending he hadn't seen her.

Jessie snorted, trying to hold back her laughter. At nearly forty-three and divorced for over ten years, Deb was a gritty woman who didn't hesitate to speak her mind, bluntly most of the time, but Jessie adored her. They'd met over a common desire to rescue a horse from a feedlot. Deb quickly became a confidante and an advocate when Jessie wanted to broach the idea of starting a rescue and rehabilitation center with her father. Deb was there when Jessie was notified about her parents and was the first to offer to relieve her of a few horses if it became necessary. She hated that she might have to take her up on the offer because of her own incompetence.

"Finally. About time you laughed. You need to find a cowboy to ride so you can give these horses a break," Deb teased, shaking her head and pursing her lips. She eyed Nathan again and frowned, suddenly serious. "I'm not sure he's the one for you. He doesn't know horses."

"Yeah, well, apparently he knows business and finance, so Justin thinks he can get the ranch back in the black. Hopefully, he does it and gets out of here quickly."

Deb nudged her arm with an elbow. "Nothing wrong with giving him a ride or two before he leaves. Ah, get it?"

Jessie snorted and shook her head. "You never learned the art of subtlety, did you Deb?"

Deb joined Jessie's laughter. "Subtlety is overrated. Enjoy life while you're still young and beautiful, Jess. Before you know it, you'll be as old as I am and regretting the things you never tried. You know the saying, 'Take the bull by the horns?' Now's the time to do it."

Deb ran a hand over the mare's neck, her attention on the horse again. "I'll take this one into the other stall. She'll be fine in a couple weeks. When do you have the farrier coming out to work on their feet?"

"Justin will give them meds here, and the shoer will be out tomorrow to do all the horses. I'm not sure when we'll be able to get that stud colt done. He's going to need more time before he trusts anyone."

"You might have bitten off more than you thought with that one."

"No, I think he just needs to adjust for a bit and realize I'm not going to hurt him," Jessie assured her. "He definitely needs to be gelded right away."

Deb laughed and pointed at Nathan, who was talking to Justin but had yet to take his eyes off Jessie. "I wasn't talking about the horse."

"WHAT THE HELL is wrong with you? Do you have a death wish?" Jessie had already finished with the horses and saw Nathan sitting on the back porch with Justin as if he was one of her guests. "I told you to stay out of the way. You could have gotten us all killed."

"That horse was crazy. I thought you were in trouble." He shrugged, and she noted he didn't sound apologetic at all. Anger seethed again, bubbling in her chest like a geyser ready to blow.

"He wasn't crazy; he was scared. I know what I'm doing."

She stood over him, looking down at him, and crossed her arms. She'd been hoping her position might intimidate him, but it didn't seem to be working. Nathan barely looked contrite and it infuriated her. Didn't he realize what could have happened?

"Why don't you stick to what you know—spreadsheets and numbers—and let me run my ranch?"

"Look, Jessie, I'm sorry, okay?" Nathan's voice drew her attention back to him. "You're right. I agreed to stay out of the way and I didn't do it." She opened her mouth to speak, but he didn't give her a chance. "The fact is, from here on out, when it comes to the horses, I will follow your orders. That being said, I can't exactly do my job without your cooperation either. So, can we head to dinner and have that discussion you promised?"

"Are you kidding me? No."

Her brother snickered beside him. "I warned you, Nathan."

She glared. "What the hell are you laughing at?"

Justin tried for an innocent look, failing miserably. "Nothing. Just go to dinner. Take *Wall Street*, here, into town and let him pick from our four-star dining establishments."

Nathan cocked his head at Justin's sarcasm. "I used to eat whatever garbage you put in front of me. I'm hardly worried about a few local restaurants."

"Yeah? Well, I hear your taste has changed a little since college," Justin teased, oblivious to Jessie's irritation with them. "Sorry, but we don't have a place that serves caviar and champagne. You might just have to make do with beer and pizza."

Nathan scowled—probably, Jessie thought, because Justin's comment hit too close to the truth. He was completely out of his element here, and they all knew it. Everything about him shouted it from the rooftops, from his expensive clothing to his inability to understand the basics of horse safety.

He'd managed to fit in better during his first visit, when he'd been completely green and needed her to show him the ropes. Jessie couldn't help but think about when she'd first taught him to ride, taking him to the river. How they'd spent that first afternoon trying to pretend there wasn't an attraction between them. Or the moment she gave in and stood on tiptoe, pressing a kiss to his surprised lips. She didn't want to think about the electric jolt of pleasure she felt when his tongue slipped past her lips. She tried to push aside the memories of him helping her unload hay and how his hands had moved over her body behind the bales, teaching her what desire felt like. She didn't want to reminisce about the many things he'd taught her or the broken heart he'd left behind.

Don't even go down that road again.

Nathan rose from the chair and moved to stand in front of Jessie, blocking Justin from her view entirely. He only took one step toward her, didn't even touch her, but she could feel electricity instantly spark between them, sizzling down her spine. It wasn't tension. That she would have been prepared for. This was different, as if her body was begging for his touch again.

Nathan's nearness sucked the air from between them, and she found it difficult to catch her breath. The look in his eyes was hot, making goosebumps break out over her arms as she remembered laying his in arms after making love, as he pressed tender kisses to her swollen lips. She saw yearning in the depths of his gaze, but it was gone in a flash, almost as if she imagined it, replaced by determination.

Nathan ran a hand through his hair, and were she in her normal frame of mind instead of this emotional upheaval, she would have laughed at how it remained perfectly in place in spite of his rough treatment. It was just one more thing that highlighted the differences between them. A few hours of work outside had her waves wild and unruly. She and Nathan had absolutely nothing in common. Why in the world did he have to be the one man who could turn her body into a live current of sexual tension?

"Jessie."

The expectation in his voice drew her eyes to his, and she realized she'd been staring at his mouth, at those lips that had teased her skin so wonderfully in the past. A blush burned her cheeks, and she prayed he wouldn't notice.

"I really am sorry. I asked you to trust my knowledge, but I didn't give you the same benefit of the doubt. We were lucky that no one got hurt."

She could read the genuine regret in his eyes, but there was something more she couldn't quite name. Nathan wasn't apologizing about the horse any longer. He stared at her intently, his gaze smoldering with desire she'd assumed was only in her mind.

"It won't happen again," he promised, breaking into her thoughts.

She took a step back from him, trying to put a little distance between them, hoping that would help her breathe again and collect her scattered emotions. "Good, it…it better not."

She tried to convince herself she had every right to be angry, but she knew it wasn't anger making her heart race like a wild stallion or causing the warmth that was settling south of her belt buckle.

"But," he added, making her want to cringe, "we still have a lot to talk about and not much time to get this taken care of. I'm only here for a week, so why don't you get ready so we can head into town for an early dinner?"

A part of Jessie wanted to refuse, if only to assert her independence, especially when she glanced at her brother and saw the smirk he wore. He knew she really had no choice in the matter—she'd have to talk to Nathan about the ranch's finances eventually.

Regardless of her irritation with Justin, she had to do whatever she could to save the ranch. This place was all that was left of her parents, filled with memories of their hard work and love. And she couldn't continue being a burden on her siblings, who were both able to keep their businesses succeeding. If dinner with Nathan was what it would take, so be it. Nothing mattered more to her than her family, not even her pride.

"Jessie, I'm only trying to help, I swear." Nathan's voice was quiet but insistent, and she felt her stomach do a nervous tumble.

"Geez, Jess, just go to dinner already. Nathan can't read your mind and figure out these expenses alone. Quit making the poor guy beg."

"Fine, but I need a shower." She glowered at her brother. "And you," she pointed at Justin, "can figure out dinner for everyone else, Mr. Big Mouth."

Chapter Seven

NATHAN WAITED FOR Jessie in the kitchen, while her sister and Bailey entertained him, reminiscing about the months he'd spend on the ranch. It felt like a lifetime ago, and he barely recognized the naïve kid he'd been in their descriptions of his antics. But when they started telling stories about Jessie as a teen, he couldn't help but be enthralled. He'd known she was a hellcat, but hearing about the time Jessie carved Julia's name into the hood of her ex-boyfriend's car when he cheated on Julia had him doubled over with laughter.

"No one messes with her family." Julia wiped away a tear, laughing at the memory.

He might laugh at the picture Julia's story created, but he couldn't stop the niggling of fear that crept down his spine when he realized her family would return the same sort of reckless loyalty for her. He was in for a world of hurt when they found out what he'd done.

"Is she still the family superhero?"

Julia cocked her head, her blond hair draping over her shoulder as she thought about the moniker. "I think so. She's been the righter of wrongs in our family as long as I can remember. Even if it was at the risk of her own hide. And, usually," she added, "it is."

"Yeah, she doesn't think much about her own safety, does she?" Nathan shook his head; the image of Jessie in the pasture with the stallion earlier made him anxious all over again.

"She comes by it honestly," Bailey said. "That's the Hart way: act first and worry about the consequences later. I think we get it from our dads."

"She's going to get herself killed one of these days," he muttered, leaning back in the chair and watching the two women prepare their own meal for the evening.

Julia paused and looked at him curiously. He'd better be careful to watch what he said around her. She was far too observant. "But, it was pretty amazing to watch. It was like she could read that animal's mind."

He'd never seen anything like what Jessie did. Seeing her with the two mares, abused and beaten, broke his heart. He'd never seen anything so brutal up close, and it made him wonder what sort of a person would do such a thing. But watching the stallion refuse to give up, then be calmed by Jessie's patience and gentle determination, made him wonder if Jessie wasn't doing exactly what she was meant to.

She shouldn't be taking people for trail rides and campouts. He'd seen the look in her eyes while she worked with each of the horses. It was pure joy, in spite of the danger. There had to be some way for her to market the ranch as a rescue facility instead of a dude ranch. He wanted to help Jessie keep that light in her eyes.

Jessie entered the kitchen, and Nathan's gaze immediately gravitated to her before he closed his eyes while taking a deep breath. He shook his head. He should have known better.

He'd assumed dinner out meant dressing up, so he'd showered and put his own clothes on again. While still casual in slacks and a polo shirt, his clothing was far dressier than her jeans and T-shirt combination. Although, he had to admit the rhinestones on the back pockets of her jeans accentuated the ample curve of her rear as she turned and reached for her truck keys.

"Ready to go, Wall Street?"

"You know I hate that nickname, right?" He slid the chair back under the table amid the laughter of all three women.

"Really?" Jessie spun the keys around a finger and arched a brow before reaching for her purse and sticking out her lower lip. "That's funny. I don't remember asking."

Nathan caught the slight smile tugging at the corner of her lips. She was beautiful when she smiled, and he wondered why she didn't do it more often.

Because it would contradict her hard-ass facade.

He arched a brow and returned the smile with one of his own. "Okay, Badass, let's go eat."

Bailey guffawed and Julia hid her laugh behind her hand. Jessie bit the corner of her mouth in an attempt to hide her smile.

She still intrigued him, as much as she ever had. No matter how many women he'd met growing up in the political limelight or at college, he'd never met a woman quite like her. How could she be so patient and tender with the animals and yet so tough on the people around her? He'd seen glimpses of the woman beneath the armor, but only enough to make him want to see more.

JESSIE DIALED THE volume up on the local country radio station as she drove into town. She wanted to avoid talking with Nathan as much possible. The more time she spent near him, the less she seemed to be able to control the heat that warmed her, forcing her to remember their history. And not the part where he left.

She kept finding herself drifting back to that last night and the way his hands had moved expertly over her body, guiding her into the passionate oblivion of desire. She swallowed as her breath caught in her chest, and she glanced sideways to find him watching her. Nathan made her uncomfortable, like she was dazed and off balance, and she couldn't have that. She'd spent too many years trying to piece her heart back together.

Jessie wasn't the type of woman who fell in love easily. It wasn't that she wasn't attracted to other men, but none had measured up to who she'd thought Nathan was that summer. Handsome and charming, he'd seemed devoted to her brother, even going so far as to evade her fumbling attempts to flirt at first. But after their first kiss at the river, they'd both known there was something special between them. At least, she'd thought they'd both known. He'd just asked for a little time to break the news to her brother himself. It turned out that she'd been the only one naïve enough to believe in fairy tales.

Jessie bit her lip nervously. She wasn't comfortable with this arrangement. She didn't understand why they couldn't just have this discussion at home, where the entire family could have talked to him about the ranch. She wanted the prying eyes, if for no other reason than to keep her on the defensive attack. Being alone with Nathan was a recipe for disaster. But she couldn't admit that to her family.

She was used to feeling completely in control, and since Nathan's arrival, that control had disappeared like early morning mist in the summer sun. He'd reawakened feelings she'd though were long gone, leaving her grasping for a handhold on her scattered emotions. Her body was not cooperating with her brain tonight.

She pulled into the parking lot of the lone pizza place in town and turned off the truck. Trying to look as nonchalant as possible, even though her heart felt like it was going to pound right out of her chest, she let her hands hang over the top of the steering wheel and eyed him suspiciously. She'd never been one to beat around the bush and didn't see the point in starting now.

"Why are we here? What are you hoping to achieve?"

He chuckled quietly, the deep, rich sound like honeyed whiskey, sending heat swirling into her belly. "What's the matter, Jess? Do I make you nervous?"

That wasn't an answer. She narrowed her eyes at him, irritated that he could read her so easily. Nathan just gave her a playboy smile.

"My friends and family call me Jess. *You* don't qualify as either any more. It's Jessie."

Jessie grabbed her purse and got out of the truck, slamming the door shut behind her. He jumped from his seat to follow her, his long strides easily making up the distance. She walked into the pizza parlor and made her way to the front counter.

"Give me a pitcher of beer and a large combination, extra thick crust."

"Can you make half of that without onions?" Nathan asked the girl taking the order.

Jessie was surprised at how quickly he'd caught up to her. "*Extra* onions on the rest," she added, secretly hoping they would fall onto his side and choke him.

The clerk, a confused high school girl, looked dumbly from one to the other. "Um, okay. That'll be thirty-six dollars and fifty-five cents." She handed Jessie a tented number as Nathan pulled out his credit card and passed it to the girl.

"Why don't you go find a seat?" he suggested, looking back at the busy dining room.

Jessie ignored his advice. She wasn't going to take orders from him. Clamping her jaw together, she crossed her arms across her chest and leaned her hip against the counter, waiting for him to sign the credit card slip.

"I would've paid for dinner, you know."

He looked down at her oddly, as if he didn't understand her annoyance. "I know. Tonight is my treat."

With a huff, she spun on her heel, hating that he seemed to bring out this juvenile, irrationally defiant side of her personality. She clenched her hands into fists, her nails digging into her palms as she made her way through the throng of families, past the jukebox and old video game machines, into a side room that was nearly empty. Finding an unoccupied pub table, she slid onto a tall stool, watching as Nathan finished paying and headed her direction.

Nathan slid onto the chair across from her and folded his hands on the Formica tabletop, staring at her silently. She waited for him to say something, anything. He just sat there, still as a statue, watching her carefully. She shifted in the chair. She didn't like being scrutinized like a specimen on display.

"What?"

"You're a tough nut to crack, Jessie Hart." He smiled, and this one went all the way to his eyes. They glimmered with humor, deep green with golden flecks. "One minute, you're gentle and coaxing with the horses, and the next you're ready to do battle with me. No matter how hard I try to figure you out, you keep surprising me." He ran his fingers over the top of the table. "I get the feeling there aren't many people who know the real you."

Jessie leaned back in her chair and quirked a resentful brow at him. "You should know better than anyone."

His smile fell, and she silently congratulated herself for a target hit. "Do you really want to do this now?"

She shrugged and forced herself to appear as unperturbed as possible. "Well, if I wait, you might disappear again."

Nathan sighed. "I apologized for that, Jessie. I was a kid."

Bitter laughter burst past her lips. "You were twenty-two, the same age Bailey is now. She would never use someone the way you did."

He clenched his jaw tightly, and she saw the muscle in his temple jump. "I didn't use you." At her dubious look, he hurried on. "I can see how it looked that way, but that was never my intention."

Jessie shook her head at him and folded her hands over the tabletop. "Maybe you could explain to me how sleeping with me, then leaving with some bullshit promise to call, wasn't using me. Because in my book that makes you a—"

His usual stoic mask slipped. "I planned to call."

It wasn't the explanation she'd waited years to hear. He hadn't even tried to feed her some lame excuse. Apparently, she wasn't even worth that. "For what, another romp in the hay?"

"Why didn't you ever tell anyone about us?"

She laughed quietly. "Did you really want me to? Do you have any clue what my father and brother would have done if they'd found out the man I lo—" She paused realizing how much she'd almost admitted to him. She would never tell him that he'd been her first—first lover, and first broken heart. "They'd have killed you."

"I'm just surprised." His voice was somber but repentant. "Most women would have jumped at the chance to get revenge for what I did. I guess I was expecting…" Nathan paused searching for the safest thing to say and shrugged. "Something different."

His voice and his eyes promised sincerity, but she felt torn. She wanted to believe him but he'd lied to her with a straight face before, and her faith had proved painfully misplaced. "Yeah? Well, it would have had to mean something." She rolled her eyes and looked around the room, unable to meet his gaze, knowing that he'd be able to read the lie in her eyes.

She felt his gaze caressing her. "Then why the hostility?"

She glared at him. "Gee, Nathan, I wonder. My parents died six months ago, leaving me a ranch to run by myself. My brother and *younger* sister have both had to loan me money, and I still can't make ends meet. Now, I've got the one man in the world I least wanted to ever see again snooping into my finances."

"Wow," he said, tilting his head to the side. "Least wanted, huh?"

"Well, after your half-hearted apology? Can we just get this finished so I can head home?"

"That's right, you're all business, aren't you, Jessie? Fine, then. Tell me about the history of the ranch."

She dragged her thoughts back to the present. "I'm not sure what I can tell you that Justin couldn't have."

"Humor me."

"The ranch has been in my family for years, long before my father was born, but my parents decided to turn what used to be a cattle ranch into a dude ranch. They were good at it, and it became a retreat for people who wanted to experience a bit of the "Old West" in their backyard. You've seen most of the renovations they made other than the addition to The Ridge."

"Just enough amenities to make it comfortable but still feel like you're roughing it," he agreed.

"We aren't one of those 'glamping' places, if that's what you're getting at."

His lips curved into a lopsided grin and her heart fluttered. Warmth flooded her belly and sank lower. She dug her nails into her palms again. *Get a grip, Jess.*

"I wasn't trying to insinuate that."

She lifted one shoulder absently in a *whatever* gesture, refusing to meet his gaze, but relaxing her hands enough to run her fingernail along the edge of the table.

"Have you always wanted to work with abused horses or was that something you started doing afterward?" He leaned back in his chair, hooking his elbow over the high back of the stool.

"It's something I've always wanted to do, but I needed to help Dad. I don't know if you remember, but Mom took care of the books, and Dad usually ran the day-to-day operations."

"What about the cattle?"

Jessie looked up as a waitress brought their pitcher of beer and frosted mugs, promising to return shortly with their pizza. She poured herself a frothy brew. "We don't have many left. Just what we used for the small cattle drives we did at the end of summer and a few Corriente to teach people how to rope. Dad and I both took care of those."

"Did you ever help your mom with the books?"

"No." She gave him a self-deprecating laugh. "Numbers have never been my thing. I hated every second of math in school, and Dad wasn't much better, so Mom kept track of everything. She and Dad went into town to meet with Brendon once a month and then again quarterly to take care of taxes."

"So you've always been hands-off when it came to the finances?"

This was starting to feel more like an interrogation than information gathering. "Basically."

Nathan poured himself another beer. He seemed completely relaxed, as if nothing she said could ruffle him. He was completely overdressed in his slacks and polo shirt, but it didn't seem to make him the slightest bit uncomfortable. It was maddening how at ease he was in his own skin. She envied him that ability.

"What about now?"

"What do you mean?"

"How much do you know about bookkeeping? How much of it would you even feel comfortable doing? I mean, it sounds like this was a three-man operation before, and now you're trying to hold it all together on your own. Or are you planning on hiring someone else to do it?"

He took a sip from his mug, and she felt her gut twist as she realized where the conversation was heading. It was beginning to sound like he and Justin had already been making plans for the ranch without consulting her. That must have been what they'd been discussing earlier on the porch. Anger began to burn her chest.

"From what your brother said, you've been forced to let all the ranch hands go. How are you going to be able to do this alone?"

"Honestly, I'm pretty hopeless at doing more than filing receipts in the correct category every month for

Brendon. I planned on letting him take care of the books for me, like he's been doing. As far as the rest, how I'm going to do it is none of your damn—"

The waitress interrupted their conversation and slid the pizza onto the table, placing a plate in front of each of them.

"So, what are your plans now?"

She blinked, trying to follow the sudden turn of conversation. This man could change direction on a dime and give her change. She was having trouble keeping up. She would have liked to blame it on the alcohol, but one beer wouldn't explain her sudden inability to breathe. "I'm not sure. I thought that's why you were here. To figure out the best option for the ranch?"

"Justin said you haven't taken in any guests since the funeral. Why not?"

Jessie felt blindsided as he jumped to the subject of her parents' death and wanted to stem his barrage of questions. "I just…I haven't. I don't know why."

He took a bite of the pizza and toppings slid off the slice, falling onto his plate with a plop. "Shit, that's hot!" He chewed tentatively, trying to swallow the pizza burning the inside of his mouth.

"I'd call that karma," she said, as she cut into her pizza with a fork, using the opportunity to think about his question.

It wasn't like there hadn't been people calling to book reservations but, even if she'd had the manpower—which she didn't—she wasn't sure she wanted guests without her parents there. It had been something they'd done as a family. Without her mom and dad heading up the events and arrivals, it would feel wrong, like she was nothing more than a poor substitute. They were the ones who had enjoyed having guests, not her.

"Are you afraid to fail?"

She looked up from her plate. Of the many things in life that scared her, failure wasn't one of them. She and failure were old friends. They went together like peanut butter and jelly. No, failing was something she did on a regular basis and, unfortunately, she was good at it.

"No, that's not it. I…" She realized she might as well admit the truth to him now. She was going to need him on her side in order to convince her brother. Jessie shrugged, giving in to what she knew deep down was the truth. "I don't want to run a dude ranch. I never did."

The pizza lay forgotten on his plate. "No?"

"A resort was Mom and Dad's dream. Not mine. I just want to work with horses. It's what I'm good at—it's the *only* thing I'm good at." The words fell from her lips before she could stop them.

He picked up the slice again, his eyes clouding briefly. "I highly doubt that. But what I saw this morning was incredible. Why not turn the ranch into a training facility?"

"Because it's not set up for training. I'd need bigger barns and more round pens. Plus what would I do with the cabins? The entire ranch is set up for guests, their comfort and desires."

"What about your desires, Jess?"

The sincerity she heard in his voice and could see in his eyes helped her overlook the fact that he'd called her by her nickname again. Her stomach did another nervous flip, but this time, it had nothing to do with feeling anxious. A warm shiver of longing traveled up her spine and down her arms as she stared at his mouth. She knew exactly what she desired.

"What do *you* want? If you could *have* anything, *do* anything with the ranch, what would it be?"

She felt tears well in the back of her eyes and closed them to the burn. She wasn't sure how to answer him, because if she told him the truth, and he laughed at her, or worse, shot her down immediately, she'd be back to square one—forced to maintain Heart Fire as a dude ranch, pandering to visitors who couldn't care less that the horses they rode had been rescued from near-death.

Chapter Eight

NATHAN SAW THE change in Jessie almost instantly. She tucked a loose curl behind her ear and tipped her head to the side, contemplative. She looked so vulnerable. It was a glimpse at the young woman he'd loved and, like an idiot, left behind. Jessie rolled her lips inward, her tongue sneaking out to moisten them. He almost groaned aloud at the small gesture.

Her eyes shuttered and she shrugged, quickly withdrawing into her shell again. "I really don't know. I've never thought about it."

"Liar," he said quietly, letting the lopsided grin slide to his lips again. Their eyes met, and she returned the smile tentatively. He immediately felt desire sink its teeth into him. He sat back, shifting in his chair, cursing his body's reaction to her. She'd made it clear she thought he was an ass. He needed to focus on the job Justin had brought him here to do, instead of fantasizing about what could never be. He forced himself to focus on the conversation. "This could be the chance to reinvent yourself and the ranch, if you want to."

She looked away, staring at the pool table across the room for a moment. "How would I even do that? You know how Justin feels about the ranch. I'm sure he's already told you his ideas about how it should be run." Her voice was quiet, hesitant, and he wondered if it was fear he heard.

Nathan didn't deny that he and Justin had discussed the matter. But this wasn't about what Justin wanted. He was here to find out what *she* wanted.

"Maybe you should start by deciding what it is you don't want." She turned those beautiful blue eyes back on him. "Take in a couple of guests this weekend, just enough to get your feet wet again, and see how you feel afterward. Figure out what you don't like about the dude ranch, and we can work it out from there. Maybe it's something as simple as hiring some help so you have more time to do what you love."

"I canceled all of our bookings."

"Bailey took a message today from a small church group down by Bakersfield, eight kids and four counselors. Their original camp was closed due to a wildfire, and they need another location on short notice."

Jessie looked panicked at the suggestion. "I don't have enough people to cover that kind of group."

"Can you call some of your old workers back?" In spite of the fear he could see in her eyes, he could also see the wheels turning as she ran through scenarios in her head. "I'll be here to help however I'm able. I'll push my flight back a couple of days if necessary."

"I might do better trying it alone," she said, but he didn't miss the humor that tugged at her lips.

It was nice to see, even if it was at the expense of his ego. "Thanks a lot. For your information, I can cook a mean omelet. And I can fix a fence now." She smiled and looked down at her slice of pizza, picking at the cheese but not eating, looking suddenly introspective and serious. "What's going on in that head of yours, Jess?"

The unshakable confidence he'd seen from the moment he stepped on the ranch slipped, and Nathan wondered if she was growing tired of her tough, independent act, as much as she wanted everyone to believe it was real. She barely looked up at him from under her long lashes. "I'm not sure I can do this. I mean, it was one thing to do it with Mom and Dad, but I don't think I can do it alone."

Worry clouded her eyes, even if she was doing her best to hide it. He covered her hand with his. "Hey, you aren't alone. You have your brother, your sister, and your cousin."

Her hand in his was warm and softer than he'd expected. Without thinking about why he did it, his thumb traced the pulse at her wrist. The tremor of heat that traveled up his arm wasn't surprising, but it wasn't exactly welcome. He needed to keep this professional if he was going to regain her trust, but he was having a difficult time keeping his body from remembering the heat of her silken skin against his, or the way she smelled—sweet like sunshine and honey with just enough spice to make it exciting.

"I promise, I will stick around and help out."

Jessie jerked her hand back as if his touch burned. Nathan couldn't believe he'd said something so stupid. He'd just reminded her of the fact that he hadn't followed through on his promise years ago. Why should she trust him?

She took a deep breath, squaring her shoulders before slipping back into her take-no-prisoners persona. "I guess I could call my friend Jennifer to see if a couple of her guys might be able to come for the weekend. At least I could make some informed decisions that way."

He tried to ignore the disappointment he felt course through him as she withdrew behind her armor again. But he'd seen a chink in it—maybe he could draw her out again.

"Since we've settled the main issue at hand, how'd you like to show a city boy around? Justin always said I'd missed out by growing up in the city, and I was always too busy to see much of the town when I was here before." He let the innuendo hang in the air, allowing her to remember what had kept him too busy to go out with Justin—late nights of stolen kisses in the barn, or that last night she'd claimed to be too sick to go to the trail ride and campfire.

"What?" She looked confused and, if he was honest, adorably surprised by his request.

"I'm sure the town has changed quite a bit. So, what do you do for fun, Jessie?" She eyed him as if he'd just asked her to walk through town naked, and he couldn't help but grin at her wariness. "You do have fun, right?"

Jessie recovered and leaned back in her chair with a mocking grin as her eyes scanned his slacks and polo shirt. "I doubt you and I have the same ideas about what constitutes 'fun.'"

"Enlighten me." He leaned back and crossed his arms over his chest. Obviously, she'd already formed her impression of the man he'd become. "Broaden my deprived horizons."

She narrowed her eyes at him speculatively. "You? Deprived? We both know you always get what you want."

He knew he was putting his life into her hands, and he wondered if he wasn't a fool for trusting her. She obviously wasn't going to forgive him for the past, but he hoped this gesture of good faith would help her realize he could be trusted this time. Especially since he had no intention of doing anything either of them was going to regret. A smile tugged at the corners of her full lips. Damn, this woman had a pretty mouth, made for long nights of kissing. When she smiled, he could almost imagine what it would be like to take that bottom lip between his again and... He quickly halted the direction of his wayward imagination.

Their relationship had been a mistake before. He was only here for a week. Last time he'd been able to resist her almost three months before giving in. Surely a week wouldn't be too hard, especially with the way she hated him now. The only problem was now he knew exactly what heaven he was missing.

She gave a short laugh and dread crept into his chest at the slightly wicked sound. "It's still too early to go cow tipping or frog gigging." Her eyes slid over his shirt and slacks. "And you're a little over dressed for mud bogging."

He cleared his throat and shifted in his chair nervously. "Frog what?"

She laughed out loud, looking far too sadistic for his liking. "Frog gigging. Hunting for frogs. To cook. What's the matter, City Boy? Don't tell me those fancy restaurants in New York have never served you frog's legs?"

He felt the pizza churn in his stomach and worried he might have turned a shade green himself. "They have, but I've never really thought about hunting them."

"Come on," she said, hopping off the stool. "Let's get this pizza wrapped up and we'll figure out something more your speed. I have an idea."

Jessie led them out the big wooden doors and dropped the box of pizza on the front seat of her truck. "Would you rather have dessert now or later?"

He found himself letting his eyes slide over her curves, hating himself for having something entirely different in mind. He quickly remembered Justin's promise to kick his ass if he fell for Jessie, letting it cool any desire. And after their talk about hunting and eating frogs, he wasn't too excited to add more food to his already queasy stomach.

"Let's go with later."

"Good, then let's hit The Feed Lot first."

"I thought we were forgoing food?"

"You'll see." Her blue eyes shimmered with what could only be called glee. He was intelligent enough to worry about what she was planning. "I'm trusting you," he said as he slid a hand to her lower back, guiding her in front of him.

"That's probably your first mistake."

An amused smile pulled on one corner of her lips and a slow burn began in his belly, traveling lower, and settling there, chasing away any thoughts of Justin, the ranch, and his resolve to keep his feelings for her hidden.

She was the complete opposite of any woman he'd ever known, any woman allowed into his family's elite circle. The women he'd dated were the antithesis of her. Too concerned with their figures to eat more than salad, none would have ever suggested pizza and ice cream. They wouldn't be caught dead hunting frogs or mud bogging, whatever that was. The only mud that touched their skin was in a spa.

Jessie slung her purse over her shoulder, and he wondered how she could be such a tomboy yet so feminine at the same time. She might be dressed in jeans and a T-shirt, but with both hugging her body like they were tailored for her curves, there was no doubt she was all woman. The rhinestones on her clothes caught the late-afternoon sunlight, glinting almost as brightly as her eyes. He was having a difficult time remembering that she was off limits. She looked back at him over her shoulder, catching him checking out her backside.

She arched a brow, daring him to continue his perusal. "Last chance to cut and run."

Nathan gave her a guilty grin. "And let you claim victory? No way." He wondered at the sudden change in her mood. Seeing this playful side to Jessie was more captivating than he remembered. "Not as sure I trust you, though."

"What if I promise it will only hurt your checkbook, and you'll thank me later?"

"I'd say: I don't think I believe you."

"That's probably smart." She laughed, a genuine laugh that bubbled from within, and he couldn't help but join her.

Two HOURS AND several hundred dollars later, Nathan stood in front of her wearing a pair of new boots, Wranglers, and an emerald button-up shirt that reflected the golden flecks in his eyes. Jessie's breath caught in her chest as she realized her mistake. In his normal attire, Nathan was handsome and polished, making it easy to remember how much the years had changed him, how he wasn't her type any longer, and how much his leaving had hurt. By convincing him to buy clothing more practical for his stay on the ranch, she'd turned him from a good looking, city slicker into a gorgeous cowboy. Her heart raced as she handed him a straw hat she'd picked out to suit him. He gave her a wary glance before slipping it onto his head and facing the mirror.

Her eyes slid over the way shirt clung to him, making his already broad shoulders appear even more so, while his waist tapered to a narrow *V*. The pants clung to him, curving around his rear and thighs. Her mouth went dry, and she licked her lips as her pulse picked up speed.

Crap! What did I do?

Nathan caught the look of regret in her reflection. "I look completely asinine, don't I?" She bit her lip, hard, to keep from blurting out the truth, and he laughed, assuming she agreed with his assessment. "I knew it."

He couldn't be more wrong. Jessie's heart couldn't take staying any longer. She made her escape as soon as the opportunity presented itself, needing to give herself a moment to rein in her stampeding heartbeat. "You need a belt," she pointed out, turning away from his reflection and hurrying to the selection of belts and buckles.

This was not what she'd envisioned when she came up with the idea of getting him some new, practical clothing for his time on the ranch. She'd only intended to keep him from standing out, but this…holy crap, if her elevated heart rate and the tingles in her belly, and below, were any indication, this idea had backfired on her miserably. She had to get her head on straight.

Nathan was here to help her get the ranch back on the right track earning a profit and that was all. He never would have come back if Justin hadn't called him. He was only doing a favor for a friend, nothing more. She didn't need any more complications, and falling for this particular city boy was a complication of the worst kind.

Giving into her feelings for Nathan again wouldn't just be stupid, it would be one step past crazy. He might look the part of a cowboy, now that he had new clothes, but that didn't make him one. If she ever felt the need for a man in her life, it was going to be one who shared her love for horses and the ranch. Not the one who'd taken her young heart and hardened it. She needed a man to stick around for the long haul, not one who disappeared after a few weeks.

No, I don't need a man at all.

She reached for a leather belt in his size and carried it back to him. Nathan spun toward her and reached out to take it. His hand brushed over hers, and her heart actually stopped for a moment. Damn! Just when she'd gotten it back under control.

At least Julia and Bailey could thank her for the eye-candy when they returned to the ranch.

Nathan narrowed his eyes, and she wondered if he wasn't trying to read her mind. "You okay? You look a little flushed."

"I'm fine," she answered quickly, too quickly. "When you're done, you should pick out a few more shirts. I'll be over by the tack."

He arched a brow, skepticism written on his face. "Are you sure you're okay?"

She clenched her jaw, willing her heart to slow down and her breathing to normalize. He was just a man, for goodness sake.

"I said I'm fine. It's just hot in here." Jessie spun on her heel, hurrying across The Feed Lot to the wall of saddles, bridles, and cinches. Anything that might put a little space between her and this man who made her feel like she was on a roller coaster—dizzy, breathless, and like she'd completely lost all control of her senses.

NATHAN WATCHED JESSIE as she leaned back on one arm beside him on the grass, licking the ice cream dripping down the side of her waffle cone. She was watching several boys playing basketball on a nearby court, as the sun dipped low in the evening sky. What in the world had he been thinking, suggesting they get ice cream and take it to the park?

Watching her eat the cone was the sexiest thing he'd ever seen. Other than that look Jessie gave him when he tried on the clothing at the western-wear store. When her blue eyes darkened, he'd wanted to drown in the hunger he saw there, to bury his hands in her dark hair, and to cover her mouth with his. Time hadn't changed the way he felt about Jessie. It was all he could to stop himself from licking the sweetness from her lips.

He needed to regain his restraint, and quickly, because if she realized the path his thoughts were taking, she'd castrate him the way she planned to do that stallion. Nathan shifted, trying to find a measure of comfort in these new jeans, but it felt like his balls were being crushed in a vice. He wasn't sure if it was the way they were cut or his body's response to watching her eat the ice cream, but he felt like the circulation to his brain was being cut off.

An image flashed through his mind of what he would look like when Justin finished with him if he found out about the fantasies Nathan was having about his sister. It worked almost as well as a bucket of ice water. Guilt welled up, cooling his desire. He'd only begun to regain a little of Jessie's trust, but Justin was relying him, and he knew how he'd feel if the roles were reversed.

He took a bite of his cone and turned his attention to another group of kids playing on the swings nearby. "What's with the foster kids at the ranch?"

"Who? Aleta and Michael?" She followed his gaze and smiled at the kids' antics, laughing as they watched one young boy twist the chain of the swing before letting it spin free.

"He told me to call him Ice, but yeah."

"Aleta's foster mom was a friend of Mom's, and she's seen how much working with the horses has helped Aleta's attitude. Michael..." Jessie sighed. "Michael's a different story. Like Aleta, he's a foster kid, but Ellie's one of my best friends. She's desperately trying to find anything to keep him away from the gang that got ahold of his older brother, who's now in jail again."

"Parents?"

"Both dead. His brother had guardianship. It's a bad situation because he idolized his brother."

Nathan shook his head. "What about Aleta's parents?"

"Her mom's in jail, and no one knows anything about her father."

He finished off his cone, popping the last bite into his mouth. Jessie was such a contradiction—tough as nails with a heart as soft as a down pillow. "You have a thing for what other people throw away, don't you?"

"What are you talking about?" She stopped watching the kids and looked over at him, frowning.

He leaned back on his hands, straightening his legs and crossing his booted ankles in front of him, staring across the lawn to where kids continued to play. "There's the abused horses, the foster kids." He met her gaze and gave her a knowing smile. "Don't think I didn't see you salivating over that hutch in the thrift shop a little while ago."

Her brows sagged, and he hated to think he was the one who'd caused the change in her lighthearted mood. "It's a good thing, Jess. Something most people wouldn't even think about." He moved his finger to touch the back of her hand lying flat against the grass. He felt the instant spark of arousal but wasn't sure which of them felt it more.

She moved her hand away from his and sat up. "I...I just..."

He chuckled quietly, shaking his head. "You're as uncomfortable accepting a compliment as I feel in these clothes."

He saw a shy smile spread over her lips and felt relief course through him that she hadn't tried to hide behind her armor again. Since dinner, they'd been able to keep this evening on an easy-going, friendly playing field, and he hoped it would make the coming days easier, especially when he had to push her to make some difficult decisions. If she didn't trust him, any advice he offered would fall on deaf ears.

"We should probably head back," she suggested, rising and tossing what was left of her cone into a nearby garbage can before making her way toward the water fountain.

He knew she was right. They should get back to the ranch, where there were plenty of eyes to watch their every move and keep him honest. Not to mention work he was supposed to be doing for her. But he was enjoying the time with her, and it had been a long time, a *very* long time, since he'd allowed himself any opportunity to have fun.

But for the first time in years, he felt free. Fully alive. He wasn't sure why Jessie was able to draw this out of him, but he wasn't quite ready to let it go and get back to his usual boring routine.

"I thought you were going to show me fun," he teased. She eyed him suspiciously. "Don't get me wrong. This is fun, but Justin said I'd missed out growing up in the city. I don't know if this qualifies as 'missing out.'"

She washed her hands in the water from the fountain and dried them on her denim-clad thighs, giving him a sideways glance. "Is that a challenge, Nathan?"

He grinned and shrugged. "I guess it might be." He loved the way his name fell from her lips. It was the first time she'd used it instead of the stupid nickname Bailey had given him, and he wanted to hear it again—as a soft sigh.

"Then we should get back to the truck because I'm about to show you something you'll never find in city limits." In his frame of mind, Nathan couldn't help but imagine all sorts of things he wanted to see from her. He had no idea what she had in mind, but if it meant spending more time looking at those blue eyes, seeing that smile on her lips and the humor lighting up her face, he'd do just about anything short of frog gigging.

Chapter Nine

JESSIE TEXTED HER brother as she and Nathan headed back to the truck from the park, asking him to saddle up two horses. She ignored his return texts asking where she was, when she would arrive, and why she was planning on riding at this hour with Nathan. If she paused long enough to think about the answers to any of his questions, she might just talk herself out of this stupid idea and remember why she didn't want anything to do with Nathan Kerrington in the first place. What made her think he would even think this was fun anyway? He probably hadn't even been on a horse since he'd left the ranch.

She eyed him slyly, seated in the passenger seat of the truck, and could almost ignore the logic and the warning bells sounding in her brain. She knew she needed to get home and check on the new horses, make sure they'd settled in for the night. She should work on the books, or at the very least, input the latest receipts into the computer program she was trying, unsuccessfully, to learn. She should make some training notes…There were at least one thousand things she *should* be doing, and none of them included spending time on an evening ride with Nathan Kerrington.

It was the first time in years she'd actually felt like someone was listening to her instead of trying to convince her to live a life she didn't want. She hated that it was Nathan, of all people. Especially since his apology wasn't really an explanation at all. She knew she was making a mistake, just like she had the last time they were together, but he'd always been able to make her ignore common sense. The man had a way of making her brain shut off and her heart take over. She must be crazy. She must have left every ounce of sense she possessed in The Feed Lot because she hadn't been thinking right since she'd first seen him in those Wranglers.

She pulled into the driveway and saw the light on in the barn with two horses tied to the hitching post in front. Bailey came out of the tack room with the bridles and hung them over the saddle horns, looking up at the sound of the truck and waving. Jessie parked the truck in front of the house.

Nathan looked at the barn and then back to her. "We're going riding? Now?"

"What's the matter? Not up for it?"

Please say no, her head begged.

Please say yes, her heart countered.

He shut the truck door, folded his hands, and smiled at her over the hood. "It's been a long time since I've ridden, and I've never been at night." The gold flecks in his eyes caught the dome light from the truck and flashed with mischief. "But I'm game to see what I've been missing."

As they walked to the barn, the light from the doorway played over the planes of his face, creating shadows and angles, giving him an air of mystery and danger. She couldn't quite make out his hooded expression, and she wondered if he was deliberately taunting her with his innuendo. Her heart immediately began to thud against her ribcage and she bit her lower lip, questioning the sanity of her thoughts again.

"Hey, Wall Street, lookin' good," Bailey said with a laugh as she approached. "We might have to change your name. I barely recognized you." She turned to Jessie. "I have your horses saddled. Heading up to The Ridge?"

"That's the plan." This was a bad idea and she knew it. He'd baited her, and stupidly, she'd let her mouth get her into trouble again. But if she backed out now, it would look like she was afraid of him.

Bailey gave her an impish grin. "Well, you have a fun ride tonight." She laughed at her own choice of words.

Jessie glared at her as Nathan arched a brow at them both. She was only taking Nathan up to The Ridge to see the changes her parents had made. She just needed to convince the parts of her body that were already warming with brazen fantasies.

She busied herself checking the saddles, finding that Bailey had already tied blankets and sweatshirts to the back of each. She'd even added a saddlebag to the back of Jessie's, but she wasn't about to take time now examine what sorts of things her cousin might have added to embarrass her.

"You ready?"

"As I'll ever be." He winked at her and untied his horse from the hitching post, surprising her when he mounted correctly and settled himself into the saddle. She raised her brows in question. "It's sort of like riding a bike," he pointed out.

"Let's see if you still feel that way in the morning when you're sore as hell." Bailey dipped her head to hide her smile as she opened the pasture gate.

Jessie went through it first and Nathan followed.

Bailey shut the gate behind him, patting his mount on the rump. "Don't worry. Grady is a solid, old boy so between him and Jessie, you'll be fine."

Nathan glanced at Jessie, and his gaze heated. "I'm sure I'm in good hands."

With the huskiness of his voice, it didn't take much for Jessie's imagination to conjure visions of her own hands on him. She turned quickly, facing forward in the saddle, refusing to look at him as Bailey burst out laughing at her obvious embarrassment.

Damn him, damn Bailey, and damn her wanton imagination.

Jessie clenched her jaw. This was just supposed to be a chance to show him something he'd never seen growing up in the city, nothing more. Why did either of them have to insinuate it was anything other than that? Why did her own imagination want to twist this into a romantic rendezvous? Her gelding jerked his nose forward, pulling against the reins she'd accidentally tightened her hands around.

"Sorry, boy," she murmured, relaxing her fingers and dropping her hand. No sense in taking her aggravation with Nathan and Bailey, or herself, out on the horse.

"Which direction are we heading?" Nathan moved his animal alongside her, looking around at the dark pasture. "This isn't exactly someplace I'd like to get lost."

A day ago, she'd have liked to have him get lost in order to avoid dealing with him. Now, with his western attire, five o'clock shadow, and seated on a horse, he looked like he'd been born on a ranch. Thoughts of getting lost *with* him suddenly seemed almost tempting. "I'm taking you to The Ridge. We let guests camp there overnight. You'll understand why soon."

He tipped his chin down, eyeing her suspiciously. "We're camping? I have to admit, it's not something I ever did growing up but—"

"You've never been camping?" She interrupted him, shocked. She'd spent most of her childhood sleeping under the stars with her siblings and their father.

He shook his head. "My family isn't really the 'camping' kind." He ran a palm over his thigh and shifted in the saddle, looking uncertain.

She laughed quietly. "Relax, Wall Street, I'm not going to molest you up here. You're not that irresistible."

He looked taken aback for a moment, but a slow smile spread over his lips and made her nervous. "So you *do* find me somewhat irresistible?"

Jessie shifted in the saddle and pressed her lips together in a thin line. She hadn't meant it that way.

Nathan chuckled, giving her a wink. "Don't worry, darlin'," he drawled playfully, his voice husky. "The feeling is mutual."

She frowned as her stomach flipped again and tingles spiraled through her entire lower half. She knew he was only teasing, but a part of her worried at how easily he'd been able to read her thoughts.

"Shut up."

She wasn't sure if she was talking to him or the voice in her head suggesting all sorts of ideas for a memorable night on The Ridge. She tapped the horse's side, urging him into a jog, knowing Nathan's gelding would follow suit. Grady, old as he was, broke into a bouncy trot and she couldn't help but grin as Nathan was jarred in the saddle, nearly coming down on the saddle horn as he pulled Grady to a stop.

"Hey! This is *not* fun!" he yelled as his horse fell behind. "Are you listening?"

Jessie slowed her gelding to match Grady's slower pace. Nathan glared at her, arching a brow. "I'm not going to admit I deserved that but, let's just say, this saddle horn almost gelded me. Truce?" Nathan held out his right hand to her.

"Truce," she agreed. "For now."

NATHAN WATCHED JESSIE as they rode. At first, she'd seemed irritated with Bailey's insinuations that she was trying to seduce him, not that he'd helped much, adding in his own innuendos. But he really couldn't help it. Watching her today, then spending the evening with her, had reminded him of why he'd been so taken with her when he'd stayed on the ranch before. Not only was she irresistible, it was actually fun to see her thrown off-kilter for a change.

Nathan had never intended to hurt Jessie. From the first moment he and Justin arrived on the ranch for summer break before their senior year of college, Nathan could barely keep his eyes off Jess. She'd just celebrated her high school graduation. She was innocent, beautiful, and full of hope for her future. The first time he'd kissed her at the river, he'd been sure he'd lost his mind. It launched a whirlwind of yearning unlike anything he'd ever felt with anyone before.

As soon as he and Justin returned to college, his father had called him, furious. Nathan had no idea how he'd found out about Jessie, but it wouldn't be the first time his father had hired an investigator to follow his children. It wasn't uncommon for senators to keep tabs on their families that way, especially *his* father. When his father pointed out how dangerous a relationship with a nobody would be for his reelection campaign, Nathan had argued. When he pressed on, insisting Nathan would damage his latest run for office and that it would cause a media circus if the tabloids found out he was slumming with some cowgirl, he balked but remained firm. It wasn't until his father threatened to destroy the Hart family's reputation if he ever returned to the ranch that Nathan took him seriously. A few casual calls to the press, and Jessie would be on the front page of every tabloid in the country, branded the whore, her family gold diggers set on luring wealthy men to blackmail and create scandal. And so he'd set aside his future with Jessie, to protect her.

Little did Nathan know that his father was more concerned with covering up his own offshore accounts, where he was hiding campaign funds, than with his son's love life. It wasn't until Nathan started his own financial consulting practice that his father had asked him to falsify the campaign contributions and join the "family business."

Learning the truth about his family too late—the unconventional and illegal parameters his father operated within—Nathan regretted his decision. He should have told his father to go to hell sooner. Jessie would have. She'd have stood up to anyone who tried to keep them apart and let the consequences be damned. He wondered what life would've been like if he'd made a different choice. Where would he have landed if his father had cut him off and he'd been forced to drop out of college? Would he have come back to the ranch to be with her? Would he have confessed his feelings for her to Justin and her father? He deplored the coward he'd been, but he'd convinced himself over the years that her feelings for him were nothing more than a fleeting summer romance.

How was it possible that she was single? He studied her long, tapered fingers curled around the reins, gently directing the huge beast with the slightest motion. She was incredibly smooth in her movements, focusing on the powerful animal completely subdued between her thighs. He was trying to ignore the longing but, so far, watching the dark waves of her hair cascade down her back as her hips rocked in the saddle had been torture for him. He'd never had trouble cooling off his libido before, and the thought of what Justin would do to him should have been enough to freeze even the hottest desire.

A small smile tipped up the corners of her mouth, and even in the moonlight, there was a joy and pride shining in her eyes as they took in her surroundings. The glow from the nearly full moon reflected in her face, highlighting the pure satisfaction he could read there. She loved this place. There was no doubt in his mind that running this ranch, helping these horses, and mentoring these kids was as much as part of Jessie as the oxygen she breathed and the blood flowing through her veins.

She held up a hand, pointing ahead, and interrupted his appraisal. "Right there. See?"

Nathan followed the direction of her finger and could make out the trail traveling up to a cliff that hung high over a wide river. The sound of the water crashing over rocks nearby created a melody with the soft *clomp* of the horses' hooves. He followed her up the short path until it ended in a wide meadow on a rocky ledge dotted with several pine trees. She dismounted and reached for Grady's reins, leading the horses to a pipe corral. "This is where we'll stop."

He followed her lead, dismounting, surprised by how tight the rarely used muscles in his inner thighs were already feeling.

She untied the blanket from the back of the saddle. "Are you cold?" she asked. "Bailey sent sweatshirts."

"I'm fine. Do you need help?" He watched her, feeling a bit useless, knowing this certainly wasn't his most gallant moment as she attended to the animals alone. He massaged his legs with his hands, feeling like an idiot but unsure how to help.

"Nope." She loosened the saddles and tied the horses in the corral before walking toward him with the blankets.

He could read the sudden insecurity in her face, surprised to see her reveal the emotion as she spread the blankets near the rocky edge and sat down. "You sure you don't want a jacket?" she asked. "I mean, we won't stay too long but…"

It was unseasonably warm for this part of California, but even if that hadn't been the case, watching her ride had created a fire in him already threatening to burn out of control. "No, I'm good."

The rasp in his voice surprised him, and she stared at him a moment longer than necessary. He didn't want her to even suspect the thoughts going through his mind right now. He cleared his throat. "This is incredible. Why didn't we ever come up here?"

His voice held every bit of the awe he felt. The location was what dreams were made of. He walked past a central fire pit to the wooden fence lining the edge of the cliff. While it provided safety, they'd been careful to make it blend with the surroundings. Pine scented the night air as the moon hung, huge and bright in the sky, illuminating the white caps of the river crashing over rocks below. The sound of the water created a symphony with the rest of the night—a slight breeze rustling through the trees, frogs and crickets, a rustle of birds high in the trees above, and the haunting call of an owl.

A slight click, like something dropping behind him, made him jump and turn. "What was that?"

She leaned back on the blanket, staring up at the stars, and folded her arms under her head, as if she didn't have a care in the world. "Probably a squirrel—or a mouse." She tipped her chin, glancing back to where he stood, still staring into the darkness where the horses relaxed. "Calm down, Wall Street. This is where you unwind and see what the city can't offer you. The horses will alert us if it's anything worth worrying about."

He watched the woman lying prone on the blanket, staring up the night sky. "Like what? A mountain lion ready to pounce?"

The sound of her laughter was rich and sweet as he edged toward the blanket, still listening for wildlife behind them. Just the throaty sound made him think of those full lips of hers again, and heat pooled, deep and unwelcome, in the pit of his loins.

He needed to put some distance between them emotionally as well. He was in trouble if getting mauled by a wild animal sounded preferable to the longing he was feeling for her again. He lay down on the blanket next her, trying to keep as much room between them as the small blanket allowed. He clasped his hands over his abs to keep from touching her again, reminding himself that he'd made the right decision for everyone when he'd cut ties with her. His family, the world he lived in, would rip her to shreds, and he couldn't do that to her, no matter how much he wanted her. Loving Jessie was a youthful fantasy he needed to bury again.

She turned her face toward him and smiled before looking back at the sky. "Bet you can't find something like this in the city."

His brows arched on his forehead. "No, I have to agree with you on that. It's definitely beautiful." His eyes never left her face, but she wasn't looking at him.

Jessie pointed up at the stars. "Somewhere…there. Right there is the Big Dipper."

He followed her gaze into the night sky, awed at how brilliant the stars were. It was an amazing sight. Pinpoints of light dotted the sky, more than he'd ever seen before. The inky sky looked like it went on forever.

"You're away from any other lights so there's nothing to dim them." She turned her head toward him and he realized he'd spoken aloud.

"If you watch, you'll see lots of shooting stars, too. You don't see many in the city."

"I don't think I've ever noticed any."

"You're kidding!"

"I told you, I wasn't exactly raised in a family that spent a lot of time outdoors." He frowned as he thought about his father and his relentless pursuit of financial success, no matter what the cost. "Or together, for that matter. My father would call this frivolous."

"Huh." Jessie sounded surprised by his admission.

Nathan turned to face her. "What?"

Jessie shrugged and raised her brows. "I would have thought you'd have it all. The house, the car, the money, the education. But you don't sound like…never mind, I shouldn't have said anything."

"What were you going to say?" he urged.

"You just sounded nostalgic. Like you would have given it all up for something else."

Nathan felt the twist of pain in his stomach as he looked back at the sky with an acerbic laugh. "You have no idea."

She looked up at the sky again. "You never talked about your family much."

"There's not a lot to talk about." That wasn't really true. He could tell her about the various crimes his father had been charged with over the years, how his mother and sister were both stuck in marriages of convenience rather than love. *Love.* He'd come to wonder if the word even really meant anything. It seemed more like trite expression. Suddenly, a burst of blue light flashed across the sky, fizzling out quickly.

"Did you make a wish?" she asked, excitedly.

"A wish?"

She turned to face him, rolling onto her side, bracing her cheek on her palm. "You're supposed to make a wish when you see a shooting star. You really did miss out growing up, didn't you?"

A sad smile slipped over her lips, and Nathan Kerrington, financial analyst to millionaire CEOs, a man used to riding in limos, eating caviar, drinking Cristal champagne, and addressing boardrooms, was struck speechless as her thick-lashed, deep blue eyes filled with innocent wonder met his. His years of business success, each dollar in his bank account and every rung he'd climbed up the corporate ladder seemed worthless compared to the unadulterated sorrow he saw in her face for his pitiful childhood. She knew a contentment and security, just in being a Hart, he'd never be able to comprehend. She had shared her pride in her family, something he'd never understood existed. Until now.

"Make a wish, Nathan." Her voice was sweet, tender, and mildly amused.

Suddenly, the only thing he could think about was Jessie and the mistake he'd made eight years ago. The cold logic that seemed to rule his every decision, in business and relationships, failed him, evaporating into the night sky by way of a shooting star. His hand found the silken curve of her neck as the inches between them disappeared. Rolling to hover over her, Nathan dipped his head, his lips finally finding hers, taking her mouth hostage as he'd thought about doing all day. He forgot the differences between them, his father's threats, the reasons this couldn't work, and the excuses he wanted to make to keep from touching her. All he knew was the uncontrollable need, held prison for the last eight years, finally set free to course through his veins.

His entire life had been ruled by self-control, logic, and order. Jessie scattered all three to the wind, making him wonder if all the things his discipline had gained him over the years weren't simply cheap imitations, his family's impressions of what his life should be.

She opened under him, soft and warm, her kiss vibrant and filled with life, like a lightning storm, so very much like the woman in his memories. Jessie held nothing back, as if every second was a celebration of life, and her fingers curled into the flesh of his triceps. His hands slid over her shoulder, down her arm bared by her short sleeves, feeling goosebumps break out over her flesh, and filling him with yearning to see what other reactions he could cause in her. She sighed softly into his mouth and arched against him.

Nathan had never known a woman to respond with such abandon. He realized he shouldn't have expected anything less. It was how Jessie did everything.

And it scared him.

JESSIE WASN'T SURE how she ended up kissing Nathan, but she wasn't about to question it. One minute they were looking up at the stars, the next she was under him with his hand on her waist, his knee parting her thighs, and hers fingers gripping his solid arms, unwilling to let him go. She couldn't fathom what part of her brain thought it was a good idea to continue letting Nathan kiss her; although at this moment, she couldn't think of anything else she'd rather do. She felt like she'd been transported back in time, except the first time they'd kissed, Nathan hadn't been this muscular, and she had gotten her heart broken. In typical Hart woman fashion, Jessie let her emotions carry her along, ignoring the consequences, knowing she would deal with the repercussions later.

Even though she didn't want to think about them right now, the worries swirled through her mind like a stirred hornet's nest. Nathan had broken her heart once before, he was sure to do it again. As much as she hated what he'd done, she'd never quite stopped loving him and hoping he'd come back.

She needed to remain focused on saving the ranch. Nathan was a distraction she didn't need now. Rekindling her relationship with Nathan was the last thing she needed to do.

When he sucked at her lower lip, she sighed and all the nagging worries and questions scattered, leaving only sensation behind. Jessie arched against him. When his tongue licked at the corner of her mouth, teasing her lips apart, toying with her, Jessie's hands slid over his broad shoulders to the nape of his neck, drawing him to her fully. She plunged her tongue into his mouth. She'd never been a patient woman, and Nathan's touch sent her reeling. It might prove to be her worst idea ever, but she wanted Nathan Kerrington, consequences be damned.

As her tongue danced with his, she pulled at his shirt, tugging at the snaps on the front, eager to feel the warmth of his skin under her palms. His hands moved up to her ribcage, and she felt his thumb trace the curve of her breast. Her entire body seemed to burn from within, pleasure cresting through her in waves, making her limbs tingle. He groaned against her lips, and she felt his fingers clench at her sides even as he began to ease himself from her.

No! Her body cried out like a petulant child.

She slid her hands to his lower back and arched against him again, feeling his erection against her thigh but unwilling to release him and face reality. If he moved away now, she was going to have to face the results of her recklessness, and she'd much rather not face that disgrace just yet. If ever.

Nathan withdrew but only slightly, his lips moved to her jaw, trailing kisses over the hollow of her throat, along the outer shell of her ear. Jessie shivered against him.

His lips moved against her skin. "See, you do find me irresistible."

She sent up a prayer of thanks at the cocky, playful tone of his voice. No harm, no foul, no broken hearts, no regrets. Just two consenting adults attracted to one another, kissing under the stars. At least, that was what she'd keep telling herself. They should be able to salvage some sort of working relationship without it being awkward. After all, they weren't kids anymore.

"I wouldn't say 'irresistible.'" She smiled as he moved the neckline of her T-shirt to the side and gently bit where her shoulder and neck met. Jessie gasped and felt heat pool between her legs.

"I supposed this is just some of the *fun* I missed growing up in the city?"

"Hmmm," she agreed, sighing as his hands found where her shirt had tugged free from the waistband of her pants. His fingers moved over the flat plane of her belly and caused spirals of pleasure to shoot through her limbs like lightning. "Among other things."

He drew his head back and looked down at her, frowning, his eyes puzzled. "There's more?"

Jessie brushed a stray lock of hair back from his forehead, gathering her courage and tried for her most flirtatious laugh. "I know you city boys know about second base."

His eyes suddenly hardened and he moved away, sitting up and adjusting his shirt. Gone was the playful, seductive man she'd seen only seconds ago, and she felt cold at the loss. A chill broke over her skin, and she ran her hands over her arms as he rose. Nathan stood and walked to the edge of the rocks and stuffed his hands into the pockets of his jeans, staring off into the night.

Jessie frowned at his back. "Did I say something wrong?" She stood and tucked her shirt back into her waistband, taking a few steps toward him.

"No."

His rigid spine and clenched fists shouted yes.

She heard him sigh into the darkness. "What river is this?"

The moment was lost. She could hear it in his voice. Wall Street had returned and replaced the playful Nathan she'd enjoyed the evening with—the one she'd long ago given her heart to. She should have known it was nothing more than a fantasy. He was back to being all about the business he'd come to discuss.

If he didn't want to talk about what just happened, Jessie could ignore it as well. She'd grown used to faking smiles and playing parts for others. Pretending the only man she'd ever loved hadn't left her behind like a one-night stand.

"It's one of the forks of the American River. The river is the reason this ranch looks so lush. It feeds several creeks throughout the property. It's also part of why it made a great cattle ranch since we don't need to rely on wells for irrigation."

"That would make Heart Fire land pretty desirable."

He sounded contemplative and that worried her. "I guess." Jessie shrugged, wondering what he was getting at.

Nathan looked back at her over his shoulder, and she could read the regret in his eyes. "Look, Jess, it's not you. I just…"

He made his way back to where she stood at the edge of the blanket, watching him. He ran his hands down her arms and reached for hers. She let him but her body remained stiff, fighting the desire to curl her arms around his waist and lay her head against his chest. She wanted to go back to the way things had been that summer, to forget the way he'd abandoned her and let her heart beat in time with his again.

"You're Justin's sister. And I don't get involved with clients. Being with you would make things…complicated."

Jessie felt her heart wither a little, but she wasn't about to let him see it. She'd been weak and let down her guard. She pulled her hands away from his and laughed at him. "Do I look like I'm still the same eighteen-year-old girl you left behind? For crying out loud, it was just a kiss, Nathan."

She was deliberately minimizing the pain twisting around her heart, stealing her breath, but she didn't want him to know how far she would have allowed her recklessness to carry her. She knew he was right to stop things between them now, was grateful really, but being rejected by him a second time stung. She reached down and rolled up the blanket before walking to the horses in the corral and tying it to the back of her saddle. She tightened the cinch on Nathan's saddle and led his horse back to him.

"And, I hate to break it to you, but any man who's afraid of my brother is hardly irresistible."

Chapter Ten

"CLOSE YOUR MOUTH, Julia. It's not that big a deal." Jessie sat across from her sister in their father's office.

"Nathan kissed you on The Ridge, and you're going to try to convince me it's not a big deal?" Julia shook her head. "I know you better than that. That man might be hot, especially now that you got him into some new clothes, but Jess, you don't…"

She knew what her sister was getting at. Jessie didn't sleep around. Technically, she barely dated anyone because she had a ranch to run and no time to waste on relationships doomed from the start. Even when she did go out with someone, it never led to more than a quick peck on the cheek. Nathan was the only man who stirred her, the only one who'd reached into her chest and grabbed hold of her heart, but she wasn't about to admit that. Not even to Julia.

"Yeah, well, he'll be gone in a few days anyway. So it doesn't really matter, does it?" She stood and tucked a file into the cabinet, leaning over to turn on the computer tower under the desk. "And clothes are just wrapping on the package. It doesn't make the man. He's still just a number-crunching accountant."

"Financial analyst." Julia grinned as she corrected her sister.

"Pain in the ass."

"Me or him?" She didn't wait for her sister to reply. "Anyway, how can you say that? He's famous, and he's here doing a favor for a friend when he doesn't have to. That alone should speak to his character, at least a little. I notice you're following his suggestions."

"You mean booking the youth group this weekend?" Julia nodded and tipped her head to the side. "That's coincidence. I just decided it was time."

"Sure you did."

Jessie glared at her sister. Julia rose and leaned over Jessie's desk—the desk where their mother had done the same paperwork Jessie found herself struggling with now. "All I'm saying is that you should cut the guy some slack. He's trying to do the right thing. That alone is respectable, especially in this day and age."

"Yeah, he's honorable."

Her sister eyed her suspiciously. "What aren't you telling me?"

Jessie hated that her sister could read her so well. With only one year separating them, the two girls could practically read each other's mind, and she knew Julia could see right through her indifference. As much as she loved her brother, she and Julia had always been closer. If for no other reason than they were both women. They'd shared a room, even when they didn't have to; clothing; and of course, secrets. Jessie wasn't sure why she was even trying to lie to Julia.

"Jessie?" Julia's mouth dropped open again, making her look like a goldfish gasping for air. "Did the two of you…when he was here before…seriously?"

Jessie looked up at her sister in shock. "I didn't even say anything."

"You didn't have to!" Julia's eyes brightened, and she smiled broadly. "Now things are making so much sense. Why you were so mopey after he left. Why you used to wait by the phone. What happened?"

"Obviously, nothing that matters." Jessie didn't mean to snap at Julia, but she didn't want to relive her past with Nathan. It was too painful, and his recent rejection still smarted, making her feel even more like an idiot.

"Okay," Julia said, raising her hands in submission. "I'll wait until you're ready to tell me. But it doesn't take a brain surgeon to know you thought you were in love. You were heartbroken after he and Justin left, and Mom and I never could figure out why." She turned to leave and paused. "Would you have slept with him last night?"

"Of course not." Jessie couldn't meet her sister's gaze. The question was ridiculous. But no matter how adamantly she denied it today, Jessie wasn't so sure she would have said no to Nathan last night. Damn it, what was wrong with her? She was just begging to get her heart broken again. "It was only a kiss."

"You *would* have," her sister said, shaking her head, her brows raised high on her forehead. "That man must be some kisser to make you forgive and forget."

"I didn't say I'd done either."

"True," Julia agreed. "But do you want him to stay?"

"Get out!" Jessie pointed at the door.

Julia held up her hands. "I'm going, I'm going." She headed for the door, pausing as she opened it. "Now I'm sorry you met him first."

Jessie threw a pen at her sister playfully, watching it bounce off the doorframe. She didn't want to think about Nathan's kisses or the way she'd responded to them, let alone the way her body was responding to just the memory of them. Heat flooded her belly, traveling lower, settling in places she'd long ignored. It had been years since she'd been with a man, years since she'd even wanted to since Nathan's departure. She told herself she'd been too busy helping her parents with the ranch. But, in reality, she was grieving the loss of her fairy tale fantasies.

Jessie reached for the phone, not wanting to let her thoughts travel any further down this dangerous rabbit trail. Then she'd be battling memories of promises made in the dark as Nathan held her, words spoken that her young heart had believed.

She dialed the one person she was certain would understand her current predicament, her best friend, Jennifer Findley.

"Findley Brothers Stock, this is Jennifer, how can I help you?"

"I'd like a miracle, please."

"Jessie!" The squeal of delight in Jennifer's voice made Jessie felt guilty for not calling sooner. Jennifer had been one of the first people at her side after her parents' accident, having lost her own parents years before. If anyone understood the trials Jessie faced running a ranch, it was her friend. "What's going on?"

"I'm in a sink-or-swim situation." She explained her financial situation and how she'd been forced to let several of their hands go. "Now, I have guests coming this weekend and need a few guys until I can hire more. Please, tell me you can spare a few."

"No problem. I have a couple guys we just hired last week, and we haven't even sent them out to rodeos yet. Let me make sure they're willing to do it, but I doubt it'll be a problem. It's easier than mending fences here." Jennifer laughed into the receiver. "When are we going to go out to lunch?"

Jessie couldn't help but feel herself relax as they slipped into small talk, discussing ranch issues, horses, and Jennifer's new baby. It was nice to catch up on the news of Jennifer's brothers and their new wives. She was just about to tell Jen about Nathan when she looked up and saw the cause of her troubled state standing in her open doorway, holding several file folders, a frown marring his brow.

"Hey, Jen. Let me call you back. I think I'm needed for a minute."

"No problem. I'll have those guys stop by tomorrow if that works for you."

"Sounds great. I'll get them settled in." Jessie motioned for Nathan to come inside and sit. "Thanks again, Jen." She hung up the phone and folded her hands. "Well, I have two cowboys coming for this weekend."

"Is that going to be enough?" The frown didn't leave his face.

"With you, Julia, and Justin helping it should be. What's wrong?"

"What do you know about Heart Fire Industries?" He laid one of the file folders on her desk and turned it toward her. She looked down at a spreadsheet showing several transfers over the past several months from Heart Fire Ranch to Heart Fire Industries, but never in the same amount.

"I have no idea what that is." She leaned back in the chair. "Dad liked to have his hands in a lot of different pots. Maybe it's an investment he forgot about?"

"But your accountant should know about it. He didn't mention it to me when I met with him, and we went over the books." The crease on his forehead deepened.

"Maybe he forgot," she suggested. She wasn't normally one to defend Brendon, having never been a fan of the guy, but she didn't like the suspicion she could see in Nathan's eyes.

"Jessie, the transfers are only coming from Heart Fire Ranch. I need to find out why and where these are going. They total several thousand dollars each month. Over four thousand so far this month alone. If you know anything…"

Was he accusing her? "I don't." She shook her head in defeat and sighed, pulling the file toward her and looking down at the long list of transfers. "How could I *not* notice an expense like that? I'd have to sign them off or something, wouldn't I?"

"Maybe, which is what has me concerned. I need to find out what this is, when it was set up, and who's in charge." He rose and started for the door, then turned back toward her. "Don't worry about it too much just yet. I'll get an answer and get the payments stopped, at least until we know what's going on. That's my job."

She wanted to say something about last night, to make sure there wasn't any sort of awkwardness between them over a measly kiss, no matter how incredibly earth-shattering it had been, but she wasn't sure how to address it. She was afraid bringing it up would make it seem like it meant more than it should. After all, she was the one who had told him it wasn't a big deal. She didn't want him thinking she was still in love with him, but she wasn't sure where she stood with him now, personally or professionally, especially when last night hadn't ended on a high note.

"We're okay after last night, right?" She hadn't meant to blurt it out that way, but as usual, her lips moved before her brain could stop them.

A slow grin slipped over his lips and her heart skipped a beat, remembering how those lips had felt moving over hers, realizing that she wanted to feel them again. She jerked her disobedient thoughts back into submission.

"Yes, Jessie, we're fine. Like you said, it was just a kiss, right?"

Jessie, not Jess. She hated hearing her words casually tossed back at her. It squeezed her chest, making her feel like she'd just lost something valuable.

Something you never really had, she reminded herself.

She tried to shove her disappointment aside and cleared her throat. "Nathan, I know you offered to help this weekend but what, exactly, were you planning on doing?"

His playboy grin faded as his eyes grew dark and smoldering. Jessie could see the heat in them, feel the sudden electric current crackle in the air between them, like lightning about to strike. "Jess, I'll do whatever you want me to."

He turned, leaving her alone in her office to catch her breath and to try to ignore the flush that traveled over her entire body as he exited down the hall.

Damn that man and his sexy mouth.

NATHAN WATCHED JESSIE in the corral with the recently gelded stallion she'd begun calling Jet. Both of the mares who arrived with him were doing well, and their physical wounds were healing. He'd already noticed that they'd put on some much-needed weight and were even showing interest when other people approached, enough that Jessie told Aleta she could start working with them this week.

But this horse didn't want anyone near him, and he barely tolerated Jessie. It scared Nathan to watch her in the corral alone with the animal. Unlike the last time, however, Nathan followed her instructions and kept his distance, trying to concentrate on the files open on his laptop. But every sound from the corral had him glancing her way, ready to fly from his chair to rescue her.

"At least you're not obvious."

Bailey made her way across the walkway to the porch of his cabin. "Why don't you just go over there and watch?"

"She told me to stay away."

Bailey laughed and shook her head. "I thought you had more cojones than that, Wall Street." Nathan glared at her. "I know my cousin, and I've seen the way she's been looking at you the last couple days."

"Like she wants me to leave?"

"Well, yes, that too, but that's not the only look she's given you." Bailey shrugged. "I haven't seen her this way...well, ever. I don't know what happened last night, and I don't want the gory details, but I don't think she'd be averse to repeating the ride, if you catch my drift."

"Bailey, your subtlety is refreshing." Nathan rolled his eyes.

"I'm just saying that she's interested in you, and I'm pretty sure you won't hurt her. Mostly because I'd kill you if you did. You know that, right?" She shot him a look through her blond bangs. "And if I didn't, Justin would."

His guilt resurfaced, knowing he'd already hurt her once before. He wondered what they would do if they found out now.

"I'm not interested in a relationship, Bailey. I'm going to help you guys and head back to New York next week to finish a job there I put on hold. Then I'm going back to my apartment."

"And what's waiting for you there, big shot?"

Nathan didn't answer, because he didn't want to admit there was nothing worth returning for. What if he gave Jessie a choice instead of making it for her? What if he'd done that years ago? Would she have stuck by him and weathered the media storm or would she have crumbled under the pressure. Jessie was a strong woman, but was she strong enough?

Bailey flopped into the chair beside him and grabbed one of the file folders, flipping through the papers before closing it again. "You two actually have a lot in common, you know. You're both too busy fixing problems for everyone else to realize you need someone to fix yours."

Nathan sighed, exasperated. This wasn't a discussion he felt like having with the young woman. What did she know about complicated relationships? About as much as he'd known when he promised Jessie he'd return. He wasn't about to have a discussion that would require admitting his life was shallow and meaningless.

"I don't have any problems."

"Sure you don't." She tossed the folder back onto the side table and stood up, looking down at Nathan. "Maybe you're right. It's probably better if you do stay away. You couldn't handle someone like Jess."

"Did you want something, Bailey, or just to be a pain in the butt?"

She laughed out loud. "And there's the real Nathan Kerrington that Justin speaks so highly of. Not this stick-in-the-mud banker. He kept telling me about all the pranks you two pulled in college, and how much fun you had the last time you were here. What happened?"

"I grew up." Nathan glared at her.

He wasn't a stick-in-the-mud. He knew how to have fun; it was just a different kind of fun. Now there was a purpose to what he chose to do for fun. He didn't have time to waste on frivolity, or the freedom he had in college to pull childish pranks. Nathan realized he sounded like his father. Visions of lying on the blanket under the stars with Jessie filled his mind, erasing the boring events he merely tolerated for business. *That* was fun, but not the kind he could have on a regular basis. She was the kind of fun that was bound to cause one of them trouble.

"Let me guess, your kind of fun consists of schmoozing clients, business dinners, and midmorning tee times." Nathan narrowed his eyes, hating that he was so predictable. Bailey pressed on, plucking the file he was reading from his hands and setting it aside. "Maybe, just maybe, you should get away from work long enough to realize life is going to keep moving ahead, with or without you, and you're getting left behind."

The truth hurt. Really hurt. He hadn't realized how empty his life really was until he'd arrived here and witnessed their family dynamic. He wanted real connections, not the charade he'd been settling for. He wanted his friendship with Justin again. He was tired of women who only wanted his wealth and fame but didn't care in the slightest about him. Seeing Jessie and Justin again slapped him in the face with all he was lacking, things he'd put on the back burner and, most likely, missed his chance at ever having. He wanted the relationship he'd given up with Jessie.

He didn't need Bailey pointing it out again. Anger swirled in his chest. Emotions he so often held in check burst free of his usual control and spilled over.

"Maybe you should realize that this rocker-country-girl thing you've got going on isn't going to get you anywhere, Bailey. Maybe you should spend a little less time criticizing my life and a little more taking an account of what you plan on doing with your own. Or are you planning on living off your cousins' generosity forever?"

Her eyes flashed and he immediately regretted his angry words. He hadn't meant for them to come out so harsh. She didn't deserve his bitterness. It wasn't her fault he'd made so many mistakes. "Bailey, I…" He glanced up at her in time to see her clench her jaw, sadness shuttered her dark brown eyes.

"It's a good thing you have me all figured out, Wall Street." Sarcasm tinged her voice and she didn't bother to hide her hurt at his snub. "You know, I'm surprised you got so riled up if I'm as far off base as you claim. I'm sure you're absolutely thrilled with your life the way it is. From what Justin's said, it's been going so well for you. All that money and prestige. How lonely is that empty penthouse, by the way?"

Bailey trotted down the steps of the porch and headed toward the main house. "Your big bank account must keep you nice and warm at night. Maybe money *can* buy happiness. You should know."

"Bailey!" Nathan yelled after her, but Bailey just ignored him and continued toward the house.

Nathan knew he should go after her, but he felt like an idiot for letting his temper get the better of him. He shouldn't have said the things he did. It wasn't like him to be abrasive, but he'd been on edge ever since he and Jessie had kissed last night. He'd been trying to dismiss it as sexual frustration, but he knew better, and Bailey had just pointed out the obvious.

From an early age, he'd been taught responsibility, logic, and money were the root of success in life. As the older of two children, they were a perfect nuclear family—one boy, one girl. His mother had gone to an all-girls college on the East Coast and studied business, but it was really an MRS degree. His father, on the other hand, had seen nothing wrong with taking whatever he wanted, whether it was in politics or business, and the legalities were of little consequence. If it wasn't legal, he'd find a way to work around the law. Money could hire people willing to do just about anything, and the large sums his father threw at his flunkies were enough to keep them quiet.

Family loyalty, love, fun, excitement, passion...none of those words were in the Kerrington vocabulary. Everything about Justin's lifestyle had been foreign and exciting to Nathan in college, drawing him like a moth to a flame. The way Jessie drew him now.

He'd dated women with far more refinement and prestige, kept company with debutantes and high society elite, yet none of them kept him awake at night, twisting in the sheets, his fingers clenching with need to touch her. None of them caused the frenzy of wild desire that raged through him in her presence, making him want to forget every bit of his genteel upbringing. To want to give in to the need to taste her lips, to feel her skin under his fingers, to hear her whisper his name.

He wanted to believe it was the novelty of Jessie, the way she was so different from any other woman he'd ever been with. She was as free a spirit as he'd ever known. She did everything completely or not at all, and when she gave her word, or her heart, she meant it. At least, at one time. He'd never found anyone else like her. In his world, people hid behind pretense, falsifying every word to raise their own esteem. But not Jessie. In fact, she didn't seem to know how incredible she was, let alone take pride in it. How the hell had he ever allowed his father's threats to convince him let go of that?

He wandered toward the corral where she stood, completely still, with her back to the horse. The animal snorted loudly at Nathan's approach but didn't look his way. The horse dropped his head and walked toward her, nudging her shoulder with his nose. He was rewarded when she stepped backward, reaching up to scratch him.

"Need something?" He was surprised when she addressed him, since she hadn't moved to look at him.

You.

He couldn't tell her that, no matter how much he wanted to. The uncontrollable attraction he'd had for her that summer came back full force, and he wondered what sort of spell she put on him. He felt tongue-tied, unable to answer, as he thought about the feel of his hands on her heated flesh. He wanted to see those blue eyes darken with desire again. What would she say if she knew his thoughts? Would she remind him of his own reservations last night?

She turned and glanced at him over her shoulder before turning her attention back to the horse. "You okay?"

"Fine."

What was wrong with him? Where was the confident ladies' man who left New York? Where was the man who had no trouble delivering crushing blows to millionaires during takeovers or flattering supermodels with half-hearted pickup lines? It was simple; he wanted her. Not just physically but emotionally. He wanted to be the man she turned to for help and the one she clung to in passion. He'd been a fool to give her up. Or to push her away again last night. He needed to talk with Justin, to clear up the past before he could move forward with Jessie, but he couldn't let her go again.

She rubbed a hand over the gelding's face, taking a few steps forward and letting the animal follow her. "You know, if you're bored, Aleta can show you where to find the grooming equipment." He saw a playful smile curve her lips. "Or you could clean stalls."

White-hot yearning shot straight through him, making the miserable jeans even more uncomfortable. He had it bad if a simple smile could cause this sort of reaction in him.

His mouth moved without permission from his brain. "Jess, there is nothing boring about watching you work."

Her eyes immediately grew serious and she stumbled to a stop. The gelding bumped into the back of her, knocking her forward a few more steps. She righted herself and licked her lips, staring at him as if trying to read the intention behind his words. She raised a hand to the gelding's nose.

"You're dangerous to my concentration," she murmured. The gelding chose that exact moment to nip at her hand, and she flicked his lip with her fingers. "No." The horse jerked his head up as if shocked by her audacity, but immediately hung his head again.

Her concentration seemed fine, and he wondered if it wasn't the current between them leaving her unnerved. "I'll make you a deal: You finish up here, and then I'll do whatever you want me to."

His comment seemed to strike lightning between them, as he left the innuendo hanging in the air. He'd seen it in her eyes, but after last night, he wondered if he wasn't tempting fate too much. He couldn't settle for one kiss. He was learning quickly that with Jessie, it was all or nothing.

Her eyes sparked with suspicion. "I thought you said that was a bad idea."

"I said it could get complicated."

"What about my brother?"

"I'm caring less about what he might think every minute." Justin would just have to get past it.

She turned away from him and ran a hand over the gelding's shoulder and down his leg before picking up his foot and patting the bottom of his hoof. He wondered if she was really working the horse or trying to avoid looking at him.

"Besides, I could probably take him after a beer and a bourbon." Her head jerked up, and he winked at her, smiling as he crossed his arms over the rail of the corral. "Isn't that how cowboys do it? With liquid courage?"

"I'm not sure what to make of you anymore," Jessie admitted as she stood, laying a hand on the gelding's back. "One minute, you're exactly what I expect: a straight-laced, suit-wearing banker—"

"Financial analyst," he corrected.

"Whatever." She pulled a rope halter from over her shoulder and slipped it over the gelding's head. "And then you do something that surprises me. I'm not surprised often."

He was taken aback by her admission. "I believe that. I get the feeling you tend to enjoy being the one *doing* the surprising, don't you, Jess?"

She smiled coyly. "Maybe."

"And you don't like that you can't figure out my intentions, do you?"

The smile slipped from her lips, and he saw her brows take a downward plunge as she turned her attention back to the horse. "What makes you think I can't figure you out? Maybe I just don't see the point in bothering."

He arched a brow. "Really?" Her armor was back and he wasn't sure what he'd said to raise it again.

Jessie shrugged, barely glancing at him. "Let's face facts, Nathan. You're leaving in a few days, and as much as I appreciate your help, it's pretty unlikely we'll hear from you again."

"Is that the kind of man you think I am?" He shook his head sadly.

She met his gaze, her blue eyes remorseful. "History tends to speak loudly. I'm not interested in repeating it."

He'd thought Bailey wielded the truth brutally. She didn't hold a candle to Jessie. Her softly spoken words felt like a knife plunged into his heart. Proving himself was going to be harder than he'd thought it would be.

"And here I thought you could read people the way you do horses. Jess, you're so busy trying to stay a few steps ahead of everyone so that you don't get hurt, you've never looked up long enough to see you're alone."

She grasped the lead rope under the horse's chin, but he saw her pinch her lips together tightly. She narrowed her eyes, and he saw the anger in them flicker to life. He might have pegged her, but in doing so, he may have ruined any chance he had at getting through to her.

"I guess it's just something we have in common then, isn't it, Wall Street? Those in glass houses should be careful about throwing stones. I don't see a wedding ring on your hand or you calling your family each evening. At least I have people I know I can turn to. Who do you have?"

She turned the gelding toward the gate and walked him to the barn as he watched her go. She was a tempest of emotion—playful one moment, turning dangerous without warning. He knew it, yet he'd stoked her ire anyway when what he'd really wanted was to take her in his arms and kiss her again, to feel his hands on her skin, and feel her hands on him. He'd wanted to explore the connection between them, to see if she didn't still feel the same way she once had. Instead, he'd managed to push her away and, in the process, accused her of doing the same thing.

Way to go, you idiot. Now you've managed to piss of two Hart women in a span of half an hour.

Chapter Eleven

JESSIE LED THE gelding into his stall, trying not to dwell on Nathan or his insult. She needed to stay focused on this particular horse. Jet was doing remarkably well in spite of still being a bit nippy, which she expected; however, she still didn't trust him enough to let anyone else work with him. She threw him a flake of hay and turned both mares out into the small pasture behind the barn so she could clean their stalls.

How dare he! How dare he accuse me of not letting people in?

She'd let him in once, like she'd never let anyone in before, and it ended in heartbreak. In a way, she was grateful for what he'd done. He'd taught her early never to completely trust anyone, never to give herself completely again. She might be alone, she might bear scars, but she was whole.

She paused the in the aisle of the barn. Why was she even angry? She knew she let people close, the ones she knew she could count on. She trusted her family with her life.

Then why haven't you told them your dream for the ranch?

Because she didn't want to open herself up to rejection again. She didn't want her dreams to be shot down without giving them a chance. She didn't want them to see her as a lost cause and abandon her.

She'd learned from an early age that people came and went in her life with regularity, like the guests who came to the ranch and stayed for a few weeks before returning to their lives. Relationships were great while they lasted, but the problem was that they *never* lasted. And once they were off the ranch, you were forgotten. Nathan had been the last and most painful. He'd promised her they would be together, told her he loved her, and then disappeared, taking her heart with him. Then her parents were gone as well.

She could empathize with Aleta and Michael, which was part of why she'd opened her home to them any time they wanted to come to a place where there was a semblance of permanence and acceptance. She wanted to offer them a place where they knew someone would always remember them and be excited to see them. Just because she didn't expect that same for herself didn't stop her from longing for it, or for someone who would see the woman behind the mask of courage she wore. Someone who wouldn't forget her. Someone who wouldn't leave her behind. Just like the kids and her horses, she was tired of being overlooked, cast aside, and left alone.

Jessie tossed two bags of pine shavings into the wheelbarrow and rolled them to the first stall, dropping them off at the doors. Grabbing the rake, she went inside, grateful for the physical labor that required nothing from her mentally. She scooped up the manure, dropping it into the wheelbarrow with a satisfying thud. She'd just started the second stall when she heard footsteps on the cement floor in the aisle way. The tiny hairs on the back of her neck lifted, and she could feel his presence like electricity in the air. She knew without looking that Nathan had followed her. She didn't want to be this sensitive to his nearness, didn't want to respond to him with a craving far stronger than she'd ever experienced before and doubted she ever would aside from him.

"Go away, Nathan."

"I came to apologize, Jess. I shouldn't have said those things."

She ignored the way her nickname slid easily from his lips and the way it made her heart trip over her ribs and start fluttering like a baby bird learning to take flight. She'd quit buying into romantic notions a long time ago, thanks to him. Now, if only she could convince her body to let them go. She set the rake against the wall and walked into the aisle way.

"It's Jessie. Jessie. We are *not* friends, remember?"

His green eyes flashed, the golden flecks lighting them from within, and she saw frustration in the set of his jaw. "No?"

"No. Let's keep our roles in perspective. You're the financial genius here to do a favor for my brother, and

I'm just his idiot little sister who bought your load of crap years ago and can't manage to keep this ranch afloat now."

His long strides ate the distance between them in seconds, but she stood her ground, staring up at him, daring him to argue. His lips were tight, set in a grim line and a deep crease lined his perfect brow. She wanted to back away, but years of working with her father wouldn't allow her to show any signs of intimidation. *Cowgirl up,* she recited the mantra in her head, although not nearly as confidently as she usually did.

"Don't do that," he ordered, staring down into her eyes, his voice quiet but insistent.

She could feel the heat emanating from him as sparks of desires burst in her chest, sending shivers over her skin. She tried to control it, to stop herself from trembling at his nearness but she couldn't stop her breath from catching in her throat. "Don't do what?" Her voice was a hoarse whisper.

"Don't belittle yourself. You are far more than that. You've always been more than that to me." His hands grasped her upper arms and he dipped his head toward her, his eyes never leaving hers. "You're a talented, kind, giving, passionate woman."

It wasn't what Jessie expected. His words were a balm to her chapped and aching heart, exactly what she needed to hear, but she knew she couldn't let him break past her walls. Who knew what damage he could cause her heart when he left again. She'd barely managed to piece together the shards last time. She pressed her hands against his chest, intending to push him away from her, but he gently circled her wrists with his fingers. Their eyes locked and she refused to be the first to look away.

"Nathan." She meant for it to be a warning but it came out sounding more like a plea.

"What, Jess?"

He placed his palms over the back of her hands and twined his fingers between hers. His touch made her weak, and she felt a wave of need break over her, threatening to drown her. She'd been so in love with him, and it had left a gaping hole in her, one she'd never managed to fill, not even with her work.

Nathan walked her backward until she felt the stall behind her. With the hard wall of his body pressing against the front of her, pinning their hands between them, there was nowhere for her to escape the explosion of yearning that began in the middle of her chest, spreading outward, heating her and leaving her breathless. Every inhalation filled her with the scent of his expensive cologne, reminding her again how out of place he was. He didn't belong here. But seeing the desire in his eyes, feeling it in every inch of him pressing up against her, made Jessie want to wrap her legs around his waist and let him take her right here in the barn.

She couldn't possibly feel this way about him again. She couldn't imagine feeling any other way about him. She needed this man. Not just wanted him, *needed* him, and that scared the crap out of her.

He was going to kiss her, and she was going to melt under his touch. There was no doubt in her mind. If that happened, she was a goner. Because, for her, this wasn't about sex; this was about how Nathan made her feel, how he'd always made her feel—understood and validated and worthy. The only other time Jessie felt that way was when she worked with her horses.

How had this man recognized the weakness in her, buried deeply, and unearthed it so easily? Panic set in. She had to protect herself. She couldn't let Nathan in, couldn't let him get close again. She shoved against his hands, using her body to knock him off balance, so he stepped backward, knocked against the handles of the wheelbarrow, and fell into the bucket.

"You can finish the stalls."

She ran out of the barn, refusing to look back at the man trying to piece together a full sentence from where he landed, inside a wheelbarrow full of fresh horse manure.

NATHAN PRESSED HIS hands into the wheelbarrow, trying to find his balance, and felt them sink into the foul muck his rear had sunken into. What in the hell was wrong with that woman?

She'd wanted him to kiss her. Almost as much as he wanted to do it. He'd seen it in her eyes, in the way she leaned into him. He'd felt it in the way her pulse raced against his fingertips at her wrist and the way her sweet breath fanned against his face when he dipped his mouth toward hers. The next thing he knew, he was butt-first in a pile of horseshit, and she was running for the house like she was on fire. He rocked himself forward, nearly toppling the wheelbarrow, and stood up just as Aleta came into the barn.

"What are you *doing*?" The girl's eyes were wide with shock as she covered her mouth with a hand. Her hand slid down slowly to reveal a broad smile. "Jess?"

Nathan flipped his hands, trying to shake the smelly mess from them, but only succeeded in getting the disgusting, wet filth on his face and shirt. "How'd you guess?"

"What'd you do?"

He quirked a brow in disbelief. "What makes you think I did anything?"

"Well, Justin was the last person she pushed into a manure pile, the first time he suggested calling you. He didn't see it coming either." She giggled at the memory. "Trust me, you got the better deal. He ended up face first."

"Great." He wiped his dirty hands down the side of his new jeans and looked around, wondering where he was going to clean up. It would serve Jess right if he used her washer since the irrational woman had caused the damage.

"I'll finish up in here. Go, shower and clean up before dinner because Jess will kill you if you come to the table like that."

"Thanks. It's Aleta, right?"

She slid the stall doors closed and reached for the handles of the wheelbarrow. "That's me. June is in the house, and she can show you where to wash those and take a shower, since you can't wash them in the cabin." She stopped in front of him. "And, trust me, you do not want to track that into the cabin or you'll have Bailey to worry about."

"I'm not going into that house with—"

Aleta laughed, her brown eyes twinkling merrily. "Jess already left. Didn't you hear her peel out of here in the truck? Go, but you'd better hurry up before she gets back."

If he was going to get his clothes cleaned and take a shower, this was his only chance because if Jess caught him in her house, she'd probably push him off the side of The Ridge.

JESSIE HAD READ an article once about yogis who could stop their pulses just by thinking about it. Right now, she'd have given anything to be able to slow hers even slightly. She wanted to believe it was anger that fueled her racing heart, an adrenaline rush that had her blood pulsing almost painfully though her temples, but she knew better.

It was Nathan—the way he touched her. The way the flecks of gold in his eyes glowed like she'd ignited a fire in him. He certainly made parts of her burn and throb. He had a way of looking at her that made her feel like she was his next conquest. And, Lord help her, but a part of her wanted to be conquered by him, knowing she would enjoy every second of it. She wasn't even sure what was stopping her from saying yes.

That wasn't exactly true. She knew why she wasn't giving in to him—he scared her. More precisely, the way he made her feel, the way he made her hope, scared her.

Nathan Kerrington dredged up images of long nights of lovemaking and mornings of waking in his arms. He made her fantasize about lazy summers, swimming holes, fairs and rodeos, date nights, and picnics in the park. All of those things were part of a serious, lasting relationship, which was something she'd never allowed herself to long for after he'd abandoned her.

She'd given Nathan everything she had to offer. Once he was gone, she devoted every waking moment to the ranch, throwing herself into work in order not to feel the emptiness in her chest or the hollow ache where her heat once beat. Everything she'd offered Nathan, she poured into Heart Fire and her horses. In spite of every effort, it still wasn't enough to keep it running smoothly in the black. She wasn't enough for either.

Nathan's words echoed through her mind: *talented…kind…giving…passionate.* Who was she kidding? Nathan didn't make her tingle because he wanted to *know* her. She'd turned her back on every one of the cowboys her parents introduced her to because their touch left her feeling frigid. How was it that a *financial analyst* could light up her body like a fireworks show on the Fourth of July? From the first time he brushed her hand, passing her in the barn, she'd felt tingles in her fingers. And that first kiss at the river so long ago—even then, she'd known there was dangerous tinder burning between them that was likely to blaze out of control.

She couldn't be in love with Nathan again. If she were to fall for someone, it had to be someone who loved Heart Fire as much as she did, someone who would share the load to make it great again, not some city boy playing cowboy for a week before heading back to New York, leaving her and her visions of a happily-ever-after ending behind. Not someone who would make her a quickly forgotten notch on his bedpost.

Happily-ever-after endings didn't exist in the real world. At least not for her. Hers was a life where things weren't always fair, parents went away and didn't come back, men who claimed to love you left and never called.

Damn Justin for asking him back here in the first place.

She pressed the button on her steering column to call her brother, intent on giving him a piece of her mind. Someone was going to take the brunt of her anger. It might as well be him. Nothing happened. She slid her hand into her purse, searching for her cell phone and realized, in her hurry to get away from Nathan, she'd left it at the house.

"Damn it!"

She seriously considered just continuing to the store without it, but inevitably, there would be an emergency. She wasn't so far from the house she couldn't turn around. She slowed the truck onto the shoulder of the road and flipped a U-turn, heading back home. Within a few minutes, she pulled up to the house and ran in the back door, looking in the kitchen for her phone near the key rack on the back wall. Not seeing it there, she headed for the stairs, assuming it must be in her room.

What a waste of a day! She still had to get to the store and back, and she'd just gone nearly twenty minutes out of her way for nothing.

Jessie opened the heavy oak door to her room, and her stomach dropped to her toes, followed by her jaw. Standing in front of her, in nothing but a towel, was the very subject of her frustration, with droplets of water clinging to his chest and hair, looking only slightly guilty. The breath seemed to stop in her lungs, even as her heart pounded against her ribcage. Her entire body ignited with desire as her eyes slid down his body and she watched him tuck in the edge of the towel. Her eyes jumped back up to his face as a lopsided grin slipped over Nathan's lips, and for the first time, she noticed a dimple in his left cheek. How had she never noticed it before? She wanted to be pissed, but that stupid indentation took anything left of her senses and scattered them, leaving her unable even to speak.

"No knock?" His eyes glinted playfully and it reminded her of why she was angry at him in the first place. His sly comment loosed her tongue.

Who in the hell did he think he was? "It's *my* room. I'm not used to finding strange men standing nearly naked in it."

She spotted her phone on the nightstand beside the bed and hurried past him to grab it, thankful for a reason to look away from his perfectly chiseled body.

How did a guy get muscles like that sitting behind a desk? Her mouth was suddenly dry, and she was finding it difficult to put together a coherent thought, knowing that a simple flick of her wrist would have him standing in front of her in all of his slick, nude glory. She clenched her hand into a tight fist to control the urge to do exactly that.

"That's good to know."

His voice was right behind her. Surprised, she straightened and spun only to smack into the solid wall of his damp chest. She jumped away from him, tripping herself and falling against the nightstand, toppling the lamp. Leaning to catch it, she lost her balance and fell into the bed on her hip.

Nathan chuckled at her clumsy attempt to right herself and offered her a hand to pull her up. She took it and tried to stand as he stepped backward, but the heels of her boots tangled in the soft down bedding and she fell again, dragging him down on top of her. His thighs straddled her knees, pinning her to the bed, bracing himself with his arms above her shoulders.

She could feel every inch of him pressed against her. The denim of her jeans and the soft terrycloth towel did nothing to hide the taut muscles of his body. She felt every part of her respond with shock waves of desire. She pressed her hands against his chest and instantly froze, regretting her decision as her fingers tingled where they touched him, sending pleasurable warmth coursing through her arms.

"Where are you going, Jess? Why do you keep running away from me?"

Why *was* she still running? Why was she even bothering to fight this? Why shouldn't she have one blissful moment? Deb's voice practically shouted in her head to seize the opportunity even as memories flooded her mind. Memories of how good they had been together, how beautiful it had been the short time it had lasted.

Any argument she might have made disappeared as he brushed a stray curl from her forehead.

"I'm not going to hurt you," he whispered.

"Yes, you will," she disagreed. Her voice choked with emotion she didn't want him to see. "You're going to destroy me."

The acknowledgment did nothing to lessen the need burning within, spreading through her like an unwelcome flood, filling her with sweet agony. Without waiting for a response from him, she curled her fingers around his nape, shutting out the warnings her mind offered, and surrendered to the sensations coursing through her, electrifying her and making her feel suddenly free. She pulled him down to meet her mouth.

The kiss wasn't slow or gentle. It was hungry, primal, and fierce. She was tired of convincing herself she didn't want him, that she didn't still love him. From the moment he'd stepped foot on the ranch, she'd felt the attraction still burning within. She couldn't deny it any longer.

Unlike their sweet, tender kisses on The Ridge the night before, his tongue plunged into her mouth, tasting, branding, mating with hers, as he buried his hands in her hair. She couldn't hold back, even if she wanted to. She didn't have that kind of control when it came to Nathan. But he didn't have to know that. She might not be able to stop herself from loving him, but she didn't need to let him know the power he held over her.

Jessie wrapped one leg around his hips and rolled him onto the bed so she straddled him, her hair hanging down over them like a dark curtain. Gasping for a breath, she dragged her mouth from his, her lips swollen and tingling.

"I can't deal with any more complications," she warned. "This has to be a straightforward arrangement. If you can't handle that, you should leave now."

He cupped his hand around her jaw, and his eyes heated to emerald fire. "Jess, I'm not going anywhere."

Jessie felt her heart do a flip in her chest as a piece broke off and soared skyward. She quickly yanked it back into place, scolding herself for the momentary elation. She'd heard that promise from him before. She had too many responsibilities to the ranch to fall for his happily ever after, forever and ever fairy tale. She couldn't let herself fall into the trap of believing in him again. Even knowing that didn't stop the longing that flooded her veins as his hands slid up the sides of her spine.

Jessie planted a hand in the middle of his chest. "Don't get all serious on me, Wall Street. We're just two adults having consensual fun for as long as we both want to."

He blinked, his brows shooting upward on his forehead, as if her words surprised him, and for a moment, she thought she saw disappointment in his eyes. It passed before she could question it, and that damn sexy dimple appeared in his cheek again, stealing her breath and making it hard to concentrate.

"Just what every man wants to hear."

She wasn't sure if his words were serious or in jest, but when his hands moved to the edge of her shirt, teasing the skin beneath with his fingertips, fire spread across her skin. The only way she was going to maintain any sort of sanity with this man was to be the seducer instead of the seducee. She grasped the bottom of her shirt and pulled it over her head, tossing it the foot of her bed.

"Make your decision." She smiled down at him and reached behind her back for the clasp of her bra, her back arching toward him.

Nathan's eyes darkened, and she felt every muscle in his body tighten under her thighs, coiling with tension. His hands found her waist, his long fingers sliding up her ribs causing shivers of delight to trip down her spine.

She wanted to cry out at that simple touch. Her entire body felt as if flames were engulfing her slowly, sweetly.

"No expectations, is that what you're saying? You're sure that's enough for you?"

Without waiting for an answer, Nathan's hands replaced hers and he unsnapped her bra, brushing aside the material to cup her breasts in his hands. His thumbs stroked the already taut peaks to aching points of agonizing pleasure. There was no way she could answer him truthfully while he was touching her, so she bit her lip, stifling the moan threatening to betray her. Jessie reached for the edge of his towel.

Nathan laughed, grasping her hand with his, and settled it against his firm abs. "There's no way I'm going to hurry this, Jess. I want to look at every inch of you."

His fingers reached for her belt buckle, unclasping it and unbuttoning her pants. His fingertips moved to her lower back, and he slowly slid them along the inside of the waistband of her pants, circling them over her hipbones and back to her zipper. Goosebumps broke out over the skin of her back and stomach, and she felt a shiver of longing travel up her spine. Nathan unzipped her jeans with painstaking slowness, and she bowed instinctively, which only pressed her fully against his groin. She wasn't sure when they'd switched roles and he'd become the seducer, but at some point, she'd lost all leverage over him. Needing his hands on her, she'd let him take control.

He stood quickly, surprising her, and lifted her to her feet, kneeling before her. His big hands slid over her rear, pushing her jeans down her thighs to the floor. With her hands on his shoulders for balance and his face at her navel, he removed her boots, and she stepped out of her pants. She could feel his hot breath fanning against the skin of her abdomen, warming her flesh, and need spiraled through her hot and fierce, making her wet with desire. He slid his hand down the back of her thigh, his fingers tickling the back of her knees, and her head fell forward with a sigh of delight. He knew exactly where to touch her to make her body turn to putty. Curling his fingers around her heel, he removed her socks while he pressed his lips to the skin at her waist.

Her body ignited, every inch of her feverish, flames of desire licking at her, melting her resolve to keep her heart distant from him, locked tightly away. Nathan's arms curled around her hips, his hands moving up the back of her thighs to cup her butt. Gripping the edge of her underwear, his lips found the curve of her belly and his eyes looked up at her, meeting her gaze between her breasts.

"Jess, you're beautiful." His lips moved against her skin, but his eyes locked on hers, as if speaking to her soul. "Every curve, every inch."

She didn't want to believe him. She was too curvy, her rear too big. She'd heard enough snide comments growing up. Unlike her sister and cousin, she'd inherited her mother's short legs and generous endowments. But when Nathan said it, when his eyes shone hot and needy as he looked at her, she didn't doubt his words. She felt beautiful, feminine, and desirable.

Nathan hooked his fingers into the edge of her underwear and slid the scrap of thin material down her legs, letting it pool at her feet. Bringing his hands back up to her hips, his thumbs trailed over the sensitive skin of her inner thigh, making her gasp with white-hot yearning. His hand traced the wet seam of her womanhood, and he slid one finger inside. Nathan rubbed his thumb against the nub as she arched against him. Jessie's knees buckled, and her fingers dug into his shoulders. Holding her to him with one hand under her rear, his lips against her belly, he locked eyes with her again and watched her pleasure.

Part of her wanted to move away, to deny herself the thrill of his touch, and to prove that she was the one in control of this situation, not him. She could never let him know how deeply her emotions were involved.

Just when her mind seemed to gain control of her body again, Nathan dipped his head. His mouth sent every thought splintering into shards of meaningless gibberish. His tongue left her forgetting her name, pushing her past caring who was in control. She cried out, bucking against him, quivering as an orgasm, more savage than she'd ever experienced, left her clinging to him, trying to stand, panting for breath.

Nathan stood slowly, his body pressing against hers, the sensation making her gasp, shivering against him in renewed pleasure. And then he was gone, leaving her on weak legs as disappointment coursed through her. She watched as he walked away from her, into the bathroom. She heard the shower turn on just before he leaned back into the room.

"Are you joining me, or did you want me to carry you?"

"What?" Her voice was still breathless.

Nathan strode back into the bedroom, and she couldn't help but let her eyes take in his physical perfection. His entire body looked carved from granite, and she felt her desire reawaken. He reached out and grasped her hand, pulling her toward him. "Where are we going?" she whispered.

"I got a shower, but you didn't." He slid his arms around her back and ducked his head, sucking her bottom lip between his.

She gasped at the pleasure spiraling through her, making her dizzy. Nathan walked her backward toward the shower before tugging the towel from his hips and tossing it over the door. He stepped inside, pulling her with him as steam enveloped them. His hands slid over her slick body as his lips worshiped her neck and shoulders. It was all she could to do to cling to him as she gave in to the sweet agony of his touch. Grasping her thighs, Nathan lifted her, and she wrapped her legs around his waist, winding her arms around his shoulders.

Nathan turned so her back was braced against the tile wall as the hot water pelted his back. The movement pressed him fully against the center of her pleasure, and she cried out, her breasts against his chest, as the water sluiced between them. The renewed fervor coursing through her surprised her, and Nathan growled deep in his throat, dropping his head against her shoulder.

"Don't move, Jess." His voice was strained. "Please, don't move."

After what she'd just experienced at his hands and mouth, her self-control was nonexistent. The water washed over his shoulder and down her breasts, making them intoxicatingly slick. His fingers dug into the firm muscle of her butt, and she could feel his restraint caving as his body throbbed against her. Nathan pressed his mouth against her collarbone, licking at the water that created a trail down the valley of her cleavage, before taking one breast into his mouth. His tongue flicked at the nipple, licking the water from her skin. Need, raw and fierce, exploded in her anew. Jessie gripped his shoulders, tightening her thighs around his hips. She wanted to feel all of him. Right now. She couldn't wait another moment.

"You can be slow later. I want you now." She inched herself down over the length of him, covering his mouth with her own. Her body enveloped his, encasing him completely as he gripped her thighs.

How could anything feel this incredible?

Her entire being surrounded him. Arms, legs, mouth, and heart, clutching him greedily as he drove into her. Her tongue swept against his as he held her against the wall, controlling each thrust with his hands cupping her rear. For the first time, she was content to simply feel, to let him guide her through the maelstrom of her desire, as he carried her to a new height of pleasure.

She cried out as the waves broke over her, releasing emotions she hadn't wanted to admit she was holding back. Nathan followed her, whispering her name against her neck, like a prayer, as he poured himself into her. She trembled against him as he continued to embrace her, unwilling let her move out of his arms. She felt wetness on her cheeks and assumed it was water until she tasted saltiness.

She was crying? She tucked her face into his neck and inhaled the sweet scent of the soap he'd used for his shower.

Please, don't let him realize I cried.

Chapter Twelve

DEAR GOD, HELP me, I've been to heaven.

Nathan felt himself grow hard again, still buried within her. He'd never responded to a woman as fiercely or been as reckless as he had with Jessie. He inhaled the sweet scent of her hair as she tucked her face against his neck and the water pounded against his back. Worries suddenly beat against his brain. He hadn't used any protection and had no idea if she was on the pill. It hadn't even crossed his mind when he saw her walk into the room. It was as if his brain took a vacation when she came in and had only just returned. They would need to talk about it, eventually. Protection was the least of his worries. There were far more pressing matters to discuss, including how much he'd hurt her.

He had seen her tears, seen the fear and pleasure in her eyes, mixing her emotions like a painful cocktail. For all her talk about them having *fun*, their lovemaking had dredged up emotions Jessie hadn't been prepared for. If there was anything he knew about Jess, she was a woman who didn't like to be blindsided, especially by something she perceived as weakness. She wanted to be in control, *had* to be in control, to feel safe. He'd just shattered that fantasy.

Feeling as if he was ripping a part of his soul away, he slid himself from within her, settling her back onto her feet and twisting behind him to reach for a container of body soap on a corner shelf. Without saying a word, he cupped one hand at the back of her neck and pressed a gentle kiss to her swollen lips, feeling guilty for being so rough as to injure her soft flesh. The tip of his tongue brushed over her lower lip, caressing it tenderly. He drew away and reached for her shoulders, turning her away from him. Gathering her thick, dark waves to one side, he pressed a kiss to her bare shoulder and felt her shiver.

"What are you doing?" she whispered. Her voice was husky, but he wasn't sure if it was from their previous lovemaking or desire reawakening.

He poured some of the soap into his hand and set the container aside. "I promised you a shower."

He stepped up behind her, letting his hands fall on her shoulders and trail over her arms. From there, his hands moved over her back, his thumbs massaging either side of her back before cupping her butt. Nathan circled his hands around her waist and slid up her ribcage slowly. She leaned back against him, sighing contentedly. His lips found the hollow behind her ear, and she dropped her head to the side, giving him better access.

His erection throbbed painfully, and it was all he could do to keep from burying himself into her again, in search of the sweet oblivion she brought. Nathan had known years ago, making love to Jessie had been incredible, but making love to Jess now was like nothing he'd ever known before. He wasn't sure he'd ever be the same. He had never felt as alive and free as he felt with her in his arms. Nathan didn't think he could explain it if he tried; this woman had marked him as hers eight years ago, but he'd been too stupid to realize it. He wouldn't make that mistake twice.

He had to make her understand why he'd done it, that he never would have let her go if he hadn't thought it was the best option for everyone at the time. Or how wrong he'd been.

His hand cupped her jaw and she tried to turn her face away from him. He knew she was trying to hide from him, but he wouldn't let her regret even one second of their time together.

One hand, slippery with soap, moved to cup her breast, massaging the flesh as the other moved over her lower stomach, holding her against him, and pulling her backward so her body molded against his chest.

"Feel what you do to me?" He gently bit her earlobe, and his hand strayed to the wet folds of her sex. "You make me want to completely lose myself in you."

Nathan wanted her to know the power she held over him when she lost control. Her head fell back onto his shoulder as he leisurely caressed her body, memorizing every curve and valley, learning what teased her, what made her quiver in his arms, and what made her beg for release. He turned her so she faced him, letting the water wash the soap from her body and tipped her face up to look him in the eye.

"What do you want, Jess?" He could see the dizzy yearning in her blue eyes but there was something else there, fear she couldn't quite hide, and she tried to turn away from him again. "Don't run from me. I need you."

He saw a flash of understanding in her eyes and a slight smile curved those gorgeous lips, as if she suddenly realized she wasn't the only one weak with desire. She slid her hand over the length of him gently and he groaned deep in his chest, closing his eyes against the explosion of raw need that burst in him.

NATHAN SAT ON the porch of his cabin, trying to pretend that he wasn't watching every move Jessie made in the barn as he thought about where he'd gone wrong with her last night. After their shower, they'd moved back to the bed. He couldn't keep his hands off her, and he didn't particularly want to, even if his body was spent. He'd missed out on caressing her body for eight years, and he wanted to make up for it. When she finally collapsed on top of him, both of them were completely exhausted, emotionally and physically. It was only then that he saw her slip into a brief moment of weakness, giving in to her satiation and curling against his chest like a purring kitten.

Nathan heard her breathing relax and thought she'd fallen asleep, but when he brushed his fingers through the waves of her hair, she'd immediately rolled away from him, reaching for her clothing as she bolted for the door, claiming she needed to feed the horses.

She tripped over Nathan's clothing, folded neatly outside the door and realized someone must have heard them together in her room. "Oh my God," she whispered, her face instantly turned bright red.

Nathan tried to catch her, but she'd already made it down the hall. Chasing her in a towel with two teens in the house didn't seem like the best idea. He let her go, praying he wasn't making an even bigger mistake.

It was nothing more than an excuse to escape. Jessie was trying to withdraw, to hide in order to process the array of emotions he'd seen in her face. And he'd seen them all. Everything from ecstasy to fear, from breathless anticipation to tight-laced control. She'd shifted from one extreme to another.

As he watched her in the barn, it wasn't hard to tell she was trying to avoid him. Her eyes flicked away to focus on the mare, shifted to him, then away just as quickly when he caught her gaze. She'd dropped the halter several times, promptly turning her back to him while she brushed the animal. Not to mention she'd taken the long way to and from the house, probably to avoid walking past him at all. He wasn't going to let her get away that easily.

Nathan shuffled through the papers in the file folder again, trying to focus on the job he was here to accomplish. He still hadn't been able to find anything that would clue him in as to what Heart Fire Industries might be or where it was located. He couldn't even find any contact information, which should have been public record. Every time he thought he found a new trail, it led to another dead end. He was back where he started with nothing but a mysterious bank account with weekly transfers of around a thousand dollars each.

"Earth to Wall Street." Julia ducked her head into his line of vision. "Didn't you hear me calling you?"

His eyes flicked to hers, and he set the file down. "Sorry. I guess I was lost in thought."

Julia looked toward her sister in the barn. "Yeah, thinking."

"Can I ask you a question?" He hadn't spent much time with Julia, since she was usually training dogs on her portion of the ranch, but he felt like he needed a fresh perspective. The decisions he recommended for the dude ranch were going to affect her bottom line as well.

"Sure," she answered, sitting in the chair beside him. "What's up?"

"Have you guys considered incorporating your businesses? There are more benefits to doing it than to leaving things the way they are. In fact, I'm surprised your parents didn't do it." He frowned. "Did they ever mention it?"

Julia shrugged. "They might have talked about it with Justin. Dad and Justin usually handled most of the business decisions with Brendon and Uncle Trevor."

"Bailey's dad?"

She shook her head. "No, Uncle Trevor is...was a friend of theirs who is also their attorney. Brendon, our accountant, is his son. Mom, Jess, and I let Dad and Justin deal with most of the financial side of things. I mean,

Mom did the books and the payroll because she was good with numbers, but she did it all on the computer unless she was delivering receipts to Brendon with Dad." Julia pursed her lips, twisting them to the side. "I got the feeling she didn't really like dealing with Brendon."

"Why?" This was the first he was hearing about any trouble with their accountant. His brows sagged. "What makes you say that?"

"I don't know. Nothing specific, really." She shrugged. "It was little things. Like one night, Brendon was supposed to meet with Justin and Dad for dinner, but Mom tried to find a reason to get the paperwork to him instead so he didn't have a reason to come to the ranch. She didn't seem that fond of him as a kid either."

"You grew up together?"

She nodded. "He's the same age as Justin. Mom used to cringe when he was over because he and Justin were always causing some sort of trouble. She tolerated him because of Uncle Trevor, but she thought he was sneaky."

"What about you and Jess?"

"We ignored them most of the time. Older boys don't really like little sisters following them around. So, other than feeling like we had another bossy older brother, we pretty much stayed away and did our own thing." A slight smile spread over her lips. "Well, except for the date he took Jess on."

"Date?" Nathan was sure he sounded like a jealous boyfriend, but he wondered why no one had mentioned the fact to him. Didn't anyone consider that the fact might have some bearing on Jessie's situation? "She dated him?"

"Just once." Julia laughed quietly and stood. "Don't worry. You don't have any competition. She barely made it through dinner with him. She said he couldn't talk about anything but the ranch. Speaking of dinner, come on. It's ready."

She cut the conversation shorter than he'd have liked, especially considering she'd just dropped the bomb that she recognized his desire for Jess. Julia headed toward the corral to let Jessie know. Nathan gathered the folders as Julia disappeared inside the house. He stood up as Jess walked by, irked when she barely glanced his way.

"I'll be right there," he said deliberately, wanting to see if she would offer him any sort of encouragement.

Nathan took a deep breath, trying to control his frustration when she shrugged. He wasn't sure why he'd even bothered to say anything. She tried to act like she didn't care one way or the other, but he wasn't buying her act. Jessie frustrated him. Talking to Bailey or Julia was easy. They were both open, friendly and easy to read. Even Justin said exactly what he felt. But Jessie…whenever he came around, she built this impervious wall around herself, like she was just waiting for him to hurt her again. After making love to her, instead of tearing it down, she'd just make it thicker and wider.

He wasn't about to let her ignore what had happened between them. He couldn't. Even now, his body reacted at the mere sight of her, at the thought of her wet and slick with him in the shower. Jessie whispering his name as she rode him to the heights of pleasure.

Enough, he warned himself.

He wanted to breach that wall, to smash it and find out why she was trying so hard to hide behind it. Somehow he had to figure out how to gain her trust again, and how he could eradicate the fear that seemed to dog her judgment.

"INCORPORATE THE RANCH?" Justin shook his head. "It's just a family business. Why would we bother?" Nathan could hear the derisive tone in his voice.

"You incorporated your clinic. Why wouldn't you do the same with the ranch?" Nathan didn't need to hear Justin's answer. His tone said it all. He thought the ranch was insignificant compared to his veterinary practice. He hoped Jessie didn't pick up on the same lack of regard.

"We're running things the same way Mom and Dad did. It worked just fine for them."

"Until there's any sort of an accident. I can't believe your parents were able to run this place as long as they did without your lawyer recommending they incorporate." Nathan passed the plate to Jessie, who looked slightly awestruck at Justin's disdain. It wasn't like him to be so openly condescending. "Look, Justin, this isn't a matter of wanting to at this point. You don't really have a choice. Otherwise, you're putting everything at risk. One accident and all of you could lose everything."

"That's a little melodramatic, don't you think?" Justin rolled his eyes and glanced at Bailey. She arched a brow but didn't give him her characteristic smart-aleck grin.

"What are you saying, Nathan?" Julia sounded worried, and Nathan saw the concern crease her brow. Was she the only one with common sense? Someone needed to convince the rest of them to see the logic in his suggestion. He looked over at Jessie, who continued to avoid his gaze. He'd seen her take her brother on already, but he couldn't figure out why she was keeping quiet now. It wasn't like her and it worried him.

"I'm saying that with these kids on the ranch, if anyone were to get hurt, and their parents were to sue, they could come after all of your assets." He pointed his fork at Justin. "And, right now, that would include everything but the clinic."

"If that's true, then Dad would have done this a long time ago," Jessie argued. "Trust me, he wouldn't have put the ranch at risk." She picked up her plate and rose. "Dad cared too much for this place to take a chance losing it. Nothing came before the ranch."

Nathan didn't miss the derision in her voice. Leave it to Jessie to jump to conclusions and assume he was attacking her parents' character. "Unless they didn't know. What if they were getting bad advice?"

"From whom?" Julia's voice was quiet.

"This is something their lawyer should have recommended to them years ago. At the very least, your accountant should have mentioned it."

"Brendon." Jessie sounded irritated, but her voice had lost the aggressive note. She slid back into her chair, frowning down at her plate as if trying to figure out a difficult puzzle.

Nathan understood the feeling. He felt like he was trying to get a clear picture through a cloudy lens.

Something wasn't right, but he couldn't quite put his finger on what it was. However, the nagging suspicion in his gut told him it wasn't going to be good news.

"That explains your questions earlier." Julia tipped her chin and looked over at him.

"Look, I'm only trying to help you guys. The first step is to find out where that missing money is going is each month, and then for you to incorporate all of the Heart Fire businesses under one entity so they can be beneficial to one another." Nathan saw Justin's head snap up. "Can you schedule an appointment with the attorney and the accountant tomorrow?"

"I can try, but what money?"

"I can't do it tomorrow," Jessie interrupted, glaring at Nathan. "I have the Findley Brothers cowboys coming by tomorrow to sign some new-hire paperwork. I have to get them settled in before this weekend."

Justin frowned at her. "Make time." He turned back to Nathan, giving him his full attention. "What money?"

Jessie's eyes snapped with blue fire. "Don't tell me how to run my ranch, Justin. I have guests coming this week and I need to make sure that—"

"Jess, stop!" Justin slapped his hands against the table and stood, his chair scraping back quickly, almost toppling over. "What is this about missing money?"

"Don't yell at me," she shouted back, jumping up from her own chair. "I just found out about it."

"How much, and how long has this been going on?"

"Hey, guys, let's settle down." Julia tried to diffuse the situation, laying her hand on her brother's arm. "Sit down." She shot Nathan a pleading look, begging him to help her calm her brother and sister.

Justin settled, but only slightly, and scooted his chair back under the table. "How much?" he repeated slowly.

Nathan looked at Jessie, who looked ready to spit flames in his direction. She was furious, but he'd assumed she would've shared this information with her siblings. He should have known better. Jessie had a stubborn, independent streak and wore it like a badge on her chest. Admitting that there was money missing would be equivalent to another failure on her part. Jessie turned away from both men, staring out the kitchen window, refusing to meet Nathan's gaze.

He sighed, regretting that he'd even opened his mouth. "About four thousand dollars a month for the past six months."

"Four thousand!"

"Justin." Julia cleared her throat in warning.

"Jessie, this is a big, complex operation, but how do you not realize four thousand dollars a month is missing from the books? That's more than half the profit each month." Justin rose and began pacing the kitchen, a move Nathan remembered from college as the calm just before the storm. He was about to launch into a full-scale attack with his sister taking the brunt of the force. Nathan felt guilty for being the catalyst.

"Julia and I have been funding this ranch for months, and you've been just throwing money away, not even knowing where it's going? I'm doing without equipment I need at the clinic, and you just keep bringing more horses in."

"I'm not the one doing the books, remember? I don't even see them, so how could I have known?"

"You could have asked Brendon, at least checked before you went throwing money away."

"I haven't been throwing it away. It's missing!"

Nathan rose and moved between Jessie and her brother. "There's no way she would have found this unless she knew to look for it, Justin. She didn't know the surplus your parents had before their accident. I don't think any of you really knew how much this ranch was making, did you?" Nathan looked at each of them individually, gauging their reaction. "But someone else did. There have been several transfers to another account. I still haven't been able to fully trace where it's going. But money is being slowly funneled from Heart Fire Ranch."

Justin's tirade stalled as he spun on Nathan, shock written over his face. "What do you mean, funneled?"

"Do either of you know what Heart Fire Industries is?" Nathan glanced from Justin to Julia, watching their reactions for anything that might be suspicious. He didn't want to believe it was one of Jess's siblings taking the money, but he'd seen families do far worse to one another.

"Other than every one of our businesses using Heart Fire in the name, I have no clue." Julia reached across the table for Jessie's hand, but Jessie pulled it away from her grasp, unwilling to accept any comfort. "Jess," Julia whispered.

"Well?" Justin glared at Jessie.

"This looks like something put in place before your parents were killed, Justin. Not something Jessie did."

Nathan glanced over his shoulder at her. "As a matter of fact, if it hadn't been for the ranch getting to the point that you had someone look at the finances closely, this might never have been discovered. Heart Fire Ranch is funding another Heart Fire entity; we just need to figure out what it is and why."

Justin took a few steps across the kitchen toward Jessie, and Nathan moved so he stood between them, trying desperately to bury the desire to punch his friend. The hurt at Justin's accusations shimmered in Jessie's eyes. "Jess, I'm sorry, I just—"

"You just thought I was too stupid and irresponsible to run this ranch. You don't trust me to be able to do it." She pushed herself away from Nathan, moving away from all three of them. She brushed past Nathan and headed for the back door, pausing to look back at them, still watching after her. "Contrary to what you believe, Justin, not every problem with this ranch is my fault." The screen door slammed against the frame behind her.

"Jess!" Julia jumped up and started after her.

"No," Nathan put a hand up. "Let me go talk to her." He looked at Justin pointedly. "I think, more than anything right now, she needs to hear that this isn't her fault."

Chapter Thirteen

JESSIE CLIPPED THE cross-tie to the mare's halter and began to groom her. In the flustered state she was in, she needed to be with her horses, allowing their quiet strength to soothe her troubled spirit. It was exactly why the teens blossomed working with the horses.

She didn't need to hide her emotions from a horse. She didn't need to lie to them. She could admit her failures and guilt without recrimination. With the horses, she could be vulnerable and open herself without fear of being hurt. Jessie ran her hands over the mare's back, wanting to release the tension from the confrontation with her brother, but it overwhelmed her. She laid her cheek against the mare's neck, breathing in her dusty, sweet smell.

Her chest ached, knowing Justin assumed the worst about her, that he believed she was incompetent, or worse, that she was using him for handouts. He was never going to believe in her ability to run this ranch. Her parents should have left it to him.

She wasn't cut out for this. She was nothing more than a horse trainer who had given riding lessons to guests. What did she know about running a dude ranch? Most of Nathan's business lingo went right over her head. What did she know about incorporating or proprietorships?

She was a trainer—that was all she knew how to do and the only thing she was good at. Her mother called it her gift, her calling, but with her parents gone and no one to share this load, it had become more of a curse.

The mare whickered a quiet greeting, and the hair at the base of her nape stood up. She knew it was Nathan even before his large hands found her waist, simply because of the way her body reacted to his presence. Goosebumps rose on her arms, and she felt a shiver of heat travel down her spine.

"Jess, are you okay?" His voice was quiet, but she could hear the strength in it. He would offer it to her if she was willing to accept it.

"I'm fine," she whispered. Jessie didn't bother to move from where her cheek lay against the mare's neck. It was a lie and they both knew it.

Nathan's hands crept up her back, his thumbs gently massaging her tense muscles. She sighed as his fingers kneaded her tight shoulders. Her brain warned her to move away from his hands, even as her body leaned back into his touch. The mare crooked her head back to look at them, curious, and Jessie patted her neck gently.

"Okay, I'll pay attention to you."

She forced herself to walk to the grooming bucket near the mare's head. She dropped the currycomb inside and retrieved a soft brush. When she turned around, Nathan was waiting. One hand curled behind her neck, his fingers winding into her loose curls, and drew her mouth to his. Flutters began in her belly, rising into her chest, warming her, then settling over her. It wasn't the fiery passion they'd shared before. This kiss was tender, touching the aching core of her, reaching the open, bruised soul that had been exposed by her brother. She didn't deserve Nathan's empathy but, oh, how she wanted it, craved it.

"Nathan," she whispered against his lips, "don't."

He brought his other hand forward to cup her jaw in his palm, his thumb brushing over her cheekbone. "I'll stop if that's what you want, Jess." His lips found hers again, sapping her will to resist him.

She recognized her weakness for this man. Like a shot of smooth whiskey, one touch, one kiss from him went straight to her head, and she was drunk with desire. It was dangerous. He was far too astute, saw too much she wanted to remain hidden. She didn't want to think about why this man, the one bound to leave, the one who didn't belong here in the first place, was the only one who'd been about to reach this emptiness in her that no one else even noticed. He would finish this job, dust his hands off, and leave. And she would be left with the broken shards of her heart, wondering why she'd been weak enough to believe him again. It was safer to stay away from him until he left next week. At least that way her heart would remain intact.

As if sensing her indecision, Nathan smiled against her lips. "Okay, I'll stop." She fought the urge to grab him by the front of his shirt and pull him back toward her. "For now."

Her eyes opened and met his. The gold flecks were bright and the dimple creased his cheek. He plucked the currycomb from her hand. "Show me what to do."

Nathan moved to the mare's side. The horse looked back at him, as if she was just as uncertain of Nathan's intentions as Jessie.

"Um, okay. You take this and brush short strokes over her coat with it."

He reached for her hand and drew her in front of him, fitting her body against his chest, laying her palm over his hand. "Show me."

There wasn't an inch of her skin, from her shoulders to the back of her thighs, that didn't feel like it ignited through her clothing. Their right hands moved in unison over the mare's back while his left hand rested over Jessie's stomach, just below her ribcage, his thumb absently tracing a path from her ribs to the bottom of her breast, leaving a trail of fire in its wake. Her left hand covered his, stilling his thumb as she tried to catch the breath that seemed to have fled her lungs at his first touch. Her entire body was trembling with want, but she couldn't seem to stop it. Deep breaths only made her inhale the scent of his soap, a spicy mix of citrus and mint, with the smell of the horse.

She felt the quiet rumble of his laughter against her back more than she heard it. "Relax, Jess. I'm not going to attack you. I promise. We're just two consenting adults, grooming a horse." The tone of his voice and the way her own words fell from his lips had her turning to look at him. He gave her a smile. "Scout's honor."

Jessie arched a brow. She'd spent years convincing herself that he was a heartless bastard, that he'd deliberately seduced her and broke her heart with complete disregard for her feelings, yet here he was, tender and teasing, so much like the man she'd thought she fell in love with that summer. She needed to get her footing with him again, regain the upper hand.

"Okay, Wall Street. You finish with the brush and I'll grab a comb for her mane and tail."

She started to move away, but he wrapped his arm tighter around her waist and nuzzled his lips against the edge of her ear. "But I like you here."

Jessie shivered against him. She wanted to be the tough cowgirl her father had raised, the one who didn't need anyone and was in complete control, but her heart was rebelling, ignoring her every warning. The more she demanded it not care, the more she was drawn to him. The more she tried to convince her body she didn't want him, the faster desire seemed to course through her veins, consuming her. She'd tried to keep her distance, but the truth was, she didn't want to. Even knowing he was bound to leave and take her heart with him again, she couldn't help the way she felt.

His teeth gently bit her earlobe and she whimpered quietly, her knees nearly giving out. Nathan laughed against the back of her neck, his breath tickling her shoulder, and she wondered if he felt the same all-encompassing craving she did. Her fingers curled around his hand, now stilled on the mare's back as his body pressed against her, hard and heated at her hips.

"I should put her away," she whispered. Nathan pulled her more fully against him, unwilling to let her go for even the short amount of time it would take for her to walk the mare to her stall.

His hand loosened from her waist but only enough for him to run his palm over her belly and grasp her hip, turning her in his arms. "You have two minutes." He gave her an impish grin, his eyes glinting mischievously, and she wondered what it meant.

Part of her wanted to remain distant from him, to continue to protect her heart. She couldn't just forget about the way he'd lied to her. Or had he? What if she'd spent the last eight years hating a man who didn't exist? What if she allowed him to prove she'd been wrong? She knew she couldn't protect her heart, it was already his, and it always had been. Why was she continuing to pretend differently?

NATHAN MOVED AWAY, giving her room to breathe again, and she gulped at the oxygen that seemed to flood the space he vacated. As he dropped the brush into the bucket and carried it into the tack room, she led the mare to the stall.

She locked the stall door and gave him a sly smile, crooking her finger at him as she hung the halter on the door. "You know, I think there's an empty cabin just around the corner."

"Is there? As a matter of fact, my cabin is just a few steps away." He closed the distance between them quickly. Unable to keep himself from touching her, he buried both of his hands into her hair, tipping her chin up to look at him. "You drive me a little crazy, woman. You know that, don't you?"

She smiled up at him, her eyes glinting mischievously. "I do."

He let his hands fall, reaching for her hand, twining his fingers in hers, starting for the doorway. "Then we should probably go."

She jumped onto his back, wrapping her arms around his neck and her legs around his waist. Her lips found the back of his neck and the burning ache in his gut turned into a raging tempest of need. Her scent surrounded him as she clung to him, her thighs circling him and her hair swinging into his face. His arousal sprang to life.

"Giddyup, cowboy," she whispered against his ear.

It took every ounce of willpower he possessed not to press her up against the wall and take her, right here in the barn. But he wanted this to be more than just physical satisfaction. He was connected to Jessie; he always had been. It was obvious she felt something for him, even it if was just attraction, but he suspected it was far more. The question was how he was going to get this stubborn woman to admit it.

After the way things had ended before, he hadn't exactly inspired her trust, let alone her forgiveness. He couldn't blame her for not wanting to be vulnerable with him. Nathan wasn't about to give up without a fight, even if it meant tricking Jessie into confessing how she felt.

Nathan pushed open the door to his cabin and carried Jessie into the kitchen, turning backward to slide her rear onto the tile counter. He turned around and moved between her thighs, grasping her buttocks and pulling her against him, leaning down until his lips were only inches from hers. Her eyes flutter closed, her dark lashes laying against her cheeks, waiting for his kiss.

"I need a drink. You want something?" He dropped a quick kiss on her full lips and went to the refrigerator. Grasping the neck of two beer bottles, he held one out for her.

Slightly confused, she blinked her eyes a few times. "What?"

"A drink." He popped the top from his with an opener and took a long swallow of the beer as if demonstrating. "Yes? No?"

She looked almost irate before she quickly masked it, narrowing her eyes before smiling at him. He could see she was trying to get a read on his sudden change of mood. "Sure."

Jessie hopped down from the counter and took the second bottle from his hand. Sliding her hand over his, she slipped the opener from his fingers before popping the cap and flipping it onto the counter. She tipped her head back and took a long draw from the bottle as he watched. Hunger curled through him, tightening his need into a throbbing ache centered under the ridiculous belt buckle he'd purchased.

With nearly a third of the bottle gone, she tipped it upright and licked the amber liquid from her lips. "Oops, look at that. I spilled." She brushed a hand over the front of her shirt and he almost groaned out loud. Sure enough, there was a small wet spot just over her right breast.

His mouth went dry when he realized what she was doing. *Damn woman is playing with fire.*

She set the bottle on the counter and, before he could stop her, she yanked her shirt over her head, tossing it at his face. He caught it with one hand and was hit with the sweet scent that was uniquely hers—hay and horses mixed with sunshine and vanilla. Nathan followed her into the sitting area where she sat on the arm of the couch, waiting for him with a half-smile curving her lips. He refused to let her see how she was affecting him, not until she lowered the barrier she'd erected around herself.

He made his way to the other end of the couch and flopped onto the soft leather sofa, his eyes never leaving hers. Nathan wasn't sure how long he could hide this overwhelming desire. His jeans were already painfully uncomfortable, and his fingers itched to touch her.

"You in a hurry?" He saw her smile falter again. It happened every time he didn't react the way she expected him to. He was finding that the trick to getting Jessie to let down her guard was to keep her guessing. "You promised me in the shower we could take it slow, remember? We never did."

"This isn't slow, Wall Street. This is a crawl." She laughed and took another swallow of the beer.

He sat up and reached for her hand, tugging her down onto the couch with him. She sank into the opposite corner of the couch, keeping a safe distance between them but with a playful grin on her lips. She was still holding back. He wanted her relaxed, open, vulnerable. He lifted her feet onto his lap and tugged her boots off. Dropping them on the floor, he began to knead the soles her feet with his thumbs.

"Oh, dear God." She sighed and dropped her head sideways against the back of the couch.

He chuckled and continued to work his hands over the arch and heel of one foot before working on the other. His hands slid up the leg of her jeans and worked on the tight muscles at her calves and ankles. "Are you nervous about this weekend?"

"About having guests again?" She opened one eye and looked at him suspiciously. "A little. Why?"

"Relax, I'm just asking." He dug his thumb into her arch, and she mewed softly, reminding him of a kitten. "Most of the time you seem to like horses more than you do people."

She grinned and eyed him again. "Says the man with my feet in his crotch. You should be careful about insulting me when you're in such a precarious position. If I had my way, it would be just me and the horses all of the time. Unless I could make it a place where kids like Aleta and Michael could come."

His hands stilled, surprised. "You want to be a foster parent?"

"I don't know. I'd like to have a place where troubled teens could come and be with the horses. An at-risk youth and horse rescue, I guess." She laughed quietly at herself. "I should probably learn to keep myself on the straight and narrow first." Her blue eyes looked up at him innocently, fear of rejection floating on the surface.

"Come here," he said, pulling her into his lap. She immediately curled her hands against his ribs, tucking her head between his neck and shoulder. *This* was where he wanted her—vulnerable, responsive, and genuine. This is where she would reveal her emotions without hesitation, where the truth would slip from her lips without restraint. It was such an exposed position. This was the Jess he'd wanted to see all along. This was the woman who melted in his arms, the guileless woman beneath the armor. The woman whose fingers were lightly playing over the ridges of his abs through his shirt, making his pulse throb in his veins and his self-control take a vacation.

As much as he loved the feeling of having her in his arms, he wanted her to see his eyes and believe every word he was about to say. He tipped her chin up. "Listen to me closely—quit selling yourself short."

She smiled sardonically. "But I'm only five foot three. I *am* short."

He frowned down at her. "I'm trying to be serious here. We are going to get this figured out."

She rose to her knees and straddled his lap, sighing as she looped her arms around his neck. "Fine, you figure it out. I have something more interesting to focus my attention on." She pressed her lips against his jaw, trailing kisses toward his neck.

He felt every muscle in his body tense as she pressed against him. She dropped her mouth toward his, pausing to nibble on his lower lip. "Now," she said, standing and unbuttoning her jeans before sliding them down her legs, "are you going to make love to me tonight, or are we just going to talk?"

Chapter Fourteen

JESSIE DIDN'T LIKE the way Nathan was breaking down her resolve. Every time she thought she had him twisted around her finger, he'd pull away and somehow get her to let her guard down. This wasn't the Nathan she remembered or the one she'd seen so far, and he'd already confused her more than any man she'd ever met. She wasn't sure she could continue to hide her heart if he kept at this tender assault.

She knew he wanted her. He'd made that blatantly clear in the barn. She could see the heat in his eyes as he looked at her, could feel it in the way his hand shook slightly against her abdomen. Then he would shut it off, like the flip of a switch.

Well, that might not be the best way to describe it, but he could certainly control it better than she could. Every attempt she made at seduction seemed to work until he turned the tables on her.

He wasn't fooling her. She knew he wanted her as much as she wanted him. She'd felt his pulse race under her hand and the way he tensed when she straddled his thighs. She hadn't missed the hunger in his eyes when she threw her shirt at him. Yet, he refused to touch her. At least, not the way she wanted him to. Not that she didn't enjoy the foot massage. It had been pure bliss, relaxing yet somehow erotic. But she was tired of talking. Right now, she wanted him to make her forget. She slid her jeans down her legs and met his hot gaze with her own.

"Jess, wait." He sat up and grasped her hips with his hands, pulling her between his knees and back down into his lap. He brushed her hair back from her face, growing somber. "I will absolutely make love to you, but only if *you* show up."

"What are you talking about? I'm right here. I'm not going anywhere."

"I mean the real you, Jess."

She immediately tensed. "Let go of me."

His hands curved around her back, his fingers closing over her shoulders, holding her close to him when she wanted to pull away. She pressed her hands against his chest, and when he didn't budge, she curled her fingers into fists, bunching the material of his shirt, and clamped her jaw shut.

He chuckled, his eyes sweeping over her body hungrily. "Jess, you are the only woman I know who could be sitting in my lap wearing nothing but a lace bra and underwear and still seem as tough as nails. Do you think it's fair that you know what you do to me, but you pretend I don't do anything to you?"

He traced the ridge of her collarbone with a fingertip, leaving a trail of fire that burned from her neck to her belly, sending sparks of desire flashing within her. She gasped and Nathan wound his other arm around her waist, even though she wasn't trying to get up any longer.

She wanted to pretend she didn't understand what he was saying, but she knew. She just hadn't thought he'd been able to tell she'd been holding back.

She should have known better. If he wanted words, she could give him those. She would tell him whatever he wanted to hear if he would stop asking for things she couldn't ever offer him again. She couldn't recover from that kind of heartbreak a second time.

His fingers traced the curve of her breast at the top of her bra, down the vee of her cleavage and to her belly button, stopping at the top of her underwear, leaving every inch of her burning with agonizing desire. She watched his eyes follow the movement of his fingers, growing hungrier with each second, before he looked up and met her gaze. The meaningless words she'd planned on saying died on her tongue as the need she'd been trying to hold back exploded within her, making her want to writhe against him, to beg for his touch.

"Are you ready for that? Be honest with me, Jess." His fingers trailed over her sex. "Because I want to make love to the real you, not the woman you think you need to be."

Her lower back bowed involuntarily, her body reaching toward his touch, even as her mind continued to refuse to give him what he wanted. His other hand moved toward her shoulder, brushing the bra strap aside. He was touching her, his fingers barely caressing her skin with feather-light strokes, but she was still feverish with need. It was agony, for him to touch her but not touch her, to feel the heat from his body under her, his heart thudding heavily against her fisted hands, to feel his erection straining against his jeans and her body throb with matching hunger, yet still have barriers between them.

His fingertips traced the curve of her breast, outlining it, as if trying to memorize the contours of her body. "No more games, no more pretending."

She sucked in a deep breath, arching toward him, needing his hands on her to put out this fire, even knowing he would stoke it higher. "I can't," she whispered, honestly, her voice hoarse with painful remorse.

His lips curved in a smile and he brushed his thumb over her cheek. "Yes, you can." He threaded his hand into her hair and drew her down to him. "You just did."

His mouth slanted over hers, his tongue plunging to twirl and dance. She let go of his shirt and curled her hands around the nape of his neck, clinging to him for a moment. Jessie looked into his eyes, seeing the same hunger and need she felt, and she pulled away from him, standing to stare down at him still seated on the couch. She allowed a seductive smile to spread over her lips, and she reached behind to unsnap her bra. She slowly slipped it over her arms before dropping it onto his lap. Arching her brow, she turned away, leaving him watching her add an extra saunter to her steps as she walked to the bedroom. She barely heard his agonized groan.

She looked over her shoulder at him as she reached the doorway. "Are you going to sit there all day?"

She turned toward him, just slightly, but enough that he could only see the curve of her breast. Nathan clenched his fists at his side. "I don't know about you, but I'm finished talking."

The look of primal desire in his eyes as he followed her into the bedroom, left no doubt that he wanted her. Nathan stepped behind her, one hand sliding over her flat stomach, pulling her against, him while the other moved to cup her breast. His lips found the back of her shoulder and her head fell to the one side with a sigh of pleasure.

Nathan laid her in the center of his bed before stretching out beside her, still fully clothed, his hips cradling her rear, her back pressed against his chest.

Jessie tried to turn toward him, but he kept his hand on her hip. "Trust me." His fingertip trailed over her arm. "Close your eyes." His lips found the hollow at the curve of her shoulder, tasting her, sending scorching shivers over her upper body.

Nathan moved his hands over the curve of her breast, gently, too gently, and she pressed herself into his hands, reaching for his wrists, intent on making him do what she wanted. He laughed quietly in her ear and deftly avoided her grasp.

"No, you don't. I'm going to enjoy every second of this. I want to watch those blue eyes of yours go dark because you want me. I want to see you as crazy as you make me feel."

His lips tickled her shoulder, his scruff scraping her skin. She moaned in exquisite pain as he cupped her breast, his thumb and finger toying with the aching peak. His free hand followed the line of her hip to where she throbbed.

"Please." She couldn't string together any other words, nothing else made sense. She only knew she needed him to touch her and now.

Nathan's fingers traced along the seam of her, over her underwear, and she cried out, her body bucking against him. She felt his lips spread into a smile against her skin, and she couldn't deny he could play her body like an instrument. Right now, she wanted nothing more than to be lost in the magic of his hands as he took her to new heights of sensation. Nathan's fingers disappeared far too quickly and she whimpered in protest as he moved her onto her stomach, his lips blazing a new trail down her spine.

One hand slid over her arc of her butt. "You have the most beautiful curves." His tongue flicked out against her lower back and she gasped. "And the most adorable dimples right here."

Every part of her body hummed with pleasure, blissful yet unsated. She wanted to touch him, to feel his skin against hers. And she didn't want to wait any longer, even if it meant she had to stop this sweet torture.

"Nathan?"

His fingers tickled the inside of her thigh as his lips found the back of her knee. She sucked in a breath again. "Hmmm?"

"You have too many clothes on," she murmured.

He laughed and let her roll onto her back. She realized the folly in it when she met his hot gaze. His eyes were smoldering, hungry and intense. The stubble from the day's beard growth scraped against her thigh, and she bit her lower lip to keep from crying out at the delicious pain. Every look, every touch, was laced with electricity. He slid up her body, letting the material of his clothing create a glorious friction between them, before he stood and pulled her to her feet.

She tugged open the snaps of the western shirt she'd told him to purchase and slid her hands over his chest, pushing the shirt from his shoulders. Her hands fell over the ridges of his abs, her fingertips barely grazing them, as she reached for his belt. His hands caught hers, moving them back to his waist.

He didn't speak, but she could read the longing his eyes. He was barely holding himself together, and she felt the flutter of excitement take flight in her chest, knowing that she held the same ability to excite him to this uncontrollable urgency. She felt the rush of feminine power that her body brought him the same agonizing pleasure she was feeling. He slid his pants and boxers down his thighs. She was dying to touch him but before she could, he sat on the edge of the bed and drew her between his thighs, cupping her breast and taking it in his mouth.

Lights exploded behind her eyes, and she dropped her head backward, reveling at the storm that raged within her. Nathan's tongue swirled around the peaks, taking her higher, as his hand slid over her hip, pooling the last vestige of the barrier between them at her feet. His hands caressed, his mouth suckled, his tongue laved, and he pulled her into his lap until she was astride his hips again. His erection pressed at her opening, begging for entrance, but he wrapped his arms around her waist and refused to let her move. He buried his face against her neck and inhaled, his hands splayed over her spine, as if he simply wanted to hold her, to cherish her for a moment longer.

His breath was hot against her skin, and while she still ached to have him fill her, it ceased being a physical ache. She felt the emotional void she'd held close for so long cracking open and letting him in, begging him to fill it.

"Nathan?" She tipped her chin down, wrapping her arms around his shoulders, her hands curling around the back of his head. The two of them were twined, almost one. "I…"

"Shh." He cupped his hand behind her head and kissed her, deeply but with a tenderness she'd never thought she'd find with him again. Her heart splintered at his gentleness, his open vulnerability. "I need you, Jess. Like I've never needed anyone before. I had no idea how much until I saw you again. I'm so sorry…for everything that happened."

His honest words filled her, caressing her soul. This was the apology she'd longed for, the words she'd waited eight years to hear. Her heart ached for what they should have had, all the time they lost. When his thumb brushed her cheek, she felt the tears on her face.

No! No, no, no! No crying!

She wasn't this woman anymore. She couldn't let him see her weak. She couldn't submit to this emotional side again. She'd never find all the pieces of herself again if she did.

She slid her hands to his shoulders, ready to push him onto his back. To take control again, to ride him and let the physical need carry her away from this place of exposure. But he wouldn't allow it.

"Don't, Jess," he growled deep in his throat, and when he spoke again, his voice came in a husky whisper as he held her close. "I want *you*, remember?"

She didn't want to feel the emotional connection, didn't want to know this vulnerability he'd unearthed in her again. It was weakness, and weakness led to pain. But Nathan held her fast on his lap while his lips found her mouth, her throat, her breast. She cried out as he entered her slowly, knowing she wouldn't—couldn't—walk away from him now. Her body clutched at him, hungry for every inch, as he buried himself within her. She held onto him as he slowly rocked his hips, his hands worshiping her as his mouth ravished her.

Need built in her, coiling in her belly, but it couldn't compare to the emotions swirling in her. She could feel it inside, trying to break through the wall that kept her distanced. She dropped her head to his shoulder, feeling the barricade around her heart chipping with each kiss and every caress. She gasped against the sensations threatening to drown her like a monsoon.

She shouldn't allow herself to feel anything for him, not when he was leaving and unlikely to return. Not when he would leave nothing but the charred remains of her heart behind after their explosive desire passed.

What was wrong with her? Where was her apathy when she needed it?

She leaned into him again, but this time he lay back on the bed. She wrapped her hands around his sides, gripping him as she rode him. Nathan reached for her hands, twining his fingers in hers and lifting his hands to the sides of his head, forcing her to fall forward toward him. He took her mouth hostage before cupping a hand at her back.

"Don't hide from me, Jess." He moved his hips against her, and she gasped. "You need me as much as I need you."

She could hear the hesitation in his voice. She realized he would stop right now if she wanted him to. He was putting her pleasure, her needs, both physical and emotional, before his own. It broke her. Tears burned in her eyes, and she couldn't stop them from falling against his face as he kissed her.

"Jess," he whispered, brushing her tear-stained cheeks with his lips. "It's okay. It's okay."

The tenderness in his voice and the gentleness of his touch, coupled with the slow burning desire, pushed her over the edge of sanity. She slid down the hard length of him and heard him groan against her throat. Every part of her burst at once, and she buried her face against his neck, unable to look into his eyes, afraid to see the judgment she was sure would be there. Her tears soaked his shoulder as he thrust into her.

"I need you," she whispered against his skin, praying he didn't hear her as they both cried out in climax.

Chapter Fifteen

JESS LAY CURLED against his chest, deliberately avoiding looking at him, and he let her—for now. Nathan ran his hands over her hair, trailing his fingers through the soft tresses, giving her as much time as she needed to gather her emotions, preparing for her to disappear behind her armor again. It had been difficult for her to let go. He'd seen the battle waging within her, every step of the way. A part of him wondered why he was pushing her. Jess didn't owe him anything, certainly not the trust he'd cast away when he'd never called. But for the first time in his life, Nathan regretted his success. He regretted the mistake he'd made.

And leaving Jessie had been a mistake, he saw that now.

He didn't care what his father threatened. Or that the tabloids and high-power circles he ran in would never understand or approve of their relationship. Nothing else mattered. This wasn't about having a woman on his arm who would make him look good, or finding someone to further his career. He wanted a woman who made him *feel* good. Justin was probably going to kill him when he found out, but as much as he loved Justin like a brother, this wasn't about Justin's happiness either. This was about Nathan feeling like an emptiness in him had finally been filled. He wanted Jess, every part of her. He wanted to go back and repair the past, to right the wrongs and correct his mistakes.

If Jess had been just like every other woman, he'd never have come back. But she was different. Everything about her was passionate, from her temper to her loving. She was an emotional roller coaster, but it was a ride he didn't want to get off. He had no idea how to make up for his mistake or how long she might want him, but he was going to find out or die trying.

Now that he'd broken down some of her walls, he wasn't letting her rebuild them.

He looked down at her and was met with her deep blue eyes, filled with pain and regret.

"Don't say it, Jess. Just stop thinking and enjoy being present in this moment a little longer." He pressed his lips to her forehead, letting his fingers trail down the valley of her back. She shivered against him and desire slid over him like a sheet, making him grow hard again.

"Don't say what?" she whispered as her fingers traced patterns on his chest.

"Don't tell me you wish it didn't happen. Or that you're sorry it did."

She looked away and sighed, her breath heating his skin. The lashes fanning her cheeks were still wet with her tears. "I won't and I'm not, but you don't understand."

"Then explain it to me."

She shook her head. "I can't do this. Not with you, not again."

His chest constricted as her words cut painfully. He knew he deserved every bit of regret she wanted to cast his way, any guilt she served him, but it didn't stop the painful ache. He prayed she wouldn't fall back into her blasé, tough girl attitude. He wasn't sure he had the strength to remove the armor again tonight. "And what is *this*?"

"I can't lose myself in you again. I have too many responsibilities now, too many people depending on me not to screw up."

"You didn't screw up, Jess. That was me."

She rose up on an elbow and looked down at him. "Yes, I did."

"When did you screw up?" She bit her lip again, fighting tears, and he fought the desire nipping at him again. "You mean the ranch?"

"I've screwed up a lot, Nathan. I'm beginning to wonder if it's all I know how to do."

"The trouble with the ranch isn't your fault." He moved back a few inches to look at her face. "I promised I'd help you, and I'm going to fix it, Jess."

"It isn't just the money troubles and the ranch. I don't think I can do this alone."

Nathan heard the catch in her voice and any desire he felt was set aside at the pain he could hear in her admission. Fresh tears burned his skin.

He hadn't meant to make her cry again. She wasn't the type of woman to want anyone see her weakness and, in her mind, tears were a weakness. But he wondered if these weren't cathartic. The mere fact that she wasn't trying to hide from him spoke volumes about the trust he was instilling in her. He rolled over so that he could look down into her face.

"Jess, you are the most stubborn woman I've ever met. Why do you feel like you have to shoulder everything?" He leaned on his elbow, letting his hand caress her neck, unable to keep himself from touching her, but trying to comfort her any way he could. "You are doing everything you can."

She shook her head, denying his declaration. "If only I hadn't convinced them to take the trip. Dad didn't even want to. I guilt-tripped him into taking Mom."

He could see the anguish written in her eyes. More than either of her siblings, she had spent her entire life working side-by-side with both of her parents daily, living in the same house. Now, on top of the condemnation she'd already heaped on herself, she was faced with their ranch going under on her watch. No wonder she worried about responsibilities. It was her nature to heal, to help, to save. Yet she was unable to save the one thing that meant most to her.

He'd already seen how she poured her heart and soul into working with the horses or the teens on the ranch. He didn't doubt she'd be the same way when the guests came tomorrow. But none of it mattered when she couldn't rescue the two people who meant the most to her, or the ranch they'd poured their lifeblood into.

"Tell me what you remember most about them." If he couldn't convince her she wasn't to blame for the financial troubles, or her own feelings of self-doubt, maybe he could help her see the flaws in her logic.

"Who? My parents?"

He nodded. "I know you got your temper from your mom."

She laughed and wiped her cheek. "Only because you were dumb enough to track mud into her kitchen right after she mopped." She ran a fingernail over his shoulder, staring at his throat. "Everyone liked Dad, thought he was friendly and fun, but I remember how tough he was. How nothing seemed to get him worked up."

Nathan didn't miss the flat tone of her voice, but he didn't want to ask anything she might not be prepared to say aloud. He could tell there was plenty she wasn't saying about her father, but she didn't seem ready to dive into that pool of confusing regrets just yet. "Did he teach you to train horses?"

"When I was younger," she said, meeting his eyes. He felt a measure of relief as the tears disappeared, at least for the moment. "But once Dad realized what I could do, he turned that part of the ranch over to me to take care of."

"How old were you?"

"Twelve."

Nathan wondered about Colton Hart. He remembered him, had liked the man and appreciated his hospitality, but what sort of man would expect a child to shoulder that sort of responsibility? Jessie was painting a different picture of the man he remembered. He was beginning to realize that Jessie's armor had been constructed far before his arrival that summer, or his abandonment after. It had been the first man in her life who'd taught her to make it strong.

"What was it he thought you could do?" His hands slid over her body, tracing each curve and crevice, reveling as she shifted into his touch.

"Dad called it 'whispering,' but it's really just understanding the horse's language." Her eyes flicked to meet his. "Like how you read people."

"Me?"

"Yes, you." She ran her fingertip over his jaw and smiled. "I've watched you do it. I don't think you even realize when you do. It's pretty annoying when you do it to me." He caught her hand and pressed a kiss to her wrist, eliciting a quiet gasp of surprised delight.

Nathan laughed. "Trust me, woman," he said, biting the edge of her hand playfully. "You are not easy to figure out."

"Good." She pulled her hand away from him, but he could read the trace of humor remaining in her eyes. This was the woman he knew had been caged inside, waiting to be set free.

"Some horses are easier to read," she said, returning to their conversation. "Take Jet, that black horse who almost killed you. He's tougher than most, but he's also one of my favorites."

She smiled broadly, and her eyes lit up with excitement as she talked about the various horses she'd worked with recently. It didn't take a genius to see this was her passion in life, her reason for getting up in the morning. "I love the challenge."

Nathan couldn't help but laugh at the sentiment. His hand cupped her breast, his thumb teasing the peak. "So do I, Jess." Her eyes grew dark, slumberous with desire, yet sparkling with excitement, but he could also see the hint of fear in them. "And you challenge me."

A knock on the door of the cabin interrupted anything she might have said. She glanced at the clock on the bedside table. "Shit!" She rolled out from under him, and he flopped onto his back, watching her quickly scan the room for her clothing.

"Your clothes are all over the cabin," he reminded her. "Your shirt is in the kitchen, your jeans are in by the couch, and I might just keep these." He held up her lace underwear on his finger.

Jess snatched them from him. "I'm glad this amuses you. Can you at least go get my clothes?"

Nathan climbed out of the bed and pulled on a pair of jeans. "I guess. But I should probably see who that is first."

She reached for him, her hands grazing his waist as she tried to pull him backward. "Don't you dare answer that door until you get my clothes for me."

"Fine." He gave her an exaggerated sigh, leaning down to sneak a quick kiss. "But this just means you'll have to buy my silence." He headed toward the living room. "Just a second," he called as he retrieved her clothes and took them back to the bedroom.

He walked in as she was hooking the clasp of her bra, her hair pulled to one side. Nathan felt the hungry desire gnawing at him as he watched her. She had no idea how incredibly sexy she was. He slid his arms around her waist, pressing against her back and letting his lips trail from her ear to her shoulder. She sighed, melting back into him, her hands reaching back to grip his thighs. If she left it up to him, he'd have ignored the door altogether and spent the rest of the night making love to her. His hand inched over her abdomen when the knock at the door sounded again, more insistent this time.

"Wall Street, have you seen Jess? She's not in the barn."

Damn it, Bailey.

Nathan vowed to extract a worthy revenge on her for this however he could and began to plot his retaliation as Jessie squirmed out of his arms and hurried for the door. She turned back to him as she reached it and gave him a warning look. He read it loud and clear—he was supposed to keep what happened between them a secret.

"Hey, Bailey." She opened the door and the surprise in Bailey's expression would have made him laugh if he didn't think Jess would find something to throw at him. "Looking for me?"

"Justin sent me to find you. He wanted me to see if you were okay and if he could apolo—" She stepped inside, looking from Jess to Nathan and back again. Contrary to Jessie's glared warning, he didn't have to tell anyone where she'd been or what they'd been doing. Her mussed hair, kiss-swollen lips, and agitation told the entire story without him saying a word.

The grin that spread over the younger woman's face made it perfectly clear she had her suspicions about the two of them. Nathan slowly shook his head and motioned with his hand at his throat for her to keep quiet, hoping Jess wouldn't see him signaling Bailey to keep quiet.

"Um, apologize," she finished awkwardly. "He also wanted to ask if you'd rather settle this with a paintball gun or water balloons."

Jessie's shoulders tensed at the mention of her brother and the reminder of how he'd hurt her tonight with his accusations. "Neither. I don't want to see or talk to him right now. Just tell him to schedule the appointment with Brendon tomorrow. Will that be soon enough?"

She turned toward Nathan, and he saw that the wall had already been resurrected. She could rebuild a wall faster than anyone he'd ever known. He had to figure out a way to tear it down, permanently this time.

NATHAN STARED DOWN at the files spread across the kitchen table. Jessie had successfully avoided him since leaving the cabin with Bailey last night. He'd hoped he could convince her to stay, but she'd followed her cousin back to the house and never emerged again. Nathan knew because he'd been watching for even a quick a glimpse of her, and so far, she'd managed to elude him, even sending Aleta out to feed the horses.

He had to focus. It wasn't going to do any good to meet with the attorney and accountant this afternoon if he didn't have everything in order. He wanted to push them to start incorporation proceedings immediately. Once that ball was rolling, he could tackle the next hurdle—getting the ranch declared a nonprofit organization. Nathan wanted to help her make the move to becoming a rescue facility rather than a dude ranch.

When she mentioned wanting to work with horses and foster kids, he'd begun wracking his brain on how best to set it up. He could see her taking it to the next step and turning Heart Fire Ranch into a place of retreat, not only for the horses, but also where families at risk, especially foster kids, could find a place to heal. He could get her accounts in order more easily if she was a nonprofit, not to mention the investors, especially local ones, would beg to be a part of funding a project like this.

Nathan wanted to give her this, to help it become a reality. Not only to save the ranch, but to see that light in her eyes again, that passion that sparked to life when she talked about the horses and how it felt to work with them. He wanted to see that glowing pride in her eyes that accomplishment would bring. And maybe to rub her brother's nose in it a little after how he'd acted yesterday.

Nathan reached for a copy of the latest bank statement, his eyes falling on the deposits to Heart Fire Industries. The company remained a mystery. Internet searches had come up empty, and records searches were proving futile so far. It was as if Heart Fire Industries didn't exist.

A knot twisted in his gut, bile rising in his throat. It wouldn't be the first time he'd caught a dummy company, set up to embezzle funds. But who would want to do that to Jessie or have the access to the ranch to make it possible to pull it off successfully? Right now, he could only see a few people with access to the accounts, and two of them were family. Both Julia and Justin seemed shocked when he'd mentioned the missing money. It could have been an act, but it would be near impossible to do anything with the ranch finances without Brendon's knowledge.

That was where Nathan was betting his money. Julia mentioned that Brendon had been a friend of Justin's since childhood. Surely, he'd know the ranch's inner workings, especially as their accountant. If Jessie dumped him, he might have an entirely different motive to get his hands on the place. Either way, Brendon was at the top of Nathan's list of suspects, and he was determined to get to the bottom of this.

His cell phone vibrated on the table, and Nathan picked it up, glancing at the screen. This was the fourth message from his father this morning. The man never contacted him unless he wanted to use Nathan to drum up family goodwill or contribute to his latest reelection campaign.

He opened the message and wasn't surprised to see yet another demand from his father that he meet him in New York. Years of rejection from his father had taught him not to get sentimental. It was nothing but a fool's game. He sent a return message letting his father know he was away on another job and would return in a few days. His gut twisted as the thought began to grasp hold. He didn't have long before he would be leaving again.

The crunch of tires on the gravel driveway alerted him to visitors, and he poked his head out the front door, tucking his cell phone back into his pocket. The unfamiliar pickup was likely the two cowboys Jessie's friend had promised to send over. The two men exited the truck and one saw him, holding up a hand in greeting. Nathan returned the gesture, albeit reservedly. Leaning against the porch rail, he waited for what seemed like an eternity, when the pair shrugged and headed in his direction.

Nathan met them at the bottom of the cabin porch. "I assume you two are looking for Jessie?"

"Yep," the first cowboy answered, looking back at the main house. "Jennifer Graham from Findley Brothers sent us over to help out for a few days."

Nathan was at a loss. He didn't have any idea what Jess needed these two to do, or sign for that matter, but no one came out of the house to meet them. "Um, she should be at the main house. I haven't seen her leave." He wondered if he should go look for her and leave these two waiting or take them inside. "Why don't you both wait on the porch, and I'll see if I can find her?"

Nathan felt strange walking into the house without an invitation, almost as uncomfortable as he had taking a shower in her room. Thinking back at how well that had turned out, he stepped inside the kitchen. He looked around and saw her keys and phone, but no one was nearby. He didn't hear any sounds in the house either. The quiet was eerie after having the teens present all weekend, but Michael had returned to school this morning and Aleta had gone with her foster mother to visit her mom in prison. He walked down the hall and poked his head into her office.

Jessie lay with her head on her folded arms, sound asleep. He was so surprised to find her sleeping, for a moment he didn't move, content to simply watch her. It was the first time he'd seen her completely relaxed. Her face was tranquil, completely serene in a way he hadn't seen yet. Even when they'd made love, she'd been battling with herself, trying to hide her emotions. But now, there was nothing to stop him from seeing the real Jessie, exposed and vulnerable. And she was stunning.

His phone vibrated again. He pulled out, silencing the notification with the push of a button. It was from Justin, letting him know they would be meeting with the lawyer and accountant in one hour at the house. When he looked up again, Jessie was awake, rubbing her eyes, and turning toward him.

Nathan leaned against the doorframe. "Good morning, beautiful. You have company on the porch."

She frowned at him. "You don't knock?"

Nathan arched a brow. "You don't say thank you?"

She moved from behind the desk, having the decency to look apologetic. "Thank you. Who is it?"

"The cowboys you were waiting for." He moved, blocking her exit, and held his phone out so she could see the screen. "Your brother set up the appointment with the attorney. They should be here within the hour."

"What?" She stopped, unable to move past him. "I love how he just makes plans without even checking with me, like I have all the time in the world."

Nathan reached for her waist and felt her stiffen. "Make time. Don't take too long with the two on the porch," he said, his hand skimming her spine, making her shiver and lean into him. She looked past his shoulder, as if she was afraid someone might see them. He loved the way she responded to him without thinking.

He tipped her chin up to look at him, and the worry in her eyes faded for a moment. "I have an idea to run past you. Come to the cabin after you finish with these two so I can show you."

She quirked a brow and gave him a dubious look. "I think you already showed me."

He gave her a lopsided grin and his fingers squeezed her hips at the thought of last night. "As much fun as it would be to show you that again, this is something else, but I think you might be just as happy with it." Jess eyed him with distrust. "I promise. Go meet with your new crew."

She brushed past him and walked into the hallway. "But, Jess?" She turned to face him. "If you want the other, I'm happy to show you that again, too."

Jess flipped her middle finger up at him and hurried out the front door.

"Is that a yes?" he called after her.

Chapter Sixteen

A KNOCK AT the front door signaled the arrival of Brendon and his father, Trevor Gray. Jessie's parents had been friends with the Grays forever, and she remembered Justin and Brendon being inseparable growing up, even playing football on the same high school team. But there was something about Brendon she couldn't stomach.

"I'm sorry. I have to get that." She rose from behind the desk as the pair of cowboys in front followed her to the door. "Thanks again. I really appreciate you both coming on such short notice." She opened the front door to see Brendon leaning against the frame.

I can't stand this cocky son of a bitch.

Brendon, surprised to see two men in her house, frowned and took a few steps backward, bumping into his father.

"Easy, son," he scolded, moving Brendon aside. "You almost knocked me down the steps."

"Hey, Uncle Trevor." Jessie greeted the older man with a warm hug around his ample waist, while her newest employees, Mitch and Clint, trotted down the porch to their truck, Brendon still giving them the evil eye.

Jessie had always liked Trevor. He'd been an adoptive uncle for the three of them since they didn't have much family around. He also didn't mind spoiling those he loved, and he'd loved her parents and the three of them as if they were blood relatives. He pressed a quick kiss to the top of her head.

"Come on; let's get this *meeting* over with. I don't know what this friend of Justin's hopes to accomplish that we haven't already done, but what do you say we humor him?" He didn't bother to hide the derision in his voice, and Jessie wondered if his feelings were hurt that they were trusting Nathan's advice over his.

NATHAN SAT AT the head of the kitchen table, looking around at the faces surrounding him. Jessie and Julia flanked him on either side with Justin on Julia's right. Jessie refused to meet her brother's eye, and he wondered if they'd even spoken since his verbal attack in the kitchen. Bailey was seated on the edge of the island. At the other end of the table sat the Hart family attorney, Trevor Gray, with his son, Brendon, to his right. Brendon hadn't taken his eyes off Jessie, and Nathan didn't like the looks he was casting her direction, as if she were property and he was prepared to stake his claim.

"So, what I'm gathering from all of this"—Trevor waved his hands at the documents Nathan had spread out for them all to see—"is that you feel Brendon and I have been remiss in our duties as counsel to the Hart family, both in their businesses and personal finances. Would that be safe for me to assume?" Trevor tented his index fingers and pressed them to his lips, waiting for Nathan's response.

Nathan had dealt with enough hard-hitting attorneys in his career to know when one was trying to put him on the defensive. He wasn't about to fall for the bait. "Yes, it is."

Trevor smiled at him, but Nathan knew it was only for show. He recognized the hostility in the man's gaze. "I see."

Brendon's eyes swung to him, malice clearly written across his face. "You think running a dude ranch is the same as running a Fortune 500 company? You have no clue what needs to be done." Trevor silenced him with a hand on his arm.

"Now, son, I'm sure Mr. Kerrington has had plenty of clients within the equine industries. Perhaps he has insight to offer that we haven't considered." He cocked his head to the side, giving Nathan a patronizing glance. "By all means, Mr. Kerrington, please, enlighten us."

"One of the things Nathan has suggested is that we incorporate," Justin broke in.

Nathan didn't miss the awkwardness that seemed to hang in the air. Justin had friends at opposite ends of this debate, but Nathan knew he was right and had their interests in mind.

Trevor laughed at the suggestion. "At this point, that's not necessary."

Nathan folded his hands over the folder on the table. "Mr. Gray, I assure you that the liability each of them faces, especially from clients, could prove devastating if anyone were to sue. It is absolutely necessary to consider—"

Trevor pinched his lips and smiled pretentiously. "I mean, it's not necessary because that's already been taken care of." He looked at Justin. "Your parents filed for incorporation just before they died. I'd been badgering your father for years about it and finally convinced him." He looked back at Nathan and gathered his own documents. "If that's the extent of your expertise, I'm sure you'll understand if we head back to town before we waste any more of our time." He rose from the chair and Brendon followed suit.

"Heart Fire Industries."

Trevor froze with his hand over his briefcase and looked up at Nathan. "What about it?"

"Is that the name you filed it under?"

This time it was Brendon who spoke up. "Yes. Why?"

"Why didn't either of you tell them about this?" Nathan stared down Brendon before looking at each of the siblings in turn. "When are the stockholder meetings? Where is the documentation? And why is Heart Fire Ranch paying Heart Fire Industries a stipend each month?"

Brendon blanched as he looked at his father. "What are you trying to imply?"

"What do you think?" It was Nathan's turn to relax as the control of the conversation shifted.

Trevor leaned over the table, bracing his hands on either side. He homed on Nathan, ignoring everyone else. "Young man, I assure you that I've done nothing short of my best for this family. They weren't told because the documentation isn't finalized. I'm sure you are aware that incorporation is a long process." Trevor's voice was overly authoritative in the quiet kitchen. As if realizing he'd begun to lose his composure, he cleared his throat and stood upright, squaring his shoulders. "And I have no idea why Heart Fire Industries is receiving any payments from the ranch, unless that's something Colton set up before his death." He looked to Brendon for confirmation.

"Six months is an inordinate delay, wouldn't you agree?" Nathan pointed out, arching a brow at the pair. This wasn't adding up, but he wasn't sure which of these two was to blame.

"I think we've wasted enough of everyone's time. The incorporation should be completed soon enough, all three businesses will be encompassed under the Heart Fire Industries umbrella, and the three of you will be equal shareholders. That is why the will was changed; to stipulate that no one may sell the property and all assets are held in equal shares. I did explain that to you at the reading, remember?"

Nathan glanced at Jessie and Julia. While Julia looked slightly shell-shocked from this revelation, Jessie was furious. As much as he wanted to, Nathan couldn't pause to guess at the reason. He had to get to the bottom of the fund transfers and stop the slow bleed on Jessie, at least for now. It would buy her some time to figure out what to do with the ranch and her future.

"Brendon, I'd like to see the records for the Heart Fire Industries account." He pointed to the statement where the transfers were evident. "Was this something Colton set up with you?"

Brendon's overconfidence disappeared like smoke in a windstorm. He shot his father an anxious glance before turning back to Nathan. "A percentage of the net income of each business is sent to an account held for Heart Fire Industries. Colton started with Heart Fire Ranch but never set up the other two before his accident."

"This isn't a portion of the net income," Nathan said. "This is a significant portion of the gross profit, putting the ranch into the red each and every month. I doubt that was Colton's intent. Why didn't you ever tell Jessie?"

"I'll look into it," Brendan muttered.

"I'm sorry." Nathan tipped his head down dramatically and pressed on. "I think I speak for Justin and Julia, as well as Jessie, when I tell you to stop any and all transfers immediately until further notice."

"You can't make that call," Trevor interrupted.

"You're right, that would be up to the equal shareholders." He turned to look at the three of them.

Justin was the first to speak up for the entire family. "Brendon, stop the payments, at least for the time being."

Brendon spun on his friend. "Justin, are you really going to trust this city slicker who didn't even know you father—or what he wanted this place to become—over me? I've known you since we were in diapers. You're going to take this joker's recommendation over mine? Over my father's?"

Nathan wanted to laugh at Brendon's scrambling. Brendon shook his head in disgust and pushed himself away from the table when Justin didn't answer. "Fine. I see where I stand."

He scooped up his paperwork, stuffed it into his distressed briefcase, and stormed through the kitchen door, letting the screen slam behind him. Trevor slowly tucked his files into his case.

"I hope the three of you understand that Brendon and I are only complying with your father's wishes. Once all of the businesses are under this umbrella, and I'm sure your *expert* here can attest to this, you'll be safer. However, it will mean more paperwork and documentation. Not to mention that you will be able to sell off portions of your shares or your entire business if you choose." He turned to look at Jessie, who had her head in her hands. "But bear in mind, everything but this house and two acres, belongs to Heart Fire Industries. That means the barns, the cabins, the rest of the outbuildings, and land…"

He shook his head. "If you have any further questions, Mr. Kerrington, please make an appointment with my secretary. I'm a busy man and I thought this was important, or I wouldn't have bothered to clear my afternoon."

Bailey slid from the counter and held the door open for him. "Uncle Trevor, Nathan is just trying to help."

As much as Nathan appreciated Bailey's vote of confidence, especially after their last argument, he wished it had come from Jessie instead.

"I know, Bailey." Trevor patted her cheek gently. "But sometimes, we go looking for help and all we find is more trouble." He glanced back at the siblings seated around the table. "I have a feeling this is one of those times."

JESSIE SMACKED HER hands against the kitchen table and stood, glaring at Justin. "You sure know how to pick your friends, don't you."

Screw this.

Jessie walked out. There was no use relying on anyone else to figure out a remedy for this situation she was in. Not Trevor or Brendon or Nathan. No one was offering her any concrete answers. She wasn't going to stand there letting everyone else decide what she should do any longer. She was going to do what she should have done months ago and take this situation into her own hands, starting now. She left all four of them standing in the kitchen. Just a few minutes alone, that was all she needed. Just some time to process the information and figure out a solution.

Sliding open the tack room, she pulled out her saddle and a bridle with one arm and jerked a blanket from the rack with the other. She dropped them outside the stall door and went in to retrieve one of her mares. Normally, she'd scold one of the kids for not grooming the horse before riding it, but right now, she needed to feel the wind in her face and the strength of her horse beneath her.

On second thought...

She reached for the bridle and slipped it over the mare's head, leading her out of the barn before hopping onto her, bareback. She saw Nathan heading toward the cabin, his arms full of files, when he stopped and looked her way.

"Jess," he began.

"Not now, Nathan." She held up a hand to stop him. "I just need some time." She tapped the horse with her heels and leaned forward to open the gate to the pasture.

"Will you just wait for two seconds?"

She clipped the latch closed. "I said, 'not now.' "

Turning the mare, she let the horse have her head and gave herself over to the animal's slow lope. She heard Nathan's voice calling to her but tuned it out as he faded into the distance behind her. She needed some time to let what her father had done sink in and decide what she was going to do about it.

Jessie rode for the one place that had always given her clarity, away from the responsibilities of the ranch, away from anyone pressing her for her time, away from the voices that blamed then demanded more from her. As the mare picked her path to the river, Jessie could hear the sounds of the water, rushing over the rocks and branches, and inhaled deeply, anticipating the comfort she always found here. It was her spot. No one, not even Julia, knew how to find it.

Chapter Seventeen

"DAMN IT!" NATHAN cursed as he slammed his hand against the gate, bouncing it from the latch.

Watching Jessie ride off through the pasture made him want to throw something. Jessie had a way of taking his self-control and throwing it out the nearest window. Why the hell was she so angry with him?

Sure, he'd been a bit thrown by the fact that incorporation papers had already been filed, but it didn't change anything. In fact, it only made him trust Trevor Gray and his son less. The truth was, no matter how much Trevor claimed to have the Harts' best interests in mind, Nathan wasn't buying it. Either Brendon was hiding something and was afraid his father would find out, or they were hiding something together. He'd seen enough backstabbing and wheeling-and-dealing in companies far bigger than this ranch to know it was just a part of the game to most people. Business was cutthroat and ruthless.

Executives didn't care who was hurt in the process of a takeover. But Nathan wasn't about to see Jessie, or her siblings, taken advantage of by those two.

"I'm only trying to help you!" he yelled after her, shaking his head as she kicked the horse into a gallop. Either she hadn't heard him or she was ignoring him. *Damn that woman's stubborn streak.*

Son of a bitch! He pushed open the door of the cabin, throwing his files on the table. They skidded across the smooth surface, some of them falling open and scattering papers across the top.

Jessie made it perfectly clear she'd never wanted him here, never wanted his help, and now she was pissed at something he'd done. Or hadn't done. He was tired of spinning his wheels trying to figure her out.

"What are you even doing here?" Nathan spun to see Bailey leaning against the doorjamb of the cabin.

"Ever heard of privacy, Bailey?"

She laughed and sauntered into the room, jumping onto the kitchen counter like he'd invited her in. "Ever heard of shutting a door?" She gave him a cocky grin. "Well?"

He sighed, wondering how she managed to ask the very question haunting him. She obviously wasn't going anywhere until he answered her. "I'm trying to help Jessie get her finances on track. At least, that's what I thought I was doing."

"Oh, you are. Or you will," she clarified. "But I mean, what are you doing *here*, right now? Why didn't you follow her?"

"Are you nuts? I have no idea where she rode off to, and she made it pretty clear I wasn't invited." He ran a hand through his hair and threw his hands into the air. "I don't even know why she's angry at me."

Bailey hopped off the counter. "For a smart guy, Wall Street, you're pretty slow on the uptake." She shook her head. "Come on," she ordered, heading for the door. When he didn't follow her, she turned and cocked her hip to the side. "Or are you planning on running back to New York now that your dad wants you there?"

"How do you know about that?"

She held up his phone and wiggled it. "You'd think someone with your smarts would lock their phone with a passcode or something." Her grin pulled at the corner of her lips. "Now, if you want to catch up to my cousin, you'd better hurry up. You *can* ride a quad can't you?"

He snatched his phone from her fingers. "You're a piece of work, Bailey. Do you know that?"

Her grin spread across her face and her dark eyes glinted mischievously. "Tell me something I haven't heard a hundred times before."

"It's not a compliment."

He scanned a new message from his father demanding he return to New York, ordering him to be at a meeting with one of his father's biggest campaign contributors in three days. How many times did he have to tell his father he wasn't interested in politics? He certainly didn't want to be connected with his father's shady dealings. Nathan quickly responded that he was unavailable until after the weekend. Jessie might be angry enough to ask him to leave but he refused to skip out on her when she had guests arriving and he was the one who'd suggested she take them in. He wasn't going to leave her short-handed, even if he might not be much help.

"Are you coming or what?"

"She doesn't want to see me."

"Holy shit, Wall Street! Stop being so dense." This was the second time he'd seen her lose her temper with him, and frankly, he wasn't sure he wanted to see it again. If Jessie's temper was fiery, Bailey's was downright frightening. "She isn't mad at you. She's hurt. Uncle Colton made her a promise before he went on that trip. He was going to hire someone else so she could concentrate on rehabilitating abused horses. Now she finds out that he was taking money from the ranch to go into a new corporation no one knew existed, as if he didn't think she could make it work. She turned down college to stay and help my aunt and uncle with this place, and now she finds out that he never really thought she'd succeed. Pull your head out of your ass already. How would that make you feel?"

Her tirade was enough to allay his frustration. If Bailey was right and that was how Jess was feeling, he needed to explain a few things to her. She was completely misunderstanding her father's intentions. "I don't think that's what he was doing."

"Then what in the hell are you waiting for? Go find her and explain it to her," Bailey huffed, her anger snuffed out.

"I don't even know where to find her."

She sighed and shook her head. "Do I have to do everything for you? Take the quad on the path that heads toward The Ridge. She's probably up there. If you don't find her there, call me and we'll go look together."

He tucked his cell into his pocket. "Any service out there?"

"It's spotty, but you should have enough to get a call through."

"I'll call you when I find her."

The grin returned to Bailey's face. "Well, that's really sweet of you, Wall Street, but I'm hoping when you find her, you'll have far more important things to do than calling me."

HE WAS LOST. There was no doubt about it. He'd known it was a stupid idea for him to just head out on a quad, even following a trail. He stopped the machine and pulled the helmet off his head, tapping a finger on the side as he tried to get his bearings. He could see The Ridge from where he was, and he was still on the path Bailey instructed him to follow, but it forked about half a mile behind him and he wasn't sure he'd gone the right direction. He could hear the river up ahead but he couldn't quite see it. The path might take him to the top, but nothing looked familiar. Then again, the last time he'd come this way had been at night, and he'd been so focused on the woman with him, he hadn't really paid much attention.

He climbed back on the quad and decided to try following the path he was on a little longer before giving up and calling Bailey. Nathan could hear her scolding him now for being such a "city boy." He was getting sick and tired of everyone assuming he was somehow incompetent because he'd grown up privileged. He might not know how to rope a steer, but he'd love to see any one of them try to navigate getting a cab in New York on an opening night. He suddenly realized how pretentious the idea sounded. In actuality, he had no doubt any of the three women could handle it, probably better than he or Justin could. He slowed the quad, wondering again if he shouldn't just turn back when he heard a horse whinny.

That had to be Jess. There was nothing else out here as far as he could see.

Nathan rode a little farther up the trail and could just make out Jessie's mare through the trees and brush surrounding a clearing near the water. He didn't want to get the quad too close in case it scared the animal, so he parked it under a tree and walked the rest of the way on foot. The mare raised her head and whinnied another greeting as he approached, but he still didn't see Jess nearby. Worry chilled the breath in his lungs. Anything could have happened to her out here alone. He glanced toward the water. If she'd tried to go swimming…

He dragged his mind back from the morbid thoughts. "Jess," he called. "Are you here?"

"Down here." Relief settled in as he walked a few feet down the riverbank and saw her sitting at the edge of the water on a log. "I should've known you wouldn't listen and leave me alone."

"Yeah, well, I guess you don't know me as well as you thought." He made his way down the slight graded slope and sat beside her.

Her eyes were filled with sadness as she gave him a sideways glance. "I don't really know you at all, Nathan."

She wasn't wrong, yet she was. Deep down, he knew they understood one another, or at least a part of each other that no one else seemed to. She'd reached into his chest and grabbed ahold of a part of his soul, showing him what was lacking in his life. She was driving him crazy trying to get her to realize she filled that void. He, on the other hand, was trying to make her see she wasn't a failure. She blamed herself for everything that went wrong but never took any credit for what she was doing right, and she was doing so much right.

He shrugged. "I'm not that hard to figure out, Jess. What you see is what you get." She didn't reply, just continued watching the water break over itself as it crashed downstream, lulling them with a ballet of white foam over the rocks. He moved to sit on the ground and leaned back on the log with his head at her thigh. "Why don't we talk about what has you so upset?"

"It's nothing."

"It's not nothing or you'd still be at the house. You're angry."

She looked down at him in surprise, hope filling her eyes, but it only took her a moment to squash the emotion. "I just need some quiet to figure out what to do now."

"What's to figure out? Your father already started the incorporation process. Now we know where the money was going and have it stopped. I'm not sure I see the problem."

"The problem is that everyone thinks they know what's best for me and this ranch." She got up and walked to the edge of the water. She was talking to him, but nothing she said was really directed at him. Her voice rose and broke. "What if I don't want to run a dude ranch? What if I just want to rehab abused horses like my dad promised? I can't even do that now without approval from Julia and Justin. I still can't make any of my own decisions. I'm stuck doing what everyone else decides. This wasn't supposed to happen. Dad was supposed to run the dude ranch, and I was going to focus on the horses." She hit her fists against her thighs. "He promised me we would take care of it when he got back. Now I find out he'd already had all of this in the works. That he had to put a backup plan in place because he expected me to fail."

Nathan could hear the anguish in her voice; her shoulders shook as she tried to control the grief coursing through her. He wasn't about to sit here and watch her go through this alone. He rose from the ground as she spun on him.

"He lied to me. Why? Why didn't he just tell me the truth? That he didn't think I could hack it."

"Whoa, whoa," Nathan moved toward her, reaching for her shoulders, but she jerked away from his touch. "Jess, calm down. He didn't lie."

She looked up at him and the hope he could read in her eyes made his stomach do a flip. He suddenly knew exactly how a superhero must feel, saving the day. Suddenly, in her eyes, he'd just offered her something more precious than gold. Her expression darkened almost as quickly.

"Of course he lied. Why else would he have hidden the money?" She turned away from him.

Nathan slid his hands over the back of her shoulders. "No, he didn't. That transfer was set up before he died, so, while we don't know why the money was being transferred, we can assume it was to be used in some way by the corporation as a whole. If he was going to continue running the dude ranch, it's highly likely that money was being set aside to help fund your rescue until it was operating independently." He turned her so she faced him again and brushed a stray curl back from her cheek. "As far as the corporation, he did the right thing. If he told you he was going to help you set something up, I'm sure he was." His thumb traced her cheekbone. "But circumstances changed before that happened."

His voice was quietly insistent, and her gaze jumped to meet his. She looked up at him, tears glistening in her eyes, and he realized there wasn't a power on earth that could stop him from kissing Jessie right now.

He didn't mean to dip his head, didn't mean to brush his lips against hers, but when her hands gripped at his forearms, when her fingers curled against him and she let out a little moan, his sanity and self-control were lost. His hands found her waist and circled her back, pulling her to him, ridding them of any space between their bodies. What started as the barest of caresses, a mere touch, quickly ignited into a raging, wild storm of hunger. Her hands slid to the back of his neck, into his hair as his lips found the curve of her ear, the indentation of her neck, and the column of her throat.

This was *not* what he came out here to do, but he had as much control to stop this now as he would to stop a tornado heading straight toward him. And being with Jessie felt exactly like that—an uncontrollable storm of emotion that left him yearning for more.

Chapter Eighteen

HOW DID SHE always manage to end up in his arms? How was it so easy for him to break down every barrier she set up? She'd come out here to figure out her future, and that included a decision to stay away from Nathan Kerrington. He was bad for her. There was nothing between them but lust, a fiery attraction that would leave her scorched and bleeding when he left—and he was bound to leave—but she was finding it increasingly difficult to not give in to the longing that seemed to pulse through her veins every time she saw him.

When he'd shown up, dusty and slightly sweaty from the ride to find her, her heart began its staccato beat and refused to slow. The man was sexy and virile. Had she not known where he was born and raised, he could have passed for a cowboy without any trouble. If he were from here, fit in here, she might consider pursuing what they had.

But he'd already made it clear, he was leaving next week. Back to the city where he belonged, back to other women she was sure he'd loved and a job that offered him far more than a broke cowgirl on a mission to save some horses. He might be adapting, learning to fit in here for the moment, but that made him even more dangerous to her heart. He might say he would stay, but eventually he would choose to leave her behind again. She couldn't continue down this doomed path. She still hadn't recovered from the last time they'd been together.

"No," she whispered, more for herself than for him, steeling her will as she put her hands against his chest. She felt his muscles tense under her fingers and tried not to inhale his musky scent. "Thank you for helping me with the ranch, but I think that now, with everything you suggested in the works, you should head back to New York."

She could barely catch her breath as she looked up at him through her lashes, waiting for a response she didn't really want to hear. His half-smile and the dimple in his cheek were the last things she'd expected to see.

"That's what you think, huh?"

"I…" She took a step backward, putting some space between them so she could clear her head and form a logical argument. Wasn't that what he dealt in—logic? Reason? "Thanks to you, the ranch will be in the black again this month, and we have guests this weekend. I don't see any reason for you to stay now."

She took another step away from him, and he folded his arms across his broad chest. He didn't touch her, but he was imposing nonetheless. "And what about next weekend or the one after that?"

He took a step toward her, and she immediately retreated. His frown spoke volumes. "I already made plans to stay through the weekend and help with the guests, Jess. They aren't expecting me back in New York until Tuesday morning to finish the merger I was working on there. Until Monday afternoon, I'm all yours."

Her heart skipped a beat, and she wondered if he was deliberately making innuendos. She took a deep breath, trying to still the desire pumping through her body. Her stomach did that flutter she was coming to expect whenever he was around.

The damn man was teasing her. She could see it in his deep emerald eyes, in the flecks that danced within them. She tried for a serious look, one that would remind him that they were discussing her future, not some weekend fling.

"Nathan, you don't even know what you're doing." She let out her breath on a sigh, realizing her own words held a double meaning as well.

What if I want you for longer? Like forever? She cursed her childish fantasies.

He took a step toward her, closing the distance she was working hard to maintain. "Jess, stop running away from me." He reached for her hand and pulled her back into his arms, holding her hips. "You're right. I don't know what I'm doing. But I'm willing to take as much time as I need to until I do." His finger traced her jawline. "Don't deny me the chance to show you I've learned a thing or two over the past eight years. I'm asking for a chance to correct my mistake."

She shook her head. "You were right to leave. Look at what you've accomplished. What happened between us was the mistake."

"You were never a mistake, Jess." His voice was a husky rasp of sound. His fingers buried in her hair, doing the most wonderful things to her scalp, making desire curl in her chest and warm parts of her it seemed only he could. "Let's be honest, neither of us knows what we're doing. We're both so used to being in control that neither of us knows how to let go. Maybe it's time we find out how and just enjoy it, for as long as it lasts."

"Nathan," she began, resting her hands at his hips. He knew exactly what he was doing to her.

She wanted to curl her arms around him, to fall against him and let him make her forget again. Her fingers dug into the firm flesh of his waist through his cotton T-shirt and she dropped her forehead to his shoulder, fighting the need to press her body into his, to feel the warmth of his lips, to lose herself in his touch again.

"I can't Nathan. I thought I could but I can't."

"I thought you said—"

"I know what I said." She could feel the heat rising in her cheeks. She didn't want to admit to him she'd been fool enough to have fallen completely head over heels for him again. "I said it was until one of us wanted out. I want out." She quickly moved away from his hands. "I appreciate you staying to help, but if you need to get back, feel free to leave."

Jessie ran to the top of the hill where the mare waited for her. She didn't wait around to see if Nathan would try to stop her. She refused to look back. If she did, she'd change her mind and give in to the desire that begged her to stay in his arms.

NATHAN STARED AT the files in front of him. He couldn't concentrate, no matter how he tried. Besides, he'd been over these same documents at least twenty times. Until Brendon e-mailed him the bank statements he'd asked for, he wasn't going to get any answers. He glanced up as yet another round of laughter, coupled with a splash and cheers from teens, came from the backyard near the pool. The church group had arrived earlier in the day, and Jess had managed to avoid him all day, staying busy with the kids. He'd seen only seen her from a distance, and she'd been so focused on the group, she hadn't even looked his way.

Right now, the only thing Nathan could focus on was the memory of Jessie in her bathing suit, water dripping over her curves just before she pushed him in. She was so certain he would leave and never come back, or that he wouldn't stay if he did, that he wasn't sure how to convince her otherwise. She didn't know it, but he'd already made arrangements to cut his meetings from a week down to just a few days, letting his partners handle most of the details with the merger. But if Jessie didn't want him back, if she continued to deny them both this chance, he was just buying himself too many free hours in the day to think about what he couldn't have. God help him, but he wanted her, and not just for a few days or a week. She had him rethinking what he wanted in his future. With that woman, forever wouldn't be long enough.

He walked to the window and watched the teens playing in the backyard as Jess directed them in a game. Water splashed and a shriek sounded from one of the teenage girls, and he saw several boys laughing. He barely remembered being that age, enjoying the freedom that came from youth. He watched Jess laugh with the boys and wave to the girl who'd ended up in the water.

He was happy to see her having fun, enjoying her guests and them loving her in return. The adult chaperones sat off to the side, in the shade of the porch, laughing at the antics of the kids but obviously thrilled to have some time to relax.

Jessie was in her element.

He'd seen her working with the horses and thought it was where she belonged, but seeing her with these kids, the way they lit up under her attention, was incredible. If only he could help her see how special she was, to see herself the way others did.

He spun on his heel and made his way to the patio where the other adults sat, absently chatting.

"She's so good with them," one woman commented.

"They love her," said another

"We need to plan an entire week here next time."

The murmurs stopped as he sat down in one of the chaise lounge chairs. "Don't mind me," he said. "Just had to see what all the commotion was about."

"Sorry," the man apologized. Nathan guessed he was the youth pastor by the way three others look to him for direction. "Are you a guest?"

"Yes, but I'm also a friend of the family. I'm staying in the first cabin."

"Then you're right beside us. I'd like to promise you a quiet night, but with this crew"—he waved a hand at the four boys now having cannonball contests—"I think they'd make me out to be a liar. I'm Steve." He held out a hand and smiled.

Nathan returned the gesture. "What does Jess have planned for you guys?"

"She showed the kids some horse basics today and taught us a little about roping, not that I was any good at either." He chuckled. "We're having a barbecue and campfire tonight by the lodge, then in the morning, we're supposed to go riding and having a picnic lunch on some ridge. She said something about doing some fishing at the river, if anyone wants to." He looked around. "This place is like an oasis, isn't it?"

Nathan's gaze remained locked on Jess, taking in every relaxed smile as she joked with two of the girls. Maybe he could cancel his meetings in New York altogether. "I've been around the world, and I've never seen anything quite like it."

The woman on the other side of Steve laughed and Nathan tore his gaze from the vision across the pool. "Something tells me it's not the landscape you're talking about."

Nathan couldn't remember the last time he'd blushed, but that didn't stop the slow burn from creeping up his neck at being caught staring at Jess. Her eyes slid over the adults and stopped when she saw him, a frown creasing her brow, and he cursed himself for being the cause.

"She's great with the kids," the woman said quickly.

"I should get inside and help get ready for the barbecue."

"Uh, okay." Steve seemed surprised by his sudden departure. As Nathan started to leave, he saw Steve lean over to one of the woman and heard, "You made him uncomfortable and chased him off."

"I didn't," she argued just before he closed the kitchen door on the rest of their conversation.

Nathan went to the cupboard and grabbed a glass, pouring himself water and chugging it quickly. He slid the glass onto the counter and braced his hands on either side of the sink, his head hanging low. Every part of his body hummed with desire for Jessie, but it couldn't even compare to the ache in his chest at the thought of leaving in two days. Jessie had him so tied up in knots, he wasn't sure which way was up any more. He doubted she did either. But he couldn't deny it. He simply didn't want to go. Every time he thought about it, it felt wrong.

"What the hell are you doing?" He muttered, rubbing a hand over the tense muscles at the back of his neck.

"That's exactly what I was wondering." Nathan spun to find Jess standing in the doorway, hip cocked to the side and her hands at her waist. She looked sexy as hell, and his body hummed to life. "I told you, I don't need your help."

"I heard you."

"Then what are you doing here?"

"I just thought I'd come see how things were going."

He was lying, but she didn't need to know that it was killing him to stay in the cabin, giving her the space she asked for, and not be near her. She didn't need to know he'd been standing at the window watching her, feeling like a stalker. But he was compelled by her, like a child near a fire. He instinctively knew it would hurt to touch, but he was powerless to stop himself.

She seemed to accept his excuse. At least, she let him believe she did.

Jess walked to the refrigerator and took out a bottle of water, twisting off the cap and taking a long swallow before smiling, looking back at the door. "I've forgotten how much fun it can be."

The smile on her face made his pulse speed up. "What's that?"

"Kids." She jerked her thumb toward the pool, where he could still hear splashing and laughter. "They're kind of like horses, slightly wild, but tamed with a little direction and the right coaxing."

She finished her bottle of water, and he couldn't stop staring at the elegant way her neck arched. She brushed past him to throw the plastic bottle into the recycling bin, and he moved behind her, slipping his hands to her waist. She stilled instantly, as if afraid to move.

"What are you doing?" she asked, her voice quiet yet demanding an answer.

"Nothing." He brushed her thick braid from her shoulder, letting it dangle down her back, while his lips moved to the edge of her ear, his breath brushing over her cheek. "Why?"

Her jaw clenched and her hands gripped the edge of the kitchen counter. "Nathan, we had an agreement. Just friends."

"Um-hmm." His hands circled her waist and drew her back against him. "Friends hug, don't they?"

Technically, that's all he was doing, but his body responded like it was far more. She was hot against the front of him. He fought the urge to kiss her neck, to taste her again, to force her reaction to him, choosing instead to remain as still as his throbbing body would allow. He felt himself harden when she sighed and leaned back into him, her body softening into his embrace. But she hung her head forward in defeat.

"Nathan, please."

"Please what?" He pulled her closer and felt the goose-bumps break out on her arms. He rested his chin on her shoulder where he could smell the sweet vanilla of her body wash. Just the scent was enough to conjure the image of her wet and soapy in the shower. He fought the groan of yearning that rolled through him like a thunderstorm.

She turned in his arms and put her hands against his chest, but her eyes focused on her hands instead of his face. "Please, don't."

His hands held her waist, refusing to let her go. "Would it make a difference if I wasn't leaving?"

Jessie's lashes fluttered as she looked up at him, as if trying to determine his sincerity. "But you will. If not this week, later." She ducked under his arm and scooted away from him. He saw the resignation in her eyes. "I can't do this again, Nathan. When you left last time, you took a part of me with you. A piece I've never retrieved."

Her admission surprised him. He leaned a hip against the counter and crossed his arms, waiting for her to say more. When she didn't, he shook his head. "I know why I didn't call, Jess. But why didn't you?"

"Me?" She backed away. "If you want a girl who'll beg you to stay, you're barking up the wrong tree. I wasn't going to be the summer fling that chased you when you wanted to disappear." She shook her head. "When you didn't call, I knew exactly what I'd meant to you."

"I could say that same thing."

Anger flared in her eyes and she clenched her jaw, pointing a finger at him. "Don't you dare. You were—"

"What, Jess?" Nathan held her wrist and pulled her back into his arms. "I was what?"

She looked away, refusing to meet his gaze. "Nothing."

Nathan held her chin between his thumb and finger. "Well, let me break down the situation then, since you won't. I was your first." Her eyes widened and she licked her lips, pressing them together. "Did you think I didn't know? I know you, Jess. I know what kind of woman you were and the kind of woman you still are."

"Nathan, stop."

"You were—are—different than any woman I've ever known. You aggravate me and confuse me, but you also excite me and make me feel things like no one else. There's something between us, there always has been."

"Whatever this attraction between us is, it's going nowhere. We're too different, worlds apart. You're smart and kind and attractive, but I know *you*, Nathan. You will wither out here. Don't you remember how antsy you were to leave?" She moved away from him, starting toward the door.

She had no idea his desire to leave had been due to his father's demanding phone calls and the increasing threats. He wasn't going to let anything, or anyone, come between them this time.

She sighed. "It's just part of who you are."

"Then I guess that leaves me with two options."

She spun back toward him, her braid whipping around. "No, that leaves no options." She raised a hand as if she was trying to ward off any argument.

He reached for her hand and pulled her to him again, continuing as if he hadn't heard her protests. "One, I can prove to you that we have several things in common. Like that you are also intelligent, and kind. Not to mention that I find you incredibly attractive."

Nathan could read the desire in her eyes and wound his arm around her waist, wanting her to feel his body respond to her nearness. "For the record, I didn't get antsy to leave. I was catching hell from someone who shouldn't have mattered." He tipped her chin up, forcing her to meet his gaze. He could see the fear there.

Her blue eyes clouded. "What's option two?" she whispered.

Nathan laughed. "Are you sure you want to know? Because it involves me carrying you back up to your room and proving to you that our differences don't matter. Why do you keep fighting, Jess? Why can't you just accept that maybe, just maybe, this isn't something that I'm just going to turn my back on a second time? I made that mistake once; I won't do it again."

She slipped out of his arms again. This time her eyes were somber and wistful. "Because right now, this is a novelty, Nathan. I've seen enough people come here for a taste of being a cowboy and it always fades. What happens when you decide staying was a mistake? That you miss your old life? Where will that leave me? Brokenhearted and alone. I won't be anyone's booty call." She walked out the back door, leaving him staring after her yet again.

Chapter Nineteen

JESSIE WAS GRATEFUL for the teens' presence and the turmoil they brought. Planning activities for them didn't afford her the luxury of breaking down the way she wanted to. She took a deep breath, straightened her shoulders, and hurried back to the pool where they waited for her next instructions. She was supposed to send them on a scavenger hunt with Mitch and Clint, but if they left, she'd be alone with her thoughts and the realization that she'd just confessed to Nathan how she felt about him, how she'd always felt about him.

She hadn't meant for the words to slip from her tongue. Once again, her mouth had overrun her good sense and gotten her into trouble.

"Jessie, we're ready." Susanne, Pastor Steve's wife, approached. "Did you find what you were looking for?" Jessie had forgotten she'd told the woman she was going in search of pens and paper. "Are you okay? You look a bit…unsettled," she finished, searching for the word.

Jessie looked back toward the house, knowing there was no way she was going to go back inside for paper or pens and risk running into Nathan again. Her heart couldn't take that now, "I'm fine, but I couldn't find enough of them," she said, feeling guilty for lying.

"That's okay, we'll manage with two teams. I can take the girls and Steve can take the boys." She hurried to her purse, bringing back a small pad of paper and two pens. "Here." She pressed the items into Jessie's hands. "You write down what they should find and I'll distract them a bit longer with a group discussion. But don't take too long, their attention span is about the same as a goldfish's," she teased.

Jessie took the paper and sat at the bar, trying to list several items that the kids would have to work to find throughout the ranch, testing them on what she'd taught them so far. She'd barely listed ten when she looked up and saw Nathan standing on the back porch watching her. Her stomach did a quick flip. Maybe her confession would be just the thing to scare him away. It sure as hell scared her. She should have never agreed to let him come back.

At least Heart Fire would stay afloat. Nathan had figured out her financial troubles, at least temporarily, and convinced her to start taking in guests again, so the ranch should be able to get back to normal operations. If she could afford to hire at least a couple of people full-time again during the busy season, and if she continued to take in guests, the ranch should do okay, even though it wasn't what she wanted to do. It was enough to get Heart Fire back in the black and get her brother to back off. She wouldn't be able to work with the horses as often, and the chance to start a rescue would have to wait until…well, who really knew if she would ever be able to do it. She was only one person.

Instead of making her feel like she was making the mature decision, the thought left her cold. This melancholy turn of her thoughts was the last direction she wanted them to take and sitting here was giving her too much time to ponder her various mistakes. She threw the pen onto the counter. Twelve things would just have to be enough for the scavenger hunt. She pasted a smile on her lips and took the paper to Susanne while sending a quick text message to Mitch to bring Clint.

If she were smarter, she'd have asked Nathan to help organize this. This was something he'd have managed well and it would've gotten him far from her for a few hours at least. But she didn't want to ask him for anything, especially now. She glanced back at the door, ignoring the disappointment she felt when she saw he was gone.

It was better this way. This was the way it had to be. *Then, cowgirl up, and quit being a baby.*

Jessie went back into the house and took the meat thawing in the refrigerator out, placing it into a giant mixing bowl. She washed her hands and walked into the pantry. This was what she did best, kept things running, kept the wheels turning, even at the expense of her own heart. She put the barbecue sauce container on the counter and went back to the refrigerator for the eggs and cheese. Justin should be here any minute to take the patties to the grill, and she wasn't even close to being ready.

Mixing the various ingredients in the bowl, she set the formed patties on an aluminum pan lined with wax paper. She tore another piece of wax paper from the roll and covered the patties, carrying them back to the refrigerator to wait for Justin. She washed her hands a second time and cleaned up her mess, wishing it was as easy to clean up the other messes she'd made in her life.

Tears stung her eyes. She was tired of doing this alone, of forgoing her wants and desires in order to please everyone else. This wasn't the plan she'd had for her life. Six months ago, she'd been preparing to finally start a rescue. She had had the full support of her father. Now, instead, she was running a dude ranch, alone, and destroying the legacy her parents had left behind. She felt her heart clench.

God, how she missed them. Even with the expectation and pressure she felt working with both of her parents, she knew her parents loved her. Trying to run the ranch without them felt like torture. It was just too much for her to bear.

Tears blurred her vision as she turned to put the eggs away, and she ran into a solid wall of muscle. She dropped the entire carton of eggs and cursed, squatting to reach for the broken pieces when Nathan held her shoulders, lifting her back to standing before burying his hands into her hair.

"Jess?" He tipped her face toward his, his lips a mere breath away.

"Please, don't. Not now." She couldn't deal with the emotional turmoil raging within her and fight her desire for him as well.

Nathan stared at her for a moment before walking to the sink and grabbing the roll of paper towels. He squatted on the floor next to her and wiped up the mess. "Okay, I won't."

He leaned forward and pressed a quick kiss to her forehead before standing to throw the wad of towels into the trash.

Her mouth dropped just as her phone rang, not giving her an opportunity to protest the kiss. "Hello?"

"Jess, I have an emergency at the clinic, so Bailey and I won't be there in time to do the barbecue. I'm really sorry," Justin apologized.

She sighed into the phone. "Okay, I understand."

And she did. The ranch wasn't Justin's responsibility, it was hers. She hung up the phone, tucking it back into her pocket.

Now what?

How was she supposed to cook dinner and entertain guests? There was just no way she could do this all by herself. This was just one more indication of what a failure she was at managing the ranch. Either of her parents would have had a backup plan. With both Clint and Mitch preparing for the ride to The Ridge the next day, she couldn't ask them to work late into the night because of her lack of planning. She glanced at Nathan.

She didn't want to ask him for help. Not only would it be admitting her failure in her business, but she'd already told him several times that she didn't need him and he should leave. How could she ask him to help her now?

"Trouble?" A frown furrowed his brow and he took a step toward her.

"Justin is hung up at the clinic." She tried to hide her frustration. "It's not a big deal. I'll just have to rethink how to set up the campfire tonight since Bailey and Julia are both gone."

"Why?" He moved to the refrigerator. "I can't teach guests how to ride or rope but I'm pretty sure I can manage to barbecue hamburgers."

"But—"

"But nothing." He took a step closer to her and kissed the tip of her nose. "I told you, I'm here to help."

JESSIE LEANED AGAINST the doorframe in the kitchen and watched as Nathan finished loading the last of the dishes into the dishwasher. He wiped his hands on the towel from the counter and turned, spotting her watching him.

"What's that look for?"

This man continued to confound her. After cooking nearly two dozen hamburgers on the grill, he'd helped her set the rest of the food out, poured sodas, served the kids chocolate cake and then insisted she stay with the group while he headed back inside to clean up. She hadn't expected a man like him, one accustomed to being served, to do so much to help her. If she'd misjudged him with something as simple as how helpful he might be with the barbecue, how else was she underestimating him? She cocked her head to the side, and a soft smile curved her lips as he came toward her.

Her fingers twitched, trying to control the urge to slip them into his thick, dark hair. It would be so easy to take the first step toward him, to let him know she wanted him for as long as he wanted to stay. She wanted to kiss him. But her feet remained rooted to the threshold, her head not allowing her heart that privilege.

He'll be gone in two days, her logic reminded her.

But there was so much she would love to do with him in those two days, to let him do to her. And what if she asked him to stay?

"Jess, are you okay?" His hand came up and he let his thumb brush over her jaw. It was enough to jolt her back to the present.

"Yeah," she said, moving to the pantry. "I think the kids are ready for s'mores." She grabbed several boxes of graham crackers, chocolate bars, and bags of marshmallows. "Were you coming out to join everyone?"

"Do you want me to?"

"I think the kids really enjoyed you earlier."

He gave her a smile, making that dimple crease his cheek, and sent her heart fluttering again. "That wasn't what I asked."

Her heart pounded in her ears, her pulse rushing through her veins, and she wondered if he could hear it. He moved to block her exit from the pantry, filling the doorway and her senses. She caught her breath as his large hand curled around the side of the door and the tiny space filled with his unique scent. Jessie tried to ignore the shiver of longing that skittered up her spine and the heat that settled over her shoulders, causing goosebumps to rise on her flesh.

Why was he making this so difficult? On the other hand, what harm would it do to just admit that she did want to spend some time with him? She'd already admitted she had feelings for him.

"I…" She had trouble getting her lips to form the words. Her mind searched for any reason she could find to be near him. "You did mention wanting to discuss an idea you had."

A slow smile spread over his lips. "I did, didn't I?" He leaned toward her, and she could feel the heat radiating from him. Or maybe that was from her because of him. "Are you sure that's the only reason you want me there?"

She willed her feet to move and bid her tongue to come up with a witty retort. Instead, her body swayed toward him, and she wondered if he really had sucked all the oxygen from the small pantry.

"I'm sorry, I don't mean to interrupt anything but the kids are getting impatient."

Susanne's voice shattered the spell he'd cast over her and replaced it with frustration. She had a job to do and it didn't include fantasizing about a guy who would forget her again as soon as his butt hit the cushy first-class seat on his flight.

"You didn't. We were just searching for these." She brushed past him, trying to ignore the icy thrill as his hand moved over her back as she held up the bags of marshmallows before handing them to the Susanne. "I didn't mean to take so long."

Jessie heard Nathan's throaty chuckle as he scooped up the box of crackers and followed her from the kitchen to the campfire. She needed to steel herself against her body's response whenever he was near, or she might as well smash her heart with a hammer now.

Chapter Twenty

EVERY NERVE IN Nathan's body vibrated with need. It had taken every ounce of self-control to keep her from seeing how she was affecting him. But, while his body might hate him—and there were parts of his body screaming at him for release right now—he'd seen her resolve begin to crumble. If it hadn't been for Susanne interrupting when she did, he was certain she would have forgotten her stubborn plan to keep him friend-zoned.

He walked to where Steve and his wife reclined as Jessie passed out several roasting forks. Steve had his hands draped over the side of a glossy acoustic guitar but started to set it aside to shake Nathan's hand.

"No, don't get up." Nathan leaned toward the man. "Good to see you again."

"You, too," he said, his fingers absently plucking the guitar's strings. "I'm glad we didn't actually scare you away."

"Not a chance."

Jessie returned to the small group of adults, and he patted the spot next to him on the oversized chaise lounge, knowing that she wasn't likely to refuse with people watching. She sat on the very edge of the seat, as far away as possible while still remaining on the same chair. He shook his head slightly at her stubborn determination and caught Susanne watching them, a smile on her face.

"Jessie, the kids have done nothing but talk about the ride tomorrow. These boys haven't stopped arguing about who is going to catch the biggest fish." She laughed and nudged her husband's leg. "And I think this one is the worst."

"Hey!" Steve protested with righteous indignation. "I *will* be the one with the biggest fish. I'm the only one who knows how to bait a hook."

Jessie laughed with the couple. "There're a lot of rainbow trout running right now. I know my brother has been using worms and doing pretty well."

"Ew! That leaves me out," Susanne said, paling as she grimaced. She turned back to the kids and pointed out a young couple on the left side of the fire pit. The boy had his arm draped around the girl and was whispering something into her ear as he roasted a marshmallow and then held it up for her to bite. "Steve, you better go and have another chat with your son."

Steve rolled his eyes and stood up. "I'll see if I can't distract them for a bit. I swear, if they aren't sleeping or eating, they're being overrun with hormones. Who's ready for some music?" he called to the group.

"I should probably help him. Sometimes keeping these kids in line is like trying to corral cats." She laughed and rose from her chair. "Oh, and Nathan, I hope I didn't upset you earlier."

Nathan glanced at Jessie and could read the curiosity in her eyes, even though she didn't ask. He shook his head. "Don't worry about it. You didn't." He leaned back in the chaise and crossed his ankles in front of him. "In fact, I think you might have helped without realizing it."

Jessie looked from one to the other, waiting for Susanne to move toward the fire pit and out of earshot before asking for an explanation. "What was that about?"

He shrugged and deliberately avoided her question, certain it would drive her crazy trying to find out. "Why are you sitting all the way over there?" She twisted around, glaring at him. He laughed at her expression. "Don't trust yourself to sit with to me, huh?"

"Hardly." He didn't miss the way she wouldn't meet his eyes when she said it.

"Liar," he countered quietly. She started to rise, but he reached for her wrist. "I'd be hard pressed to even try to steal a kiss unless I wanted Susanne to send Steve over. What do you think I'd do with eight teens, two counselors, a pastor, and his wife out here?"

"Make me uncomfortable," she countered, but there was a ghost of a smile on her lips.

"What if I promise to behave?"

She eyed him skeptically. "I don't think you know how."

He pulled her down toward the seat. "I'll keep my hands to myself. That's the best I can offer." He gave her a lopsided grin. "Now, what you choose to do with *your* hands is a different story."

She shook her head but let him drag her down beside him, and he slid his arm around her shoulders. She was stiff beside him as he pointed out the young couple. "Do you remember being that age?" When she only shrugged, he went on. "It's pretty cool the way Steve and Susanne watch over the kids but still give them their freedom. I never had that opportunity."

She looked up at him. "No?" He heard the surprise in her voice. He knew she thought he was nothing more than a spoiled, rich kid. She had no idea that privilege came at a price.

"My father and grandfather are politicians, so everything we did was scrutinized. I couldn't leave the house without security." He looked down at her, tucked under his arm, warmth filling his chest when she seemed genuinely interested. "Made dates sort of awkward."

She laughed quietly, relaxing against his side. "I get the feeling you managed just fine."

"Not until I went to college. But that is a story better left untold."

"A regular ladies' man, huh?" She curled against his ribs, letting her head rest against his shoulder.

"Nope, I was a complete nerd and had no idea how to even talk to a girl."

She sat up and looked into his face. "I doubt that."

"I swear. But then in college I met this loud-mouthed, short-tempered hillbilly, and he taught me everything I know."

"Seriously? Justin?" She clicked her tongue. "That explains so much," she teased.

He let his fingers play with the long waves of her hair. She sighed, and he realized that this was the most relaxed he'd been in a very long time. Like the earth had stopped spinning and they were the only two people left. As a matter of fact, he couldn't remember ever feeling this way, at least, not since that summer. But even then, the sneaking around, while exciting, had made it difficult to ever relax with her. "Jess, what would you think about turning the ranch into a nonprofit organization?"

She yawned and covered her mouth with the back of her hand. "For what?"

"You said you wanted to rescue abused horses, and you light up when you work with the teens. What if I could help you turn this place into sort of a camp for at-risk youth to connect with horses, like you said you wanted?"

"How would that even work? I mean, what about the overhead like hay and vet bills?"

"Investors. You would need to find sponsors and donors."

Her eyes had slipped closed, and her voice held a husky, sleepy tone. He knew he was losing her to sheer exhaustion. "I don't know anyone who would donate."

"I do. I could make a few phone calls," he offered.

The only reply was the sound of her soft breathing. She'd given in to her fatigue and fallen asleep on him. Nothing was going to make him move. He didn't care if he stayed on this chaise lounge all night if it meant holding her in his arms.

JESSIE WOKE THE next morning feeling more refreshed than she had in years. She reached her arms above her and pressed her toes toward the foot of the bed, arching her back. She blinked against the sunlight streaming through her bedroom window and rolled over, reaching for the down comforter when her hand landed on the hard, muscular abs of the man in bed with her.

She yelped in surprise, jerking her hand away, as Nathan opened one eye and smiled at her. "Good morning, Jess."

She scooted away from him. "What the hell are you doing in here?" She pushed herself up on one elbow to look at the clock. "It's six in the morning. Why are you in my bed?"

"You don't remember?" He gave her a devilish grin.

No way.

She would've remembered making love to Nathan. Like riding her first horse, or every tumble she'd taken since, making love to Nathan was something she'd never forget as long as she lived. Even now, lying on the opposite side of the bed from him, her body was humming with desire.

As if he sensed her hesitance, he laughed. "I'm kidding, Jess. Nothing happened." She wasn't sure she believed that entirely either. "We were talking on the patio while the kids made s'mores and you fell asleep, so I brought you to your room."

She checked her clothing and found that she was still wearing her T-shirt and underwear but no jeans. She arched a brow at him and he grinned again.

"You wouldn't have been comfortable in jeans. I was just helping you out." He gave her his most innocent look—a look designed to charm the pants off her, had she been wearing any.

"Nathan." Her voice was a warning as she scooted farther toward her side of the bed.

He moved quickly, hovering over her, pinning her between his hands at either side of her shoulders. "Jess, come on. Nothing happened. Can't we just enjoy the last couple of days I have on the ranch without overthinking every detail?" His eyes held a question she wasn't sure she could answer. His hand found her cheek and he caressed it. "Please?"

His words hit her like a semitruck. He was leaving in two days, and it was likely that she would never see him again. Never get the chance to feel like this in his arms again. This man who'd reminded her what it was to be a woman, to feel again. The man who'd likely saved her ranch and encouraged her to follow her heart. Her palm brushed over the five o'clock shadow covering his jaw, and she shivered at the delicious rasp against her hand. This was exactly what she'd tried to protect herself from—the broken heart that would follow his departure. But for all her reluctance and reservations, she hadn't been able to stop her heart from plunging forward. Why was she denying them both these last few days? It wasn't going to make losing him again hurt any less.

"What are you thinking about, Jess?" His voice was gravelly, and it was sexy as hell, warming her from head to toe.

"You," she whispered. "Me."

He bent down, barely brushing his lips against hers in the softest, most gentle kiss she'd ever experienced, and she felt her entire body explode with yearning. Her fingers dove into his hair, and she pulled him closer, wanting more. Nathan ended the kiss too quickly, rolling away from her and off the bed.

"You have eight kids who are going to be demanding breakfast in an hour. We need to get up."

"What?" She blinked dumbly, wondering what just happened. "But…"

His eyes shone with mischievous humor. "But nothing. Get up, lazy bones." He reached for her hand and pulled her to standing. Without warning, he met her at the edge of the bed and slid his hands down her back, cupping her rear and making her shiver as she caught herself with her hands on his waist. She felt his erection pressing hard against her belly. There was no doubt that he wanted her as much as she wanted him, but he was denying them both. His mouth sought hers, his tongue sweeping against hers, scorching her, branding her as his. Suddenly, he picked up her jeans from the floor and pressed them into her hands.

"Shower, and make it quick. I'll start pancakes in the kitchen."

"Wait, what…" He turned and hurried to the door before she could figure out what had just happened. She raised a hand to her lips, still trembling from his touch. "Nathan?"

He stopped and looked back at her over his shoulder, grinning. "Don't worry, Jess. I have plans for you tomorrow."

He headed down the stairs, leaving her to speculate about what his plans might entail. She threw the jeans onto the bed and rubbed her hands over her arms. She wasn't sure what he had in mind, but now that she'd decided to take full advantage of his last few days on the ranch, her plans included him, naked, in her bed again.

NATHAN SEARCHED THE pantry for the pancake mix. It had almost killed him to lie with Jessie pressed against him all night long and do nothing. Sure, he could've left her and headed to his cabin, but he wasn't a complete idiot. With only two days left to convince her that this was a relationship worth fighting for, he needed to prove to her that he wasn't going anywhere for long. He just had no idea how to do that. He cracked several eggs into a large mixing bowl and poured in the mix. Maybe Bailey or Julia would have some ideas—if he dared confess his feelings about Jessie to them.

Nathan heard boots tromping into the kitchen. Justin stopped short in the doorway, and laughter burst from him. "Well, look at you, getting all domestic."

Justin's teasing didn't bother him. "Keep it up and you get to go hungry this morning."

"I don't care; this is too good to pass up." He jerked his phone from his pocket and took a picture of Nathan cooking.

"Hey," Nathan yelled, swiping at Justin's hand, nearly grabbing the phone. "If I see that picture online, I'll kill you."

"Yeah? You and what army?"

"No army. I'll just call Tatiana Banks and tell her you're looking for a wife." Nathan knew the barb would hit its mark. The only time Justin had given in and had a one-night stand in college, she'd turned out to be a crazy stalker who camped outside their dorm room for weeks.

Justin cringed. "Fine, here, take the phone." He shoved the device toward Nathan. "Please. Just don't call her."

They laughed easily, the way only longtime friends could. Nathan knew that if he wanted to tell Justin about his feelings for Jessie, now was his chance. He heard the shower turn on overhead and he had a hard time dragging his mind from the visions of Jess under the water, his hands moving over her soap-slickened body. He shot Justin a sideways glance as his friend retrieved a cup and filled it with coffee.

"So, what did Jess con you into helping with today?"

"She didn't *con* me into anything; I offered. She wants to take the kids up to The Ridge on horseback then fishing at the river."

"Listen to you. You'd think you'd been out here a lot longer than a week." He laughed into his mug. "We might turn you into a redneck yet."

"I'd like to do something nice for her tonight. To thank her for letting me stay."

"Would you, now?" Justin arched a brow, pausing with his cup halfway to his mouth. "That'd better be the only reason."

Nathan didn't meet his friend's gaze.

"Dude, please tell me you haven't gone and fallen for my sister. You're not her type, any more than she's yours."

Nathan prayed Justin couldn't see the truth written clearly on his face. This wasn't the way to break it to him.

"Besides, I love ya, man, but I know your track record, and I've seen you on enough tabloids. You'll break my sister's heart, just like the rest of the women you date, and then I'll have to break your neck. She's not like one of your models." Justin sat on the edge of the kitchen table.

"Jessie'd never fit in with your crowd. Remember how your parents reacted when they met me?" Justin rose and dumped his coffee down the drain before slapping Nathan's shoulder. "Besides, you don't stand a chance. Jess would never fall for a city boy. She needs someone to stay here. She'll never leave the ranch. This place is her soul."

Nathan knew everything Justin was saying was true, but every point he made felt like a stake to Nathan's heart. Justin wasn't bringing up anything he hadn't thought of already, but he'd been so taken by the way she made him feel, that he'd pushed these things to the back of his mind. They were things they could deal with later.

But Justin was right. She wouldn't fit into his lifestyle of high-power dinners and yacht club soirees, nor would his family ever accept her. When his father had threatened to ruin Heart Fire, and Jessie, if he ever went back, he had known he had to cut ties with Jessie and Justin to protect them. Even now, if he wanted to, his father could raise enough red flags that it would be near impossible for Nathan to get Jessie the donors she was going to need to fund the ranch. It was better to keep his whereabouts quiet, at least for a little longer.

What was he thinking? Jessie deserved far better than a man who wanted to keep his relationship with her hidden, like she was a dirty secret. One who'd abandoned her at the first sign of a threat, even if he did believe he was doing the right thing. She deserved someone who adored her and wouldn't, *couldn't*, leave her side. Someone who would stand up for her, no matter how high the price. Someone who knew how to unload hay and saddle a horse. She needed someone who could do the chores around the ranch all day and love her throughout the night. And, even if he wanted to be, it wasn't the man he was.

Just the thought of another man holding Jessie in her bed, another man making her smile, sent an ache of emptiness through him. Jessie was his. He didn't even want to think about another man driving her wild, making her want to try to seduce him. He threw the eggshells down the drain and flipped on the disposal.

"You okay?" Justin gave his friend an odd look.

"I'm fine." Nathan knew his voice belied his clipped words. He was pissed—at Justin, at his father but, more than anyone, at himself. "I just said I wanted to do something nice. Forget it."

"Need any help?" Jessie sauntered into the room, her damp hair hung in waves around her face, and as she reached behind her to pull it back on her head. She hurried over to the griddle where he'd already started the first batch of pancakes. "Or are you trying to burn breakfast?"

Justin laughed and rinsed out his mug, leaving the cup in the sink. "I should have warned you not to let this guy cook," he teased. "This rich kid's pretty much helpless unless he's counting money."

Nathan frowned and clenched his jaw hard enough for it to hurt his temples. He knew Justin was joking, but he wasn't an imbecile, and he didn't like having his upbringing thrown in his face. That wasn't who he was either. He'd worked hard to shed that reputation, to prove himself as more than the son of a senator. More than a rich kid with a trust fund—because that trust fund had been a nonexistent illusion, a smoke screen for his father's criminal activities. Nathan had never seen a dime.

"You all right?" Jessie slid her hand down his arm, and he felt anger curl through him. He moved away from her to flip the pancakes and gain control of his raging fury.

This entire situation was ridiculous. He should be able to stay with her if he wanted to, to love her if he wanted to. *Wait…love?* Denial started spinning excuses in his head. He didn't love Jessie. He *couldn't* love Jess. He'd already established a long time ago that "love" was a word that meant nothing.

"Nathan?"

"Good morning," Susanne chirped as she entered the kitchen. Jessie passed her a mug and poured her some coffee. "The troops are up and clamoring for food. I've got them staged on the back patio for now." She laughed as she accepted the mug of steaming coffee. "Jessie, you have no idea how much I needed this."

Nathan was grateful for the interruption—if for no other reason than it derailed his outrageous fairy tale notions of romance. He had no idea where this relationship was going to end up but he wasn't going to let a few semantics ruin what they could have. She was his, and he wasn't giving her up.

Chapter Twenty-One

NATHAN SPENT THE entire morning watching Jessie laugh with the kids, taking them up to The Ridge, keeping them herded like cattle as Mitch and Clint pulled up the rear of the group. Everyone was having a great time on the ride. Everyone but him. He kept replaying his conversation with Justin and wondering why he didn't just tell his friend how he felt about Jessie.

He cared about Jessie more than he'd ever cared about anyone. He knew what they shared was special: She was a one-of-a-kind woman and had opened up doors he'd locked for years, even a few he'd forgotten about. He couldn't imagine a day without her. *So, why didn't you just say that?*

Because he was afraid Justin wouldn't believe him. They might have spent years without communicating, but Justin knew him. He'd filled his loveless life with other women, not caring how shallow those relationships had proven. In fact, he'd wanted them that way. Nathan had spent his entire life trying not to be like his father, but in the end, he'd become just like him, living the life his father had laid out for him. Instead of shedding the life of privilege and entitlement, he'd embraced it with both hands. Sure, he had become successful in his own right, earning more than most men ever would, but it wasn't enough to fill the void. He'd gone searching, letting the hollow pursuit lead the way down this path he had grown to hate.

He had to find a chance to talk to Justin, to make him understand how he felt about Jessie.

"Kinda quiet today," Steve said as he rode up beside him. "Susanne told me there was some tension in the kitchen this morning." He chuckled. "I'll never understand how that wife of mine seems to get herself into the middle of everything."

"I've just got a lot on my mind."

Nathan hadn't really said anything, but Steve nodded as if he understood. "Could it have something to do with a pretty girl who fell asleep on you last night by the fire?" Nathan turned to look at the other man. "I don't mean to pry, but I've seen the way the two of you look at one another." He laughed and looked at the kids ahead of them. "We all have. The two of you were all the girls wanted to talk about when they went to their cabin last night, according to Susanne."

"We're just old friends."

"Friendship is a good place to start. But I think you have more than friendship in mind," Steve agreed. "Looks like she does, too."

"I'm leaving on Monday to head back to my regular life." Nathan said. Dread made his stomach roll, coiling it up in a knot that made him feel sick.

Steve shrugged. "When are you coming back?"

"I'm not."

"I see." Steve wiped a hand over his mouth. "I know it's none of my business, but why wouldn't you? You don't seem thrilled about leaving, so what do you have there that's so much more important than what you have right in front of you? You said it yourself the other day; you've never found anything quite like it." He turned his solemn brown eyes toward Nathan. "Trust me, when you find a woman worth fight for, you fight for her." A smile crept to his lips as Susanne looked back at him and waved. "I know."

JESSIE SET UP one tent, while Mitch and Clint set up the tents for themselves and directed the kids on setting up theirs. They'd been perfect employees—great at entertaining the kids, full of boundless energy, and neither complained at doing any of the tedious chores. In short, she was planning to talk to Jennifer early next week to feel out the possibility of hiring them full time. They were exactly what she needed on the ranch, whether she took in guests or only horses.

She watched Nathan as he and Steve unsuccessfully tried to set up their tent, laughing at their own incompetence. She wandered over to where they stood, pausing to throw the horses some hay in the corral.

"You boys look like you need some help."

Steve chuckled, looking up from the directions as he tried to pry two mismatched poles apart. "What gave it away? That we are the furthest from being done or because even my wife can put one up faster than I can?"

Jessie looked over at Susanne, who was sliding the last pole into her tent, and shrugged. "It's a woman thing. We read directions."

Steve made a promise to Jessie. "I'll tell you what, you put this one together with Nathan, and I'll be in charge of the kids at the campfire tonight and let you get some sleep." He shot a glance at Nathan and immediately handed off the instructions, walking toward his wife.

"What was *that* about?"

"I'm not exactly sure, but I think it has something to do with the fact that Susanne and Steve have aspirations of becoming matchmakers."

"Oh." Jessie wasn't sure whether Nathan would balk at the idea or not. This morning since walking in on him and Justin at breakfast, he seemed withdrawn. She wasn't sure whether they were moving forward or if he wanted to take a leap backward.

Nathan stared down at the instructions in his hands. "I think we need to talk tonight."

Her heart stopped for a moment before her stomach dropped to her toes. "Okay."

It didn't sound promising. In fact, he sounded apologetic. She took a deep breath, preparing for the stab of the knife that would cut out her heart. If she busied herself with the tent, maybe he wouldn't see the pain she knew she couldn't hide. She squatted down on the balls of her feet, stuffed a pole through the top of the nylon tent, and moved to the other side to repeat the movement with the next pole.

"Jess." Nathan's voice was quiet, gently cajoling, and she looked up without wanting to. "It's not what you think."

"I'm not thinking anything," she lied, quickly looking away.

Nathan moved to squat beside her and took her hands in his, his eyes gleaming with intensity. "We've already established what a bad liar you are. There are just a few things you and I need to figure out. Get some of the stuff in here," he said, pointing at her forehead, "out into the open and deal with it. For both of our sakes."

Her heart thudded painfully against her ribs. Since she had no real baseline to establish where this conversation might lead, he was scaring her. It could be anything from him wanting to say good-bye now to him not wanting to say good-bye at all. Her initial instinct was to hide, to run away from either extreme, and remain safe in the cocoon of the ranch, sheltered from anything and anyone who might demand more of her than she was comfortable giving. But Nathan was different. In spite of her fear and their past, she wanted to give him everything, to give a relationship with him a chance. Now if only she had the nerve to tell him how she felt.

"All right," she agreed.

"But we should probably get this tent up first." He looked back at the laughing teens. "And feed this crew."

"Bailey is bringing dinner when she comes up."

He arched a brow. "Bailey's coming?"

"In a little bit. She's fixing dinner at the house and bringing it up, along with dessert. Then she'll stay with me in my tent and help fix breakfast in the morning. Why?"

"Just what I need." Nathan shook his head. "Another ball breaker watching me like a hawk."

Chapter Twenty-Two

NATHAN WATCHED AS the sun dropped low, ready to fall behind the edge of The Ridge and dip into the water of the river. The kids were already laughing around the campfire. Clint and Mitch were stoking it into a bonfire with very vocal supervision from Bailey, while Steve strummed away on his guitar. He'd been surprised when Bailey pulled the guitar from the items she'd stashed in the back seat of the truck. She'd remembered everything, including the blanket and special dessert he'd texted and asked her to bring for Jessie. He owed her; maybe he'd rethink that revenge he was planning for her interruption at his cabin.

She'd even thought to park the truck far enough away from the group that he could have some privacy with Jessie while they watched the sunset. He needed to remember to get her a special gift for this. Bailey might be a ball breaker, but she had his back.

Spreading the blanket in the bed of the truck, Nathan opened the back door and called Jessie over. "I need some help with this."

She frowned but made her way toward him. "What's wrong? I thought we already got everything out and—"

Nathan pulled her toward him and pressed her up against the truck before dipping his head to capture her lips. He'd been dying to kiss her since this morning when he'd left her warm and rumpled in her bed, promising a special surprise. This might not be the Ritz, but with the sun melting behind a few hazy clouds tingeing the sky pink, purple, and blue, holding this beautiful temptation in his arms, this moment was worth a million dollars.

His tongue swept against her lips, coaxing her to open to him. She didn't disappoint, sighing as she allowed him access to her sweetness. Her arms circled his waist, her hands gliding over his back as she drew him closer. Nathan groaned against her lips. When a loud burst of laughter came from the campfire, Nathan eased away from her with painstaking slowness, unsure whether he was annoyed or grateful for the company. As long as they were present, he wouldn't let his desire get out of hand.

Jessie whimpered quietly in protest, her fingers digging into the muscles of his back, making his erection strain against his jeans. He brushed his thumb over her jawline as he withdrew.

"Don't you want your surprise?"

He smiled down at her and loved the flicker of excitement that lit her eyes. There was no doubt about it. Jessie thrilled him like no woman ever had. He might not be willing to call it love, but he was willing to admit what they shared was special.

"That wasn't it?"

"Woman," he scolded, chuckling quietly, "you're selling me short. I can do better than that." Grasping her hand and bringing it to his lips, he kissed the back of it. "Come here and see."

He took her to the back of the truck where he'd laid out lemon meringue pie and two bottles of her favorite beer. Nathan slid his hands onto her waist and effortlessly lifted her into the back of the truck before joining her.

"How did you do this?" she asked, awed.

"Bailey helped," he admitted. "I wanted tonight to be special." He sat against the back and pulled her down between his legs, brushing her hair back from her face. "Jess, do you realize how much you mean to me? This past week has been incredible." He saw the tears in her eyes as she bit down on her lower lip. "I didn't mean to make you cry."

She shook her head. "It's not that, it's…Nathan, thank you."

He tucked a curl behind her ear. "For what? The ranch?"

"Yes…no." Her fingers ran over his hands, caressing his palms and sending jolts of desire straight to his groin. "I've spent a long time blaming you…for not calling, for never coming back. I wasted so much time and energy trying to be what I thought everyone else wanted that I forgot to find out who I was and what I wanted. And I would have gone on that way, but you reminded me that it's okay to want something for myself." She twined her fingers with his. "For letting me be me again." She looked up at him, her eyes shining with gratitude and, dare he believe, adoration.

"Jess," he whispered.

"Wait, let me finish."

She laid her hand against his chest, and he felt the muscles contract. In fact, every muscle in his body seemed strung tight, ready to snap at the slightest provocation. The thought of leaving her sent pain spiraling through his chest, constricting his lungs, making it impossible to breathe.

"It's been a long time, even before my parents died, since I felt I could really be myself. With my parents, especially my dad, I had to be tough and independent to work with the other guys. Justin and Julia went away to college, but I stayed to help them. They needed me, and part of me liked that, but I had to play a role for them. I thought I had to keep being that way if I wanted the crew to take me seriously. That role stuck, and I've been playing it ever since. It's become such a part of me, of who I am, that I've forgotten how to be anything but the hardass you accused me of being."

"Jess, I—"

"No, I was," she interrupted. "I *am*."

She stopped him with a hand over his mouth. He smiled against her palm and nipped at her fingers playfully. She gasped slightly, her chest heaving, and he pressed a kiss to her hand. Her eyes darkened and he recognized the same need he felt swirling in their depths.

Jess scooted from his lap and straddled his thighs, cupping his face in her fingers. "Nathan, I don't know what will happen after you leave tomorrow, but I don't want to make the same mistake twice. I didn't tell you last time how I felt. I care about you, a lot. Honestly, more than I want to. I know we're different, and we really have nothing in common but…"

Her words tapered off, as if she was afraid to say any more, and her lashes dropped to her cheeks. She looked up at him again from under them. "Say something, please?"

He slid one hand to her back, pulling her toward him, letting the other bury itself in the thick waves of her dark hair. "Jess, I think we are more alike than you realize." He met her gaze, willing her to read the truth in his eyes. "I care about you more than I've ever cared about anyone else. I always have."

She shook her head. "You don't have to say it back. I just wanted—"

"I'm saying it because I mean it." He brushed his lips against hers. "You mean more to me than anyone ever has. I may be leaving tomorrow, Jess, but even Jet, with his snapping teeth, couldn't keep me from coming back."

JESSIE FELT HER heart shoot into the heavens and burst like one of the stars in the night sky. She was certain that every one of the guests could see it happen. She wasn't sure she believed they really had a chance at making this work. She wanted to ask him how it would even be possible. Before she could speak, his mouth found hers, sending her senses spiraling into the sky with her heart. She didn't want to talk, didn't want to argue, she only wanted him. Her arms curled around his shoulders, and the kiss quickly turned from gently seeking to intense and feverish, leaving her breathless when the teens' laughter broke through the haze of their yearning.

A slow blush crept over her cheeks, burning her face, and she was grateful no one could see them. "I should get back."

"Why? Bailey is taking care of everyone. She insisted we have dessert and a little privacy under the stars."

Bailey had no idea how much this meant to Jessie—or maybe she did. Either way, Jessie owed her big time. She would need to thank her cousin appropriately for the gift. Jessie scooted to Nathan's side and curled herself against his chest, her fingers toying absently with the front of his shirt, and smiled up at him.

"I'll agree to a few minutes, but you have to keep this PG. I don't want my guests to wonder what sort of a ranch I run."

He chuckled and pulled her closer, pressing a kiss to her forehead. "No promises."

Jessie sighed, content for the moment simply to be in his arms. Knowing he planned on returning as soon as possible made it easier to let herself relish the complete adoration she had for him. She didn't kid herself, thinking he felt the same way she did—why would a man like Nathan fall in love with a mousey cowgirl with dirt under her nails—but knowing he cared was enough for now. Still, a nagging doubt gnawed at the edges of her mind. He'd promised to return before and had never come back.

"What are you thinking about?" he asked as he brushed a few waves back from her face and looked down at her.

"Nothing."

Nathan grinned. "Liar."

She returned his smile. "Fine," she said, sighing dramatically. "I'm wondering how soon it might be before you are able to come back."

"I have a couple of meetings early in the week, and then I need to meet with my father before I leave New York and head back to LA to check on my place there." She tried to catch the frown before he noticed it. "What?"

Wearing Wranglers, boots, and denim shirts made it easy to forget that he was worth a small fortune and how important his family was. But listening to him talk about business trips and his jet-setting lifestyle with the upper elite and his family, she wasn't sure there was any room in his life for a struggling horse trainer. She pinched her lips together and shook her head.

"Jess," he warned, tipping her chin up so she was forced to meet his gaze. "Don't go second-guessing me—us. Let's take this one day at a time. Right now, that means enjoying the stars in the back of your truck with eight teenagers pretending not to watch us from their campfire."

She eyed the group, gathered around the fire, laughing at one another. Bailey was doing a great job keeping everyone entertained, but people were definitely taking notice of the couple in the back of the truck. She could make out the soft smile on Susanne's face and the wink Bailey shot her. She only wished she felt as confident about their relationship as everyone else seemed to.

SUNDAY AFTERNOON, AS Jessie watched as the kids climbed onto the beat-up bus to head back home, Susanne came up and gave her a quick hug.

"We had so much fun. I'm so glad you were able to do this for us."

Jessie smiled back at her. It had been emotionally trying to do without her parents, but the group reminded her how much she enjoyed the presence of guests, watching others love her home almost as much as she did. However, this part was exactly what she didn't like about the dude ranch—saying good-bye.

"I'm so glad you guys came. I hope we'll see you again soon."

Susanne winked. "Of course you will. We have a winter camp for the kids as well, and this place would be beautiful with a small dusting of snow."

Jessie laughed. "Well, that's about all we get most years, but it's plenty as far as I'm concerned."

Steve and Nathan finished loading the luggage into the bottom compartment of the bus and Steve clapped his hands together. "You about ready, wife?"

"Oh, I forgot my purse in the cabin. Jessie, why don't you walk with me to go get it?"

Steve rolled his eyes as he turned toward Nathan. "Women. They can never keep track of anything."

"Pshhhh, you hush," she replied, waving a hand his way. She didn't leave Jessie a chance to refuse as she put an arm around her waist and dragged her toward the cabin. As they arrived on the porch, Susanne faced Jessie. "I didn't really forget my purse. I just didn't want everyone to hear."

"Hear what?"

"That man loves you, and I think you love him."

"What?" Jessie wasn't sure what to say to Susanne's bold, and obviously irrational, statement. "Nathan? No, we're just..." What were they? Was Nathan her boyfriend? It seemed to simple and explanation for how she felt. "I don't exactly know what we are."

Susanne laughed quietly. "Yeah, Steve and I were like that once, too. I don't mean to meddle, but I can see you two care about each other very much. I'd hate to see you waste too much time fighting it. Trust me. From my experience, it's not worth the fight. It just wastes time and hurts."

"It's complicated."

"When isn't it?" she said, laughing again. "Whatever the complication, you can work through it if you love each other enough."

And there is our problem—we don't love each other—I love him.

There was no sense in denying it any longer. She loved Nathan Kerrington. She'd never stopped. From the moment he'd first stepped on the ranch eight years ago, he'd shattered every preconceived notion of what love should look like. He still turned her world on its head, but she realized she didn't want it any other way.

She loved the way he didn't balk at her temper, the way he could see through her moods to figure out what was underneath, the way he could bring out every emotion she tried to hide. He saw past the front she put up for everyone, moved past it to appreciate the woman behind the mask. Nathan had seen something in her no one had ever tried to find before—not her family and not her friends—and had shown her it was okay to be herself, to want and need and desire something for herself instead of sacrificing every part of her for others. And her heart didn't seem to beat fully unless he was around.

Susanne smiled and placed a comforting hand on her shoulder. "You should see your face right now. It says it all." She shook her head and looked back toward the bus. "You need to tell him whatever it was you were just thinking. He needs to hear it."

They walked back to the bus, and Susanne gave her one last hug before getting on the bus with the kids. Steve shook Nathan's hand and reached for Jessie's. "It was a pleasure to stay here, Jessie. Be sure to save us a week for winter camp. I'll have Susanne call and set it up, if that's okay."

"I'd love that."

"Drive careful, Steve," Nathan said.

"I will." The man eyed Jessie and met Nathan's gaze again. "And you remember what I said."

Jessie was curious about the interchange but didn't want to pry, any more than she wanted Nathan to ask her what Susanne had said. Nathan moved closer and slid his arm around her waist, pulling her to his side as they waved at the departing bus. His fingers slid down to twine with hers.

"Alone at last." She could read the wicked gleam in his eyes, as the green flecks practically glowed with heat.

She laughed, and put one hand against his chest. "Hardly. Bailey is cleaning the cabins, and the guys are in the barn. Not to mention, Aleta is coming back later tonight."

His head dropped forward, his chin against his chest, as he sighed loudly. "And here I thought I had you all to myself."

She laughed at his mock disappointment. "Come on, let's go get something started for these guys to eat. They're going to be raiding the kitchen if we don't feed them soon." She shook her head at him. "Once we get them out, you can have me all to yourself."

Nathan spun her into his arms, walking backward with her in his embrace. He tipped her chin up before pressing a quick kiss to her lips. "You have yourself a deal."

THE KNOCK ON his office door surprised Justin. He hadn't scheduled any appointments after lunch, so he could sneak in a few minutes to gather his weekly receipts for Brendon when he headed into town later in the week.

Brendon's head peered around the edge of the door. "You mind if I come in? I wanted to talk to you about Jessie."

Speak of the devil, Justin thought.

"Aw, man," Justin said with a groan. "We've already had this discussion. She just wasn't interested."

Brendon slumped into one of the chairs in front of Justin's desk and waved him off. "I know that, although I still wish she'd give me another shot." He lifted his booted feet to the edge of Justin's desk and crossed them at the ankles. "I was wondering how much you know about this Kerrington guy. How much do you really trust him?"

Justin paused his perusal of a receipt and set it aside. "He was my roommate in college. He's one of my best friends, I trust him. Why?" Justin could feel a headache coming on and rubbed his thumb against his temple.

"I don't know. Dad didn't like him at all." Brendon shrugged a shoulder. "I just...I couldn't shake this feeling there was more to him, so I looked up a few things when we left your place the other day." He reached into his briefcase and pulled a folder out, dropping it over the pile of receipts in front of Justin. "His family has a pretty colorful record—several indictments for fraud and conspiracy. His father's got tax evasion charges against him now. Is this really the guy you want giving you business advice?"

Justin looked over the documents and printed-out newspaper stories. Nathan told him years ago that he'd never been close to his father, but one of the articles showed him at an event with his arm around his father's shoulders. They'd been out of college for years, only staying in touch by phone. It was a long time and people changed dramatically in less, but he couldn't believe that Nathan would cheat him.

"I called him, not the other way around." Justin frowned as he pushed the folder back toward Brendon. "Just because his father's a crook, doesn't mean he's one. He's a financial analyst."

"So?"

"So, I'm sure there are much more lucrative businesses he works with, and could steal from if he wanted to, rather than a failing dude ranch. He's already worth a small fortune."

"Justin, we both know Heart Fire Ranch is worth a boat load of cash, even struggling. Land can be pretty tempting. If he could get his hands on it…maybe seduce either of your sisters? I'm sure that money would go a long way toward paying his father's attorney fees. Why use his own money when he can use yours, or your sisters'? Not to mention that some of his ideas, they aren't what's best for your family."

"Like what?"

"Well, like stopping payments to Heart Fire Industries, for one. I didn't want to hurt her, but your father wanted to set those payments up so that Jessie didn't drain all three of you dry with these horses of hers. You've seen how much of a toll they've taken on the finances in just a few months."

Justin wanted to disprove Brendon's theory, but he couldn't get his conversation with Nathan over breakfast this morning out of his mind. He couldn't still the nagging doubts circling his mind.

Brendon's feet hit the floor as he leaned forward, bracing his elbows on his knees. "You know him better than I do. But you know what they say about the apple not falling far from the tree." He stood up to leave. "Just keep an eye on Jessie. I'd hate to see her get hurt if this guy is using her. Who knows what he's telling her when you're working here at the clinic?"

Brendon glanced at the receipts Justin had been sorting. "Did you want me to take those with me?"

"No, I'm not finished with them." Justin walked Brendon to the front of the office, holding open the door. "Hey, Brendon, thanks for keeping an eye out for us. It means a lot."

"Anytime, bro. You know I've always got your back."

Justin watched as Brendon slid into the driver's seat of his Mercedes and pulled back out onto the main highway. He didn't like the suspicion twisting in his gut, demanding answers for questions he hadn't thought to ask. How could he have just assumed Nathan was the same as he had been in college? They were both different now, older, wiser, more worldly.

The news clipping of Nathan with his father haunted Justin. They looked pretty cozy for men who didn't get along. He grabbed his keys and flipped the closed sign on the door. He wanted to get home and talk with Jessie. A little reassurance from her would go a long way to settling the unease beginning to gnaw at him.

As usual, lunch was a chaotic fiasco filled with laughter and good-natured ribbing. Mitch and Clint acted more like twin brothers than friends. Jessie reminded herself to call Jennifer to ask about hiring them. Bailey, as was her custom, was a complete smart-ass but Jessie was beginning to wonder if there wasn't something more than friendship brewing between her and the quiet Clint. She found it difficult to imagine her cousin dating a cowboy, especially after all the years of her complaining about them.

Jessie rinsed off the last plate and slid it into the dishwasher before wiping her hands with the towel on the sink. She turned toward the table where Nathan was seated, watching her. She'd felt his eyes following her all through lunch.

Jessie felt like a fumbling idiot when she'd dropped several bottles of water out of the refrigerator and then followed them with the mayonnaise container. Nathan's knowing chuckle didn't do anything to lessen the nervous shiver of yearning that shook her, but when she met his gaze, she could read the same longing in the heated desire she saw in his eyes. She leaned back against the island, her hands at her lower back.

"Well, I'm going to head over to the clinic," Bailey announced. "Unless you want me to stick around." She arched a brow at her cousin, a playful smile curving her lips.

"I think we can manage. Thanks, Bailey."

"I'll just bet you will," she teased. Bailey headed for the back door. "Have fun!"

She'd no more closed the door when Jessie crooked a finger at Nathan.

"You think that's all it takes, woman?" he asked.

"Absolutely." It felt good to tease him, to laugh and enjoy the new ground they were breaking on their relationship.

Nathan moved toward her, his arms wrapping around her waist, lifting her from the floor onto the island and stepping between her thighs. "This has been the longest two days ever. I can't wait to get you upstairs."

Heat seemed to course between them, igniting an impatient demand in her. She wanted him, minus his clothing, right now. She cupped his jaw between her hands and dragged him toward her, biting his lower lip gently. "What are you waiting for?"

Nathan growled and captured her mouth, his tongue dancing with hers, sending her senses twisting in a tornado of desire. She clutched at his back, begging him to take her without words.

"What in the *hell*?" Justin yelled from the doorway.

Jessie jerked backward in surprise, but Nathan held his hand against her cheek for another moment before turning and standing in front of her, protecting her from the full brunt of her brother's wrath.

"I told you to stay away from my sister." Justin clenched his fists at his side, and Jessie could see the dark fury in his eyes. Why would Justin care who she dated? It was none of his business.

"It's not what you think, Justin."

"Sure it's not. I know all about your father's trouble with the law. Is she just a pawn to help you get him out of trouble, a way to get your hands on the ranch? Some kind of publicity stunt?" His eyes flicked to Jessie's. "Or maybe she's just another notch on your bedpost?"

Nathan held his hands up as Justin approached. "I know you're upset, Justin, but I'm not after the ranch. I don't need your money."

Jessie slid from the island and stood by Nathan. "Justin, stop."

"Really?" he went on, ignoring her. "I had a visitor at the clinic today. He gave me a quick rundown of our financial situation, how stopping payments could ruin the rest of us, and how Heart Fire Industries was set up because my father wanted to make sure that Heart Fire Ranch and my sister's kind heart didn't drain us all into oblivion. Then I get here and find you groping her. He warned me you were going to try to use her."

Jessie's mouth dropped open in shock at the accusation in her brother's words. "Brendon?"

Nathan clenched his jaw hard enough for the muscle in his temple to tick. "And you trust him? Over me?"

"He's not the one trying to screw my sister. He also isn't trying to fund a defense for his father against fraud charges." Jessie looked up at Nathan in shock. "Oh, you didn't know about that, Jess? Then you probably don't know about the fact that this isn't the first time. His family has quite the record." Justin shoved against Nathan's chest, knocking him back a step. "I thought you said you didn't talk to them. The picture I saw in the paper, the one of you and your father during his campaign last year, looked pretty chummy."

"Is that true?" Jessie took a step away from him.

"Justin, you've always been my best friend. You have no idea what risk I'm taking to help you, what could happen if it comes out that I'm here. Why would I try to con you?"

Justin looked at Jessie. "If it's so dangerous for us, then why did you come?" Nathan's eyes dropped on Jessie. "Her?"

"Justin, stop. Please," Jessie's voice had lost its defiant tone, leaving her sounding defeated and confused. Nathan tried to meet her gaze but she refused to look at him.

"You know, I sure as hell didn't think you'd stoop low enough to use my sister." He looked over at Jessie and shook his head. "I have no clue who you are anymore."

Jessie couldn't listen to any more. Her stomach was roiling, and she was going to be sick. She'd fallen for it again. Not only had she jeopardized the ranch and her siblings, but she'd made a fool of herself over this man again. She'd believed his lies again. She had to get out of here, away from the two of them. She moved toward the door.

"No, Jess," Nathan began, turning toward her. "At least give me a chance to explain."

She didn't want to hear anything else—no more lies, no more excuses. She didn't need one more reason to feel like more of a failure than she already did. With one hand on her stomach and the other held up, she ran from the room. But not before she saw her brother's arm cock back and heard his fist connect with flesh.

NATHAN CAME TO on the kitchen floor with his jaw throbbing but stinging with cold. He tried to push himself up on an elbow.

"Hang tight, Wall Street."

Bailey.

She removed an ice pack from his jaw and squatted down, looking at him. "You're gonna have a helluva goose egg, and it's gonna leave a bruise." She roughly placed it back, letting her hands dangle between her thighs. "I thought you were smart. Why in the hell would you let Justin think you were using Jess?"

Nathan, still slightly groggy, tried to remember exactly what had happened. He remembered wanting everyone to leave so he could take Jess upstairs, her kissing him—*oh, crap*!

How had Brendon even found out about his dad? So far, his father's lawyer had managed to keep the charges under wraps from the media. At least, that's what his father said. With politics, money talked, and lawyers weren't the most trustworthy if leaking news might get them a leg up on the opposition or some cash in their pocket.

Damn lawyers.

"Bailey, did you read my e-mail? The one from my dad?"

She tipped her head to the side. "Of course I did," she answered unapologetically. "I wasn't going to take a chance that Jess might get hurt. Just because Justin trusted you didn't mean I—"

"Who did you tell?" he interrupted.

He saw the regret flash in her dark eyes. "It was when you first got it. I asked Uncle Trevor to check up on you. I had no idea, Nathan. I'm sorry."

"It's not your fault Justin's jumping to conclusions. If he would've given me a chance, I could have shown him I refused to help my father." He looked up at her from the corner of his eye, trying to see around the ice pack. "I'm not trying to con Jessie."

She stood up and helped him to a chair. "I know that. You think I'd be helping you now if I thought you were?" She grinned at him. "I'd have kicked you while you were on the floor and helpless."

"I have no doubt," he muttered, trying to figure out how he was going to convince Jessie of the truth. "Where's Jess?"

Bailey handed him a bottle of water and two aspirin, twisting her lips to the side of her mouth and biting the corner of her mouth. "She told me to tell you to leave tonight and not to come back."

Chapter Twenty-Three

NATHAN'S PLANE TOUCHED down, a day earlier than
he'd planned, and he rubbed his eyes as exhaustion
sapped what little strength he had left from his limbs.
He had barely made his way to the luggage carousel and
grabbed his bag, when he turned to see a limo driver
holding a sign with his name. Gratitude flooded him as
he climbed into the luxury vehicle and poured himself a
scotch, downing it in one gulp, praying it would dull the
ache settling in his chest.

He rubbed at it with the heel of his hand before scrubbing his hands over his two-day beard growth. He must
look like a mess with his rumpled suit, crooked tie, and
unshaven face. Not at all the man who'd left New York
only a week ago. But his haggard appearance didn't hold
a candle to the way he felt inside.

Jess had disappeared, not even allowing him an
opportunity to defend himself. Justin, his once best

friend, had immediately assumed he was trying to con them, and there was still the matter of Jessie's financial woes. He wasn't stupid enough to believe that one meeting with Brendon and his father would be enough to remedy her situation. Stopping the mysterious payments had only been a Band-Aid on a gaping wound.

The car pulled up to his hotel. He waved off the porter, carrying his own bag and pulling out his key as the elevator doors opened. Looking around, he found himself struck by the ostentatiousness of the building. Everything from the mirrored walls to the gold filigree trim screamed of money and wealth, yet there was a stench surrounding it now. Maybe it was simply the lack of fresh air, he reasoned. Purified air enveloped him, but he missed the scent of pine and dust and horses. And the sweet citrus vanilla scent of Jessie's soap that clung to her, in spite of working outdoors.

Nathan shook his head, trying to rid his mind of the visions that plagued him since he'd come to on the kitchen floor. He made his way through the hotel suite and dropped his bag on the bed before heading to the liquor cabinet. It was practically calling his name from the tray on the bar. He filled a glass with scotch, adding another two fingers for good measure. He let his body fold onto the couch, staring out at the city skyline through the wall of windows.

It didn't matter that it was barely four in the afternoon. He wanted to get drunk enough to forget it all—the ranch, the fury and betrayal in Justin's face, the pain he saw in Jessie's eyes.

He wasn't sure how she could believe the lies Brendon spewed, especially after the night they'd just shared. He'd just told her how much he cared, that he'd never felt this way for anyone.

But not the complete truth.

He hadn't told her about his family's criminal history or how he was helping the federal government indict his father for hiding campaign money in offshore accounts. He didn't tell her about his father's threats in the past to destroy her family's reputation, about the risk being there put them in.

Or that you loved her.

He tossed back the rest of the glass. Love. His mother *loved* his father; his parents claimed to *love* him and his sister; his father *loved* his job. What did it even mean? After years of hearing it tossed casually from the lips of shallow, vindictive people, it should mean nothing.

Except he'd wanted to say it to Jessie.

He'd found himself with *I love you* ready to tumble from his lips several times over the past two days, but he'd stopped himself with the excuse that it wasn't real, that they were playing in a fantasy. That soon, one of them would wake up. But he knew that wasn't true either. He'd spent the last eight years chasing the memory of her, trying to find a way to fill the void that had been left in his life after losing her the first time. How long would it take this time?

Nathan got up and refilled his glass. He knew he was well on his way to getting drunk, prayed he could just pass out and wake tomorrow with a new perspective. Maybe he only felt this way because he'd been in such close proximity to her for the last week, working together almost twenty-four hours a day. Maybe coming back to New York was the best thing for them both, giving them the distance they needed to put this relationship in perspective. Maybe he'd be fine in a couple days and find that it was nothing more than a mutual attraction based on lust.

If that were the case, why did his chest ache? Why did he feel so empty? Why couldn't he stop thinking about the way those blue eyes had looked up at him with complete trust last night? Knowing Jessie believed he'd failed her was going to haunt him. He needed to drown his pain in this bottle tonight because he knew the answer to each of his questions—he'd just lost the only part of his life worth living for.

JESSIE STOOD IN the barn, staring at the stalls around her. She needed to work Jet, but she wasn't in any frame of mind to give him the attention and focus he needed. What she should do was saddle one of the mares she was training and take her to the river, someplace where she could think without Justin's voice in her ear. She headed toward the tack room and grabbed the bucket of brushes, but instead of haltering the mare, she leaned back against the wall and slid to the floor, burying her face in her hands and fighting the tears that burned her eyes.

What was wrong with her? Why couldn't she do anything right? Was she just doomed to tear their entire family apart? How in the world had she fallen for his lies again? When was this pain going to stop?

So far Julia and Bailey had both jumped to Nathan's defense, citing jealousy as Brendon's motivation for disparaging him. Justin, however, was just as certain that Brendon was right. Confessing their relationship years ago hadn't swayed Justin. In fact, it had done the opposite, as he claimed it proved Nathan had always been a liar. The arguments had gone back and forth for hours after Nathan had left, with no one backing down.

Jessie, on the other hand, wasn't sure what to think. She found it difficult to justify the man who'd made love to her with the con artist Brendon and Justin claimed him to be. But that only made her distrust her own judgment that much more. A con artist wouldn't have advertised he was using her. Not being able to tell he was faking would have been the point. She ran her fingers through her hair, her chin sagging forward, while the sharp ache in her chest stabbed like knives, clawing into her, tearing at her psyche, ripping her confidence to shreds. She was an idiot.

"Jess?" She looked up to see her sister wander into the barn, her latest dog in training, a massive longhaired German shepherd, at her leg. "Are you all right?"

"I'm fine." The words didn't connect with her tone. Even as she started to push herself to standing, she found she didn't have the strength to move. The dog moved toward her and buried his furry head under her chin.

"Somehow I don't believe you, and neither does Moose."

Julia sat on the ground beside her, letting the dog lay between them, his head resting on Jessie's leg as she stroked the top of his head. "I think this one's a winner, Julia," she murmured, smiling down at the golden brown eyes that looked up at her sadly. "He's a sweetie."

Her sister ran a hand over the shepherd's back. "He's pretty intuitive. He whined until I followed him out here and found you."

"Why would he do it, Julia? What would he hope to gain? A failing ranch? He has money. He doesn't need this place to help his father unless it's just for good PR like Justin said." Jessie shook her head. "But even that just doesn't make sense."

"Which is what Bailey and I have been saying all along." She sighed. "I know Justin is upset, but I think once he stops and listens, really looks at the evidence, he's going to see that Nathan wasn't trying to betray him. The man was—*is*—in love with you."

"Okay, then why would Brendon lie?"

"He didn't." Jessie's eyes snapped up to meet hers. "Not really. Everything he said about Nathan's father was true. He just let Justin make assumptions from there." Julia shook her head. "You know Brendon. He was a sneaky, conniving kid, and he's always been so cocky that you'd eventually get together with him, like he has you in his back pocket. He can't stand you falling for someone other than him." She shook her head and Moose rolled his soft brown eyes to look up at Julia's face before turning them back to Jessie. "I don't trust him, and neither do the dogs. I don't always trust my instincts anymore, but I sure trust theirs."

Julia's voice was sadly reminiscent, reminding Jessie of Julia's own tumultuous past relationships. Jessie reached for her hand, trying to comfort her sister. "And Justin—"

"Is being a fool," Julia cut her off. "He's upset, Jess. Ever since Mom and Dad died, he wants to take care of us. He's trying to watch out for us." She shook her head and scratched behind the dog's ear. "But we're grown women. We don't need him to protect us. Look, I don't remember much about that summer Nathan was here but, I do remember how happy you were. When he left, something in you died. You changed. This past week, I've seen that spark in you again. The one we only see when you're with the horses. I understand you're afraid to believe in him after the way he left the last time, but you've changed. Why can't you believe that he has, too?"

Jessie sighed. If Julia was right, Jessie might have just let the only man she'd ever loved slip away again because she'd been too afraid to let go of this belief that she was destined to fail her family again, too afraid to trust her instincts. Instead, she'd run away and failed Nathan, the man who still held her heart.

NATHAN FORCED A broad smile to his lips and clapped the CEO on the back. In truth, he should be the happiest man in the room. He'd just finished conducting a merger between two Internet tycoons and had earned three times his usual substantial fee. But, as he stepped into the elevator, begging off celebratory drinks, the success felt shallow. As the doors closed, he sighed and loosened his silk tie, aching to get back to his penthouse to pack. He'd already called and moved his flight up, wanting nothing more than to get back to his office in Los Angeles to pick up where he'd left off. Well, there was one thing he wanted more, but Jessie still hadn't called him.

He wanted to give in and call her, but wasn't sure it would do any good. She'd told him to leave, hadn't even given him a chance to explain, so he doubted she'd have taken his calls anyway. Instead, he was going to use this time to prove to her he hadn't been lying. The first step was to figure out who was officially the CFO of Heart Fire Industries. Then he wanted to find out why and where all of the money taken from Heart Fire Ranch had gone. It had only been three days since he'd left the ranch, but in a quick cursory check, he'd seen that since the halt of the weekly payments, the mysterious account had been depleted by several daily withdrawals. He had to find out who had made them and why.

Nathan pulled out his cell phone and dialed his secretary. "Cassandra, I need a flight scheduled to Sacramento Airport tomorrow. And this time, I need a hotel and a rental car."

"You're leaving again, already? You haven't even gotten back to your office yet," his secretary complained. "I have a ton of phone calls for you to return, and you probably forgot about your appointment with the investors you told me to schedule last week."

He had. He'd called her after Jessie told him her dream for the ranch. If he could talk them into investing in her idea, a rescue for abused horses and a retreat for at-risk youth, her money problems would be solved. Nathan ran a hand through his hair and rubbed his temple, trying to massage away the migraine forming behind his eyes.

"Okay, make the flight for Friday; then clear my weekend and the week after." She sighed into the phone, her exasperation with him evident. She'd been working with him since the beginning of his career, and he knew she was indispensable. "Just do it. After today, I think a raise is in your future."

"Are you trying to bribe me, Mr. Kerrington?" Cassandra laughed quietly at him and hung up the phone.

Nathan went cold. He knew she was joking, but bribery, extortion, conspiracy, tax fraud...white-collar crime seemed to run in his genes. Justin's accusations weren't too far off the truth, but Nathan refused to become like his father. He would never stand for what he'd done, what he continued to do. Nathan wasn't going to tarnish the rest of his future because of his family or their threats.

He caught a glimpse of himself in the mirrored reflection of the elevator. In his high-power Armani, Rolex, and two-hundred-dollar tie, he was the picture of high finance and wealth. He looked just like his father.

He jerked the tie loose and ripped it from his neck, unbuttoning the shirt at his throat. He was finished with this lifestyle. He'd earned enough money over the past few years that he could support Heart Fire Ranch singlehandedly if Jessie would let him. Nathan couldn't wait to turn his back on everything he'd worked for—the success, the fame, the recognition—and work with her, side by side in the middle of nowhere in those uncomfortable jeans and dusty boots.

Guilt and regret knifed through him, slicing him to the core. She'd trusted him and he'd let her down. Let her believe the worst. Let her believe that he didn't love her more than everything else.

God, how he loved her.

He couldn't deny it any longer. The past three days—hoping his phone would ring, praying every caller was Jessie—had been hell on earth. He needed her the way he needed blood in his veins. The way he felt for her had only grown stronger being away from her. She hadn't just made him *feel* more alive, she'd been the air he needed to breathe. And he was slowly suffocating here without her. Jessie wasn't like the other women. She didn't make him try to be better; she made him a completely different man.

Nathan didn't blame Justin for feeling the way he did, for immediately turning against him and believing the worst. Nathan had kept secrets from him about his family. Finding out the person you were trusting with your financial information was from a family of criminals, then to see that man kissing your sister, Justin had been blindsided.

Justin had seen the trail of broken hearts Nathan left behind in college. Nathan had scoffed at the tabloids over the years when they featured him with another famous actress or model he'd left behind. But, coupled with his relentless pursuit of success and the money that followed, a legacy from his father and grandfather, not telling Justin had sealed his fate. Why would Justin want that for his sister? No one would.

Nathan was going to fix this. He was leaving this crap behind, and he was going to remedy this situation with Justin, once and for all.

"ABOUT DAMN TIME you're back. You were supposed to meet me in New York."

Nathan looked up as he entered his apartment to find his father pouring himself a drink from Nathan's supply of twenty-five-year-old Scotch. "What are you doing here?"

"Now, is that any way to greet your father? You sound disappointed." Nathan watched as he swallowed the drink. His father looked haggard, older than he had the last time he'd seen him. But he supposed a criminal trial had that effect, especially when you were losing. "Are you finished playing cowboys? I need you here to work your magic on a few campaign contributors and help deposit the funds into the proper accounts."

His father ambled toward the couch, putting a finger into the knot of his tie and working it down as Nathan dropped his keys into an antique bowl beside the door.

"Had me followed again? I'd have thought you'd be using every dime on your defense." He slid his hands into his pockets and turned to face his father. "I already told you I'm not having any part of this. I'm sorry you made some bad decisions. I'm not getting involved." Nathan took a step toward his father, narrowing his eyes as the man took a step backward.

"Shut up! Anyone could be listening. They could have this place wired."

Nathan simply glared at his father, waiting for him to reveal his motive for lying in wait in Nathan's apartment. His father's dark brown eyes grew cold and he narrowed them at Nathan. "I thought you got my point when I told you to stay away from that family. I warned you what would happen if you didn't."

"What are you going to do? Threaten to disown me again? Cut me off? I'm not a kid anymore. I've got more money behind me to protect them than you do to ruin them, and they have far less to lose than you do. If you go after them, who knows what information might fall into the Feds' hands. There are doctored books, bank routing numbers, and so many contributors who would love to hear how you cheated them. I'm sure the prosecutor would just love for your son to change his mind and testify against you." Nathan turned his back on his father and carried his bag into his bedroom. "Look, I'm tired. I've just landed from my third flight in three days. I don't have the energy to deal with you tonight."

His father followed him. "What's gotten into you? You never minded my business decisions when I was putting you through college or while you were a struggling intern." He jerked at Nathan's arm.

Nathan shook his head, feeling sick to his stomach. "You disgust me. The people you've crushed to get to the top, the lives you've ruined just to stay there…I'm glad I got away from you before you dragged me down, too."

"That's right, Mr. High and Mighty. You've never had any underhanded dealings on your way to the top of the ladder, have you?" Nathan's father stabbed a finger at his chest.

Nathan crossed his arms, letting his father take his best shot. He wasn't going to let the man threaten him any longer. He wasn't always proud of his choices, but at least he could say he stayed on the right side of the law, even if it was a fine tightrope at times.

"I've never crushed people along the way. I would never slander a family just because they didn't serve a purpose for me."

"This is about that damn cowgirl whore and her brother again?" His father laughed. "You can't possibly be serious about her."

Nathan cleared the space between them in only two strides, grasping his father by the front of his shirt. "If I ever hear you talk about Jessie again, or her family, you're going to wish a criminal trial was the least of your worries."

His father tried to brush Nathan's hands away, looking surprised when he didn't let go. "You won't do anything. Besides, you wouldn't want to see anything happen to that nice ranch or anyone on it."

Nathan loosened his hands, letting his father stumble backward to catch his balance. "I wouldn't advise you to test me, Father. I think we both know that you will come out on the losing end of this battle. I promise you that."

At that, his father did something Nathan had never seen him do before—he gave up.

"You *have* to help me. I can't go to prison, Nathan. I'll be ruined." His eyes were wild, desperate and pathetic, as he searched the room like a trapped animal looking for an escape.

Nathan turned away from his father, squaring his shoulders for the verbal assault he expected, but he was too worn out to care any longer. "You're already ruined.

You destroyed your reputation and the family name. You've thrown it all away." He ran a hand through his hair. "It's over, and you lost. You got caught. Pay the two million in fines and serve your time. They'll probably only give you probation anyway."

"I'll lose my job. You're really going to let your mother and sister suffer, too? I didn't raise you to be a selfish bastard."

"Are you kidding? You were the best teacher I could have had." Nathan gave him a sardonic laugh. "As far as Mother and Katrina are concerned, I'll take care of both of them. Now, get out." He pointed toward the door. "Don't come back again, because I won't be here."

"But, where—"

"Gone." Nathan opened the front door of his apartment. "Good luck with your trial, Father. You're going to need it."

JESSIE LED JET into the corral. Today would be his first ride since arriving on the ranch and, as long as everything went well, a major milestone they'd achieve together. Thanks to Moose, who was now ever-vigilant and present, she'd finally stopped crying herself to sleep, phone in hand, wanting desperately to hear Nathan's voice. And Jet was learning to trust people again, due in large part to the extra time and attention she'd shown him this past week while trying to keep her mind off Nathan. She glanced down at the dog trotting quietly beside her. She hadn't expected him to stay after her talk with Julia in the barn, but after thirty minutes of tears, when her sister rose to leave, Moose refused to lift his head from her lap. Julia informed her he was doing exactly what he was trained to do as a therapy dog—heal pain and distress— and insisted he stay.

Jessie had to admit she loved having him around, especially after everyone went home in the evenings, leaving her in the large, abnormally quiet house alone. She'd begun sleeping in one of the guest rooms, unable to even think about going near her room or shower without tears threatening. Her heart may have scabbed over, but in some ways, she was afraid that this time she would never completely heal. There would always be a scar from Nathan Kerrington, and it was painfully ugly.

"Stay, Moose," she commanded the dog, giving him the signal her sister taught her. Moose lay to the right side of the gate while she walked through but never took his golden eyes off her as she walked Jet to the middle of the corral.

"Don't you dare make me look stupid, Jet." She muttered the warning to the horse under her breath. His ears flicked back, listening to her voice. "You know I'm not going to hurt you."

She put one foot into the stirrup, holding the reins with her left hand, and stood, letting the horse feel her weight. He raised his head slightly, and she felt his muscles bunch, but he relaxed as he turned toward her. "Good boy," she murmured. "This is going to be so easy for you."

Jessie swung her leg over Jet's back and lowered herself into the saddle slowly. His rear instantly curled under him and she continued to soothe him with her words, watching his ears twist back and forth as he decided whether to put his trust in the person he'd come to know or fall back on his past experiences of abuse and betrayal.

She ran her fingers over his neck, coaxing him, all the while, inwardly pleading with him to believe in her, to trust her and know she cared about him too much to hurt him. She wanted him to feel the truth through her caress on his neck and the tone of her voice as she spoke. She needed him to remember that, while other humans had treated him badly and done unforgivable things, she wasn't like them. His body began to relax under her, and he started to lower his head, moving forward into a walk.

She let him find his own way around the corral, barely directing him, but wanting to cheer for the progress he made. The simple fact was that he'd chosen to put his faith in her.

Why couldn't you do the same with Nathan?

Jessie froze in the saddle, and Jet immediately tensed beneath her. "Easy boy," she murmured.

Nathan had gentled her the same way she had the scared animal. And, just like Jet, she believed she had her reasons to distrust him. But, instead having faith in Nathan, she'd run again, regardless of the fact that he'd given her every reason to believe in him. She'd rejected Nathan and the knowledge crushed her. She was an idiot. She'd thrown everything they'd shared away because of an accusation. She should have known better.

"I guess you're smarter than I am, boy."

She had to make it right, somehow.

Chapter Twenty-Four

NATHAN SHIFTED IN his Wranglers and boots in the white pickup he'd rented, intently watching the entrance the bank. He should have listened to his gut when it told him Brendon was trouble. From their first meeting, Nathan hadn't trusted him. Watching him walk into the bank now confirmed his suspicions.

Sliding out of the driver's seat, he followed Brendon into the bank, watching as the other man sat down at a desk and waited for an account manager. Nathan walked up behind him and placed a hand on his shoulder. "Morning, Brendon. What brings you here?"

Brendon spun and rose to his feet. "What are you doing here? I thought you left."

"I did." Nathan settled into the chair next to Brendon and let a smile curve his lips. "And now I'm back." He leaned back in the chair as if preparing for a long visit.

"You know, it's odd that we should show up here at the same time."

Brendon sat back down, one brow raised in question. "I think it's *odd* to see you here at all, City Boy. What happened? People didn't buy your bullshit urban cowboy act, so you had to come back here to try to look important? Sorry, we don't have enough money around here for your kind of white-collar criminal."

Nathan's smile widened slowly as he met Brendon's anxious gaze. The accountant wasn't nearly as confident as he wanted Nathan to believe he was. Nathan could almost smell the fear seeping from his pores.

"You know, it's funny you, of all people, should mention white-collar criminals." He slid a hand into his pocket and pulled out his phone and a business card, shifting his eyes from the card back to Brendon's face. "Contrary to what you told Justin, my name is clear and my record is clean as a whistle, but thanks to my father's case, I've been in close contact with federal investigators."

"So?"

"They were pretty cooperative when I asked them to look into what appeared to be someone embezzling from Heart Fire Ranch."

He watched Brendon's face redden as he shifted in his chair. The man refrained from commenting, but Nathan saw his fingers grip the arms.

"When they contacted the local authorities and suggested we set up a sting, I was more than willing to do whatever I could, as well as provide any resources I had to protect Jessie."

He punched a button on his phone and played back a recording of Brendon on the phone with Nathan's secretary while she pretended to be a bank representative. Brendon paled, his mouth falling open, as he heard the woman inform him there was trouble with the Heart Fire Industries account and that she needed the account holder to come in to correct the error.

"Which brings us back to this bank and your business here." Since the meeting with Brendon and Trevor, Nathan had suspected the accountant of routing money from Jessie's ranch into his own hands. He was the only one with the ability to hide the crime without creating suspicion. Nathan pressed several buttons on his phone, dialing the number on the card but not putting the call through just yet.

"You think I'm the one taking money from Heart Fire." Nathan noticed it wasn't a question or a denial of culpability. "You're wrong."

"Am I?" Nathan leaned forward in his seat. "The account holder is told to come solve and issue with Heart Fire Industries, and here you are. That account is now nearly emptied out. But, of course, you already knew that, didn't you?"

"What?" This time, Brendon paled. "No, there's nearly fifty thousand in that account."

"Not anymore."

Brendon was on his feet, flagging down an account representative, dragging the disgruntled employee back to the desk. "I need you to look up this account." The bank employee eyed Nathan who remained rooted to his spot, phone still in his hand. "Now! What in the hell are you waiting for, you imbecile? Do it now!"

Either Brendon was a tremendous actor or he had no idea the account had been emptied. Nathan didn't think he was faking his frantic state.

"Sit down, Brendon," Nathan ordered. "The man will do his job better without you screaming in his face." He sent the call and put the phone to his ear. "We need some assistance at First National."

"Who are you calling? The police?" Brendon's eyes shot toward the front doors as if contemplating his escape.

"I don't think so," Nathan said into the phone, ignoring Brendon's questions. "Let's find out what's going on before we call in the troops."

"You don't understand." Brendon ran a hand through his hair. "I…he said…"

"Who said?" Brendon had his attention now. There was no doubt Brendon had set up the account and the money transfers that had nearly sent Jessie into bankruptcy, but his reaction to this news made it clear there was someone else involved.

"Sir, this account had a final withdrawal yesterday and is showing a zero balance. There are also no pending deposits, per your request. Now," he said, glaring at the two men at his desk, "if you don't mind, I was helping a customer."

Nathan nodded and saw two officers enter the building. Brendon had buried his head in his hands, muttering, as Nathan rose and motioned for the officers. "Brendon, you might want to call your father, or a good defense attorney."

"What? No!" He jumped up from the chair. "Wait, it wasn't me!" The officers reached for Brendon's arms, twisting them behind him roughly as they clipped a set of handcuffs over his wrists.

"Brendon Gray, you have the right to remain silent."

Nathan walked toward the front door, wanting to feel satisfaction now that Brendon was in custody. But hearing that almost fifty thousand dollars had been stolen from Jessie made his heart sink. The chance of them ever seeing that money again was slim. He'd failed her after all. He was too late.

"HEY, JESS! I heard some interesting news today in town." Bailey breezed into the office, eyes alight with mischief, and plopped into the chair in front of Jessie's desk as Moose trotted up and dropped his head in her lap for attention.

She barely looked up from the computer and the pile of receipts and invoices that seemed to never end. She really needed to spend some time figuring out this computer program. Nathan could've helped—

Stop! she warned herself. Thoughts of Nathan only led to tears.

"I don't need to hear gossip, Bailey. Don't we get enough of it in this town without you spreading it?"

"You don't even want to know when it's about Heart Fire?"

Bailey had her full attention now. "What about the ranch?"

The last thing she needed was people talking about her. She was in the black for the first time in over six months, thanks to Nathan. Enough that she'd been able to convince Jennifer to let her hire Mitch and Clint full time. She didn't want to risk anything driving them away, especially small town gossip.

"Brendon Gray was arrested."

Jessie's eyes widened in surprise, and she dropped her pen. "What?"

"Thought you didn't want to know," Bailey teased, laughing.

"This isn't funny, Bailey. What was he arrested for?"

"Embezzling." A knot began to tighten in Jessie's belly, fear gripping her, coiling around her chest as she waited for Bailey to go on. "From what I hear, Nathan nailed his ass to the wall right there in the bank."

Her heart dropped to her toes. Nathan? He was here? When had he arrived? Why hadn't he come to the ranch?

"Once they started questioning him, he started singing like a bird. Keeps insisting he was set up."

"Wait, go back to the beginning. Nathan is here, and Brendon's been embezzling money? From us?"

"Yes, yes, and apparently." Bailey slapped her hands against her knees and stood up. "Justin canceled his afternoon appointments and closed up the clinic to head into town to meet with Uncle Trevor. He wants to see what all of this is about and what sort of ramifications it might have."

"Where's Julia? We need to get into town."

Bailey shrugged. "She's not home, so she probably took the dogs out on some training exercise. Do you want me to drive?"

"No, stay and wait for Julia. Then you two meet us in town. I've got to find Justin." Jessie hurried into the kitchen and snatched her keys and purse from the counter. "Tell Mitch and Clint to just finish working the two mares, and I'll be back later."

"Jess!" Bailey chased her down the front steps of the porch. "You realize what this means, right?"

She nodded. "Justin was wrong."

Bailey's smiled spread even wider. "It also means Nathan kept his promise to you."

"We'll see."

ALL HELL WAS breaking loose in the small sheriff station when Jessie finally made her way inside. Two deputies tried to calm Uncle Trevor as he threatened everyone within a five-foot radius with slander and libel lawsuits if any rumors left the building. He should have known it was already spreading through the entire town. Several people had stopped Jessie on her way inside to ask if she'd heard. She could see Brendon holed up in the sheriff's office with his head in his hands, while Nathan leaned against a doorway as Uncle Trevor continued his barrage.

"Jessie, thank goodness you're finally here! Will you please explain to Deputy Dip-shit over here that Brendon has been acting in your family's best interest and that you weren't taken advantage of. This man," he said, flinging his hand in Nathan's direction, "seems to think Brendon has been stealing money from the ranch. I think with his background, Officer, you should be checking his credentials and handcuffing him in that office instead."

She'd never seen her uncle so worked up. He was always in control and never lost his cool; however, right now, he looked ready to pull his salt and pepper hair from his head.

"Sir, please relax. Your client needs you right now, and if you can't settle down, I think you need to recuse yourself from this case," the deputy said.

Nathan looked hard as steel, his eyes barely registering any tenderness as they took in her presence. "That would probably be best anyway, Gray. Seems like this might be a conflict of interest."

Uncle Trevor shot daggers at him, lunging toward the doorway, only stopping when the deputy wrapped an arm around his chest and forcibly pulled him away. "That's it! Into this room." The deputy pushed her uncle into one of the other smaller offices as Justin came running into the office, pushing his way past her, freezing when he saw Nathan.

"What in the *hell*, Nathan?" Justin spun to face her. "Please, tell me you're not a part of this."

"I just got here. I don't even know what's going on." She turned back to Nathan. "What *is* going on?" Jessie looked from one man to the next, waiting for someone, anyone, to provide some sort of answer.

Nathan pushed himself from the doorframe and ambled toward them. Jessie clenched her jaw.

Was he seriously going to strut toward her like he had nothing to prove? Like some sort of superhero who'd just rescued the damsel in distress? She might be itching to throw her arms around him, to feel him under her hands, but she wasn't about to tolerate this macho bullshit from him any more than she would from her brother.

"Does this look like an Old West shoot out? Spit it out already, Maverick. I don't have all day."

The corner of his lips curled into a grin and that damn dimple sunk into his cheek. "I've missed you, Jess."

Her heart might have done several flips in her chest at his words and the way her name slid from his lips. Not to mention the way the green in his eyes seemed to skim over her from head to toe, heating every inch of her along the way, but he didn't need to know any of that. She folded her arms and cocked her hip to the side, waiting for him to answer.

"You had our accountant arrested for embezzlement?" Justin's voice was strained, and Jessie could tell he was aching for a fight.

"Brendon is CFO, and the only person with access to the Heart Fire Industries account, the only person who could touch that money. He was the only person able to access funds from each one of you, and now, the Heart Fire Industries account is empty. If he diverted those funds, Justin, that's embezzlement, whether you trust me or not."

Jessie noticed Nathan wasn't quite able to keep the hurt from his eyes at the thought of Justin not having faith in him. She looked at her brother. He was torn, and she could understand why. He'd known Brendon since they were kids, but what else was it going to take to convince him Brendon had lied?

"Is this about Jessie?"

And again, it was none of his business *who* she dated. She turned to her brother and shoved a hand against his chest, knocking him back a few steps.

"About me? Why would anything be about me? It's always about you and Julia or the ranch. Nothing is ever about what I want." She pushed against his chest again. "What goes on between me and Nathan is none of your business. I don't remember asking for your permission, Justin. Whether you realize it or not, I'm an adult woman who makes her own choices. The way Mom and Dad taught me."

Justin looked down at her and grabbed her wrist gently. "Jess, you don't know what you want or need." His sweet, mocking tone made her feel like a child, and she was done with him treating her like she needed his help.

"Don't 'Jess' me. I didn't ask you to take Dad's place. I love you, but that's something you can't do." She jerked her wrist away from him, angry tears filling her eyes. "Why can't you see I don't need your protection?"

"Because you do," Nathan moved closer to where she stood.

"You have no right to be involved in this discussion at all." She turned on him. "You lied."

"I didn't—"

She held up a hand. "It may have been a simple omission to you, but you didn't tell me about your family. I trusted you."

"I know you did. I just didn't know where things were going between us." His eyes flicked toward her brother and back. "How was I supposed to bring up something like that?"

She looked between Nathan and Justin. "What is it with the two of you?" She slapped her brother's arm. "You think you need to guard me like a vestal virgin." She shook her head. "Guess what? This isn't the Roman Empire, and I'm not a virgin."

"Jess!"

"And you're so worried about what Justin will think that you can't make a decision. You need to grow a pair. Maybe stand up to my brother. Unless you lied, and this really was just a fling to you."

Jessie turned to Deputy Chase McKee, who looked confused by their family drama. The poor guy had known Jessie and Justin forever and had just returned to the force. Jessie wondered if he wasn't getting far more than he bargained for. "Do whatever you need to: press charges, book Brendon, whatever. Let these two handle everything. It seems to be what you do best anyway. I have a ranch to run."

Jessie walked out of the office, leaving every man in the building staring after her, and for once, she didn't care one bit if it made her the family failure. This time, if she failed, it would be on her own terms, and she would do it splendidly.

"SHE CAN'T DO THAT," Trevor yelled, as he rose from the desk. "Justin, you need to talk some sense into her."

Justin looked from Nathan to the father and son, both cuffed like common criminals. "Let's figure out what's going on." Nathan nodded and headed toward the office where Brendon waited with the sheriff, but Justin stopped him with his hand. "You better believe I'm going to kick your ass for hurting my sister when this is over with."

"You already did," Nathan argued.

"Then I'll do it again." Justin said, not leaving any further room for argument. He sat on the edge of the sheriff's desk and let Nathan take the chair. Then he addressed Brendon "I don't know what's going on, but as your friend, man, seeing how your dad is losing it in the next room, you might want to appoint someone else."

Brendon ran his shackled hands through his hair, hitting himself in the forehead. "I didn't do this. Not really."

"Wait," Nathan warned, glancing back at the sheriff. "Do you want your father in here?"

"Don't say anything, son, until I can make some calls." Trevor's voice carried through the thin walls of the offices, while they could see the deputy trying to calm him again.

"I don't need an attorney. I didn't do anything wrong." Brendon's voice was tired, but it didn't stop the sheriff from pulling out a pad of paper and a small recorder.

"Then tell me what happened, Brendon, because I really don't want to believe you'd do this." Justin shook his head, disappointment showing.

"Before your parents went on their trip, your dad came in and said he wanted me to open an account and to set up recurring transfers from the ranch equal to fifty percent of the monthly income. He just said it was to help Jessie down the road and that he'd explain more once the companies were incorporated. Something about rescuing horses." He buried his head into his hands again. "But then they were killed. I never touched that money, Justin." He looked up at all three men. "Not once in the six months the account was open. I should have said something but, honestly, I forgot about it until this guy came asking questions."

"Jessie was drowning in debt, almost declaring bankruptcy, and you *forgot* about the account?" Nathan knew he sounded dubious, but the man's story was asinine. "This is just your word against a dead man's."

Brendon shook his head, slowly. "No, my father knew. He set up the incorporation. He and your father were the first ones on the board of directors. After the trip, they were going to add the three of you. And I'm not the only one with access to the account; I'm just the first listed because I'm the CFO. Justin, you've got to believe me, man. You're like a brother to me." He looked up at Justin with watery eyes full of regret. "And you know how I feel about Jessie. I would never do this to her."

Nathan's jaw clenched at hearing Brendon even mention her name. He gripped the arm of the chair to keep from pulverizing the man.

"I think we need to have a chat with Trevor." The sheriff's voice broke through the rage blinding Nathan. "Maybe he can shed a little light on this situation."

"I don't need light; I need air. The stench of bullshit is beginning to choke me." He rose and walked out of the office, the glare of the sunlight reflecting off the windshields of cruisers, nearly blinding him.

He leaned against one of the cars and took a deep breath, the heated air of late spring rife with car exhaust nearly choking him. Or maybe it was the fact that his accusation against Brendon wasn't going to hold up in light of the man's recent confession. Someone had stolen that money from Jessie, and he hadn't been fast enough or smart enough to stop it before it happened. He slammed the heel of his hand against the car's hood and stood, raking his hands through his hair in frustration.

"Damn it!"

"You know, I don't think you need a vandalism charge with everything else on your plate right now."

Nathan spun, his pulse speeding up at the sound of Jess's voice. "I thought you left."

"I did." She shrugged. "But I came back."

"Why?"

He wanted to tell himself to shut up, to stop asking questions and just be grateful for her return, but his mouth operated without consulting his brain. The same way his feet moved without his acknowledgment. Nathan buried his hands into her hair, not waiting for an answer, and sought her mouth. He didn't need to hear the words from her; he could feel it in the way her body melted against him, in the sigh that left her lips, in the way her hands moved over his back, hungry for him.

"Jess," he whispered, pulling back only far enough to lean his forehead against hers. "I left to keep you from getting hurt. My father's a criminal. He's been stealing money and hiding it in offshore accounts all my life. He saw you as a threat to his operation and said if I ever returned here, he'd destroy your family. I was young and stupid and powerless to stop him if he carried through on his threat. So I let go of you and tried to convince myself I'd done the right thing."

His thumb traced her cheekbone. "But when Justin called, I couldn't let the ranch go under. Not if I could help. And since I'm telling you everything, when I went back, he wanted me to help him falsify his books, but I refused. I never actually lied to you."

His hands curved around her jaw, his thumb caressing the hollow of her cheek. He needed her to believe him.

She smiled up at him, her hands covering his. "Nathan, thank you for telling me the truth about your family, but as for the lying, let's mutually agree you walked a fine line in a gray area."

"I should have known you'd have to have the last word." He smiled down at her, relieved. "I should have told you."

"Yes," she agreed. "You should have, but—"

Trevor pushed open the door of the station as one of the deputies followed him and Brendon outside. He had a broad, evil grin on his lips when he turned toward Nathan. "Well, looks like the charges against Brendon were dropped. Prepare yourself for a lawsuit, Mr. Kerrington. It's going to be an expensive one." He looked past Nathan to Jessie and shook his head. "Your father would be so disappointed."

Nathan felt the agony come off Jessie in waves, and the fact that this man would say something so deliberately cruel and hurtful infuriated him. He wasn't about to let it happen. "Sue away, Gray. I have the truth and million-dollar lawyers at my disposal. I doubt we'll lose. You, on the other hand…" Nathan shrugged.

Trevor laughed. "Then, by all means, take your best shot, young man. I'd be glad to drag this out long enough that you end up with nothing left. Not to mention how the world would love to hear about the financial tycoon who went after a frail old man living on nothing but his retirement. You play chess, Mr. Kerrington? This is what we call, 'check.' "

Nathan took a step toward the old man as Justin stepped between them. "Don't. Not now," his friend muttered. "Let's go back to the ranch."

"It will really be a shame to see another Kerrington reputation go down in flames."

"Ride with me, Nathan." Justin ordered. "We need to talk."

Jessie looked up at him, worry creasing her brow, but Nathan knew his friend, and there was a wide chasm between them now that needed to be bridged. Jessie might have said differently, but Nathan knew, as much as Justin's accusation had wounded her, she adored her brother and longed for his approval.

"I'll meet you at the ranch, okay?" He pressed his lips to hers briefly. "We'll finish our discussion then, too."

She chewed at her lower lip. It might have been less than a week, but he needed this woman. Unfortunately, right now, her hulking linebacker of a brother stood between them. He walked Jessie to her truck and went back to meet Justin in front of the police station.

"Excuse me, Mr. Kerrington?" A deputy met him at the front of Justin's truck. "Could we speak with you for a moment?"

"Go ahead," Justin said. "This can wait until you're finished."

Chapter Twenty-Five

NATHAN EYED JUSTIN as he climbed into Justin's pickup and fumbled with the recording device in his pocket. This wouldn't be his first time going undercover for the police, but he didn't want them taping any personal conversations about Jessie if he could avoid it.

"Is this where I get to ask about your intentions for my sister?" Justin's jaw clenched, and Nathan could tell he was trying to control his temper as he backed out onto the road. "Dude, you slept with my sister. I never would have done that to you."

"Not without telling me first," Nathan finished for him. Justin rolled his eyes and gave him a frustrated glare. "You're right. I should have told you there was something going on between us. I should have told you about it when I stayed with you at the ranch that summer. But I was trying to protect you, and her. My family held a lot of sway back then, and when they threatened to destroy your parents' business and your future if I didn't stay away from her…" Nathan shook his head. "How was I supposed to tell you that?"

"They couldn't have done anything."

"That's where you're wrong, Justin. They could and would have." Nathan ran his hand over the small device in his pocket, muffling what it would pick up. "Money can buy a lot of things, Justin and my father had plenty at his disposal to bribe people to destroy your family. I couldn't take that chance. I cared too much."

"So you blew her off, never called? God, I feel like a fool for telling you how worried I was about her then. The whole time, you knew it was because of you. And then you just took off, like our friendship meant nothing. You were the closest thing I had to a brother."

Nathan took a deep breath. What could he say? Justin was right. He could hear the disgust in Justin's voice.

"What about now?"

"I've cut all ties to my father. He's going to lose his case and will be too hard-pressed trying to stay out of prison to worry about me."

Justin eyed him. "I mean, what about you and Jess?"

"It was—*is*—confusing. I don't know where she stands, Justin, but I always planned on coming back. There's nothing on earth, not even you, that's going to convince me to leave her again. Unless it's what she wants."

Justin slammed on the brakes, veering onto the shoulder of the road, and put it into park. "You love her?" Nathan didn't deny it—nor did he look away. "I thought you didn't believe in falling in love."

"I don't. I didn't," he clarified. "But Jess—" He didn't know how to explain it, but Jess had taken all his plans for his future and turned them upside down. She made him wonder if his entire life had simply been one long wait for her to step inside and show him the way to right his wrongs.

"Yeah, I get it. It's Jess. She has a way of throwing a wrench into things when you least expect it." He arched a brow and laughed quietly. "And it's usually for the better." Justin pulled back out onto the highway. "I guess I can learn to deal with the two of you together, provided you don't hurt her again."

Nathan chuckled and shook his head.

"What's so funny?"

"You. Thinking you could stop me."

Justin shot him a warning look. "I knocked you on your ass once already. Don't make me do it again."

"You know she wants to turn the ranch into a horse rescue, right?" He watched Justin's shoulder slump.

"How is that even going to be possible? With how expensive horses are to keep, without guests, how would she even feed them?" Justin shook his head. "And now? How can we recoup a loss like this? Fifty thousand dollars?"

"I have some big investors lined up for her." Justin looked over at Nathan suspiciously. "I met with a few while I was in New York, and I have three lined up here in California willing to make some big start-up donations, if she becomes a nonprofit."

"To rescue abused horses?"

Nathan nodded. "I think your father was trying to get the dominoes all lined up for it before they went on the trip—the incorporation, the transferred money. Jess made a comment once that she thought your father lied to her. After what we just heard from Brendon, it all makes sense that your father was trying to set this up for her to start her operation."

"Why didn't he just tell her?"

Nathan shrugged. "You know your father better than I do. Maybe he wanted to surprise her. Maybe he didn't want upset you."

"Me?"

"Justin, you're pretty hard on Jess. You jumped on her about the missing money before you even gave her a chance to explain." Justin opened his mouth to defend himself, but Nathan didn't give him a chance. "I know you love her, and I don't know all the history, man, but Jess adores you, and she feels like she's always letting you down. You can see it in her eyes."

Justin ran a hand over his face, scrubbing his jaw, and shook his head. "I guess I've dealt with things badly after Mom and Dad died. I just didn't know what to do."

A companionable silence fell between them, neither feeling compelled to speak until Justin pulled the truck off the main highway onto the road to the ranch. "Who took the money, Nathan? I don't think it was Brendon."

"You want my honest opinion or what I can prove?"

"Either." He shrugged.

"I think it was Trevor and that he used Brendon as a patsy."

"His own son?" Justin sounded doubtful.

"Who else knew your father was incorporating the businesses? Who else is on the board of directors and has access? Who else would your father have put that much trust in?"

"Then shouldn't we confront him?"

"With what? Conjecture? Suspicion? A theory?" Nathan shook his head and pursed his lips. "Unfortunately, I have nothing else to go on. I can't just make accusations, and if it's him, he's done a great job of making Brendon look suspicious while still shining enough doubt to make the evidence circumstantial."

"But, if Mom and Dad hadn't gone on that trip, if they hadn't been in that accident, none of this would have worked."

"*If* it was an accident." Nathan had seen the police report. A single-car accident, probable cause was determined to be the driver falling asleep at the wheel. The brakes hadn't been applied as they left the road. No one in the small town even suspected foul play.

Justin pulled the truck onto the shoulder of the road again and spun the wheel, making a U-turn, leaving a cloud of dust behind them.

"Are you saying that son of a bitch killed my parents?" Justin's nostrils flared, his eyes wide with disbelief and rage. "That he destroyed our family for money? My father was his friend. We grew up with him."

"Justin, slow down or let me drive," Nathan warned. "I don't know, but it's what I suspect. Proving it is an entirely different matter."

"I'll get us proof. I may have to beat him to a pulp to get it, but if he killed our parents, he'll admit it."

It wouldn't do them any good to alert Trevor that they were on to him. Nathan needed to get a recorded confession, not an assault charge, but he'd been wondering how to get to Trevor's office to confront him about what he'd done. Justin was making this easier. Now, he just had to figure out a way to get Trevor to confess to what he'd done.

JUSTIN PUT ON the breaks and pulled into the parking spot, barely taking time to throw the truck into park before leaping from the driver's seat. Nathan chased him, trying to catch him before he headed into the office, hellbent on revenge. "Justin, wait. We need them to confess."

Justin stopped, his boots skidding on the sidewalk in front of the office building. "You really think he's going to give up anything? You said it yourself, he's done a great job of hiding behind the suspicion he's cast on his own son."

"Well, you can't beat it out of him." Nathan realized he didn't put it past Justin to do exactly that. Not that he could blame him. If Trevor had murdered his family, he'd want to do the same.

"Or maybe I can."

Nathan caught the secretary at the desk inside watching them argue on the sidewalk. They had to do something, or she was going to alert Trevor of their presence. "Just follow my lead, okay?"

He wasn't entirely sure the best course of action to take, but he couldn't let Justin go in half-cocked, ready to beat someone. Getting a confession was their best shot.

Nathan knew they didn't have much time before Jessie realized they weren't following her and started looking for them. He loved that woman, but she would jump into this fray without even thinking of the danger to herself. He didn't want her here for this.

Nathan pulled the door open and gave the secretary a flirtatious smile. "Well, hello. How in the world did Trevor manage to find such a lovely secretary?" He turned to Justin, whose face was still red with fury. "The lucky devil." He shot Justin a look of warning and saw the understanding dawn in his eyes.

"How can I help you, gentlemen?" She appeared stoic, but Nathan didn't miss the way her body language relaxed when Justin looked her way. "Justin, I'm surprised to see you here again so soon."

"We have some documents for Mr. Gray. Is he in?" Nathan offered.

"He's with his son, and I don't think—"

"It will only take a second, Christy." Justin cut her off. "I don't think Uncle Trevor remembered these were coming today, and I need to have him sign them. He'll be a bear if they don't get turned in."

She didn't look pleased but jerked her chin toward the door. "He came in irritated, so let's not give him another reason. Go ahead."

Nathan and Justin made their way into the spacious office and shut the door behind them with a soft click. Brendon was just coming back into the main room with a file in his hands.

"Was this what you—" He stopped short when he saw Justin and Nathan standing in front of his father's mahogany desk.

"Hurry up. We need to shred—" Trevor, who had been watching his son, turned to see what had startled Brendon. "What the hell are you doing here? I told Christy not to disturb me."

"I'm sure you did." Nathan ran a hand over the top of the desk, noting the fine craftsmanship. "Nice office. You have expensive taste for a small-town lawyer."

"Get out of my office before I call the police." Gray's voice was quiet but dangerous.

"You know"—Justin slid into one of the leather chairs and put his dirty boots on the desk—"I think that might be a good idea."

Nathan didn't miss the fact that Brendon still stood in the doorway, his fingers tightly gripping the file, his knuckles white, and his face ashen. He walked toward him, and Brendon's eyes shot toward his father. "I wonder if the police might be interested in the file you seem to want shredded so quickly."

Trevor placed his hands on the back of his chair and smiled a cold, heartless grin. "I have nothing to hide. By all means, feel free to look at it before I finish cleaning my office."

Nathan narrowed his eyes. The man was too cocky, far too confident, for someone who'd only been released from handcuffs and whose son had been accused of embezzling less than an hour ago. It had to be a bluff.

"May I?" Nathan held out his hand, and Brendon looked to his father for confirmation. He stuck out his bottom lip and nodded. Nathan opened the file and flipped through the pages. It was nothing but car repair receipts from a local mechanic. He clenched his jaw. This was nothing. How could his instincts be so off? Did he just have it in for these two?

As if reading his expression, Trevor laughed. "Find anything interesting? Now, if you don't mind seeing yourselves out."

Nathan dropped the file in Justin's lap. "You know, it's odd that you haven't heard anything about the incorporation. It's been well over the usual six weeks. You'd think after six months, you'd have checked on it." Trevor's lips pinched into a thin line, and he refrained from commenting. "Unless you have them already. In which case, there should be a meeting of the board."

"Is that the case? Because I can call my sisters and have them down here in just a few minutes." Justin held up his phone and looked at Trevor expectantly.

"What are you trying to prove, Kerrington?" Trevor ignored Justin who tucked his phone into his pocket and began flipping through the receipts.

"What are you trying to hide?" Nathan countered. A commotion from the entrance had all four men turning their heads to the doorway as Jessie burst through it.

"Get away from me, Christy, or I swear you'll be sorry."

"Sir, I tried to stop her, but—"

Trevor held up a hand and waved her out. "I'll take care of this." His eyes skimmed over his son, and he shook his head. "Just like I always do."

"What is going on?" Jessie asked. "I tried calling you. Then I came back and found your truck parked—"

"Nathan, these are receipts for Dad's truck." He rose and slapped the file on the desk. "What in the hell did you do?"

Trevor arched a brow and laughed. "Why wouldn't I have receipts for repairs on your father's ranch truck? I'm his attorney."

"Attorney," Nathan said, "not accountant." He reached for the file again. "Where is the documentation for Heart Fire Industries?"

Brendon, who had been like a statue in the doorway, took a step backward and looked ready to run. Nathan grasped his arm. "Don't even think about it." Nathan turned back to Trevor. "You can show us or the police can find it when they tear this place apart."

Trevor shook his head and laughed bitterly. "You should know better than anyone, Kerrington, that you need to show cause. You have nothing on me."

"We have an account with four names on it right now: Colton and Melissa Hart, Brendon Gray, and Trevor Gray. With two of those now deceased, there are only two people who could touch the money in that account." He smiled when he saw the old man blanch. "You've done a terrific job proving your son's innocence. Thank you for that, by the way."

Trevor quickly recovered. "You seem quite sure of yourself, Mr. Kerrington. But, let's be honest, you're guessing. You have no way of knowing anything."

"Are you sure? Certain enough to stake your freedom on it? With as much money as I have, you'd be surprised at how resourceful my investigators can be." He raised his brows as he waited for Trevor's response. The two stared at each other for what seemed like minutes. Nathan was surprised everyone else in the room remained silent, as if waiting to see who caved first.

A quiet knock sounded at the door. "Sir, is everything okay in there? Do you need me to phone the police?" Christy's voice was tentative, but it seemed to spark Brendon into motion.

He ran for the door and Justin moved but not as quickly as Jessie. She grabbed Brendon by the front of his shirt and shoved him back against the wall. "Don't even think about it. No one is leaving until we have the truth." She stepped closer to him, her nose barely reaching his chin. "I don't care how I have to get it, either. Someone nearly drove my ranch into the ground, and I'm ready to extract a little payback for the fifty thousand dollars stolen from me."

"I didn't do it, Jessie," Brendon whispered. "I set up the account and the transfers, but that was all." His eyes flicked to Justin who stood behind her. "I swear."

"Shut up, Brendon." Trevor's voice rumbled in the room, savage and cruel, like the growl of a feral animal.

"I'm not going to jail for you." Brendon ground out the words as Jessie released him.

She turned on Trevor. "You? You took the money? Why?" She moved toward his desk. "You're family!"

"No, we aren't." Trevor turned vindictive eyes on Jessie. "I took that failing cattle ranch and turned it into a successful business for your father, and do you know what he gave me? Nothing."

"You were on the board of Heart Fire Industries," Nathan said. "That put you on the payroll. But I'm guessing that wasn't enough for you, was it?"

Trevor raised a brow and tipped his head. "Would it have been enough for you? Tell me, Mr. Kerrington, what are you getting out of helping these two?"

"I'm helping a friend."

Trevor looked at Jessie pointedly and laughed. "Sure you are."

"So, you decided to set up the transfers and withdraw the money?"

Trevor laughed bitterly. "Not exactly."

"You had *me* set it up so your hands were clean?" Realization dawned on Brendon's face. "You always planned for me to take the fall for this, all of this, didn't you?"

"Son, you're hands are clean, too. They don't have anything."

"I'm not going down for you. I swear I won't," Brendon vowed, pointing at his father. "Where is the money?"

"It's safe."

"In some offshore account with your name." Nathan strode toward the desk, knowing Trevor was trapped in his own lies. "You know, Brendon, I'm sure the police would go much easier on you for your cooperation. As a matter of fact, I'm sure Justin and Jessie might be willing to testify on your behalf if you were to tell the police what you know."

Justin took a threatening step toward his friend. "Or I could just beat the crap out of you now."

"Brendon isn't going to say anything, because he doesn't know anything." Trevor smiled his evil grin again.

Brendon looked from his father to Nathan, as if unsure who might offer him the best deal. He narrowed his eyes at the man behind the chair and took a step closer to Nathan, glancing at Justin. "I'll tell you everything I know, but you have to promise to do whatever you can to make sure I don't serve any time."

"Done," Nathan said. Jessie's mouth opened in protest, but he shook his head. Justin clenched his fists at his sides, and Nathan could tell he wasn't happy with the compromise either, but neither of them realized how important this was. This man's testimony was exactly what they needed to make a case and try to get her money back.

"The money is in Germany. I have the account information."

Trevor's face colored with rage. "Shut up, Brendon!" He lunged across the desk, but the chair blocked his attack.

Nathan shoved a paper at Brendon. "Write it down. Names, account numbers, routing information."

"I need to call the police," Jessie said, pulling out her phone.

Nathan was just about to tell her about the device hidden in his pocket when Brendon passed him the paper with the bank information.

"He cut the brake line." Brendon's voice was quiet but anxious.

"You son of a bitch!" Trevor's voice was thick with rage.

"He had someone do it. I don't know who."

"How do you know?" Nathan asked. "Did you see it?"

Brendon shook his head. "He told me. And I have his receipt for the hotel where it happened."

"You killed my parents?" Justin dove toward the old man, and Nathan jumped into action. He couldn't have Justin getting arrested for assault when they had to make this an open-and-shut case. They didn't have it yet.

Jessie looked like she was in a state of shock, her face pale and her hands trembling. She let out a pained wail that chilled Nathan's heart. He wished he'd been able to warn her. Suddenly, she pushed past her brother. Nathan let go of Justin and both of them reached for her arms, barely catching her before she got her hands on Trevor.

Jessie struggled against the two of them, and Nathan was shocked at the difficulty they had holding her back. "I'm going to kill you, you bastard."

"You can't do anything." Trevor chuckled under his breath. "I'm not stupid. You have nothing more than his word on this. And I can give you proof that *he* stole that money from you."

"I don't care about the money." Jessie paused long enough to glare at Brendon and then turned back to the man across the desk, the man she'd trusted for most of her life. "I want my parents back. You said it was an accident."

"I have the name of the man he paid to do it." Four sets of eyes turned to Brendon.

"I thought you said—"

Brendon cut Justin off. "I lied." He looked at his father. "That's right, Dad. I'm not fool enough to trust you. I followed you. I even talked to him. Let's see who gets the better deal with the police."

Trevor pointed a finger at his son. "You're finished. I will destroy you."

Several officers burst into the room with Christy peering from behind. "Freeze! Everyone, hands into the air."

"Officers, I'm so glad you're here. These people are trespassing, and these two have already tried to attack me." He pointed at Jessie and Justin.

"Nice try," said the deputy who'd fitted Nathan with the device as he pulled his handcuffs out and walked around the desk. Another deputy cuffed Brendon. "You're coming with us Trevor. You are under arrest for the murder of Colton and Melissa Hart. You have the right to remain silent—"

"What the hell? These three came in—"

"Trevor, we got everything we need." Nathan reached into his pocket and pulled out the recorder, no bigger than a pen cap. "And since Brendon wants to be so very cooperative, I'd say you're pretty well screwed. Check and mate."

Chapter Twenty-Six

NATHAN DISCONNECTED THE call on his cell and looked across the yard to where Jessie was unloading two new geldings from the trailer with Moose protectively standing at the gate. He caught his breath as she led the first emaciated animal out. It never failed to shock him when he saw the condition most of the animals came to Jess in—beaten, worn down, and pitiful—but she was able to restore them, the way she had with him. He wanted to do the same for her.

He walked down the porch steps and stood at the fence, clearing his throat to get her attention without spooking the animal. She looked at Deb. "Can you hold him for a second?"

Jessie hurried to the fence, worry creasing her brow. "Well? What did they say?"

"It's over. Trevor is trying to work out a deal, but Brendon rolled on him, so they have plenty of evidence. Apparently, he didn't trust his father and made sure he could blackmail him if the time came." Nathan shook his head. "I thought my family was dysfunctional. Trevor's going to prison for two counts of murder, Jess."

Jessie's eyes misted. She still missed her parents, but Trevor Gray was responsible for their death and was going to pay. She, on the other hand, was going to turn Heart Fire Ranch into a refuge her parents would have been proud to be a part of.

"Thank you." He could hear the catch in her throat as she leaned over the fence and pressed her lips against his, laying her hand against his cheek. Jessie took a deep breath before clearing her throat.

"Are we ready to place the ad for an on-site counselor for the teens?"

Nathan sighed and rolled his eyes playfully. "And we're back to business." He pinched her chin between his thumb and index finger. "Focus on me for two more minutes, please."

He kissed her gently, relishing the fact that he could do it whenever he wanted to now, without worry that his father might come after her. Now that his father's trial had begun, he was far too concerned with trying to make himself look like a wronged victim to worry about how Nathan's defection from their elite circle would look.

Desire swirled through him. He loved this woman more than he'd ever thought possible. He wondered if he could convince Deb to do this evaluation alone so he could take Jessie into the house. They hadn't made love since his return, even though she'd tried to convince him otherwise, but he wanted everything to be perfect.

"Will the two of you stop?" Bailey's voice broke through his haze of need.

Nathan pressed his forehead against Jessie's as she laughed. "Bailey, it's a good thing I adore you because if I didn't…"

"But you do, so you won't *do* anything." She had her arms crossed and a satisfied smiled on her lips. She waved a hand between them. "You have me to thank for this. Just remember that, Wall Street."

"You know, I don't work in New York anymore. You can stop with that name."

"You'll always be Wall Street to me. Embrace it." She turned to Jessie and grew serious. "Ellie called. Michael's brother made parole, and she wants to bring Michael out here so he doesn't start running with that crowd. She wanted to make sure it was okay."

"Of course it is." Jessie frowned and turned to Nathan. "You don't mind having a teen boy and Ellie staying for a while, right?"

"Jess, I know that your full house was just part of the deal. Trust me." He pressed another kiss to her lips. "I'm getting the best part of the bargain."

"Ugh!" Bailey threw her hands up. "You two are making me sick. I think I just threw up in my mouth a little." She turned and headed back toward the barn, laughing. "I'm going to go help Mitch clean stalls. Horseshit is preferable to you two."

Nathan laughed and caught Deb's eye over Jessie's shoulder. "Okay, I've distracted you long enough, but come find me when you finish. I'm going to try to get a few more donor meetings set up. I think at the rate we're going, we might as well set up a charity event. People love what you're doing here, Jess."

She cocked her head to the side, her dark waves falling over her shoulder like a curtain. "I didn't do this, Nathan. You did."

"Oh," Bailey yelled as she stopped at the barn door. "The new sign is up if you want to see it."

Jessie turned toward Nathan, her eyes alight with glee. He'd been hoping to take her to see it tonight, just before sunset. Glancing at the sky, he could see the sun just passing the midafternoon mark and sighed. He'd have to make it work.

"Okay, hop in the truck and let's go see it."

"Bailey, help Deb," Jessie called as she ran for the truck. Nathan headed inside to grab her keys and the package he'd hidden in his cabin.

JESSIE STOOD AT the entrance of the ranch and stared at the new sign for Heart Fire Ranch. Beautiful scrollwork surrounded the new addition that declared her home an equine rescue and rehabilitation program. Nathan stepped up behind her and wrapped his arms around her waist.

"It looks good," he murmured against her ear, causing shivers to crest over her in waves. "Are you happy?"

"I am." She turned in his arms to cup his jaw in her palms. "I have no idea how you managed to do this so quickly, but thank you."

"I just called in a few small favors." Nathan shrugged as if he hadn't done the impossible for her.

Somehow he'd managed to expedite the incorporation document Trevor had never filed and found a few donors willing to commit to several hundred thousand dollars toward funding the rescue. She'd be able to start upgrades to the barns and break ground on a covered arena. Now, they had begun the process of setting up the facility as a camp for at-risk teens as well, which was bringing in a new group of donors who wanted to help. Nathan had worked a miracle and made her dream a reality.

She stared at him in awe. "Just another day at the office, huh, Superman?"

"Something like that." Nathan gave her that cocky, lopsided smile that sent her heart racing, the dimple in his cheek deepening. "We should probably head back to the house. I have an architect faxing me his proposal for the new lodge today."

"Are you sure you want to do this? Give up your office and apartment in LA? That's a big move."

Nathan curled his fingers around the back of her neck, and she felt the sizzle of heat spiral in her belly. "I have never been more certain of anything. That isn't my life anymore. You are." He brushed his lips against hers lightly.

She smiled against his kiss. "You won't miss dating all those starlets and models?"

Nathan nipped at the corner of her mouth. "Who said I can't—oomph!" Nathan grunted as she playfully pressed a fist into his ribcage. He pulled her close. "I have everything I want right here."

He deepened their kiss and she sighed against him, wishing for a moment they were back in the house, where she could remove every shred of clothing separating them. Jessie leaned into him, rocking onto her toes, every part of her tingling with desire for him.

"Let's go back," she whispered against his mouth. "I have something I need you to do."

Nathan slid his hands down her back and cupped her rear, pulling her up against him. She could feel his need for her through their clothing. "Hopefully it's the same thing I'm wanting to do."

The blare of a horn scared her, making Moose start barking in the back of the truck. She jumped backward away from Nathan. "What the...I'm going to kill him."

Justin pulled his truck to a stop beside them and rolled down the window. "You two are pretty sickening. You know that, right?"

Nathan drew her back into the circle of his arms again and she shivered with delight. She loved how he seemed to crave touching her, the way she did him, but it was beginning to frustrate her that they hadn't made love since his return. He'd moved into one of the cabins and wouldn't budge, even when she pointed out how ridiculous it was for him to stay there when she had a perfectly good house with a large bed she was happy to share with him. Yet he continued to deny her, deny both of them, really, without explanation, and she was unsure why. His request that she trust him was the only reason he would give. She was willing to give him that concession, but she wasn't sure how much longer she could wait.

"You're just jealous."

"Hardly." Justin laughed and shook his head. "The sign looks good. When is Deb bringing the next group of horses?"

"This week. She found these at a stockyard in Nevada. Underfed and heading to slaughter, but otherwise healthy. I'll be prepping some stable mix to help them gain weight later if you want to help."

"Sure." He jerked his chin at the sign. "When are you going to change it to include the camp?"

Jessie couldn't help the smile from spreading over her lips. She still couldn't believe that she was actually going to be able to start pairing her horses with kids in a therapy program. None of this would have been possible without Nathan, and it just made her love him even more. She just wished she was brave enough to actually tell him. She was too afraid he wasn't ready for it, and she might scare him away. They'd agreed to take this relationship one day at a time, and she was trying to be patient.

It wasn't working.

"Later, once we start having camps. Probably in the summer. I still need to hire counselors who know about horses and want to work with troubled teens.

"Yeah, that should be a piece of cake," Justin said, pursing his lips. "I'll keep my ears open. Are you two heading back?"

"Yes."

"No," Nathan said at the same time.

"We're not?"

Nathan smiled. "Not just yet." He turned to Justin. "We'll meet you there a little later."

Justin's brows rose. She knew that look. These two were up to something. She watched her brother drive away before she turned to Nathan. "What are you planning?"

He tried for his best look of innocence and shrugged, but she wasn't buying it for a second. "Nathan, don't make me push you into another pile of manure."

He took a step closer, the spicy scent of him enveloping her, his nearness causing her heart to skip and jump in her chest as warmth spread through her limbs, making standing upright difficult. His hand curled into her hair, and she gasped at the delicious feel of his hard body cradling her softness. She looked up to see the gold flecks dancing mischievously in his green eyes as his lips curved into a wide smile.

"Jess, you don't want to do that today. I promise." He took her hand and led her to the truck, opening the passenger door. "Just be patient."

He climbed behind the wheel, and she marveled at how much had changed. A few weeks ago, she'd argued with Justin at the mention of Nathan on her ranch. The idea of letting him help had sent her into fits of rage. Now, in spite of their past mistakes, she trusted him with her truck, her ranch, her finances, her dreams, and her heart. She felt her chest swell with emotion. He'd taught her to feel again, to dream, to hope, and to believe.

For so long, Jessie believed she was nothing more than the family failure, doomed to repeat her mistakes and hurt those she loved. Nathan had saved her from herself, made her see that she was a diamond, rare and beautiful, even if she was still a little rough around the edges.

"What are you smiling about?" He glanced over at her as he drove.

She flipped up the console and scooted closer to him on the bench seat, twining her fingers in his. "You. You've been pretty amazing, Wall Street."

"Ugh, please stop calling me that." He cringed and she laughed.

"Okay," she agreed. "You hardly look like the same guy Bailey brought from the airport. No more suits, no more ties. Now if I could get you to stop using hair products," she teased as she ran her fingers through his still perfectly tousled hair. "But I do like the scruff." She ran a hand over his rough jaw and laid her head on his shoulder.

Nathan laughed quietly. "I'll admit I don't miss the suits, but no gel? That's just uncivilized." He pressed a kiss to the top of her head.

"Nathan, what's going to happen with your family?" She felt him tense before he inhaled deeply.

"I guess it depends on what happens during the trial. My father will probably be found guilty, but I doubt he'll serve time. He'll lose his job, but I'm sure my grandfather will find somewhere to plug him into one of his businesses, not that those are any more legal. Honestly, I refuse to worry about it. He made his bed."

"You couldn't forgive him?"

Nathan stared at her, surprise clear on his face. "You're kidding, right? Jess, he threatened your entire family if I continued to see you. I'm still not sure how far he would've gone, but I do know someone would have been hurt."

"You underestimate us Harts."

"After seeing you try to leap over that desk after Trevor, I won't make that mistake again."

She shook her head and looked out the front window. "We're going to The Ridge?"

He just smiled and drove up the path before turning the truck around and backing up so they could sit in the bed and see the river below. He reached into the backseat of the truck and pulled out a bottle of champagne with two plastic glasses and a blanket.

"My, aren't you prepared. I don't remember you mentioning you were ever a Boy Scout," she teased.

"Nope. I owe Bailey again."

"She *does* keep rescuing you, doesn't she?"

Nathan moved around the truck, but she opened her door before he could. It was nice that he wanted to be a gentleman, but she didn't want to wait any longer than necessary before touching him again. She hurried to the back of the truck and dropped the tailgate, coaxing the dog down and jumping into the back.

"Woman, you make it difficult to spoil you. Could you stop being so independent and let me be a gentleman?"

"Get your butt up here, and I promise I'll be a lady for ten minutes."

Nathan jumped into the back with her. He spread out the blanket and opened the bottle of champagne before pulling her down to sit between his legs as they both faced the river. Jessie leaned back against his chest and sighed, relaxing as his arms came around her and he poured them each a glass.

Nathan held his up. "To new beginnings and the healing to come."

"To the future," she agreed, tapping her glass against his. She sipped the drink, letting the bubbles tickle her nose. "You know, this is the first time I've ever had champagne."

Nathan drew back a few inches. "Are you serious?"

She laughed at his surprise. "I'm more of a cold-bottle-of-beer girl, but I could get used to this." She sipped the drink again.

He took the glass from her and set them both on the wheel well. He looked worried and her stomach twisted with dread. "Jess, I want to give you everything you've never had. Everything you've always wanted."

She smiled up at him, her heart ready to burst with tenderness for this man. "You have, Nathan. You've done that and more. You are the only person who found out what was buried inside me—my hopes, my dreams, my fears. You've helped me face my demons and conquer them. I can never thank you enough." She turned to face him. "I love you, Nathan. I have nothing to offer you but me, but—"

"Stop, Jess." Nathan cupped her face in his palms and smiled at her. "This is *my* proposal, and you're not going to take control of this, too."

"What?" Her butt dropped to her heels. "What did you just say?"

"Jessie Hart, I love you. I've always loved you. I can't believe I was ever stupid enough to let you go. I've done so many things wrong with our relationship." He slid a hand into his pocket and pulled out a small box. "I wanted to prove to you that I could do this right—the champagne, the sunset, not touching you this past few weeks when it's nearly killed me."

Jessie laughed even as her eyes misted over. He flipped open the box and revealed an elegant oval diamond solitaire surrounded by smaller diamonds set in a filigree design. It sparkled like the sun on the water as it dipped to the horizon. "The ring."

"It's beautiful."

"Jess, marry me. Let's build this crazy dream of yours together. Let me help you build new dreams, find new hopes. I was a prisoner and never even knew it until you. Without you, I'm only half a man. You've changed me, Jess. You've freed me to be who I always wanted to be, to let go and just let it happen."

Nathan brushed away the tear slipping down her cheek, and she reached up, covering his hand with hers. For the first time, she didn't feel like a failure. She was full—of strength, of life, of love. Nathan made her whole, complete and perfect. There weren't any words to express to him how she felt.

Jessie wrapped her arms around his neck and pressed her lips to his, letting her mouth tell him what her words couldn't. He responded as if they spoke a language only the two of them heard. Lips meshed, tongues danced, bodies twined. Suddenly, Nathan drew back.

"Is that a yes?"

She laughed. "Yes! Now will you please take me home and make love to me?"

"My pleasure."

Julia Hart knows how much good she does training therapy dogs—it's what helped her overcome her own trials after a past relationship turned unexpectedly violent.

Dylan, a former soldier, has run out of hope for recovery. Plagued by nightmares and flashbacks, he doubts anything will help him overcome his PTSD. When his brother convinces him to try one last time, he agrees to get a therapy dog—if only to prove it won't help.

Dylan didn't expect to find Julia or that he could begin to hope again. But when Julia's attacker, Evan, is released from prison, Dylan and Julia will have to face the past together.

Continue reading for a sneak peek at the next book in T. J. Kline's Healing Harts series,

TAKING HEART

Coming in June 2015 from Avon Impulse.

An Excerpt from

TAKING HEART

Chapter One

SERGEANT DYLAN GRANGER heard a series of loud *pops* as bullets hit the stone wall beside his head and rock dust crumbled into his face. He ducked further behind the wall. Their position had been compromised again, and this time, the entire unit was under attack by insurgents.

"We're not going to make it through this, Doc. We're taking too much fire," Michaels yelled at him.

"We have to make it through this. I haven't lost a man yet." Dylan ignored his partner, the junior medic of their unit, and checked the pulse of Sergeant Jefferies, the communications expert he was attending to. The soldier's blood was warm on Dylan's hands as he tried to stem the flow from the gunshot wound to Jefferies's abdomen. It was bad, but if he could get the bleeding to slow, he could save him. After seven years as a Special Forces Medic, Dylan had seen more than his fair share of wounds.

"You hear me, Jefferies?" The soldier's eyes rolled back, but he tried to nod. Dylan could see the fear in his face, knew he was close to giving up.

The desert sun beat down on the three of them as bullets whizzed past, and Dylan looked back over his shoulder where the rest of the unit had managed to hunker down behind a secondary shelter. At least they were covered on all four sides. He, Michaels, and Jefferies were sitting ducks behind a solitary low wall. He had to get Jefferies to the shelter, where they would have cover and he could focus on stopping the bleeding.

He signaled to the rest of the unit for cover and noted their affirmation. "Come on, we're making a break for it," he told Michaels. "You keep pressure on the wound, and I'll carry him."

Dylan slid his weapon over his shoulder and wrapped his arm under the officer's armpits as they prepared to drag him to safety. They had to move *now*.

"Just leave me, Doc," Jeffries muttered.

Dylan could see it in Michaels's eyes. He agreed and knew their best option was to leave the injured man behind.

Not on my watch.

"Shut up, Jeffries. You have two kids to get home to. Michaels here is going to hold the compress tight, but you need to help. Press on his hands." Dylan nodded to Michaels, and they made a run for the building behind them.

The world exploded into broken rock and dust. Heat and fire surrounded them, swirling through the air. For a moment, Dylan wondered if he hadn't just found hell on earth. He lifted his head carefully, the entire world around him ringing, spinning, as he tried to regain his bearings. It took him too long to realize he was pinned to the ground under Jefferies's dead weight. The weight of a mangled corpse. Using his forearms, he dragged himself from beneath the fallen soldier and saw Michaels to his left, face down. Dylan crawled to his side, tugging at him.

"Michaels!" He rolled him onto his back and saw the blood and dirt smeared over his face.

"My leg, Doc." Dylan looked down and saw that the man was bleeding out. He wasn't going to make it. Another explosion rocked the earth beneath them. "Grenades." Michaels' voice was barely a whisper. "Fall back while you can, Doc. Go!"

Dylan's felt something hit the side of his helmet, and his vision blurred before going completely dark.

HE REACHED FOR his head and bolted upright, sweat pouring from his body. He woke from reliving the nightmare again. It had been a year since he'd left Afghanistan behind. A year since the attack on their base that had left most of his unit KIA. A year of this new kind of hell on earth.

Dylan looked at the clock and reached for the glass of water on his bedside table, hating the way his hands trembled. He balled them into fists, willing the tremors to stop, and clenched his jaw so hard he thought it would snap. He wanted the nightmares to end, wanted his life back, wanted control over this. But what the doctors diagnosed as post-traumatic stress disorder, he called the end of his world.

He'd saved hundreds of men in his service, and now he couldn't function even one day without panic attacks, pills, and doctor's visits. Nothing remained of the man he'd once been—confident and capable. He looked up and saw his brother standing in the doorway of his room.

"You okay?"

Dylan hated being such a burden on Gage, but after returning home with a bullet wound in his head and burns that ran from his neck, over his right arm, and down his chest, he knew he would never have survived without him. His brother refused to give up on him, taking him in and putting his own life on hold to help him regain some semblance of a life.

"I'm good," he lied, popping open the prescription bottle on the nightstand.

"You sure you want another one of those? I thought your doctor said to taper off."

Dylan glared at his brother. The doctor had warned him about the risks of the medication they had him on, as well as taking more than they recommended. After becoming addicted to the painkillers early in his recovery, he had to be especially careful about which medications and how much of each he was taking. He didn't want to go through that battle again, but right now, it was the only thing keeping him from giving up entirely. He could understand the trap so many returning soldiers fell into, finding only pills and booze could help them escape the nightmare that lived inside them, haunting them even while they were awake. The pills let him fall into a dreamless sleep, where the faces of the men he hadn't saved didn't look at him with accusation in their eyes. The pills kept him from contemplating the other option to avoid their eyes: the loaded pistol hidden under his mattress.

"Dylan, you've tried everything else. Nothing is working. Can we please just call them up and see what they think?"

This discussion again? Dylan shook his head. He didn't want a therapy dog. If the medications and therapy he was already getting from three different doctors couldn't control his PTSD, how would a dog help? He didn't even like animals.

"No. We've already been over this. If I can't take care of myself, how am I going to take care of a dog?"

"What have you got left to lose?"

Technically, Gage was right. He had already lost everything he valued in life except his brother: his job, his independence, not to mention his sanity. He owed it to Gage at least to try to have some semblance of a normal life so his brother could find one for himself again.

"What if we go and it doesn't work?" Dylan asked, voicing the concern he didn't want to admit. It was really the crux of the matter. They'd already tried everything else with little to no success. If this didn't work, he would be forced to face that he was doomed to live in this hell forever, or until he ended it.

Gage raised both hands, palms out. "Then no harm, no foul, and I won't mention it again."

Dylan untangled himself from the sheet and sat at the edge of the bed, his feet landing on the cold hardwood floor. He might as well get up, since he wouldn't be able to sleep again tonight. "You know I can't afford it, and the military isn't running their PTSD-Canine therapy program anymore."

"I know." Gage moved into the room and reached for Dylan's empty water glass. "But I've been looking around at private trainers and other foundations to help. Or I'll pay for it."

"I can't keep surviving on your charity."

"Hey, enough." His voice was as unbending as his loyalty. "We're family. You took care of me for years when Mom got sick and Dad was drinking. You put me through college and got me to this point. Let me help you for a change, Dylan."

Dylan ran a hand over several days' worth of beard growth. He knew his brother was afraid he'd given up on life. A part of him *had*. If this last ditch effort was what he needed to do to assuage any misplaced guilt Gage had, he'd suck it up and prove to him that a dog wasn't going to fix what was messed up about him. He was broken, in ways that couldn't be fixed.

"WHAT'S THE MATTER, Wall Street? Cat got your tongue?" Julia grinned at her sister's fiancé across the table.

Nathan had been living on Heart Fire Ranch with Julia's sister, Jessie, long enough to realize what life in the country was like. Sometimes it included the barn cats leaving half-eaten mice as a prize for those they adored.

Granted, stepping on that "prize" in bare feet tended to put a damper on the rest of your day when it happened first thing in the morning. The prim-and-proper financial analyst still looked shocked.

Nathan shook his head, trying to keep a straight face as he reached for his coffee. "One day, I might actually get used to these things, but I will never enjoy them."

Jessie winked at her sister. "Don't let him fool you. He's already found several perks to living out here." She turned Nathan. "Like the fact that you claim bad cell service when you want to ignore calls from clients. And what about your new addiction to fishing?"

"I see your point," Nathan said, shrugging before winking at Jessie. "I can think of a few other perks, too."

"And that's my cue to leave," Julia said, jumping up from behind the breakfast table. The Great Dane asleep at her feet opened an eye and looked up at her. "Come on, Tango, let's go."

The dog immediately responded and moved toward the door as Julia put her mug into the dishwasher. As much as she enjoyed sharing breakfast at her sister's house, as they'd done almost daily since their parents' death a year ago, with Nathan there she felt a bit like a third wheel on days when her brother, Justin, and cousin, Bailey, didn't join them. She knew Jessie and Nathan were still finding their footing, and she wanted to give them the space they needed to get reacquainted after eight years apart. They didn't need a little sister tagging along.

"You coming back for lunch?" Jessie looked at Julia expectantly, and Julia could read the excitement in her sister's eyes. "We have our first group of kids coming in for a camp this week. Bailey's cleaning out the cabins for them today."

As nice as it sounded to spend time with both of them, she'd made arrangements to see some dogs at the shelter later. "Normally, I'd be happy to let you use me as an indentured servant," she teased. "But I can't today. Rain check?" The sound of Julia's ringtone had Tango's ears lifting as "Who Let the Dogs Out" rang through the kitchen.

"Ugh!" Jessie covered her ears. "Will you please change that? You have no idea how much I hate that song."

Julia smiled at her sister. "Yes, I do, but it makes me laugh, so no." She glanced at the screen, not recognizing the caller, and pressed the button. "Heart Fire Training, this is Julia."

"Hi, my name is Gage Granger. We've spoken a bit by e-mail about a PTSD dog. I'm calling for my brother."

"Yes, Mr. Granger. I remember." Julia waved to her sister, motioning that she had to take the call, and headed outside with Tango following at her heels, as if understanding an unspoken command. She opened the door of her beat-up pickup, and he jumped inside, sprawling across the bench seat with his head half hanging out the lowered window. As she turned on the truck, she listened to the man on the other end explain his brother's circumstances. The more he spoke, the more she realized this was going to be like many of the other severe PTSD cases she'd dealt with, and it was going to take intense training with both the dog and new handler. She felt the butterflies flutter to life in her stomach, realizing they would have to stay at her home in order for her to train them to work together. She hadn't had any unmarried men at her facility since—

Stop! This is not Evan; this is not the past.

"When would your brother be available to come to my facility?"

"To travel?" The voice on the other end of the phone sounded surprised. "I don't know if that will be possible. Dylan doesn't…he isn't…"

"Mr. Granger, I understand that travel could cause some anxiety for your brother, but because each person has different symptoms and varying degrees of PTSD, I need to meet him to be able to match him up. His dog has to be a partner who can work with your brother's specific needs in mind. Part of that is training the dog to relate to your brother and his triggers."

"The dog's training is tailored to Dylan's needs?"

"Exactly, and I'll teach him to work with the dog. I really need him here in order to see which dog pairs up with his personality best. If you're with him a lot, it would be best if you come as well. Based on what you've told me, I have a few dogs that might work for your brother, but you'll need to plan on staying three to four weeks. "

"You have accommodations for both of us?"

Julia pulled into her driveway and ran her hand over the dog at her side, trying to ignore the nervous tremor she could hear in her voice and the shake of her hand. "You're both welcome to stay in my home, that way we can work with your brother and his animal consistently.

But, if you prefer, my sister has cabins on her adjacent property as well." She couldn't help but hope they would choose to stay at Heart Fire Ranch instead. "How soon can you get here?"

"We can get a flight out tomorrow. I'll make sure of it." She didn't miss the desperation in his voice. In the last four years of focusing her training on dogs to serve people with PTSD, she'd met so many family members who wanted miracles the victim wasn't ready for. It was a recipe for disaster if everyone wasn't on board for the journey.

"Mr. Granger, as long as your brother wants this as much as you want it for him, you'll be pleased with the results. If not"—she took a deep breath, knowing that it wouldn't do any of them good to sugarcoat the truth— "you'll both be wasting your time and setting yourself up for disappointment."

There was a pregnant pause from Gage. "Ms. Hart, you're our last hope."

"Tomorrow?" Dylan stared at his brother. "Have you lost your mind? We can't leave in the morning."

"Dylan, it's already arranged. All you need to do is pack."

Dylan had hoped that letting his brother do the leg-work would dissuade him from this pointless pursuit. There was nothing a dog, even a therapy dog, could do. He'd already seen the brochures and read the information about how they were supposed to help with mood swings and anxiety, but if pills and alcohol couldn't touch them, how was an animal going to do anything? He ran a hand over his beard-roughened jaw, his fingers running over the marred flesh on his neck. The burns and scars had been covered with intricately colored tribal tattoos starting behind his ear, but they didn't make the truth hurt any less. He'd been the only man from his unit to survive the attack, and he still wasn't sure why. This wasn't living.

Dylan saw the hope in Gage's eyes. He really thought a dog was going to make a difference? *Whatever.* It wasn't worth fighting over. If Gage wanted to take a few weeks off work and stay at some training facility, fine. He'd see soon enough that this wouldn't help.

"Fine." Dylan shook his head in defeat and ran a hand over his close-shaven head. "I'll have to call Dr. Miller and let him know."

"I've already called him." Gage tossed a basket of Dylan's laundry onto his bed and began to fold it. "For the record, he thinks it's a great idea."

Dylan clenched his jaw. He appreciated his brother's help, but he wasn't completely incompetent. He felt the always-present anger simmering just below the surface. "I'm not an invalid. I can still do my own laundry."

Gage looked up, eyeing him curiously. "I know you can, Dylan. I wasn't implying you couldn't."

"Then stop coddling me like I'm going to break. I'm already broken." Dylan felt the familiar curtain of rage coming down over him, but he was helpless to stop it. It didn't matter how many pills they gave him or how many behavioral exercises he tried, when an episode came on it was like a flash flood and drown him every time. He reached out, throwing the hamper from the bed. "This is pointless."

"Dylan..."

"You know damn well I can't get on a plane, what that will do to me."

"Fine, we'll drive. It's only all the way across the country." Gage grabbed a pillow from the bed and slapped it into his brother's hands. "You want to be pissed? Go ahead. You want to throw things? Be my guest. But use this, and you clean up whatever mess you make." Gage turned on his heel and left the room.

It wasn't the reaction Dylan expected but instead of cooling the storm inside, it built, gaining momentum until he felt it swirling in his chest. He growled in rage, throwing the pillow at the wall and looking around the room for something else to throw. It only pissed him off more that every surface was already cleared. His brother had learned that lesson after Dylan's last episode. He clenched his fists, trying to still the fury building within. Every muscle in Dylan's body seemed to tense as he fought for control, bracing his fists on either side of the doorframe. He couldn't stop his fist when it rose of its own accord and slammed against the wall, putting a hole in it.

The pain radiating up his arm was enough to shake him from his fury, but self-loathing filled the vacuum left behind once his anger dissipated. He backed up until his legs hit the bed. His knees lost strength, unable to hold him as the adrenaline left him weak, and he dropped to sit on the edge of the mattress. Dylan looked at the bottle of pills on his nightstand, sweet oblivion that would make him forget, at least for a short while.

Just this once.

It was a lie. It wasn't the first time he'd made that promise to himself, and he was sure it wouldn't be the last, but he wasn't about to take the steps down that dark path again. He looked away. He wouldn't cave. Dylan buried his forehead in his hands, rubbing at his temples with his fingers, his right hand skimming the scar that ran from his temple to the back of his ear. He'd have been better off if that bullet had killed him.

Chapter Two

"JULIA, YOU CAN'T just let two strange men stay here."
Her older brother, Justin, stood in front of her door,
refusing to let her exit. His hulking frame would have
been intimidating to anyone else, but she knew he was
a pushover.

"It's not the first time I've let clients stay, Justin. I just
sent home a very sweet mother and her son last week."
She brushed past him and trotted down the porch steps,
heading to the dog kennels with Tango on her heels. She
didn't need Justin reminding her of things she'd already
put behind her. "We grew up on a dude ranch. We've had
strangers living with us all our lives"

She hoped he'd let this drop, but as he ran after her,
he pressed on. "There is no way you're staying here alone.
Not after what happened with Evan."

She stopped and froze midstep, not bothering to turn
to face him. "Don't ever mention him again, Justin. Ever."

"Julia—"

"If you mention it again, I swear, I will find another vet for my dogs."

"You can't just keep pretending he doesn't exist." He reached for his sister's shoulders and turned her to face him. "Now that he's out of jail, do you really think a restraining order is going to do you any good?"

"I'm being careful, Justin, but I can't put my life and career on hold for one creepy guy. He's gone. I'm not taking unnecessary risks, and I'm watching my back. So are the dogs. In the meantime, I still have a life to live and people who need my help."

Justin pulled her into a protective hug. She understood that he felt responsible to watch out for her and Jessie since their parents' car accident nearly a year ago, but Jessie had already asked him to stop trying to parent them. It was annoying enough when he tried to be a protective big brother.

"I want to be here when they arrive today."

She shoved him away and threw her hands in the air. He just wasn't going to give up. "Oh my goodness, are you even listening to yourself? I don't need your protection. Stop!"

"Little sis, you're not big enough to stop me." He gave her a grin and headed for his truck, leaving her to shake her head as she walked the rest of the way to the kennels.

Julia knew Justin wasn't wrong. At well over six feet and nearly two hundred and fifty pounds of solid muscle, she was no match for him physically. Few people were, but she had spent most of her life outwitting him, and her stubborn streak knew no boundaries. Julia went into the kennel's small kitchen area and prepared breakfast for the various dogs, mentally running through the characteristics of each of the animals.

It took a special dog to be a PTSD therapy animal. From what Gage said on the phone, Dylan was a man who liked to be active and would need a dog that could keep up with him. A smaller dog would never do for him, but luckily most of her dogs were large animals. She had a few extra-large dogs, like Tango, but she was leaning toward a shepherd mix named Cruise. He was smart, sensitive, and intuitive to moods. Plus, he'd already shown a good aptitude for picking up training quickly. It was one of the trickier sides of PTSD. The dogs had to adapt quickly and learn commands based on the needs of each individual, usually while they were both at the facility.

Julia set the food in front of the dogs and went into her office at the back of the kennel, staring at the picture collage on her wall of animals she'd trained and placed in homes over the years. Her eyes were immediately drawn the beautiful black lab in the right corner and her eyes misted. Misty had been a shelter rescue who had performed amazingly well, better than most of the dogs she worked with in her ten years of training. When Evan had called her looking for a dog that could help with his diabetes, alerting him to low blood sugar episodes that had become worrisome, Misty had been a perfect choice. If only she had listened to her instincts, or Misty's.

Julia turned away from the board, not wanting to think about the mistake that had been paid for with

Misty's life. Misty was the reason she'd started scent training each of her dogs since. She'd learned a lesson from Evan that she'd never forget—people lie.

Her phone vibrated on her desk, alerting her of a message. Grateful for the interruption, she opened the screen to see a message from Gage that their plane was early, and they would get a rental and arrive at Heart Fire shortly.

"Come on, Tango. We need to change the sheets before they get here." The dog lifted one brow, as if questioning her. She laughed and pointed at him. "Don't give me that look. I get enough flak from Justin. I don't need you taking his side."

The dog jumped up from the floor and moved to her right side. She reached her hand out and laid it on his massive head, rubbing behind one ear. "I think there might be some peanut butter treats in the house. What do you say?"

Tango barked once loudly and nudged the door open with his nose before looking back at her.

"I knew you'd see it my way."

DYLAN STARED OUT the window, barely paying attention to the landscape passing in a blur down the highway. The trip had been less eventful than either he or Gage expected. The only point he'd had some trouble coping was when the engines geared up for takeoff and the whine had nearly thrown him back. He'd felt himself slipping, his vision fading as his mind took him back to that day. Gage had nudged his arm, forcing him to focus on the present, and guilt overrode the flashback.

"You okay?" Gage glanced his way. Dylan hated the constant worry he could read in his brother's eyes.

He couldn't keep doing this to his brother. He'd become nothing more than a burden, the way their alcoholic father had been. Dylan had been the one who had stepped up from a young age, far too young for the responsibility of taking care of his mother and younger brother. To know that Gage might one day resent him, the way he did his father—he couldn't let that happen. As much as he didn't think a dog would help him, it might at least do enough good that he could give his brother back the freedom he'd lost when Dylan returned from Afghanistan.

He shifted in the seat of the Camaro his brother had rented. The old Dylan would have been itching to open the car on the long stretch of highway, to press his foot to the floor and let the powerful beast fly over the asphalt, like Icarus soaring toward the sun. But that man had become mortal, dying the day a bullet grazed his temple and a grenade exploded beside him. He fisted his hands, trying to control the anger that rose to the surface whenever he thought of what he'd lost.

"Yeah. Where is this place? BFE? How much farther?"

Gage checked the GPS navigation. "About five miles. Just off the next exit."

Dylan's brows drooped. "Not much around here, is there?"

Gage shrugged as he turned off the highway. "Maybe that's a good thing."

"I don't like it. There's a lot of trees and ground cover. Too many hills."

He knew it might not make sense to anyone else, but the hills and wooded areas made it harder for Dylan to see anyone approaching. He might not be in combat any longer, but that didn't stop him from scanning the woods for enemies. The doctors claimed it was just part of the PTSD, but he hadn't met a soldier yet who didn't continue to watch his back, even at home.

It was the same reason he'd done Internet searches on this training facility while his brother was sleeping. He not only wanted to get a lay of the place, but he wanted to know what he should expect. He was surprised to find out it was run by a woman. He'd even watched a few of the videos posted on her website. As much as it looked like she knew what she was doing, he wasn't sure how much a dog trainer could understand about a PTSD case like his without having been in combat. The woman in the videos looked more like a cheerleader than someone who knew anything about fear, trauma, or death.

Dylan crossed his arms over his chest as they approached the entrance and a sign welcoming them to Heart Fire Training Facility. As they pulled up to the main house, Dylan saw his brother's eyes widen. The house was a sprawling two-story ranch style with a wraparound porch, but what really caught his attention was the beautiful woman seated on the steps waiting for them.

"Damn."

Dylan chuckled at his brother's response. He couldn't help but agree. She was much prettier in person than she'd been in her videos, and that was saying a lot. He turned to say something and found his brother staring at him. "What?"

"You laughed."

"Okay?"

Gage stopped the car and turned it off. "That's the first time I've heard you laugh since you came home."

Dylan clenched his jaw, reaching for the door handle. His brother was right, and it had actually felt good, until he realized that he was the only one in his unit still able to laugh. Guilt washed over him as he thought about the families who had lost loved ones because of his failure. He climbed out of the car, refusing to respond.

"Hi, I'm Julia. You must be Dylan?"

The woman moved down the stairs, a broad smile on her face as she extended her hand. Immediately a monster-sized dog bounded down the stairs and sat at her feet, staring up at Dylan. He tucked his hands into his pockets, his mouth turning down as his brows bunched in a frown. He wasn't about to put out a hand where this beast could bite. The dog cocked his head to one side, studying Dylan, and then he opened his mouth in what looked like a grin, his huge pink tongue lolling to the side.

She laughed. "It's okay. Tango is a big teddy bear." She seemed to catch herself. "Unless he's on alert and working."

He wondered at her hesitation and looked back at the dog, and the teeth he could see inside the sloppy grin. "Teddy bear, huh?"

His brother moved around the car and reached for her hand. "Hi, I'm Gage. We spoke on the phone. This is Dylan."

Dylan nodded at her, not moving to approach as he looked around at the facility. He assumed from the barks, yips and howls that the solitary outbuilding was a kennel or training area. The rest of the property was open with pine trees surrounding the back of the property into the hills. She had landscaped the front with wildflowers and grasses that looked native yet too orderly to be natural.

"If you want to grab your bags, I'll show you to your rooms," she offered as she turned back to the house.

Dylan didn't miss the fact that the dog rose and followed behind her. He met his brother at the truck of the car. "That dog is a monster," he muttered. "If you think I'm taking something like that home, you're the crazy one."

"You're not crazy; just give it a chance, will you?" Gage looked around the side of the car, making sure Julia couldn't hear the criticism. "What's the worst-case scenario? That you get to stare at her for three weeks?"

Dylan glared at his brother. The last thing he needed was any sort of romantic entanglement. He couldn't even take care of himself right now. "You go right ahead."

"You can't be serious. Are you blind?"

Dylan shrugged. He hadn't missed anything—not her curves, not her smile, not the white scar at her temple, and certainly not the way her dark brown eyes seemed to dance as she spoke. But he had nothing to offer, and he wasn't selfish enough to sentence anyone else to the hell that was his life now. It was just easier to avoid any emotion, even the good ones. Hurt followed too closely at every turn.

"Are you two coming?" she called from the doorway. Dylan shut the trunk as his brother headed toward the house.

That smile was on her lips again as she opened the door, and he felt stab of jealousy at the opportunity he'd just passed up for his brother. He didn't fault Gage; under different circumstances, he would have taken a shot at her. Dylan had always hoped to be married by now, maybe with a kid or two, but now, with a different sort of future ahead of him, he was glad he'd never taken the plunge. He had enough guilt on his shoulders without a wife and kids to disappoint. Gage held open the door for him and followed Julia inside.

The house was tastefully furnished, more for comfort than in any particular style, but it was homey and welcoming. He thought he smelled cookies as they passed the kitchen and continued down the hall.

"I put you guys in the back of the house. There's a back door just off the hall and these two rooms adjoin." She looked pointedly at Dylan. "If you need anything, just let me know. I'll do my best to make this an easy transition for you."

The sympathy in her dark eyes made him cringe. He didn't want this woman feeling sorry for him. He didn't want anyone pitying him. He was a special ops medic, had completed some of the most difficult military training the world had to offer, and here he was with a dog trainer assessing his ability to care for some mutt?

He inhaled deeply, stuffing the rage into the recesses of his chest. Now wasn't the time, and she wasn't who he was really angry at. That he could recognize the fact was a step in the right direction and would make his therapist proud, but it wasn't enough for him. "Thanks, this will be fine."

Dylan went into the room and dropped his bag on the bed, while Gage moved into the next room. Julia stood in his doorway and stared at him, making him wish she'd hurry up and move on. "Is there something else?"

"You don't really want to be here, do you?" Dylan didn't detect any judgment or condemnation in her voice. She was simply stating a fact.

His brother appeared at her shoulder. "He's just tired from the stress of the trip," he offered.

She glanced back at Gage then back to Dylan and arched a brow, doubtful. "Tired, huh?"

Clearly, she didn't believe Gage's excuse. She wasn't just a pretty face. This woman had a brain. Dylan didn't want to lie, so he just kept his too-honest mouth shut, setting the variety of anti-anxiety pills, sleeping aids, and pain medication on the top of the dresser.

"I'll make you a deal, Dylan. You unpack and relax a bit. Feel free to use the pool in the back or wander around the property. Then, after dinner, we'll go out and you can meet some of the dogs. If you still want to head home, you can give up and fly out tomorrow. We'll just call it a minivacation."

"What's in it for you?" Dylan narrowed his eyes. In his experience, people didn't offer something for nothing. "If I don't take a dog, you don't get paid."

Gage glared at him, his eyes warning Dylan to shut up, but she laughed at him. "I offer the PTSD dogs as part of a nonprofit foundation. Anything paid for the dog goes back into the organization to rescue more dogs for training. I only take a small salary. It's enough to meet my needs."

He hadn't expected that. Nor did he expect the way her eyes softened as she continued. "It doesn't do anyone any good for you to get a dog you don't want. You won't connect, and the dog won't be able to reach you. This is a partnership between you and your animal. It can't be forced. We might even go out there and find that I don't have one to fit your needs."

Dylan hadn't thought about that. He'd assumed that any dog would work, especially since he didn't think this would do any good. The fact that she was being completely honest with him, even if that meant failure on her part, made him want to trust her, at least a bit. He stared at her intensely, trying to figure her out. He couldn't help but feel some of the weight on his shoulders lift as she smiled at him and her face lit up.

"Well?" The monster-dog plopped down at her feet, laying his head on his paws, and looked up at him. He felt his resistance caving.

"As long as it's not a horse like that one, I'll give it a shot."

"This will be great." She turned and patted Gage on the arm. "You'll see."

Acknowledgments

WITH EVERY BOOK I write, it seems like the list of people to thank grows longer and more significant. First, I want to thank my wonderful editor, Rebecca. This was a tough one for me, as you know, and without you every step of the way, I don't know that it would have ever come to fruition. You took a very rough lump of coal and turned it into a diamond.

I have to give the biggest of hugs to my partner in crime, Codi Gary, who has talked me down from the ledge on a near daily basis and knows exactly how to read my mind. I'm so grateful for the day you game into my life like a tornado, my sister from another mother. You're the best, but you already know that.

For all of my writing friends who never act like they are tired of hearing my endless questions, complaints, doubts, and worries—Candis, Heather, Shelly, Jen, Jodi, Kristin, KC, Kimberly, Leanne, Alexis, Tracie, Julia,

Mary Chris, and Lashell—you keep me sane and continually functioning. I think without you I would crawl into a hole and become a blubbering mess.

For my readers, without you, I'd be nothing. Your support, encouragement, and kind words mean far more than you will ever know. I sit down every single day with you in mind and want to give you my very best.

For Mama, my biggest fan, for always being the first to remind me to trust in myself and the abilities you gave me. You have always pushed me to reach new heights and seek out the difficult in order to become better.

And I need to thank my husband and children who have spent far too many evenings fixing their own meals, cleaning the house, and taking care of matters so that Mom can do what she does, living in this imaginary world of my own creation. Thank you guys for always reminding me that I have my own happy ending firmly based in the reality of our home. I love you!

About the Author

T. J. KLINE was raised competing in rodeos and rodeo queen competitions from the age of fourteen and has thorough knowledge of the sport as well as the culture involved. She has written several articles about rodeo for small periodicals, as well as a more recent how-to article for *RevWriter*, and she has written a nonfiction health book and two inspirational fiction titles under the name Tina Klinesmith. She is also an avid reader and book reviewer for both Tyndale and Multnomah. In her spare time, she can be found laughing hysterically with her husband, children, and their menagerie of pets in Northern California.

Discover great authors, exclusive offers, and more at hc.com.

About the Author

T. J. Kraus was raised competing in rodeo and rodeo queen competitions from the age of fourteen and has thorough knowledge of the sport as well as the culture involved. She has written several articles about rodeo for small periodicals, as well as a nonfiction how-to guide book, and she has written a nonfiction health book and two inspirational fiction titles under the name Tina Klinesmith. She is also an avid reader and book reviewer for both Tyndale and Multnomah. In her spare time, she can be found laughing hysterically with her husband, children, and their menagerie of pets in Northern California.